Richard Tregaskis
Classics Collection

China Bomb:
A Novel

Richard Tregaskis

China Bomb: A Novel

Published by JMFdeA Press

For information address:
JMFdeA Press
P.O. Box 235737
Honolulu, HI 96823
www.jmfdeapress.com

Paperback ISBN: 978-1-956695-08-3
E-Book ISBN: 978-1-956695-09-0
Audiobook ISBN: 978-1-956695-10-6

JMFdeA Press chose to keep the content and punctuation in the Richard Tregaskis
Classics Collection as RT originally wrote it. We feel RT's flavor would have been
diluted by making changes to adhere to modern rules. There are certain words RT
used that will show the reader the era in which RT lived. Richard Tregaskis was a
kind, generous, big-hearted man who continuously put himself at great peril to tell
the stories the world needed to know. He used some terms that are not acceptable
today. Richard meant no malice. He was writing about his enemies. JMFdeA Press
did not alter RT's works out of respect for him, and to also show how far as a
society we have matured some. On Sept.18, 2021 there was a rally "Justice for J6" in
Washington, D.C.. Have we really evolved in today's time to
be a more tolerant society?

"As a young boy, I enjoyed reading about the heroes of our Nation. In reading the Landmark book version of Richard Tregaskis' *Guadalcanal Diary*, I was inspired by the courage and sacrifice of the Marines and sailors who fought and persevered in that very difficult battle—the first land offensive of the US in WWII. It inspired me to serve later in my life, but more importantly, taught me about the importance of exhibiting will, courage, and resilience when things were hard. Thanks RT for telling the story of these great Americans and so many others over the course of your life and career."

Robert B. Neller
General USMC retired
37th Commandant of the Marine Corps

Contents

About the Author

After graduating from Harvard *cum laude* in 1938, Richard Tregaskis became a journalist and a staff member of the International Service. RT was anxious to get to the heart of the action to be able to tell the heart stories of the valiant men putting their lives on the line for our country. He was sent as a correspondent to cover operations of the Pacific Fleet at the outbreak of World War II. His experiences in the South Pacific became his first book. He wrote about war in a unique way and *Guadalcanal Diary* earned him a permanent spot in American literature and set the genre of war correspondence. It continues to be essential reading by U.S. military personnel.

Tregaskis was also with American forces in the European theatre following the Allies of the invasion of Italy. While there he was hit by German shrapnel. A piece went through his helmet and part of his head, and out the other side of his helmet. After learning how to speak and use his right hand again, he continued writing. In short time, came *Invasion Diary* and *Stronger Than Fear*.

In 1947 he journeyed for two years around the world. He spent most of that time observing the Nationalist-Communist war in China, from which he barely escaped. From those amazing experiences came *Seven*

Leagues to Paradise, Last Plane to Shanghai, and *China Bomb: A Novel.* RT was compelled to write about the dangers of indirect insurgencies, and why they are successful. Since WWII, we had constant emerging enemies who brought new kinds of war. Tregaskis wrote about all of them.

RT felt compelled to pen *X-15 Diary: The Story of America's First Space Ship,* which describes the full story of the X-15 hypersonic manned rocket ship, first of its kind in the race to space. There are the many stories of the men and women who worked tirelessly in this great chapter of American history.

Vietnam Diary, another seminal war correspondence book, was the first definitive eyewitness account of this new style of guerrilla combat. Tregaskis spent four months in the thick of the war to gather the compelling stories of courageous men fighting in these vicious battles. Due to his special skills and extensive travel in Vietnam, RT was contracted to write about one of the largest war-time construction efforts in history. His book, *Building the Bases The History of Construction in Southeast Asia* was an incredible undertaking which only he, with his talent and expertise, could write. It covers every major construction by the U.S. Navy Construction Battalions (Navy SEABEES), and other military and civilian engineers and their stories as the events of the war evolved.

Amidst writing for motion pictures and television, RT delved into fictional biographies. *The Warrior King: Hawaii's Kamehameha the Great* was created out of his love of Hawaii after he made it his home. It is an exceptional historical story of the legendary leader of the Hawaiian Islands. Tregaskis transports the reader back in time to when the Hawaiian Islands were under the rule of many kings and the events that transpired to create a one Hawaiian Nation, governed by one ruler for the prosperity of all of the Hawaiian people.

RT left behind a halfway finished love story, *The Secret of the Taj*, about Mumtaz Mahal who inspired the creation of the Taj Mahal. It was out of his passionate love of his wife, Moana, and their assignments to India, that this manuscript came to fruition.

In 1964, Richard Tregaskis was awarded the George Polk Award for reporting under hazardous conditions for the book that became Vietnam Diary. The helmet he wore in 1943 in Italy when a shell fragment pierced through it and into his skull is on display at the National Museum of the Marine Corps, along with a copy of *Invasion Diary*. Although RT had challenges with Type I diabetes, he never complained and it never stopped him from telling the important stories of the times as they were happening. During his life Richard Tregaskis clambered in and out of jeeps, fighters, bombers, trucks, and choppers while carrying his pack and notebook into the battles of nine wars. He was a special war correspondent who was able to sense the problems of the men in the heat of battle, while having an extraordinary ability to understand the strategy of war.

Introduction

By the time Richard Tregaskis wrote China Bomb in the 1960s, we had lived through WWII and the Korean War. We were still in the midst of the ever frustrating Vietnam War and China was emerging with the atomic bomb. They conducted their first test in October 1964 and appeared to be making fast progress.

It was many tense years that felt like "the enemy" was constantly all around us and infiltrating our society in order to take over. While RT wanted to explore other themes in his writing, he fervently felt that his mission was to call attention to indirect insurgencies. Already one fifth of the world's population was communist and seemed to be gaining a foothold in more countries. If Vietnam would have been taken over, the assumption was the other Asians countries would fall to communism as well.

The dangers were the same since RT wrote *Guadalcanal Diary*—an enemy, warfare, and danger to democracy. When he started writing, the letters flew onto the page. Sometimes he would handwrite and sometimes he would clack at the typewriter. I would put it together into a draft, he altered it, and so on until it was finished. He was already a seasoned reporter. He wrote in the included Rough for Novel Outline on March 9, 1964, "As Hemingway wrote at the age of 44 when he had written For Whom the Bell Tolls, with his age and experience a man should be able to write a good novel." He told me that fiction had a way of being able to get to the heart of a matter in a way non-fiction could not.

RT's first book was *Guadalcanal Diary* which set the genre for war correspondence books. No one knew about the tins of sardines crammed in his backpack. If anyone asked about his copy of a manual authored by the founder of Boston's famed Joslin Diabetes clinic, RT would say it was autographed by a special friend. Leaving Guadalcanal, RT returned to Pearl Harbor to write. In the field he filled a small notebook, and when at camp would transcribe them into a larger journal. When his adventure was finished, he had several. Daytime, the Navy locked him up to work with his notebooks and locked up the notebooks at night. The bloody experience of Guadalcanal changed him. He was stunned to be alive, and glad for it. The battle on that feverish island changed all those who survived it, yet these men couldn't bring themselves to talk about their experiences. RT told their stories. He saw, felt, and brought readers into the pangs of homesickness, the tales of scrounging, or the moments of humor.

Leaving the Pacific, RT went to the European theatre. The size fourteen boots Marines called his PTs, for "Patrol Tregaskis," went along. Eventually, luck deserted him. In a battle in Italy, on a hill called Mount Corno near Cassino, RT was hit by German shrapnel. A piece went through his helmet, a part of his head, and out the other side of the helmet, leaving a gaping jagged hole. Somehow, he staggered to the lines of the American 38th Evacuation Hospital, dragging along the helmet. There, managing to convey the word "diabetic" to a doctor, Major William Pitts of Charlotte, N.C., who performed the tedious, massive surgery. Within a few months, RT had learned again to talk. RT read poetry to practice speaking. He again learned to use his right hand, and was back to duty writing *Invasion Diary* and immediately afterward, *Stronger Than Fear*. The helmet he wore is now displayed at the National Museum of the Marine Corps.

Although their paths did not cross in the Solomon Islands, a man he knew in college days was at sea in the waters of Guadalcanal at the same time RT was on the island. This man became President John F. Kennedy. While President Kennedy was in office, RT wrote *John F. Kennedy and PT-109*. The President loaned RT his personal logs and notes for research. At Harvard, RT and Jack Kennedy were swimmers, and close friend Torbert MacDonald captained the Harvard football team. At competitions for the varsity swim team backstrokers, RT trounced Kennedy for a slot on the team; it was a special year—they beat Yale. As press secretary Pierre Salinger took RT into the Oval Office, the first thing the President said was, "Pierre, RT beat me out for the Harvard Varsity Swim Team." RT replied, "Sir, if I'd known you would be President, I would have let you win." Amidst the laughter, one could note that neither President Kennedy nor Congressman MacDonald ever forgot that competition.

In 1962 I was introduced to RT at the beach by my neighbor. The next day, I started working with him as a secretary. He was already researching *Vietnam Diary*. I took a photography course and traveled with him to Vietnam many times to cover the war. This was almost like art come to life, for in RT's book *Last Plane to Shanghai* (which was published before meeting me), he wrote about a male journalist meeting a female photographer. Against many odds, the characters fell in love and covered a dangerous assignment in the midst of the China Civil War. RT considered Martha a worthy literary achievement.

Together, RT and I tackled the communist regime in *China Bomb: A novel*. RT felt a great urgency to share how such indirect insurgencies happen and why they are so successful. Set in the near future, it explored what every American in the late 1960s feared—China building a nuclear bomb. Americans were all war-torn with Vietnam continuing, and here was an enemy emerging with a new kind of war with more dangerous weapons. It was vital for people to understand the importance of this instead of being lackadaisical, despite our weariness. I am including an outline for this book as well as correspondence. There is another tidbit for you to get a sense of what was being taught to people across the globe. It influenced them to see Americans with "imperialist" ideals in a certain light. They viewed Americans as a threat to world peace while we perceived them as a threat to world peace.

RT and I went to many places and had innumerous adventures while writing books, magazine and newspaper articles, and screenplays. A scrupulous taker of notes, meticulous researcher, and diligent questioner, RT shared in the ordeals of the men he chronicled. While participating, he was uncommonly brave, and two generations of American fighting men accepted him as a member of their team. They talked about him, angular and tall, a bit over six foot six, soft-spoken and very thin, always writing, watching, questioning, and taking photographs at the height of battle. In addition to these traits crucial to the military historian, RT brought another quality to the battle lines— it distinguishes the great in both soldiers and civilians—he cared deeply about the affairs of the everyday man. I was never happier than I was with him, even in the uncomfortable bush being eaten by insects with the enemy nearby.

Over our many trips to India, we went to Agra. RT became enamored with the woman who inspired the Taj Mahal. He wrote a complete outline and half a manuscript of a fictional biography called *The Secret of the Taj* about Mumtaz Mahal, but did not finish it.

In 1964 RT and I were on an assignment in an area called Ladakh. It is the famous roof of the world where the Himalaya and Karakoram of India nearly meet the Pamirs of Russia. It is a high, cold, desolate moraine. Indian soldiers peered through binoculars at Chinese soldiers who peered in return over their own sandbags. We flew over the Karakoram in an unpressurized Indian Air Force plane, with oxygen bottles, then landed at the lowest elevation—11,000 feet.

We carried RT's insulin kit and an odd assortment of food and drugs. He acquired a blister on his foot from a faulty stirrup adjustment. We flew immediately to Kashmir. There, in an Army hospital, the gangrene set in. He went into a 4-day coma and his foot turned black. The doctor told me there was no diabetes of this severity in India. I thought – I know, they just die. I never left his room and helped my husband. They evicted me, but I went right back anyway. He recovered—I believe due mostly to that RT will-power that was so powerful. He immediately returned to writing.

We had a rare, special relationship. We learned to play out our minds back and forth and the mental stimulation was exhilarating. I was grateful to always be in synch with my husband. RT was a man of courage and he inspired me to travel on assignment with and without him to cover the 1971 Indo-Pakistani War.

One of his favorite books to write was The *Warrior King; Hawaii's Kamehameha the Great* for he was much taken by the story of Kamehameha. RT was thrilled to share more about his home, beloved Hawai'i. He needed to exercise for his diabetes. Hawaii was ideal to do his daily exercises of swimming. Who wouldn't want to swim in the warm Pacific ocean with the Hawaiian trade winds tickling you every day? RT went to Grey's beach and liked chatting with the regulars. In the tropics, he loved wearing as little as possible at home because the temperature rarely dipped below 66°. Living in Waikiki, we walked almost everywhere because everything was centrally located. Often we visited Don the Beachcomber who was my first employer in Hawai'i. Friends constantly stopped by our home at any time. Once John Steinbeck spent the whole day with us lounging on our large lanai with a mural of a beach although we were two blocks away from the real thing. Those years were truly special.

In 2000 I reprinted some of his books. In 2016 a publisher approached me to turn s few of RT's books into e-books and audio books. It was a great success. Now I am thrilled to introduce The Richard Tregaskis Classics Collection through JMFdeA Press to share his complete legacy in audio and digital format as well as print while providing new personal stories and memorabilia. Look for *The Secret of the Taj* as well, for I am trying to finish it for my love.

RT was one of the few civilians to receive a purple heart for bravery in combat. He was a courageous man who made it his mission to share the reality of war as it was happening with details that was not normally covered. In 1964, the Overseas Press Club presented Richard Tregaskis with the George Polk Award for first-person reporting under hazardous circumstances for the book that became *Vietnam Diary*. In 1973, Marquis' "Who's Who in America" asked for a quote; RT sent these words: "Reverence for truth, thank God, continues to be a great American ideal. Beauty makes life most pleasant, and humor cushions the worst moments. But courage remains the most valuable of all. My life in many wars has shown me that America has ample stores of all of these values in the face of the most severe mortal dangers."

I want to extend my deepest aloha to the American Heritage Center at the University of Wyoming where the Richard Tregaskis Papers are housed. I have sent them a large part of RT's correspondence and research. They provided me scans of some of the memorabilia I am sharing with you. It is my hope to have his entire collection scanned to aid researchers with their work.

Please visit the estate's website about RT at richardtregaskis.com to learn more about this fascinating man who I loved deeply and his extraordinary books. Visit jmfdeapress.com to add to your collection of his compelling historical works.

Much aloha,
Moana
May 2021

Sept 12
With Deepest Sympathy
to Beautiful Shakti
4 years and she's
still serving time
at the typewriter!
But if it's any
consolation Ganesha
Desai's loves her
passionately!   Love

Photographs & Archives

Dongfang Hong, The east is red
Designer: Zhang Yuqing
1965, October
Publisher: Zhejiang renmin chubanshe

"Dongfang Hong originally was a folk song. In the 1930s, it was popular among the communists in Yan'an, with lyrics about the anti-Japanese struggle. In the early 1940s, the text was rewritten again, to become a hymn to Mao Zedong:

"The east is red, the sun is rising
China has brought forth a Mao Zedong.
He works for the people's welfare.
Hurrah, He is the people's great savior."

A so-called 'song-and-dance epic' was made in the early 1960s, in 1965 a film version was released. During the Cultural Revolution the song was played everywhere, all the time, and in fact replaced the official anthem of the People's Republic of China." —Kent Wang

Obtained through the International Institute of Social History
IISG BG E12/606
https://hdl.handle.net/10622/DFE2DC3E-65A0-4772-A02E-999069AE6B47

人民公社万岁
人民公社好幸福万年长

TITLE:
Renmin gongshe hao xingfu wannian chang.
'The people's commune is good, happiness will last for ten thousand years.'
Ca. 1960

China tried to make the countryside into an investment. After all 80% of the population lived in rural areas. Collectivized agriculture was seen as the solution. Mao Zedong established a campaign called The Great Leap Forward from 1958-1963. It did allow for maximum extraction of surplus from farms, leaving famine. While farmers contributed to the "greater good", they received no healthcare and no schooling, and less food. By the time it was abandoned in 1961, there was massive environmental and economic destruction. Even more devastating was the 15-55 million deaths due to starvation and forced labor. It is considered the largest famine in history.

This poster was inspired from a photograph of the musicians, which was published in *China Reconstructs*, October 1959 p.12, with the caption "Celebration of the 1958 bumper harvest at a people's commune in Anhwei [Anhui] province". The photographer is Tung Chang [Dong Zhang?].

Obtained through the International Institute of Social History
IISG BG E16/40
https://hdl.handle.net/10622/64062D78-A930-4710-A1CA-A15451F41B6D

March 9th, 1964

ROUGH FOR NOVEL OUTLINE

(In Far Eastern foreign relations, there is no issue more frightening to the Amerk average American than the thought that the Chinese Communists may have a nuclear bomb. Pont of impact, no other news development in all Asia could be important or apt to throw our foreign policy, and in fact all of our lives, into a tizzy. Amongst any possible intelligence development, this is the giant one which would overshadow any others in any other part of the world.

The Vietnam war has intensified our apprehensions about China to the million/th magnitude. The Vietnamese campaign, and the Laotian debacle before it have served, as if we needed any reminder, to remind us that the Chinese Communists are committed to an aggressive, Leninistic form of aggression. The growing schism between the Russian and Chinese Reds has underlined the fact that China prides itself on her unrelenting animosity towards American or any other Western power which may intervene in her attempts to Communise all of Asia.

This novel is an attempt to bring to focus our apprehensions about Red China, and to weave some didactic themes about the mis-conduct of our war effort in Southeast Asia through an exciting suspense narrative and love story.

I am especially well qualified by experience on the ground and in my writing endeavours during the last 15 years to handle this job.

Since the end of World War II, we have been engaged in a cycle of Leninistic wars. The pattern of these wars has been very slow to dawn upon us, though by the time of the Vietnam campaign, our leadership at least seemed to be aware of the way the pattern works.

Right after World War II, Russia began a campaign of conquest following the lines which Lenin had laid down in such of his writings as WHAT IS TO BE DONE and ONCE STEP FORWARD, TWO STEPS BACKWARD. Stalin used this doctrine as the basis of two books which were best sellers for many years in Russia, PROBLEMS OF LENINISM and FOUNDATIONS OF LENINISM.

The basic idea is the Communists states intervene in civil wars wherever they may be raging, and attept to turn the insurgent effort into a Communist movement.

This is done by indirect, as the Communists train the insurgents in doctrine and supply them with weapons, especially including propaganda weapons. The basic idea is that a conquest is not carried on directly by armed forces of the aggressor, but by training a nucleus, or vanguard in the country at war, and lending support while that vanguard leads the reserve or budkof the people in the country, to overthrow the government and set up a Communist, one-party regime.

This kind of insurgency achieved remarkable results in China, Chechosovakia, Korea, Cuba, Burma, Laos, and many parts of Africa and nearly succeeded in Malaya, the Philippines and Greece.

3

From this brand of insurgency which we call Leninism sprang our techniques of counter-insurgency which were first developed in Greece and most recently led to the involvement of many interesting war techniques in Vietnam. But because of a public lassitude and failure of the leadership to end the journalistic and writing fraternity to make clear what was going on, the blood and sweat expended in our Leninistic war efforts went largely without appreciation. In my non-fiction writing, like my syndicated articles and magazine stories, and in VIETNAM DIARY, I tried to call this pattern to public attention. My principal effort in faction along this line was LAST PLANE TO SHANGHAI, a love story which attempted to dramatise the issue in terms of one man and one woman in the midst of the China Civil War.

Just about the time the leading Americans seemed to be getting an understanding of the mechanism which the Russina Communists first and the Chinese Communists after them were using, the Chinese began to pay attention to the need for nuclear energy in their weapons arsenal. As usually happens in war history, we were just beginning to understand the mechanism of the current war, when a new kind of war was being prepared by the enemy. We had just begun to understand how to cope with insurgency with out techniques for anit-guerrilla action, when China began to give evidence of equipping herself with nuclear weapons.

4

It seems that the Russinas are loath to launch a
nuclear war, as it would bemuch too expensive for both sides,
and probably with the inclusive, but the Chinese have no such
scruples, and seem inclined to use whatever weapons they can
discover to further their unrelenting campaign of aggression
against capitalism, and particularly American capitalism.)

END
PRECEDE

STORY AND CHARACTERS

I will go into the basic situation of our story first,
to sum it up quickly, and then delineate the characters.

BASIC SITUATION: And American import-export businessman
in Bangkok,
Jack Eagles, a former OSS man in World War II days, hears about
an unprecedented amount of smuggling of high power batteries
and generators into Red China.

As a trader, he is familiar with the smuggling mechanism
from Hong Kong and other Southeast Asian ports in to the China
mainland, he makes it a point to maintain a friendship with
the Chinese smugglers, who consider their trade a legitimate one.
The evidence brought to his attention by some smuggler friend
arouses his curiosity. The smuggling of batteries and
generators through the "Smuggler's Islands" north of Hong Kong
itself is not strange, but the quantities reported by the
smugglers are phenomenal, and some of the items included in
the shipments are very suspicious. One is a case of Geiger

5

counters and a case of clamp-machinery which could be used in implosion, the technique used in small nuclear bombs to force the uranium elements together so that a critical mass can be created and an explosion generated. Eagles, a middle-aged man who maintains his reserve rank as a lieutenant colonel, knows very little about atomic energy or nuclear weapons, but thinks he recognizes a significant trend in the list of smuggled items.

Eagles is one of the hell-for-leather China buffs who served the US brilliantly during the China-Burma-India campaign in World War II. Many of these men -- OSS officers, pilots who flew with Chennault during the war and afterwards, for Civil Air Transport during the China Civil War, Army and Navy men who fulfilled their tours of duty and because enamoured of Asia -- stayed in the area as soldiers of fortune. Like Eagles, most of them married and built families. Many of them, like Eagles, ~~show~~ chose Thai, Vietnamese or Chinese girls as brides. But there is a camaraderie, frequently mixed with business rivalry, amongst them.

Eagles' closest friend, Hank Chancellor, is one of this group. Hank, though now in his middle years, is still active as a pilot (and pirate) and he has worked with Eagles on many deals, some of them virging on the illegal, some definitely linked with American government (CIA) efforts.

Knowing the compartmentation of the CIA, the difficulties

of negotiating with them, their cumbersomeness and their

frequent failure to do anything about a pressing issue without

overwhelming, incontrovertible proof, Jack Eagles seeks out

the help of Chancellor on the problem. They plan to make a

little expedition on their own to Hong Kong to check up with

their smuggler friends.

At the outset it should be made clear that these aging

soldier of fortune types are prompted in their involvement not

by conventional patriotic motivation, but by a kind of stubborn un-

willingness to share their Southeast Asian preserve with the

brigands coming down from the north. They would be the first to

protest that they don't want to get shot up or spend a lot of

money on a patriotic enterprise -- but their history since they

got out of the service at the end of World War II has indicated

that they don't like Communists and what the Communists do to

a country. They had all had first-hand experience with the

kind of one-party dictatorship of a small nucleus which is the

usual result of a maoh touted Commonist revolution. Supposed to

bring a new measure of social betterment, the Communist

revolutions, everywhere they have been involved, have led to

a repressive police state with firstx worse social injustices

by far than the imperialism it was supposed to replace.

In several crises involving the United States, Jack

Eagles, Hank Chancellor and the others have been helpful to

our national effort: flying supplies and paratroopers to the

Kerens in Burma when we were interested in reinforcing Burma's

position along the confused Chinese Communist frontier, bringing

7

in military materials and dropping parachute reinforcements
to the northern provinces of Thailand (and in Eagles case,
helping to train Thai paratroopers) and most recently in
flying air lift supplies and reinforcements to Laotian
guerrillas resisting the efforts of the Communist Viet Minh
to build airfields and consolidate the Red position in the
Plaine des Jarres.

Chancellor and Eagles make a trip to Hong Kong on their
own, and seek out the assistance of their eminent smuggler
friend, Lok Wei. Lok takes them up to Sha To Kok,
the principal smuggler's island, so they can get a first hand
look at the principal source of the suspicious items.

Lok Wei is the head of a famous smuggling family, and
is well known not only to the underworld but also to enterprising
members of British and American Intelligence. The intelligence
agents wouldn't want Mr. Lok to go out of business, because he
and many other smugglers like him are too valuable as sources of
information and suppliers of transport for agents going in and
out of China. As a matter of fact, the leaders of intelligence
make it possible for Lok and the other valued
smugglers to work more efficiently -- they supply the Chinese
outlaws with new, more powerful engines, and even, occasionally
with new boats so that they will be able to circumvent the
Communist coastal patrols.

In a daring and dangerous night expedition, Chancellor
and Eagles check up on the smuggling shipments, and see
conclusive evidence that they are in fact being made.

Then they get Lok to run them in to the Chinese
coast to try to find out destination of the shipments. Their
checkup shows that the shipments are not going into the Chinese
coast north or east of Hong Kong, but apparently are destined
for a point to the west. A chase of a smuggler's boat is
fruitless when they lose him about 40 miles west of Macau.
This is a startling development, because the natural assumption would
be that the nuclear materials were going in to Canton, an
air field near Canton or farther to the north and east opposite
Formosa, where the suspected atom bombs could be used for the
anchluss of that fated island possession of the Republican
Chinese.

Eagles and Chancellor hear through the grapevine -- at
Jingles, the restaurant known as PG and the Mandarin-Hilton
circuit in Hong Kong that a CIA cloak and dagger man coming
through Hong Kong enroute to India. They decide theymust get
to him and ask for help, even though they don't yet know where
the atomic supplies are heading.

The CIA operator, a relative stranger to Asian undercover
operations although a scholar with experience in Hong Kong and
Taipai, turns out to be a bust. His name is Dr. L. D. V. Simoleon,
he is supposed to be on a mission to the Himalyan frontier in
India, and he is very disrespectful and uninterested in the
findings of Eagles and Chancellor.

His principal complaint seems to be that the evidence
is not conclusive enough, and the Americans don't even know where
the stuff is going. It's the same old complaint that Jack and
Hank have heard ever since they were rookies in China, but the

ẖüẗẍẗẖẹ additional complaint, that they don't know where the material is going, they apologise for. If Simoleon will bear with them, they promise that they will get a more definitive rundown -- and ask only that he will recommend to the powers that be in Washington who might be able to help them when they get all their information together. He is evasive about this. They regard him as an over-educated *precious* academician, and he chalks them off as unadulterated pirates with obvious axes to grind— *and furthermore, decidedly gauche.*

INSERT A:
for prefatory note:

I've been convinced in my writing history that in a novel a play or a work of fiction, you can sometimes come closer to the heart of an important matter than you can with literal non-fiction. This is what I tried to do with the essence of modern war on individual terms, in my first novel, STRONGER THAN FEAR; in my second novel, LAST PLANE TO SHANGHAI, I tackled the phenonmenon of Leninistic war, and tried to clarify in terms of the two characters in thelove story. In the latter, besides wanting to sugarcoat a didactic pill, I was much interested in the character of the woman, and I feel that she will stand up as a worthy literary achievement ẉïẗḥ whether or not the didactic purpose of the book is achieved.

I must point out that I've ẚḻṣẉẖạḏ alsø had considerable experience with dramatic fiction, as a screen and TV writer. My earliest literary experience in college was narrative technique, my honors thesis at Harvard having been concerned with the narrative technique of Kipling.

Experienøe has taught me that in mnay cases the writer who essays fiction is unable to come to the truth about his theme because he simply doesn't know enough about that theme ƒor the people or scene involved in it.   By this time I should be in a good position to meet the qualifications for the type of novel I outline here. As Hemingway wrote at the age of 44 when he had written FOR WHOM THE BELL TOLLS, with his age and experience a man should be able to write ~~his best~~ novel.

July 25, 1950

Mr. Louis Ruppel
Editor
Collier's
New York

Dear Lou,

It was swell of you to be so understanding about
the Korean assignment. When I thought it over, talked to
my doctor, and listened to what Marian had to say about it,
I was convinced that after all it wasn't such a good
idea for me. It also wouldn't have been fair to Twentieth-
Century Fox to pull out in the middle of a project they
had assigned me to, even though I was being hired on a
week-to-week basis and they weren't too sure they were
going on with the project.

The biggest reason, though, was in the matter of health.
During World War II, although I had diabetes then too, I
didn't have to take insulin. I handled the disease with
diet. Now, on an insulin regime, I seem to have more
difficulty keeping the thing under control. It seemed wise
to me to wrestle with the diabetes a bit longer before
going out on a deal as rugged as the Korean war. Maybe I
can whip the thing down somewhat before the next Little
Hot War breaks out, or at least before the big war in
1953. I hope when there are further developments on Southeast
Asia or the Iran-Iraq-Arabia area, you'll send me out to
do a job for you.

Meanwhile, I'd like to suggest a piece along this line:
How to Beat the Russians At Their Own Game. On the trip
around the world I made for True in 1948-49, I was struck time
after time with the expert methods the Russians were using
everywhere to engineer their world revolution---a shapr
contrast to our own bungling. Everywhere I went is seemed that
the Russians were carrying on the Third World War by starting
civil wars--but they were doing it cheaply, by remote control.
One saw few Russians in Chian, Siam or India or in Western
Europe, but when you checked, you always found out that the
revolutionary leaders were being sent or had been sent
to Russia for indoctrination, then sent back to do the
Communist business. If anyone objected that the Russians were
interfering in foreign affairs, the Russians had--and have--
a good answer: therevolutionaries are nationals, not Russi

2

     In contrast with the Russian method, our technique seemed inept and with ineffective. We sent American advisory groups in, and the nationals, like the Chinese, disliked and distrusted us for this rather obvious insult to their touchy national pride.

     Instead of sending in droves of Americans, who always look like imperialists, we should do what the Russians do: we should take the small groups of literate men, intellectuals and patriots who are the leaders in any given country, and bring t them to the U.S. Here they would see how well men live, how automobiles, refrigerators, handsome houses, television and radio sets, clean and healthful food are available to the average person. They should be given fellowships at American universities--because most of the leaders are serious, earnest men--and they should have all their expenses paid so that they could roam around the country at will. After a few months they would be able to see for themselves how much better the U.S. way of life is than the Russian. Then, going home, they would lead their countries towards our way. No coercian would be needed, and the Russians would be beaten at their own game.

     Another Russian method could well be copied by us: the paper war. A Tass correspondent whom I had met on the Western Front told me in 1948, in Shanghai, that the biggest import from Russia into China was newsprint. It was being shipped into China at giveaway prices; you saw it in processed form, in the mountains of pamphlets and leaflets and broadsides which the Chinese intellectuals disseminated to further the leftist cause.

     Our propaganda efforts counted in other media could also benefit from some imitation of the Russians. The Commies in China offered specific, concrete examples as benefits of their system: like raises in the pay of labor, more land for farmers, etc. In Europe I was told many times that the Voice of America is a fizzle because it is not as direct in its propaganda as the Russians. Europeans often told me that the Voice of America programs of music, intermingled with laudatory accounts of American history, are ineffective. Programs, I was told, should tell how much the average man makes in America, should emphasize the fact that he has a refrigerator, car, and a good house with a bath and hot and cold running water, works only forty hours a week, lives on plenty of butter and meat. These things, it seems, are more interesting to hungry and poor people than political ideals.

     I have a lot of material on this subject gathered on th round the world trip. The stuff seems Bm especially importan nowadays. Do you think so too?   Best,

LIST OF CHARACTERS

WASHINGTON

CIA Chief   Charles Hudibras & wife Isabella

                Driver, Joe

Director SE Asia Section Walter Montgomery

                Secretary, Lucy

Special Assistant   David Soloretha
  To the President

Senator   Samuel Smythe

President Luscome Landers ("Red") & wife Edythe

                Secretary, Virginia

Chairman JCS   General Harold Morman

Byron Daniels, NY Herald Tribune

Casey Ford, CBS

Admiral Joe Bloomfield, CNO

White House Doc. Bill Beech

Lt. Merlin Berns, works in COMSUBS, Pentagon

Witness Capt. King, Spec. Forces

QUEEN ELIZABETH HOSPITAL

Emergency Clerk George Wong

Nurse   Miss Chang

Intern   Smiley

Dr. Siu Yung

BANGKOK

Freeman Blake & wife Aurengsem

   Malay girlfriend Bintang

Miss Patpong &
   Eric Carlson (husband)

List of Characters/2

MISC.

Point Meng Wan

Suburb: Man Cheong

Edward Wolring

CIA director re: Vietnamese Buddhist demonstrations

Ching tu base

Hoihow suburbs

Mx蕪

Man Cheung=controlled money

USS BAILEY

Capt. Bowles

SEVENTH FLEET

Adm. Andrew Kerr (command)

Capt. Lew Morheim (carrier)

CHINA & HAINAN

Premier Wan Li-san

       Secy. Miss Wen

Mary's brother Ching

Ambassador to India Dr. Ho Ching-Kuo

Engineer (Technician) Chau

Technician Ching-Kuo

Technician Cho (p. 214)

Assistant Driver Private Chang

Driver Sgt. Pung Yin-su & wife Mei

Wing On

Wing Run

CHINA & HAINAN, CONT.

Comrade Ling

Tak, Pung's friend

Wong Chu
Kong (netsman) (Litzu)   =drinkers of Kaoliang

Mei Ling

Kei Ying, her roommate

Party Chief Nhay

Farmer Dinh & wife Hanh
     radio op. N. hu

The Shau Ling (village chief)
              Nhap Dat
     Secy. Cao
Tung Ku-Hainan Coastal Area
P.C. Yu Min & Lt. JoLi-Ren
Ching Nam - Junk Captain

List of Characters/3

FAMILIES

Nooley: wife Emma
         kids Michael Jr. & Sean

Paisan: girlfriend Noh (Nyam Noh & Nam Ky)

         wife Zoe
         brother Joe

Muhlbach: girlfriend Mio

BARRACUDA

Elgin (seaman)

Rubinchik & Halsey, Signalmen

Sam JR. and James

Commander Wilson

Navigator LCdr. Stan Hammond

Communicator Lt. Bosworth

Exec. LCdr. Joe Battersby

Ensign Grundler

Lt. Frisbee (damage control)

Chief of Boat Bert Colvin

Elec. Counter Measures Operator Bentley
                         navigator
Lt. Percy Smith, stanby/& mess officer protestant lay reader

Chief Jones, Seaman on snorkel

Assistant Bennett -- Hodges

Lt. Bert Holloway, diving officer

Subrad at control; Pirelli & Bob Jones

Bob Jones

List of Characters/4

HONG KONG & DETACHMENT

CIA Chief Arthur Lowery
    Driver Ling

Asst. Mil. Attaché, Col. Morgan

Hank Musgrave

Mary Wu & Sen (son)

AMS Bureau Chief George Yerby

Gladys Wo

Chen Xiu Yu
    Chok Lun Tau = thugs
    Au Chow

Mary's sister Wen

Mil. Attaché Col. Croy

Eddie Ming

Peterson & Taylor

Capt. Frank Hope

Sgt. Paisan Veracruze

Maj. Mike Nooley ("Red")

Maj. Paul Gresham

Lt. Kurt Helmantholer

Sgt. Polk
Sgt. Espinoza
Sgt. Hildebrand
Sgt. Hanson
Sgt. Hing
Sgt. O'Connor - Jack
Sgt. Roberts - Bob
Sgt. Wohl - Bull
Sgt. Bissell
Sgt. Jones
PFC Muhlbach (Muley)
PFC Jim Trotter

Agents Santos & Nicholson

Author's Note

We often hear the baloney that Chinese nuclear power could somehow menace the Continental United States. The fact is that China could not afford a long-range missile system even if her science were up to it—which it is not. The Chinese missiles, like their air power, are strictly local, and from hunger, like most everything else in Communist China.

And until now, the "nuclear power" which Peking brags about has been atomic bombs, nuclear firecrackers like our first A-bombs.

However, the hard-working Chinese have been knocking themselves out to develop a really modern weapon: the Hydrogen Bomb, which even in medium size is 1,000 to 2,000 times as powerful and destructive as the A-bomb.

We must fear the Chinese H-bomb, even if there is only one (and only one doesn't come easily even with unlimited funds).

It is not dangerous to us at home, but if the Chinese Communist dictator in an unbalanced moment should decide to load it on a moderately obsolete aircraft and go after the U.S. Seventh Fleet in Asian waters, it could destroy the Fleet—or any other American concentration of power in Southeast Asia.

The apparatus of modern war, with its emphasis on espionage, so-called Intelligence and clandestine missions, is supposed to warn and prepare us against such an emergency. But nothing ever goes the way it's supposed to progress in theory, a human factor which besets Asian wars as well as wars anywhere.

Could the Communist Chinese get away with this kind of madness? And could we stop it? It would have happened. Perhaps it did. Right about now.

FEBRUARY, **1967**
RICHARD TREGASKIS

For certain Marines, Green Berets, Submariners and Fly Boys, and for Moana, Maudie, and Ley-to —without whom this novel would not have been truthful.

— And for Bill Bird, a great guy
and very generous-hearted too --
also one of the brave men.
From his friend
Rich. Tregaskis
Honolulu, Oct. 24, '67

1

October 7

THE BIG AMERICAN-MADE JET WEARING THE BOLD COLORS
of Japan Air Lines swung past bare island peaks poking from wide
blue waters. The plane's wings tilted toward the sheltered harbor—one
of the world's greatest. The aircraft swung west, past the clustered
main hump of Hong Kong Island, the asparagus-bed of concrete towers marking the business section. The harbor spread a proud array of
ships anchored in orderly tiers. There were freighters of almost every
flag, set out in a monument to the orderliness of British Imperialism.
But it also looked like, and was, Communist China's principal window to freedom, and her main access route to the splendid, manufac-
tured goods of the west—all the cameras, autos, machinery, trucks,
refrigerators she could afford. That wasn't much, considering that her

principal resource was oceans of unskilled and illiterate labor. Hong Kong was the escape valve of a quarter of the world's population constrained in a repressive absolutist dictatorship. It was the Asian meeting place of capitalist and communist, the Berlin of Southeast Asia.

Hank Musgrave, sitting in the third seat of the tourist cabin aboard JAL:543, left side, had no such geopolitical thoughts about it. He was thinking about Hong Kong as American servicemen of the area often did, as the wildest and the most exciting of the Asian cities for a vacation. More specifically, he thought of Mary Wu, the full-bodied taxi-dancer, a refugee from Shanghai, whose physique promised and delivered a pneumatic bliss expected because of her profession, but whose Asian wit provided salt for the dish before and afterward. He had known many courtesans, but never one as bright as Mary. If she had been born to a middle-class American family, she would undoubtedly have earned a Ph.D. at Vassar, summa cum laude. Geography, a simple matter of geography.

Hank, a lean-faced individual of thirty-four, dark-haired, sharp-minded and sharp-tongued, realized that Mary might be gone from Hong Kong's Asia Ballroom. Their girls didn't usually stay long. If they were exceptionally attractive, they drifted into more intimate quarters as the mistresses of one or another of the Colony's numerous officialdom, British or Chinese. Or they went the other way, down—down into the cheaper dives.

Because new girls kept coming in by the thousand from China's inexhaustible labor reservoir, the competition was murderous.

The little Japanese stewardess, elegant and fragile in her kimono, came by to check seat belts. This JAL stewardess was probably the highest type of Japanese beauty, but compared to Mary Wu, she was short-legged, flat-chested, shy. It was true that her complexion was a masterpiece of Benares silk. And the back of her neck seemed satisfactory, for whatever that was worth. Hank drifted into a sudden, almost embarrassingly vivid projection of Mary's full-chested and long-legged beauty—a re-creation of the way she looked when she came out of the bathroom smooth and naked as a yellow dolphin that first time they had made love, at the Hong Kong Biltmore. Then she had executed a fraction of a Go-Go step and said:

"Hank—big boy. Shall we get to first things first?"

He was jerked back to the present when a piping, pleasant Japanese girl's voice made the PA announcement about the Hong Kong landing:

"Fasten your seat belts, please, and no smoking," and then, the same repeated in Japanese.

Hank's mind was still flooded with the warmth of Mary Wu, and her instinctive attractiveness even when she was being businesslike. Hank thought beyond the remembered female smoothness and the vibrant masses of hips and thighs. Mary Wu, with all her curves in the right places, was not the be-all and end-all. Even now, at this stage before he had yet seen her, when he was heading for a week's diversion in Hong Kong, he thought of his profession—about doing a piece on Red China for American Media Service, out of Hong Kong. He could dig around a little here and pick up some of the latest leaks out of Canton, Shanghai, and Peking.

Hank congratulated himself on the fact that he was not completely the slave of amorous imagining, that his professional instincts persisted even among the ramblings of a vivid libido. Of course, he reflected wryly, he had just enjoyed a week of booze and female companionship in Tokyo, and made out with four different Japanese broads. Probably his nonchalance about the temptations of the flesh wasn't such a triumph of the will after all.

As the big jet sloped toward the Kai Tak runway, Hank's mind stayed in a practical groove. The office—would they send him back to Delhi, or, influenced by the latest wave of scare thinking in New York, re-direct him to Singapore to cover the current Malayasian alarum? Would the Hong Kong bureau chief, George Yerby, have some late word from New York? Would American Media Service give him the expense account he had asked for, to pay for the flat in Delhi? When you asked for any kind of expense increase, the New York office always had a way of transferring you to another place, figuring you had been too long where you were and were getting wise to the local expense-account racket. He would have to contact George right away anyhow as soon as he got to the hotel. Maybe George would be at the airfield to meet him. He had sent George a cable from Japan.

But when the passengers filed through the long customs hallway and out toward the busses, George was not there, nobody was there. Hank's ego deflated as he moved toward the busses. He could get a bus to the Peninsula Hotel and then hop a cab to the Shamrock, a struggling little Chinese hotel out near the Asia Ballroom. That location and the price were the only advantages. The blasted AMS skinflints and tightwads. He had only a hundred bucks left of the money he had set aside for the vacation—and that had to pay for Mary Wu.

A few minutes ago, he had been the glamorous foreign correspondent, buoyed up with his expectation of a liaison with the sexiest courtesan he had ever known or could imagine, entertaining her in the most cosmopolitan city of Asia. Now he was kicking himself for being the most unimportant ink-stained wretch of a tightwad news service.

At the Shamrock, he checked into one of the $7.00 (American) rooms, washed his face with the pitcher of cold water in the john. Hong Kong still rationed water and the taps wouldn't be turned on again until 7:00 p.m. Then he went up to the Garden Bar on the top deck to drown his sorrows. He would drink up a little nerve, and call Mary. To hell with George, he could wait till tomorrow.

He belted his double Scotch and one after it, and headed for the room, to telephone his pneumatic Chinese love.

He asked the operator for the Asia Ballroom, and waited for the piping, singsong voice he expected. Usually, the girls wouldn't connect you by phone with one of the hostesses.

This night was no exception. "Mary Wu not here."

He was going to ask if she had left permanently, when the phone connection clicked off. And in the same moment, the Shamrock operator cut in: "Telephone for you, Mr. Musgrave."

A familiar dry voice with a curling New England accent came on: "Hank—this is Freeman Blake; heard you were in town."

"I'm heading west, Freeman," Hank said. "Back to Delhi. Stopped here for a couple of days of R & R. How'd you know I was here?"

"Blake knows all—naturally. And I hear you've been trying to reach a mutual friend, Mary Wu."

"It looks as if you do know all."

"Natch. And you won't find her at the Asia Ballroom anymore. She's gone what you might call straight."

Hank wondered what the Silver Fox was up to? He remembered Blake well from many geopolitical adventures in the Bangkok vicinity.

Freeman Blake was a bona fide import-export dealer, with all the usual implications of the trade: smuggling, contraband, bribes, assistance to the CIA and British Intelligence, some surviving idealism in the choice of warring revolutionary factions—and there were plenty of factions to choose from in Southeast Asia. In Freeman's case, the idealistic scruples were a lot more considerable than with most of the breed. Hank knew how many times Freeman had stuck his neck out to help the revolutionary groups supported by the CIA: viz, the Karen rebels in Burma, the anti-Sukarno guerrillas in Sumatra, the supposedly peaceable charter-plane services which flew helicopters into Laos during the American struggle in Vietnam.

Hank asked: "How's Aurengsem?"

Aurengsem was Blake's beautiful Thai wife, a lady who also had good family connections with the ruling clique of Thailand. Blake had chosen her, like everything else in his local environment, with a maximum of calculation and above all, a sharp eye for economic utility.

"She's fine, thanks. Say—Hank—how about coming by tomorrow morning—to see me at the Hilton. First thing. Say—nine o'clock. It's very important."

The sound of the words reminded Hank of the start of several of his "Sneaky-Peepy" patriotic involvements in the past, one of them with Freeman Blake, in Bangkok.

"Okay," he said. "At nine o'clock." He hung up the phone and there was a cheering note in his bleak isolation. At least somebody had noted his arrival in Hong Kong, and seemed to give a damn. Hank began to whistle. Blake was always involved in something exciting—if you could get it out of him

2

HANK WAS ON TIME WHEN HE KNOCKED ON THE DOOR
at Room 423 at the Hong Kong Hilton next morning—the fourth floor, facing the rather déclassé Hong Kong section called Wanchai. This was the most reasonably priced exposure in the hotel, with somewhat less of a view than the other three sides, although Hong Kong was unique in that almost any building seemed to command superb vistas of harbor and mountain; an Asian version of San Francisco.

Freeman, thought Hank, naturally *would* stay in one of the lower-level rooms in the Hilton. He chooses the Hilton, of course, because it's centrally located, one of the favorite meeting places for Caucasians, and if he lives on one of the lower floors it doesn't do too much violence to his hard-dying conscience of thrift. Wiliness with a buck probably still is No. 1 in Freeman's list of the virtues.

Freeman opened the door; he was tall and silver-haired, he wore his wavy hair with exact precision, like a carefully tended warrior's helmet, as a badge of distinction and respect. His eyes seemed strangely hooded—as if the mystery of the Asian epicanthic fold had somehow, by a kind of osmosis, rubbed off on him. But this time Freeman looked pudgy around the face, and even his carefully tailored Hong Kong suit failed to hide a slight convexity in the middle. Maybe the soft living of the Bangkok cocktail set was making its mark. Or perhaps it had been too long since he was involved in one of those up-country sub-rosa operations. Those exercises in the boondocks tended to pep up one's physical tone and shave the flab from waist and hips.

Now, he squinted up and down the length of the hall, waved Hank into the room and locked the door. Then he turned up the volume of the hotel music system to full blast, so that the sound was a blaring of drums and brass. It was the simplest method of thwarting possible hostile "bugs" which an enemy might have planted near you.

Hank raised his voice above the sound. "What are you doing in Hong Kong? I know it takes a lot to get you away from Aurengsem and the kids."

Freeman shrugged the question away: "The usual monkey business." The big New Englander's stock evasive technique was to overconfess whatever he might be accused of, and thus turn it into a joke.

But that moment he turned to the issue on his mind. "Hank—you knew Mary Wu. You knew her—perhaps very well."

Hank said: "Yeah. Since you know all and see all, you undoubtedly are aware of that. Where is she now? And what's the big mystery about her?"

He sensed that Blake was about to retreat, now when he hadn't even advanced at all. Blake stretched his full six-feet-two, slowly extracted a mahogany-shaded Meerschaum with a curved stem, and knocked it against the palm of his other hand.

He walked to the wide pane fronting the indigo swath of the Wanchai section of the harbor. Down there, in the dense traffic stream of freighters trading with China, a neat gray American destroyer turned like a drifting toy, her crewmen trying to catch a mooring. Freeman was being deliberate with great effort.

"What's eating you, Freeman?" Hank asked. "I haven't seen you this distracted since you and Whitey Wilbur were dropping guns for the Karen revolution."

Freeman's face broke into a characteristic wide, cockeyed smile, and he watched the first of the harbor sampans begin to cluster around the destroyer. She had anchored now, and blue-uniformed, tiny figures of crewmen were unshipping her gangway. "Yeah, it's not too different, in a way. But—well—I'm hesitant. I'm afraid you might tip off the story, the way you did that yarn about the Karens, incidentally, way back when."

Hank said: "I got that story fa'r and sqa'r, stranger. You want me to promise this will be off the record, not to be offered to the readers of AMS? If so, not a chance."

Freeman sat down puffing. "Yeah. Hell of it is—I need your help. I know I can trust you more than 99 percent of the shanty types among the newspaper people. I know most of the correspondents would knife their grandmother for a one-minute lead on a story.

"But you were a Marine in 1946, and a trusted correspondent in China and various of the civil wars the Commies started after World War II. So you know what the Commies are up to; that they can't be trusted, that they're a bunch of bastards that stand on your privates until finally they agree to negotiate; then they get off and you tip your hat and say 'thank you very much.' You know all that."

Another pause. "And besides, when we've needed you in an emergency, you've come through several times when the heat was on. But this is one—I can't even tell you the first thing about it."

Hank got up. "Maybe I better just leave," he said. "As usual, Freeman, you're telling me nothing. Not even where I can find Mary Wu—and yesterday, at least, that was first on my priority list. Are you going to tell me that much? That's little enough."

Blake looked stricken. He shook his head. "Look—*this* is absolutely top priority. Nothing else can touch it. And I can't even tell you where *she* is: it's all too delicate."

Hank had had enough. He started for the door. "Freeman, you're hopeless. As long as you've known me—if you can tell me only that it's absolutely top secret, and secret and won't give me a hint of what's at stake, the hell with it. You seem to want me to jump into an Agency job on fiat, but you don't think enough of me to tell me the first thing about what it is.

"So I'm not taking any chances. AMS is a nickel-nursing dispenser of commercial news, that's true. But I do work for them. And you haven't shown me any heat in this so-called emergency."

Blake motioned Hank back into the chair and turned to watch the destroyer again. "You can't just go now. This is an important one. You see that American tin can down there?" he said pointing out the window, as if that was somehow dreadfully important. "You see, there's already a U.S. station ship on duty in the harbor, another destroyer. That's all the U.S. needs at the moment—the one stand-by warship to evacuate the Americans in Hong Kong Colony, if need be—if something busts between Uncle Sugar and Charlie up north. Understand? *But*, here is another tin can coming in. She's the *U.S.S. Merritt A. Edson*"

Hank made a face: "Is that the big story you're talking about?"

Freeman laughed. "Not per se." He turned to face Hank. "You knew Mary Wu pretty well, right?"

"Sure," Hank said. "Considering that she was a dancehall girl, and at the time she seemed to have made up her mind to keep on with that vocation, I knew her not wisely, but too well. However, when I checked there last night at the Asia Ballroom in Kowloon, she wasn't anywhere around. She's gone off somewhere—maybe she's picked up with one of the Chinese sub-officials in the lower-grade British hegemony hereabouts—so I decided to run the best course of valor and give up the whole chase. I might not like it if I found her —and as I said, this Hong Kong visit is dedicated wholly to Rest and Recuperation."

Freeman was standing, his feet braced, and Hank could see Freeman had decided it was time for some kind of final pitch. "All right," Blake began, "you've been trustworthy, reliable, you've been motivated in the past. You've even bled a little bit and won a couple of Orders of the Purple Shaft in our various cold wars since the end of World War II, including Vietnam."

He turned and looked out the window towards the U.S. tin can. A thin trickle of officers in white uniforms was heading down the gangway toward the captain's gig, which danced in the ultramarine chop of Hong Kong Harbor. "The *U.S.S. Edson* is going on a mission that's as top secret as any ever has been. I want you to look up Mary Wu, because she can get some G-2 that's related to the thing we're on."

"Okay, so what's the G-2 that you want?" Hank asked. "I never did get any dough for helping you in your so-called import-export operations in the past anyhow—might as well not break my record with any vile drachmas now. Or will there be money in it this time, perchance?"

Freeman sighed. He knew he was a long way from getting what he wanted yet. "All right. First, I've got to have your absolute promise that none of this will leak out—not, at least, in any way in less than one month from today."

Hank could feel his hackles standing up. Now suddenly he had been pushed too far. "You've got a helluva nerve, Freeman. You forget that your priority table is all upside down from mine. My first priority is getting a story. Yours is Agency monkey business, *Gott mit Uns*, my country right or wrong, and all that. The rest of it doesn't matter. You want me to get Mary into some act where she might get hurt or killed, and you won't even tell me enough about it so I'll know what the hell I'm doing. You're so scared of the Goddamned story you can't even give me a clue what it's about. What kind of cockeyed newspaperman do you think I am? No, you made your pitch, and I'll just shove off and say 'thanks a lot, but no thanks.'"

Freeman wouldn't leave it quite at that. He couldn't allow a final edge as rough as that. He smiled. "Hank, please, don't tip it. And think it over. Maybe we can make it more attractive to you. Let me know." He was picking up the phone when Musgrave left the room.

Since his first instinct at that moment was to drown the continuing vexations of this Hong Kong stay with alcoholic libations, Hank headed for the International Press Club on the 25th floor of the Hilton.

On the edge of a glassed-in patio, Hank sought a bar stool and a Scotch. Mid-morning was a slack hour. Only two other determined barflies were seeking the solace of the Press Club today at 10:20 A.M.

Looking again at the harbor, Hank watched that now-familiar destroyer at the mooring buoy. How could a single, ancient destroyer be a key to a story of such highly nervous top-secret priority? It must be tied in with an intelligence mission into China. A penetration into Amoy? Something like that.

But why should it perturb Freeman this much? He watched the ship. The captain's gig had disappeared, a liberty boat was turning around the gangway, and a long freight barge had already tied up next to the lean gray flank of the destroyer. An incredible number of Chinese coolies in rough work clothes—an unbelievable number even in Hong Kong which like China is such a great laboratory case for birth control—were swarming over the sharp gunwales of the *Edson*. The neater dungaree-blue uniforms of the *Edson's* work party were swallowed up by the inundation. It was clear the loading party was driven by more than ordinary urgency.

Then, in the club bar enclosure, Hank noted two strangers who were then sliding onto bar stools at the far end. They were Caucasians, but very clearly strangers to the Press Club because they demonstrated none of the unathletic suet which is wont to accumulate with unathletic civilian pursuits like newspapering in the regions of the jaw and midriff. The compelling thing about these Caucasians was that he knew they were familiar to him from somewhere, and there was something wrong about their being in civvies. They were military types.

The taller was fair-haired and blue-eyed, lean and muscular, just a shade over six feet, a good natural heavyweight. There was a lightness and good-nature about his face, coupled with abundant athletic muscular resolve, which struck some vague but potent currents of memory, if Hank could isolate them.

The other man was squarish, in the same age bracket, about twenty-eight or twenty-nine, but dark-complexioned. He, too, moved athletically, with the resilience of someone used to up-hill and down-dale chases on foot.

These two were clearly oriented in Hank's direction, and the taller, officer-type smiled somewhat uneasily. Before they reached Hank, he remembered they were Green Beret, Special Force troopers he had known in the plateau-jungles of Central Vietnam, somewhere up on the Laotian frontier where a vast dispersal of Special Force troops tried to seal the borders against traffic from North Vietnam. The taller man had been the captain of a B-Detachment. Musgrave knew that, and knew almost instantly that it had been near a Montagnard base called Plei Mrong. And the name came, too, Eric Hope.

The sergeant-type was Spanish or Mexican, North American-Spanish. It was a strange nickname, Hank knew: something Italian. Paisan, that was it, a weird mixture of Italian and Spanish, Paisan Veracruze. Hank could see him now, in the Montagnard camp, in one of the thatched buildings that were the Special Force headquarters. He sat in the cool of the plateau-night, shave-headed, bunch-muscled in a T-shirt, presiding over an earnest poker game with beer and a huge can of homemade popcorn for the nighttime enjoyment of the group before they went out to set a counter-guerrilla ambush.

"Mr. Musgrave? Hank Musgrave?" Hope smiled earnestly with far more ease and tact than a twenty-eight-year-old Army captain ordinarily had a right to—except perhaps a general's aide, and Hope had once been that, too, in a distinguished Army career.

"That's right," Hank told him. "I remember you from Plei Mrong, up on the Ho Chi Minh Trail and I remember Veracruze, too. You still in the Army?"

Captain Hope seemed inordinately pleased with the recognition, and the names, but the question abruptly sapped some of his steam. He mumbled: "No—kind of R & R. You working on a story here?"

"No. It's R & R for me, too. Great to be on R & R in Hong Kong, especially if you believe it stands for Rape and Riot. Can I buy you guys a drink?" Hope looked around uneasily, hesitated, seemed to do a violent double-take of the *U.S.S. Edson* so intimately revealed through the wide plate glass of the Press Club window.

"Thanks, thanks a lot. But it's crowding chow time. Maybe you could join Paisan and me for lunch."

Hank wanted to explore the situation a little further. "We could have lunch at the Press Club," he said.

"No, not here," Hope answered too quickly. But he recovered nicely: "I mean, I've got a favorite place, only a few minutes away from here. We can have a quick drink, and go there."

"Okay," Hank told him, knowing that it was going to be indeed a very quick drink. Captain Hope had something very urgent on his mind.

The "favorite place" turned out to be an alley off the downtown thoroughfare called Pedder Street, not a restaurant at all. The torrential foot-traffic of Pedder Street, the bustling thousands of Chinese wearing the clothes of the Western world, here had faded into a trickle of Asians in dark sharkskin pajamas and slippers. There were the inescapable darting children you would expect, and the inevitable strings of laundry hanging between concrete porches.

Hope and Musgrave walked ahead while Veracruze followed carrying in his hand a transistor radio blaring out cacaphonic "ying yang" Chinese music.

Captain Hope spoke quietly and earnestly against the protective sound of the radio while his eyes watched the narrow thoroughfare ahead, where it descended toward the waterfront.

"Listen, Hank—all our mutual friends in Hong Kong know about your record as a correspondent—that you're not about to tip off a story if it's high on the secret list—or at least the parts of a story that are most sensitive. I know this myself from the time you were up with my Special Force detachment in Plei Mrong."

Hank said: "If it's too secret, don't strain. Just don't tell me about it. I might find out about it by myself, anyhow—so we'd both be off the hook."

Hope laughed. "Okay. I won't give you any 'Spook' talk about 'Our Friend', or 'That Guy', or 'The Person We Know', when you're supposed to guess that it's Freeman Blake I'm talking about, right now. I figure the Spook business is a regular part of the form of warfare these days—but right now, when time is short and we've gotta get some action quick, I'm not going to pussyfoot." He laughed. "Besides, I don't think anybody's going to be able to bug us in this alley, while Veracruze is blanketing us with ying-yang."

Hank liked Hope's forthrightness. "Go ahead."

"All right. A week ago, while you were out of Delhi, somebody at the level of the Chinese Ambassador there defected to the U.S. Embassy. I think it was the Ambassador himself, but I'm not sure.

"Nobody knew about the defection publicly, but this guy was real hot at the U.S. Embassy. He spilled his guts, to the effect that the Chinese Reds seem to have an H-bomb, ready to go. And they're going to use it.

"This time, it's not a little firecracker or a nuclear device on a tower at Lop Nor, but the 'Big Boy' itself. According to this guy, the Chinese have got only one. And no missiles to deliver it. Plan is to drop it from a bomber. He didn't know about the type, but he had pretty good proof, from the Chinese big noise—Wan Li-san himself —that it was the only one they have.

"The Chinese big shot in India was supposed to come back to the Embassy again, but he never made it. Just disappeared, and the Chinese made the official explanation that several members of the staff had been called back to Peking for consultation."

Now, Hank was beginning to get the story, in italics and capital letters, and he certainly wasn't going to ask Hope how he happened to start telling it now. But Hope got around to that:

"You have to know this much, and a lot more—even though it's a mortal secret—so you can do what the local Agency types want you to do. Freeman Blake is too damned cautious, he wasn't willing to get his neck out a fraction of an inch to tell you about it—or promise any government funds until he checked with somebody else. "But the Agency knows and I know that you've worked with them, and that you have a pretty good sense of obligation not to spill something that might embarrass our government, if it's absolutely top priority."

Hank said: "Never mind the bouquets. Why are they so hot to get me into this act? What can I do for them?"

Hope jumped after it: "Okay. We know that, from the leak at the Chinese Embassy in Delhi, the bomb is supposed to be dropped on the sixteenth of this month, and that the target is supposed to be the U.S. Seventh Fleet, which will be showing in the South China Sea in the next week. And that's where your friend Mary Wu comes in.

"They know—I mean the Agency people know—that you were a pretty intimate buddy of hers. They know that she, in her present job, might get some dope we're absolutely desperate for and find out something we've got to know yesterday if not sooner: where the bomb is, right now."

Hank said: "I'd like to know how I can do it, if at all. Also what 'her present job' is. And if she can get the dope that they want, what's going to be in it for her? You know as well as I do, Hope, that when the Agency types get mixed up in something like this, it isn't usually the Agency people that get hurt, it's the ones with colored skin, the indigenous personnel that get smashed.

"So, if I'm to do this bit of gumshoe work, where does she get off? And where do I come out on the story?"

Hope said: "You're way ahead of me."

But Musgrave wasn't, really. He was trying to play it cool, but all sorts of jet-fires had been lit in his head, and Hope could sense it. He rushed ahead.

"Ordinarily, the boss types who run me would have taken this proposition in stages. They'd ask you if you'd do a little 007-type work for them, to talk to Mary Wu—who now works for an import- export house here, incidentally—and find out if there have been any shipments of light, high-yield solid electrolyte batteries from here into some South China port. They'd tell you nothing about why.

"I say solid electrolyte batteries because those would be a good tip-off that the H-bomb has been sent in to wherever it is. We'd heard from our Chinese friend in India that there was a shortage of certain parts for the bomb which would be likely coming in from Hong Kong.

"So now you know damned near as much as I do, and I wouldn't have spilled any of this to you if we didn't have a big rush now— in fact, a desperate, mad scramble—to find out where the bomb is— and at absolutely maximum speed.

"This Goddamn thing is breathing on our necks, we're desperate to get information, the Washington people are spilling money everywhere to get a result—and that's why they're after you right now as a good lead to get some dope from Mary Wu, without tipping off anything to her."

The light-blue eyes turned toward Hank, and he heard or felt a kind of sigh as Hope added: "And that is a most unworkmanlike and unskilled way to make a pitch at an intelligence source. Especially since I haven't mentioned the vulgar matter of money, yet. There could be a thousand bucks in it for Mary Wu if she gets us the dope as to where those electrolyte batteries went to in South China—and by the way, a couple of thousand for you if you can put these pieces together intelligently."

It was all pretty upsetting, and Musgrave was thinking that in all his experience in this era of sub-rosa war which has been with the world since the end of WW II, he had never heard a less "Spooky" or "Sneaky-Peepy"-type intelligence recruiting speech. But he would have to grant that, considering his own background and state of mind, no recruiting speech could have been better designed to make him want to pitch in and help—even though he knew that he was losing out on a great story.

Before he could say anything, the hoarse, high-timbred voice of Veracruze interrupted. "Cap'n," he was saying. "Over on the right, the house with the blue terrace, about hundred meters, third floor. Looks like a guy watching us with binoculars. He's got one of them black suits on. In the back of the building, just behind the wash line." And he added: "But don't look up there right now, keep on goin'."

Somehow, Hope had made an instantaneous appraisal without moving his head, and he was talking still as if addressing himself to Musgrave: "Okay, Paisan. You keep an eye on him, we'll keep on walking. Main thing I want to know if it's binoculars, or a listening device."

Hope kept moving his lips silently, as camouflage, while Veracruze reported: "No, it's binoculars or field glasses, Cap'n. It don't look at all like one of them listening cones. In a minute, you can check it yourself, if the wash don't blow."

By this time Hank, too, had fixed on the building in question, and the wash on the third floor. He could spot a figure in black standing beyond fluctuating pennants of children's drawers hung out on a line, but the binoculars escaped him.

Hope was going on as cheerfully as ever, still without turning his head towards the house in question: "We've got to expect to get bugged. The Unfriendlies have got agents all over Hong Kong, and we know they've been watching any Americans that look any different from the tourists. But I don't think they've got anything on us, yet."

3

HOPE HAD CHOSEN ANOTHER SCENE IN WHICH TO FINISH his briefing, his sales pitch, and his instruction manual for the job.

The spot was his room at the Empress Hotel, on the Kowloon side. Of course, he and Hank couldn't talk at all on the crowded Star Ferry crossing the Harbor from the Island and, Hope reflected, during the trip Hank could contemplate certain advantages inherent in attempting the mission; like the Good Green.

Hope filled Hank in: "The reason Mary Wu might have a tap on the shipment of high-yield solid electrolyte batteries out of Hong Kong is that it happens she works for an import-exporter named Chen who is a dealer in electrical stuff.

"A shipment of high-yield solid electrolyte batteries sent by an export agent out of here into China, would probably have some other label, and it would probably be manifested in the cargo lists as something else, like a fork lift or an electric generator.

"We've run through a little of this stuff with the British intelligence here, without telling them anything, and we haven't *found* anything. We're trying everything. The time is too damn short for leisurely methods."

Hank interrupted: "Excuse my ignorance, but what exactly does a high-yield solid whatever-it-is have to do with the H-bomb?"

"Okay," Hope said. "It's just one of the things that the 'Nuke' boys say is a very likely indication, so we're checking it out.

"I don't know exactly how it works either, but as it was explained to me, the hydrogen bomb, like the atomic bomb, has to get squeezed together to get exploded. Imploded, to be exact. You know that much.

"And the kick for this kind of squeezing has to be supplied by some lightweight batteries with plenty of power.

"The nuclear Sneaky-Peepy boys say this is one item that the Commies are in short supply of—they might reach out to get it in Hong Kong. You know you can get everything here. Everything in the world—and fast—if you've got the money."

Hank said: "And you say that Mary Wu would be able to put a tap on this kind of shipment, right?"

"If anybody could, she probably could, as Chen's secretary. And, to state it boldly, we figure you are our best avenue of approach to Mary Wu."

"And how do you know this is the Mary Wu that I knew? After all, Mary Wu in Hong Kong is like Jane Smith in England, they come by the hundreds. Besides, the one I knew was a dancehall girl. Could she be a secretary to a big import-export firm chief so fast?"

"Blake says she is. She learns fast. He has a pretty long arm on her—and you, too."

Hank smiled. "I know that. But why don't you just get the British to raid the firm—and grab their papers?"

"We're trying to keep it all as clandestine as we can. We can't take a chance of tipping it off to the Chinese—or tell the British the whole fact of the matter. If we're going to have to make a raid, it's got to be completely in the black. Blacker than that if we can manage it."

*

Considering that it was supposed to be the largest business of its kind in Hong Kong, the office of the Tiger Importing Company, Ltd., wasn't at all imposing, Hank thought. It was a third-floor walk-up next to a big jewelled-sweater workshop, in a surprisingly old building for Hong Kong on Nathan Road, the main artery of Kowloon.

Hank knocked at the frosty window lettered with the Tiger name, and walked in.

The room was a large, bare office on the British model, with lines of cramped desks ranged in it, and a staff of young Chinese clerks, male and female, working furiously over ledger books and piles of paperwork.

Beyond the large workroom, a couple of private offices were shut off by frosty-paned doors. Hank picked out an attractive slip of a Chinese girl, and addressed himself to her, thinking that it would be just like a standard G-2 foul-up to get the wrong dope on Mary.

But when he asked the sloe-eyed clerk, she unwittingly confirmed the G-2. "Miss Wu inner office," she said. "Over there. Secretary to boss." He moved as indicated, toward the door saying Chen Yu, President and Managing Director.

Next to that imposing entrance was a smaller one. The door was marked, on frosty glass, Mary Wu, Secretary, with corresponding Chinese characters. First there were the characters for Mary Wu, using her Chinese name Wu Mei-Yan.

The other characters gave him a start—the squiggles indicating her position. Translated literally, they meant "secret archives," the same characters for the title of Secretary. It struck him instantly that if and when he had unravelled all of the preliminaries and succeeded in establishing some personal contact with Mary again, he might find a discouraging wall of silence when it came to prying into essentially a secret affair to her. Also, if she were in the direct pay of the Unfriendlies, and he were too talkative, she might tip off everything he knew about the bomb plot. The usual jitters beginning an Agency job.

He was hesitating, about twenty feet from the boss's door, when Mary came out, carrying a secretary's notebook. She didn't appear to see him, and closed the door very rapidly behind her, effectively cutting off the view from and into the boss's chamber.

She was wearing a white silk blouse and heavy tweed skirt, and sensible shoes. Hank remembered well the clinging evening gowns, the *cheongsam* skirt slit up the sides practically to the hip, which had been her working uniform when she was the most successful of the taxi-dancers at the Asia Ballroom; No, two, that is, within the sub-category of hostesses who spoke English.

In the moment, he noted that the sober costume didn't obscure the shape of the slim figure, the bosom exceptionally full for a Chinese. And the ridiculously short skirt in vogue among females these days revealed that the taut curve of those lengthy golden legs was still very much with her: more important, that she was still aware of it. Hank's heart beat with the same high excitement he remembered from many pleasant hours of expectation in the days of her earlier career.

But she seemed businesslike, preoccupied, apparently not to see him at all. She moved, as he had always remembered she moved, as erect as a queen, proud of her figure and with inherent grace. And the clear-cut beauty of her face, the chiseled arch of her cheekbones, the clean line of her jaw—these were still much with her.

He watched her face carefully to see whether, if she remembered him immediately she would seem to be friendly. As she moved toward her office, she took in his height, his sandy-colored hair. Her flash of recognition was immediate: "Hank!!" Her face did brighten, but her smile seemed faint, and he fancied he could see her glancing around the room to see whether the female office workers were watching her. Those black eyes, with their perfect upward slant, also turned momentarily to the boss's door. Then she seemed to decide that she would talk to him out there, rather than take him into the privacy of her office. Possibly, he thought, she wanted to put him off to a later meeting farther from curious spectators. But his cry to her was uninhibited, and probably dangerously so:

"Mary! *Ising wan!*" He had called her by the familiar Cantonese word for lover or sweetheart. The sound almost struck him dumb. But at last he managed: "It's damn near thirteen months since I saw you last."

He could see her mind picking that up, and now she repeated it all in Cantonese, and in a firm and audible voice, obviously for the benefit of the office onlookers.

And she went on, in the same clear Cantonese: "You just got into town, and you found me here through my former neighbors."

"*Hai loh!*" Hank agreed, meaning "definitely yes," following her lead in Cantonese.

Then she rushed on very softly in idiomatic American, the Vietnam idiom which she knew well: "Number Ten thou'! I'll get zapped, you stay around here." That would approximately translate: "Worst thing you could do is to come here. Might make real trouble for both of us."

The whispered instructions continued at top speed: "You want to see me, make it old tea place up on top. Twenty hundred tonight. You better bug out. Bye!"

Hank grasped instantly what she meant: he must leave, immediately or sooner, and meet her tonight at one of their favorite places, the tea house up on top of the Peak, that mountain at the top of Hong Kong Island, at eight o'clock.

She was wearing a polite expression, and glancing at the boss's office door, when he left. To reinforce the construction she was attempting, as he left, she called out to him, for the benefit of the office, in Cantonese: "Sorry I can't see you any more! I have a new life now!"

✳

Hank checked in with Hope by telephone to Hope's room at the Empress, shortly after, using the form of anonymous indication which he knew was standard for Spook conversations that might be bugged: "I talked briefly to our friend and won't be able to make a date until tonight." Hope answered in the correct noncommittal mode: "Too bad. But will you call me as soon as you can, tonight?"

"Sure thing."

✳

Hank took the funicular up to the Peak at eight o'clock, and saw her standing on the concrete platform just outside the station at the very top of Hong Kong Island. It was cool there, and she wore a western-style tweed jacket. He might have bustled right up to her, but he saw that she was bristling some kind of warning, and from the drop of her right hand he gathered she didn't want to be recognized in this congested and illuminated spot. Instead, he fell in behind her as she

• 26 •

walked along the concrete ramp from the funicular station to the tea house.

The tea kiosk was crowded, as usual. It was full of Chinese tourists, and the clatter of conversation and tea dishes. Mary walked into the terrace overlooking the bright harbor lights, and was shown to a table at the edge of the terrace. He followed her in a few moments, staged a recognition charade, and took a chair at her table. Now she was quite different from the Mary Wu of the Tiger office. She was soft and feminine, although very much on edge, almost tremulous.

"I thought it was better to meet up here," she said speaking English, with her eyes flicking around the close-packed tables filling the room.

He gave the waiter their order for jasmine tea, and told her: "I wondered why you mentioned this place."

"Meeting this way, in the tea house, could be a believable accident," she said. "If they should find out."

At the table they made small talk, purposely in Cantonese, so that if anyone were listening in, the conversation would seem to be only a re-establishment of social relations after a period of a couple of years.

"I had to quit the dancehall business, for the sake of my son. You remember Norman."

He certainly did remember Norman, the son whom she had managed somehow to spirit out of Communist China when she escaped. When he had seen Norman last, he was a cunning Buddha-head of about three, and he knew well that because of Norman, Mary had had an ironclad rule against taking any boy-friends up to her apartment when she was working as a dancehall girl. Other places might be all right for business dealings on occasion.

He knew that Norman's name, like her English translation of her name Mei-Yan, had evolved from the Chinese. His name in

Mandarin—he had been born in Shanghai—was *Yung Gan*. That became Ho-han in Cantonese when Mary managed to reach Hong Kong. The translation of Ho-han into Norman in the British colony was easy.

And Hank knew how much Norman meant to her. The boy stood for the one great love of her life, her bridegroom in Shanghai. Later on, that husband, Wu, had been liquidated by the Communists as a kind of accidental byproduct of one of their so-called re-education programs.

Most of her family had been 're-educated', which translated into individual education-in-a-concentration camp, or more crudely, brain-washing. Her father and mother had both been casualties of this system. Then Mary had worked her way into the southern provinces of China, next to the free sanctuary of Hong Kong. There, she utilized her obvious feminine assets with a local Communist chief to arrange papers for a passage over the border into Hong Kong, for son and self. It had been this experience—using her sex appeal to further her route to freedom through a chain of Communist local chiefs—that got her started in the dancehall hostess business in Hong Kong. A lucrative profession for her, anyhow, in an over-saturated labor market. But during that experience in Hong Kong's Asia Ballroom, she had kept Norman well away from an involvement with her means of livelihood.

Now she smiled: "I had to decide whether I would grow into a professional wild pig," she said, "or change my profession altogether. I studied shorthand and typing, I even learned Stenotype. I had the advantage of speaking English—and especially, American.

"I thought I might get into an import-export business, and work up to be a secretary of the company, and get a squeeze of the profits. I thought I'd make nearly as much as I was earning at the Asia

Ballroom." She spread her hands, palms up, in a shrug of futility. "But I'm a salaried employee, still. No percentage."

Those words were music to Hank's ears at the moment. They indicated that she was short of money, and that the reward he could promise her for information would probably fall on receptive ears.

After the tea, they made their way along the dark concrete path which edges the top of the slope overlooking the city, the Harbor and the lights of the ships. He made sure they were well away from any neighbors in this lover's lane, and turned on a transistor radio.

"Mary, you know I always had a soft spot in my heart for you and Norman. I wrote two letters to you right after I left, last time. One came back. Marked 'unknown'. First thing I did when I came back to Hong Kong this time, was to try looking for you at the Asia Ballroom. But no dice.

"I found you at the Tiger Import-Export Company—but not through your former neighbors in Kowloon as you wisely suggested for public consumption back at the office. I found out through some American friends of mine, American servicemen who are here."

He saw her eyelids flicker at the mention of American servicemen, and that she had long since guessed what he was about. He knew that in the past at least, she had been violently anti-Communist, and she generally liked Americans. He was careful to hold the carrot of the thousand dollars constantly in sight, and also to simplify what she had to do. He said nothing about the over-all plan. All these friends of his needed, he said, was to know whether the Tiger Import-Export had sent solid electrolyte batteries into South China, and in which part of China they ended. Could she find out? If she could, she would have the thousand dollars American, beautiful folding green, on the spot.

They stopped at a concrete wall and looked down toward Wanchai, the forest of splashing neon there, the airy, curving string of electric bulbs outlining the rigging of a ship of war, probably the American destroyer *U.S.S. Edson.*

"Hank," she began, still with a nervous edge in her voice, "I've got other problems than just maintenance for Norman. I've brought my sister in already on the shark circuit." He knew what she meant: that she had paid seagoing smugglers to bring her sister in illegally from Red China. He was also heartened because now she was convincing herself that her financial need was great, that it justified what she would have to do. "That cost one hundred and twenty-five dollars, the American-green kind, and about fifty dollars extra in grease for the local *Sien-jong.*"

Hank knew now that she was bargaining. She had the inherent Chinese knack for haggling, an art fostered by a long history of need and tragic shortages. She was going to up the ante somewhat before she got the information he wanted—but, at least, he was convinced now, she was going to play ball. Judging from the alacrity of her response, she also did have some definite information about the solid electrolytes and where they had gone in China.

"I think maybe I could get my friends up to fourteen hundred or fifteen hundred—but no more than that." Then following through with the solid bargaining technique of deprecating the product—a technique which he had learned the hard way over the years in Asia: "After all, Mary, you know how these things go. This is only one bit of information that the masterminds add up with other bits to get some kind of a cockeyed picture."

"The masterminds are cockeyed on both sides," she said with a tight smile. "But I like your side better. On your side, the big shots can't afford to be so cockeyed, because on your side, the public knows more about what's happening. On your side, if a war gets too cockeyed, people know about it and get it changed. But on the communist side, it's all buried." She laughed. "And I do mean buried, like the soldier corpses. Like the doctor who buries his mistakes."

As she talked, in the shadows where the plane of her face gleamed like perfect ski-slopes, golden snow contours, he felt a wave of regret that this was turning out to be a simple bargaining session. He remembered some such before. "This, too, on a business basis."

She thought he was getting restive, and added: "All right, Hank, I think I can find out. The batteries, yes, there were some. I remember them, and I remember how much heat there was to get them on their way." She added parenthetically, "You know why I've been so jumpy: the Tiger Company is what you call a payola of the Communists. Naturally, the heat is on me. We'll have to find out where the shipment went in China. Canton first. From there, I don't know. But I can find out. Maybe, if you could take out a room in another hotel—you're staying at the Shamrock, aren't you? Why not make it the Mandarin? If you do that, I'll come up to your room."

Now the slope of those long-lashed eyes turned in his direction. She turned her body skillfully so that the long curve of her throat caught the gleam. It was like Mary, the quintessence of Asian femininity, to know exactly what and how much she was projecting, the old flower-like charm he remembered from the Asia Ballroom days. It was like her never to forget the delicacy and perfection of the Asian Peach, the Mandarin symbol of femininity. As with almost all Asian women he had known, the awareness of femininity never slept. Asian women, he thought, were great in business because they never forgot the power of their femininity.

"I'll check in at the Mandarin in the morning," he told her. "Call me in the afternoon and I'll tell you what room number. Can I see you about eight o'clock tomorrow night?"

She smiled her faint, intriguing half-smile. "Probably," she said.

"Eight o'clock, then." However, he remembered the big rush to get the intelligence, and added: "Or better still, if you can get that dope, come by at lunch time. That would be even better. I'll be there from eleven o'clock on."

When she said she would try, he had visions of her waiting for her boss to step out so that she could check the Tiger Company files. And momentarily, he wished for the old days, when they had been alone and she was so completely free in her speech, her beauty, her wit. Toward the end, even her favors had been free, simply because she liked him. Now a shadow of constraint like a steel brace seemed to have taken her over. Her wit was only a shadow of its former self.

One thing he must check with her. "Mary—your boss—you're not —mixed up with him, are you?"

At last he saw the broad smile he had missed, the white arch of those beautiful teeth which had somehow, through all the communist miseries and privations, and her current nervous privations, retained their perfection. "You know, Hank, I tend to think pretty straight. I don't get 'mixed up' about the essentials. Chen Yu is my boss, and I can see that he's pretty deep in something with the Communists. My sympathies are with your side, money or not." And he was sure that she was telling the truth.

She laughed: "Of course, in this case there's the handsome green, too—to reinforce my ideals."

Then the steel frame of anxiety clamped over her again. As they were about to part, she said, "I'll call you, tomorrow morning. Better leave me here." She walked back along the concrete path toward the crowded tramway station, and he watched the grace of her motion. She was a beautiful woman still. And he wondered, with such a woman couldn't I make it? I could stay in Asia, do the lucrative two-minute TV feature spots about what they're thinking in Hong Kong or Calcutta or Singapore (as if anybody knew), and raise a brood of golden-colored kids like Freeman Blake's brood. But he thought, not right now, not this moment, anyhow. Because again, he seemed to be caught up in something just as exciting, if perhaps less pleasant— one of those huge, clandestine, important stories, only the biggest ever to come down the pike.

He hurried back to the hotel to phone Eric Hope; he tried to reach Hope several times at his hotel, but the operator kept saying the line was busy. When at last Hope got the message, and called back, he explained: "I've been on the damn phone all the time. I'll tell you about it later. How did you make out?"

"Everything went fine," Hank told him in the proper Spook form of indefiniteness. "There's a lot I want to talk to you about. When can I see you?"

"I'll be over there at your hotel in half an hour; see you then."

Eric was on time, and he explained his busyness against the usual background of hotel music. This time, he first checked the closet and the phone for signs of bugging. Then he stretched wearily, and said: "There are a lot of people checking in to my command. My own party people—like Paisan. A million things to do—yesterday. You understand."

Hank said he did, and Hope charged ahead: "I'll tell you more about it later, but first, tell me what happened, and what you need."

When Hank told him about the successful beginning with Mary, Eric was happy. He said he thought he could stretch things to the fifteen-hundred-dollar figure.

Then he was heading for the door, plainly a man with too much to do. But he was still forceful; "You'll get it tomorrow," he promised. "Definitely."

Hank said: "Goose it along as much as you can. The earlier in the morning you can get it, the better."

"I'll bring the money to you here before ten o'clock. Okay?"

4

October 9

WHEN HOPE CAME BY HANK'S ROOM AT THE SHAMROCK IN the morning, he had the $1500 for Mary, in anticipation of the goods she would deliver.

"There were only a few snags getting the loot," he said. "The boss says I should convey to you that 'no information, no money' is the principle."

Hank could see he was uneasy delivering this budgetary message.

"I understand the accounting department," Hank told him. "But Mary's already got some of the dope, we know that, and it looks good for the rest. I wouldn't be surprised if she knew all about why we're interested—even though I told her nothing except the fact that we wanted to know about the solid electrolyte batteries."

Hope stood up to go, and saw the *U.S.S. Edson* still surrounded by lighters and junks, still taking provisions aboard. He stopped momentarily to watch the process.

Hank asked him, "Is that the ship in the big plan we're involved in?"

Eric weighed the question, but his face still shone with honesty. "Not definitely," he said. "It's only one of the alternatives. You know how it is, you have to be ready with a dozen alternate solutions for one problem."

Hank didn't push. His first priority—to make the move to the Mandarin. To be there when Mary called.

He pulled out a JAL bag and put the money, fifteen hundred-dollar bills, into an envelope. Whoever had sent the money had chosen the denominations wisely. In the free currency market of Hong Kong, the larger denominations were always at a premium because they were easier to store and smuggle.

As Hope was leaving he said: "You'll call me later in the day, as soon as you know anything?"

"Right." Hank was thinking what that money would mean to Mary and to him, and Hope still hovered a moment at the door. "This is my luggage for the move to the Mandarin," Hank explained. "But don't worry, I won't let any porter carry it."

Hope reached in his pocket and extended a fountain-pen-tear-gas gun. "You've got no way to protect it. This is better than nothing."

He hesitated one minute longer. "I don't know whether you know how to use that gadget. It's really not much use unless you shoot it right in the guy's face. It'll blind him for a few hours."

Hank realized why Hope had been such a good, practical leader and instructor up in the Vietnam Montagnard country. He could get right to the heart of the instruction matter without excessive verbiage: "When you hit this lever, it punctures the cartridge with a kind of faint bang, and a cloud of tear gas comes out. But you've got to aim it right in the guy's face, and clear out pronto. Otherwise you get gassed, too. This is a fresh one. It should have a pretty good charge, but you gotta change your cartridges, they tend to get worn out and lose their zapp pretty fast. Otherwise, the guy pulls a knife on you while you pull your gas gun, and pfftt! Nothing! Except you've got a red necktie, the self-renewing kind."

✳

Hank checked into the Mandarin at ten-forty, and Mary phoned at about eleven. "I'll see you there at twelve-fifteen."

Hank had time to say: "The room number is 913." Then she clicked off.

He had hung up his coat in the empty closet and ordered luncheon to be delivered at 12:10. She would be on time; she always was punctual, like a good businessman.

This room, too, had a good view of the deep-blue of the Harbor, and at the far right end, the slim gray seagoing knife-blade of the *U.S.S. Edson*, still inundated by working parties, and surrounded by lighters and junks. But this time he wasn't watching them. He was remembering the last time he had met Mary in this same hotel, one deck below, in room 817. It was funny how that number stuck in his head.

Actually, nothing important had occurred in that room, in the sense of historical or even social happenings. But the love-making there had been something else.

Mary had a fantastic golden body, and she loved love-making with a frankness and devotion-to-the-art shared by few people in history except perhaps the ancient Greek followers of Astarte, and especially the Hindu adorers of Shakti, the believers in physical love for its own sake; and the Polynesians of the Pacific, who had a similarly healthful approach.

Hank wondered if her new career as an embryo executive had dimmed her appetite for a good thing in life, perhaps even the best. Maybe he would yet find out.

He remembered that on this same date, when he and Mary had been enjoying this best of the personal recreations, in room 817, he had fallen asleep exhausted, delightfully exhausted. Then, that night, he had come awake at 3:30 in the morning and he saw her standing beside the bed, a slick golden dolphin with every curve in precisely the right place, and she was setting beside him a glass of cold milk and a plate of crackers. Where she had managed to conjure them at the unseasonable hour he couldn't fathom, but that little bit of thoughtfulness made a strangely penetrating impression. It was incongruous that something so inconsequential should wield such an emotional punch. But life, he thought, is like that, little things are always popping out of nowhere and bowling you over when you least expect it.

That night in room 817 was the last he had seen of Mary till now. He'd had to shove off the next day on some five-alarm drill for India, by urgent order of American Media Service. When that hoo-haw had subsided—it was one of the troubles along the India-China border—he had written to her at the Hong Kong address he knew, on the Kowloon side, but the letter was returned with an English script notation on the envelope: "Party Unknown, Return to Sender." Later, he had written to her at the Asia Ballroom, and heard nothing from that one.

Mary was a free-swinging wit with the intelligence and earthy humor which distinguish the Chinese common people—or which did until they were swallowed up in the Communist police state. And she had an extra facility—a pride of body which always kept her athletically trim, clean, and well-groomed.

It was an unbeatable combination, coupled with a tremendous language adaptability, which had made her the most sought-after hostess at the Asia Ballroom. And strangely enough, she was not as much physically trammeled as one would have expected in a champion of this profession. Always, she had been able to kid an American client, no matter how grimly determined and straight-faced he was in his pursuit of his particular amatory excitement, and she could keep him at bay practically as she wished by well-chosen, flamboyant flights of humor.

Hank remembered the time she once told him about, when a young American soldier acquainted her with his distinctive libidinous preference.

His preference was about as crazy as they come in the weirdo catalogues of sexual repression. He wanted to cut two round holes in a newspaper. She was to wear it momentarily as a kind of breast plate to enshrine for him her already notable mammary development.

Mary, more than equal to the situation, had hooted to him an old homily out of the Buddhist Good Book, the *Dhammapada*

"Let a wise man leave the small pleasure, and look to the great."

Not only had this aphorism given this frustrated character pause, but, as she explained: "It made a man of him—again."

Hank had asked her who the lucky guy was, not without an edge of jealousy.

"That's classified information," she said. "Only for the eyes of those who 'Need To Know'." But what she had done for this nameless client was like what she had done for Hank.

Hank was at that time shattered by the break-up of his first and only marriage, to the All-American beauty from California who had known from the beginning that he wasn't good enough for her. Her mistake: marrying a newsman. His: marrying her.

At this time, Mary had reminded Hank how to be a man at a bad time in life—and did it in the most pleasant way. He would always be grateful for that, and possibly a lot more than grateful.

She arrived one minute early, this time, at his new room in the Mandarin, just after the waiter had left the wheeled luncheon tray. She was immaculate as ever, wearing the same tweed suit with a fresh white blouse, but her face showed faint lines of strain. She closed the door quickly, and told him: "I don't think anybody was following me." But she looked as if she had left a whole family of ghosts in the hall-way. "Of course," she said, smiling, "I don't want the Great King Chen to know I'm seeing you. I don't want to die just yet."

She looked around uneasily. "Can we talk here?"

He turned up the volume of music, pulled two chairs to the roller-table.

"Sure. But first, I've got some food for us." He took the metal lid off her plate. "Do you want a drink?"

"No, thanks," she said and smiled. "Bad for the figure." She never did drink much, and she had also learned an enlightened American taste: high protein, particularly steaks.

She started right out with the business at hand, while she plied a knife and fork, with un-Asian dexterity. He remembered that she preferred knife and fork over chopsticks, because she had once said: "If you want to eat in a hurry, and you've got something to eat, chopsticks are about as much help as a bottle of Patou."

Now she said: "I haven't got much time. I better talk fast. Twelve solid electrolyte batteries were sent on August twelfth. They were taken from emergency kits for elevators. But all the rest of the stuff was left behind, only the batteries were sent in a packing case, and they were manifested as 'elevator repair kits', which was just partially true.

"The ship was China Coastal Line, British registry, and it went to Canton. The hard part was to find out what happened after that. I did. They went to Hainan, the island of Hainan. The port of Hoihow, to use the Cantonese name. Haiko is the Mandarin name, since the Commies took over."

"You're sure of it; sure of that destination?"

"I saw the lading slip, which showed a stop at Canton, but that the batteries would be sent on with a lot of other things to be dropped at Hoihow."

This was it, the important dope. If the batteries were dropped off at the island of Hainan, that was probably the final destination, since it is the extreme southern point of the Communist Chinese state—and incidentally, probably one of the best and most convenient places from which a hydrogen bomb attack on the Seventh Fleet might be launched.

As Mary was cutting her steak, the fork slipped and bounced to the floor. When she picked it up and started to cut again, it rattled against the plate. He knew she was riding on a thin edge of nerve, and told her: "Mary, would it make you feel better if I followed you when you went back to the office? I could see if anyone was trailing you, and I could watch out for you a little if anyone should try to jump you."

She laughed, the gentle, feminine, yet insistent laugh like wind chimes, which overcame her no matter how incongruous the situation. He remembered it well, it was pleasantly characteristic. She said, before her laughter had stopped: "Hank! With your height, you'd be a great one to trail me through the streets of a South China city. About as obvious as a detective eight feet tall, in your country."

She was absolutely right. "So okay, it was a bad idea, But I could hire somebody, some local type, to watch over you."

"Never mind, Hank. It will be all right." Her nerves had snapped to a tight pitch again: "I am worried about one thing."

He got up to fetch the airline bag and the money. She divined that he had misread her: "I don't mean the money."

He crossed the room to get the money bag. It was a tribute to her in these strenuous times that she was as un-pushy as she had been as a dancehall girl, when money came to her with the greatest of ease, and she could deliberate how she was going to take it, and from whom. She had a basically American generosity and open-handedness.

She went on: "It's what all this means—naturally, I'm curious. About what it all means. When you asked especially about these batteries, I began to put together some things I remembered from the time the shipment was sent. About that time, Chen had a couple of visitors who I know were from the Commie side, just out of China. They wore the blue, worker-style tunic Papa Mao always had; Chen kept them away from me, he addressed them as 'doctor', and they were the right age and look for scientists. That is, like a mechanic with extra mathematics, but unable to talk except of 'Q-forces', or 'I'll extrapolate in this parameter', meaning 'I'll take a guess'." She pronounced the phrase as a Chinese might, deliberately using these carried-over English words: "Extra-porate in this pel-ah-metah."

He knew exactly what she meant and marvelled again at her brilliance in picking up and understanding an obscure but very pertinent phrase in a strange language. And the significance of what she was saying was that these were Chinese scientists who had come down to spur along the shipment through the necessary mechanism, and Mary, with her usual perspicacity, had apparently divined that the batteries were involved with the nuclear bomb.

In one minute more, she made that clear. "So if you want me to, I'll try to find out more about this bomb—if it is a bomb. I heard the learned technician using that Mandarin word, *Kgwa-hua*, and I know that they use that word for bomb, too, and I also heard King Chen use the Cantonese word biggest, which is *ting tsai*."

She said: "You know Hank, I try to live my own life and keep my family alive and no *'dwai bu-shu'*, and it's a hard enough job to keep that little corner of the world alive. But sometimes you border on things that will involve a lot more people.

"In a case like that, you think that you and your family are only one of millions that make up the bigger unit. And I know which bigger unit I'm in favor of. All you have to do is compare the life of the family unit on this side, with the communist side. Their side is like being in jail—plenty of people in your cell, always, listening for you to say something that'll send you up for re-education or discipline. But those people in your jail cell, sharing your slop bucket and every two inches of space, aren't your family. And certainly not your friends. Was there ever a *friendly* jail?

"So I'll do everything I can to stay on this side, and when it comes to helping, I'll help this side."

She laughed. "Even aside from the normal preoccupation with feathering my nest with good green. So, if you like, I will try to find out more about this bomb, when I have a chance to get to the records. Good or not good? *Hau* or *Bu-hau?*"

She had used the literal phrase, rendering it directly into English, which had been one of their favorites when Hank knew her, and which translates approximately into "Okay?"

"Decidedly okay," he told her, still without revealing more than that about the story. But he had to warn her: "This is big stuff, you'd better watch it. I don't want you getting hurt, and what you've told me is enough. It's plenty, and all I asked for. You could find out if it's the biggest bomb, the hydrogen bomb that makes the atom seem a peanut. But don't stick your neck out. I happen to want to see that beautiful body kept in one piece. I remember it not wisely, but too well."

She took a mouthful of steak. "Not wisely, but too well?"

"A literary indiscretion of one of my worthy predecessors in the writing line," he said. "And it's certainly true about my remembrances of you. I think it was Shakespeare. You know that name?"

She nodded. "But not as well as Kung Fu-tzu, or his partial successor in the Communist state as the sage of China, Mo-tzu. Mo-tzu wrote: 'All-embracing love is the cause of benefit to the world.' Too serious?"

She levelled the heavenly curve of those eyes in his direction and his heart accelerated. She touched his wrist with the golden peach-curve of her hand, and he remarked on the perfection of the dimples there, the miraculous smoothness of those fleshly valleys.

She said: "Hank, I learn from you, always. You know worlds I don't know, you always make me awake to them."

He told her, and meant it: "With you, I learned about still other worlds. I haven't forgotten those particular worlds you taught *me* about."

She took his hand and placed the back of it against the golden curve of her throat.

"Women can always teach men—the dummoxes—about those certain worlds. Men can make war or build empires or fortunes, whatever they do to spread their strength around. But the women's world is there first. Women know it by instinct and they have to show it to the men, isn't that right? *Hau* or *Bu-hau?* Okay or not okay?"

"Okay—by all means!" he said. "And I agree this world is first, it's like—like they say, it's basic. You must continue your instruction; for instance, in the next day or two."

She smiled, he heard the silver chime of her laughter. "First things first, Hank," she said. "I still think so."

He gave her the envelope and she put it in her purse without counting the money. "This will help to pay for Norman's education."

"There will be more of the same if you find out more about the *Kwag-hua*, the bomb. But don't take chances. And if you want to reach me, call me at the hotel and I can meet you any time. Or if you can't, have your sister call and tell me where or when."

She was leaving. She kissed him lightly, the smooth, taut, cool cheek against his face, her skin peony-fresh. The touch moved him.

"I want to quote another of our Western sages, a European kind of Mo-tzu called Anatole France: '*L'amour, c'est le contact de deux epidermes.*'"

"French?"

"Yes. Love is the touching of two skins."

"He *was* a sage." She laughed. "That man France—he knew first things first."

She left, saying: "Don't come with me. I'll phone you. And later, I'll give you some more of the instruction we talked about."

He watched her go, thinking: If she has Gods, may they keep her safe.

*

As he put in his call to Hope at the hotel, he thought how much of that priceless instruction he'd had from this Daughter of the Phoenix.

Eric Hope came over to Hank's room at the Mandarin for the meeting.

He gave the room the usual check-over for bugs and the hotel radio volume went zooming as usual to approximately the volume of a Go-Go concert. Hank conveyed Mary's G-2 to him, and he was much enthused.

"I'll have to take all this info to the Big Cheese myself, as quickly as I can," he said. "No telephone calls that might risk anything, or get anything wrong."

He reached into his pocket for an envelope, and he suddenly was a shamefaced schoolboy excusing himself for truancy.

"I brought the money for you. But one of the big shots said the extra money paid to Mary would have to come out of yours."

Hank was very little disturbed: "I'll bet the big cheese in question was Freeman Blake—it sounds like his Yankee ideas of thrift."

"Right." Eric hesitated. "Believe me, Hank, I threw him every pitch I could think of."

"I know. Matter of fact, I expected it. Main thing is, they came through with the money for Mary right on time. I really sweated that one out. Nothing's more predictable than the delay and screw-up of the government paymaster—except maybe the niggardliness of Freeman Blake. Also, it's a pretty safe bet that there will always be one or more budget-minded types like that in a big government operation, especially the Sneaky-Peepy type."

Hope had one more item which had evidently been much on his mind. "Hank—you know what our general mission is. I expect now it will be in Hainan.

"We'll need a good interpreter. I know you're pretty sharp with the local lingos. Do you dig Hainanese, or whatever the language is over there?"

Hank nodded. "I don't know just what dialect they speak. But I think maybe I could hack it between Cantonese and Vietnamese. Why? You want to take me along?"

Hope mumbled: "I dunno. Obviously, the big cheeses trust you. And there isn't time to look around for the perfect interpreter, who speaks all the Hainanese dialects. We need dependable people quickly—dependable more than anything. And you know about us Green Beret types—you don't seem like a straight leg at all."

"Straight leg" was Green Beret slang for anyone who didn't have parachute training; literally, one who didn't know the value of the bent knee when hitting the ground in a jump. It also was a Green Beret term of disrespect for regular infantry, or anyone else unfamiliar with the Special Forces.

Hank laughed. "Thanks a lot for considering me almost good enough for the privilege of risking my neck on a heroic kamikaze mission."

"Well, would you do it, if I could swing it?"

"I might. You'd have to let me know how long a time and—"

"The job's going to have to be done in a week. It won't be long."

Hank said: "Let's play it by ear for a bit. You'll have to talk to the big shots, Freeman and whoever else there is. I'd have to justify the time off, for American Media Service, and all that. But maybe it's still the best movie in town."

"All right." Eric was leaving. "Call me if you hear anything more from Mary."

*

Cranked up by a journalist's conscience, Hank Musgrave had to use the rest of the afternoon to talk to George Yerby, the local AMS chief, and that stretched into dinner. Naturally, Hank said nothing about the bomb and the anti-bomb expedition. The afternoon was pure froth.

He and George went to the Hi-Ball Restaurant for some extravagant Chinese dishes like shark's fin, almond cream and crackly pork, and talked about office politics, and the latest gossip about the correspondents in Tokyo, Hong Kong, Bangkok, and Delhi.

Hank checked several times with the Shamrock operator for messages. None. George and he went then to the Blue Sky, a taxi-dance night-club, and sat around with a couple of cute Asian slips of girls. George was struck with the fact that Hank seemed unhappy with his Blue Sky hostess: "Something wrong with the talent?"

"It's fine," Hank said. "But I was thinking about some real big league talent I know. Real Da Kine. And I don't mean my ex-wife."

George had a much-better-than-average memory. "That girl wouldn't be Mary Wu?" He saw assent in Hank's face. "I thought so. That was a real superwoman in any nationality. Whatever happened to her?"

"Dunno," said Hank. "But I'd like to."

5

October 10

WHEN HANK GOT BACK TO THE SHAMROCK ABOUT MIDNIGHT, he found there was a message in his box. Somehow it had been overlooked, probably in the ordinary slippage between languages. He would have to talk to people here in Cantonese, imperfect as his might be, instead of counting on their knowledge of English.

The message was marked 8:24 P.M. and it said: "Please call *Fu-ren*, Phone 62415." The name *Fu-ren* was a kind of code which he remembered with a glow of *gemutlichkeit*. He had used the word *Fu-ren*, meaning approximately "female mate" or "female lover" as a term of endearment for Mary. But he had forgotten, until now.

He went up to the room to phone the number, and when he opened the door, he had the strange feeling something was wrong. He noted a peculiar scent, like wet clothing, and flipped on the light. No one was visible in the room, but some prescience was jolting him wide awake. He checked the closet door, expecting at least a dead body. Nothing there.

The bathroom door was ajar an inch or two, and the room was dark. He shoved open the door and reached to flick on the light, then something smashed him with bright tendrils of pain. At that moment, he saw something move, a Chinese head with slick black hair, a face violently twisted and notably pocked with scars, and then he blacked out.

He came to with a pulsing head, on the cold floor just inside the bathroom. Something dripped into and obscured his eyes, warm and liquid. He put up a hand and felt a gash on the top of his head, a crenellated puffiness and sogginess, an agonizing soufflé.

He fumbled for his wallet. Still there. He pulled it out and saw the money was untouched and the credit cards intact. His watch still on his wrist. His heart was beating like a bass kettle. Must have been out a while.

How could that bastard have surprised him like that? He had had enough of that before to know better: a flat-footed Japanese schoolboy. If it was connected with Mary, what was the thug after? Mechanically, he checked the room: a couple of bureau drawers were opened; the briefcase, an attache-case type, was left wide open, the papers flipped through.

He opened the room door carefully. Nobody in the hallway. He tried to collect his senses. His head was a balloon, shot full of pain. Judging from the gash, he estimated he'd been conked with a sharp-edged object—maybe the barrel of a gun. But he didn't remember seeing it. He stared at his watch, at last registered the time. It was twelve-thirty-five, and if he remembered correctly it had been twelve-twenty when he came in.

He walked into the bathroom, and looked at the wound in the mirror. A mess. The blood had smeared across the top of his head and congealed as far down as his eyebrows.

He mopped it with a washcloth: not too deep. Bleeding had stopped, but it was swelling. He daubed it with antiseptic.

He took a couple of aspirin, and decided it would be better not to make any complaint to the police, or to the hotel management.

Mainly he was worrying about Mary. If they were onto him, it might get to be a lot worse for her. He found her phone message in his pocket and asked the operator for the number. It was busy.

Was this catastrophe? He didn't know yet. He checked the bureau drawers. They had been thoroughly ruffled through, everything upside down; but at a quick look it didn't seem that anything was missing. He moved to the briefcase and inspected the sheafs of copy paper, notes, printed stuff. He saw that one of the notebooks was gone. His last notebook, which he remembered as shiny, red spiral-bound. Not there. Significant? That would be the one which had to do with the last part of the recent stay in Tokyo. Notes about Zengakuren, the Japanese leftist party, good for their egos, if the Commies picked it up. But fortunately, he remembered in a flash there were no notes about Mary, Freeman Blake, or Hope. Not one.

His diary was gone, too, running notes of the year, very summary. Didn't matter. Fortunately, he hadn't written in it for the last two days.

He asked for Mary's number and heard a strange feminine voice: "Wey?"

He inquired in Cantonese: "Mary Wu there?"

Hesitation, then the voice inquired tremulously: "Who is speaking?"

"Hank Musgrave. Who is this?"

"Liang—Mary Wu sister." Then another pause, a choking sob, and a torrent of English: "Mistah Hank—I am—very upset in heart. Mary is much injured by another."

"Speak Cantonese," he instructed, and that unloosed a torrent. He caught most of it and it chilled him. Mary had been close to her apartment in Kowloon, when she had been jumped by two men, and beaten up, but bad.

Fortunately, a policeman had come along before Mary could be finished off, but she was seriously enough hurt: "Many broken bones." Exactly what the injuries were he couldn't fathom—any more than you can get a straight account of anything from a witness to a traffic accident right after it happens. And first reports are usually too pessimistic, as well. Mary was in the Queen Elizabeth Hospital, an emergency case.

Mary's sister, of course, was at Mary's apartment, with Norman, her son. The boy was okay, asleep. But Hank knew something would soon have to be done to protect the child and the sister. Communist agents are specific in their efforts against the families of a human target. He had seen it in China, the Malayan War, the Korean War, the Philippines, and Vietnam.

He told Liang he would go over to the hospital immediately and call her later. And he phoned Hope at his room in the Empress.

Hope was sleepy, but responsive: "Hank—I tried to reach you before. The boss man has been wanting to see you. Shall I come over there?"

"No. I'm going to the Queen Elizabeth Hospital. Our friend has been beaten up. It sounds bad. I've got to get over there. I'll come by your room afterward."

"Okay. I'll be here."

*

His cab turned in to the emergency entrance just behind the clanging bell of a slab-sided ambulance. In the darkness of the courtyard, beneath the sign saying "Emergency Admitting", stretcher bearers were busy.

He checked with the man at the admitting desk, a plump, tiny Cantonese with grizzly hair. Hank showed his credentials, proof of being a working journalist with the feature service.

"Accident cases always coming in," the clerk said, coolly inclining his head towards the body on the stretcher. "What can I do for you?"

"I'm interested in—an assault case," Hank told him, thinking how dreadfully impersonal that sounded. And a wave of fury caught him like a blast of heat against the thugs who had smashed Mary. I'm not a stranger to bloodshed, it has been a daily fact of life in my job. But sometimes, as now, the involvement gets very personal.

Hank bribed Wong with a U.S. five-dollar bill and slipped another five to the tiny Chinese nurse whom Wong introduced, and he followed her through endless corridors to a large dimly lit women's ward.

The nurse silently led the way and stopped. The form supposed to be Mary was inert, the head a hard cone of bandages with no face: black-shadow patches indicating eyes, nose, and mouth.

He shouldn't have felt panic, but was she awake? The face gone, he couldn't tell whether the eyes were open. Were they watching him? He bent over to look more closely and brushed against the tube of an intravenous feeding bottle, now put aside. It was an indistinct small form with a white cocoon for a head, and features like a child's drawing, inexpert blobs of dark. An enormity, that it should happen to her, the golden girl. Probably his fault. No, the Commies. Their fault, as usual: The No. 1 advocates of violence in this generation. Each generation seems to have such bullies. Commies or otherwise.

The nurse, a young slip of a girl with her hair drawn back severely, was jittery.

"Must go," she whispered hoarsely. "Men not supposed to be in women ward this hour."

"Okay." He followed her out of the ward into the white bareness of the corridor, salved her anxieties with another five-dollar benediction and started operations to get Mary out of the ward and into a smaller room. His exploratory expedition, conducted by the nurse, led to a front office, where he arranged with a stuffy old Anglo-Saxon battle-axe with a pince-nez to have Mary moved tomorrow to a better room. The private rooms were all booked out. But there were ways. He managed a semi-private one in the Elgin Pavilion. This was arranged by a guarantee payment of $200 American. No corruption. It was all official and according to the British rulebook —cash on the barrelhead, in advance. He knew better than to try to bribe the ancient and incorruptible Anglo-Saxon custodian.

Before he left the hospital, he went back to the ward and found the same little ward nurse, a Miss Chang. In the frantic search for Mary, he hadn't yet heard a clinical report on her injuries.

Miss Chang remembered: "Multiple facial fractures, I think there were four, but she'll be all right. She's not on the critical list."

"Could she talk at all?"

"Nothing that we could hear."

Miss Chang was going on with the impersonality of a textbook: "There's a nose fracture, one or two maxillary fractures, and a malar fracture, underneath the eye."

That bastard: Chen. I'll fracture his maxillary, and a few other things, too. If Mary can't talk, tomorrow I'll bring a notebook and pen, and maybe she can write the answers. Then we'll take care of Mr. Fracturing Maxillary Chen—or whoever did it.

*

He stopped at Hope's room at the Empress and phoned Liang from there. He told her Mary was resting comfortably, a benign if bloody lie, that he'd arranged to have her moved to a semi-private room. He also told Liang he'd come by the apartment in the morning. It was now two-twenty-two A.M.

He told Hope: "We've got to get some surveillance over Mary and her sister and the kid, at her apartment. Immediately, if not sooner."

Hope agreed, and put in a call to his superior.

Hank sat on the couch, watching the harbor lights, while Hope phoned. "Mr. Lowery? I've got our friend with me. He's pretty tired now."

Hank heard the telephone receiver squeal with vehement verbiage. "Get over here with him as soon as you can. It's damned important." Then the squeaky sound went on undistinguishably, urgently.

Hope laid the phone down and sighed. "I'm sure you heard most of that. Mostly, it was beefing because I took so long to catch up with you. Knowing him, I'd estimate he just got a hot foot from the big boys back home. He doesn't ordinarily get that excited.

"Will you come with me right now? We can run over there in maybe half an hour. The ferries have stopped, but we can get a bumboat. He's sending a car to pick us up beside the Queen's Pier."

"Okay, but I'll probably fall asleep in the car,"

"That's fine. As long as you can walk when we get to the Chief's house."

6

AT THE SAME MOMENT WHEN HANK MUSGRAVE AND ERIC Hope walked out of the Empress Hotel toward a waiting cab, something closely related was happening in Washington, D.C. It was 2:32 the previous day, there.

President Bascombe Landers was sitting in his favorite small office above the balcony in the White House. With him were Special Assistant David Soloretha and the Chairman of the Joint Chiefs of Staff, General Harold Morman.

The President held a cup of coffee in his hand. He took a swallow. "I don't care whether the plan is safe or not, Harold. We can't intervene in China with massive overt force. Even though I know that it would be much more secure in the military sense. An airborne division could do the job without fail, but think of the world insecurity that would follow that kind of expedition! The inevitable upshot would be—we would certainly be in an official war with China, and possibly with Russia. You understand that, don't you, Harry?"

General Morman was still protesting. "But Mr. President, is this not the most important single target in the world today? Doesn't it deserve the kind of effort which is guaranteed to succeed? Suppose your small force fails—and the Chinese bomb is dropped on the Seventh Fleet. Aren't we in a war anyhow? According to our JACOSIP estimates—"

"What are JACOSIP estimates?"

"JACOSIP—it stands for Joint Army Command Operations Intelligence—" he hesitated. "I guess the "P" stands for 'Preparation.' Some hu-hu like that. Anyhow, based on our intelligence levels, our bright boys have estimated that American forces will *never* be called on for less than a divisional land operation in the SEAPOR, the South East Asian Position of Readiness. It's just not mathematically sound."

"Harry." There was a deadly coldness in the way he pronounced the name this time, and Soloretha knew that General Morman was going to feel the heavy edge of the Presidential two-handed sword. Now it swung.

"Mathematical principles be damned, Harry! I'm talking about what can be done in the present world political situation, what we can get away with and still get the result. Don't tell me what your computing machines—human or otherwise—have figured can and can't be done. I know what we can risk, and what is 'safe.' You know the computing machines are only giant idiots—morons. Their only virtue is speed: speed in simple calculations.

"I have a good human brain. One good grade human brain. The equivalent of ten million of the latest IBM machines. My brain is picking the 'safest' course, already. All I want is for you to make sure that our present mission into Hainan doesn't fail."

General Morman gulped. "Yes, Mr. President—we will make sure." But he was not completely subjugated. "This split authority— with Hudibras really in command—makes things difficult—"

The phone rang—the red one which carried traffic with the Capitol and the Congressional Office Buildings. The President answered it: "Why? My God. You mean he's already filed? Tomorrow? Well, Bill, you better get to him right away. Ask him to call me directly. No, I'll call him." Handing over the receiver, he explained to Soloretha: "Senator Smythe has pushed through a resolution for an investigation of CIA operations in Southeast Asia. Malaysia, Vietnam—and you know it'll hit Operation Typhoon. He says this is the first big step in his 'Secrecy in Government' campaign. Says he's going to eliminate censorship of all budget items—drag everything out in the open. 'Open military budgets, openly arrived at,' he says. We'll have to get right after Smythe and tell him he's got to back off—that it would tip off our whole operation into Hainan."

The President turned to General Morman: "You'll excuse me now, General." Morman stood up, acknowledging the dismissal.

The President nodded curtly and picked up his blue telephone. "Get me Hudibras at the Plastics Factory." A brief wait, then: "Charlie, I appreciate that last bit of information on Typhoon—name of the place and all that. But we need a lot more—faster than ever— Senator Smythe has started the investigation. He's putting the heat on. That means I want *you* to put on more heat than that."

Soloretha interjected: "Mr. President, you wanted me to remind you—ask him to get more people on Typhoon."

The President nodded. "Oh, yes. I want you to get more people into that show down there—Lowery's intelligence show. Never mind how. Just get 'em and get 'em workin', and get me some intelligence! All right. Well, let me know. But pep it up—call me and let me know."

＊

Hope and Musgrave took a night cab to the Hong Kong waterfront, found a grinning walla-walla driver whom Hope knew. The cool night air revived the weary Americans. It was difficult to talk in any but anonymous terms, despite the insistent noise of the knocking diesel engine. The black-clad boatman and his crew of wife and two slender sons were too close.

Hank asked Hope guardedly: "Eric, do you think my girl will be all right? Will they leave her alone where she is?"

"We'll keep an eye on her," Hope said. "I'll ask the boss. I think he'll send somebody to look out for her right away. You know, you're just damned lucky she wasn't killed."

Hank said: "I know. Like I was lucky in Vietnam: I had a fractured skull instead of getting killed. Lucky! Anyhow, I asked the matron to keep visitors away from her except Liang or me. I'm sure my friend wouldn't want her son to see her now. He'd have the fright of his life."

"We can get to Mr. Big about having somebody watch Mary. And the chances are, nobody can reach her before we do." He paused. "Listen—I don't want to seem hardboiled, but—why do you think they didn't finish her off?"

Hank gulped. "The cop came by—that was all."

Hope was looking across the square at the top of the stairs. "I see the car waiting for us."

Hope waved and the car, a large black sedan, moved from a parking space and rolled towards them.

Hank said: "It looks as if your Big Chief believes in protective local coloring—a conservative British car. What is it, a Daimler?"

"Yeah. And he goes wild just at the *thought* of the car I've been driving here in Hong Kong. It's a Porsche 911, a real gone rear-engine car about as conspicuous as a Ferrari V-I2 would be among the Morrises."

The Daimler stopped beside them. A large Chinese in chauffeur's uniform sat at the wheel.

"Good evening, Ling," Hope said.

"Good evening, sir," the driver answered, his English enunciation impeccable.

As the car started up, Hank asked Hope in diplomatic terms: "This uniform and all that—is that protective coloring?"

Hope grinned. "The best. Everybody who is somebody in Hong Kong has a limo and a chauffeur."

*

The mansion stood at the head of a dimly lit, winding road on the heights overlooking Deepwater Bay, on the Peak of Hong Kong island, a fashionable section. The sign at the gate said "Croy." A tall, bearded Sikh, wearing a turban and carrying a long-barrelled shotgun, let them into the courtyard.

Ling parked the car beside the brightly lit front door, and led them past a Chinese manservant and into a book-lined study with large windows showing a view of the South China Sea, south of Hong Kong, and the creeping inchworm lights of junks; then into a bright inner room.

There was a desk with a draftsman's swinging lamp mounted over it, and in the bright illumination of the fluorescent tube, two men bent over an assemblage of papers. One, sitting at the desk, wore a conservative suit with neat beaver tie. Heavy-framed glasses perched on his nose and he could have passed for a young instructor in an Ivy League college.

The other man was shirt-sleeved, he was considerably taller and more substantial than the instructor-type at the desk.

When Hope and Musgrave came into the room, the shorter man, seated at the desk, stood up. He looked at them over the tops of his glasses. Hank saw that his eyes were light-colored and wide, strangely owlish and inexpressive.

"So you're Musgrave," he said. "I am Arthur Lowery. This—" he indicated the husky man in shirt-sleeves, "is Colonel Croy. Colonel Croy is the military attaché at the Consulate—and this is his house."

Croy was as wholesome-looking a man as Lowery seemed weird and offbeat. The Colonel in his early forties, with graying hair, a ruddy, healthy-looking face and a broad body. A consular errand boy, Hank decided.

Lowery said impatiently: "Let's go into the radio room." He led the way through a hall to a heavy wooden door from which an edge of bright light could be seen, and the sound of clattering teleprinter came.

Croy explained: "This is the after-hours communications room of the Consulate."

Lowery knocked and immediately pushed the door open.

The first thing Hank saw was a table with two teleprinters along one wall of the windowless room, and a thin youth sitting in front of one machine which clattered at full gallop. A wide table in front of another wall carried a maze of electronic equipment—unscrambling devices and decoders, tape-recorders, computers, banks of transistors and diodes in complex array. The third and fourth walls were covered with maps of Southeast Asia and Hong Kong. Lowery walked to the teleprinter-in-use, and read the message over the shoulder of the operator. Then he turned to Hank, his face a curious mixture of respect and critical disbelief. "Another message about you, Musgrave," he said.

"Back in Washington, they still haven't grasped the fact that until this moment I hadn't met you. But you should know that to them there are no compartments in our effort. And in this case it is a fact: Freeman Blake and I are in the same compartment. It's that kind of high-priority emergency."

Lowery pulled chairs out from under the edge of the table, and arranged them opposite an overstuffed chair beneath the wall maps.

"Let's sit down here. It's a fine and properly noisy place for an agency conference—and we can be sure of having the latest radio communication on tap, at the same time.

"Musgrave, we've been pursuing you for many hours. You have a source bringing good information. She's a dancehall girl? What's the latest you have from her?"

Hank felt himself reddening. But in that moment Hope sprang into the conversational breach. "She has had bad luck, she's in the hospital. It has upset Musgrave considerably."

The warning seemed to have made little impression on Lowery, but he said: "Sorry." And Hank thought no wonder Hope calls him "Mister." A real cool fish.

He seized the moment to make his pitch. "She's in bad shape now in the Queen Elizabeth Hospital—and I'm very concerned about her. Can someone be sent to watch over her night and day? I'm afraid Chen and his boys might work her over some more, or finish her off."

Lowery said: "Maybe."

"It'll have to be better than that." Hank felt his scalp prickle with anger. Then he said, tactfully: "You know the information she has brought us so far. There can be a lot more—if she's alive and well."

"Okay, we'll look after her. You can tell me the details of where she is, but first I want you to summarize for me all the items you've been feeding us."

Hank saw a sudden glint in Lowery's eye. "Ordinary expenses shouldn't be an obstacle. If you're low on funds, we can take care of it without trouble.

"Now, I want you to go over the things you have learned from her, and we'll check them against what we know."

Hank laid out the whole schmeer once more. When he had finished, Lowery actually looked pleased.

He said, "Good. We'll take care of Mary Wu immediately. We'll have someone watching that hospital room all the time." And to Croy: "Better give him a Band-Aid for that bang on the head."

Croy said: "Yessir." He led the way out of the room, saw that Hank got bandaged and then Hank asked him: "Is there a couch hereabouts? Either I find one, or go to sleep standing up."

"Yes, in the living room. You can sleep until we've finished with Hope. Then Ling will drive you both back to the ferry." He added: "The boss says you have a good knowledge of Cantonese, Mandarin, and some of the dialects, is that right?"

"Generally true. Not very good on dialects like Hakka, Fukien, and Szechwan, though."

"All right. You'll have plenty of work, so get what sleep you can." He added conversationally: "This whole operation is way up in the air—flying eight directions at once. And it's ten times as bad in Washington. Trouble is, it all came up so suddenly. We didn't have time to prepare."

Hank said: "Did you ever see a military emergency where people were prepared for what happened? You're always prepared for everything, except what happens. So you always have to get everything done yesterday."

"That's right," said Croy. "Lowery hasn't had four hours sleep all week. More than I could get by with in my middle-age. A Gung-ho type, that boy."

Something about the phrase "Gung-ho" didn't seem to fit Lowery. Croy sensed Hank's reaction and smiled. "I mean the new-model, ice-water type," he explained. "I've puzzled over him, but he at least lives for something bigger than he is—that's more than most of us do."

"What's that bigger thing?"

"The country—right or wrong. Not a bad dedication for an Agency type. It simplifies things considerably."

That moment, the communications room door swung open, spreading a wide patch of yellow light, and Lowery stuck his head out. "Croy, I want you to call that local light—the millionaire. The one with the friends on Hainan—what's his name, Ming? You can leave word with the household that he should phone me first thing in the morning. It looks as if we're going to have a big problem doing everything in time—and I've got to find out if he can be any help to us."

Sinking onto the overstuffed couch, his bones reaching out for the sleep-giving embrace, Hank was conscious enough to ask Croy before oblivion took him: "Sometime later, will you explain what all that means?"

"I'll try." Croy looked after Lowery with something like admiration. He added: "If anyone can bring this complicated job off, I think Lowery is probably the one."

It was still dark when Hank woke up to see that Eric Hope stood beside the couch. Hank jumped up.

"I'm ready to go," he said.

Hope smiled. "You haven't forgotten how to wake up in a hurry."

"I've spent too many years in wars to forget that."

Eric nodded. "Lowery's got it all set up for a stake-out at Mary's room, and at the apartment. Her son will always be watched."

Hank stretched. "Good. Is Lowery going to do anything about Chen?"

Hope said: "You mean beat it out of Chen?" Hank nodded. "I'm sure he will—but first, he'll get all the dope he can out of Chen, the more judicious way."

Hank looked at his watch. It was six-twelve. "If you're ready, I'll head back to Kowloon with you. I want to check on Liang and the hospital."

"Want me to come along with you?" He was bright-eyed, fresh-faced still. He seemed to have the same resistance to the effects of sleeplessness as Lowery. "You might need some help."

"Fine."

✳

On the Kowloon side, Hope and Musgrave stopped at Mary's apartment on the way to the hospital. Her flat turned out to be a walk-up in a side street off Nathan Road, the main thoroughfare. It was a new building with the dank scent of fresh cement still haunting the hallways.

As they reached Mary's fourth-floor apartment, a crew-cut Chinese man, aged twenty-four or twenty-five, was waiting for them. Hope gave him a password: "Foxtrot." The Chinese stood aside for them. Hank was surprised and pleased to see that Lowery's organization had arranged the stake-out so quickly.

In the hall outside Mary's apartment, two Chinese kids, five or six years old, were playing the international children's game of Bang-Bang. In this case, one circled the other on a tricycle while they pretended to be shooting at each other, making appropriate "Ka-chung! Ka-chung!" sounds.

Hank instantly recognized the boy crouching at the center. It was Norman. The other boy must be a neighbor. Norman stopped the game and stood at a kind of attention when the Americans came up. He was taller and thinner now than Hank had remembered him, but had the same well-modelled features. He had obviously recognized Hank, but waited politely for him to speak.

Musgrave identified himself in Cantonese: "I'm Hank. You remember me?"

"Yes, Mr. Hank," he replied in faultless English, with the same gravity of manner which had always appealed to Hank. "You told me stories. About the Communists in China."

At that point, Mary's sister Liang opened the apartment door looking very much on guard, ready to jump into a retreat. Hank saw that she was smaller than Mary, older, not nearly as good-looking. She had evidently been weeping since her eyes were red and swollen.

Hank introduced Hope and himself, greeted her in Cantonese and her face brightened.

She said, in a rapid Shanghai dialect of which he understood a good deal: "Many thanks for helping us. We owe you very much."

"Nothing. We are going to the hospital to see Mary now. What have you told Norman about it?" Although Norman was standing beside them, he surmised the boy couldn't understand Cantonese, especially the Shanghai-ese variety.

Liang answered: "He knows that his mother had an accident."

Hank said; "Better wait a day or two before you take Norman to see her. She can't talk now—also too many bandages. And one other matter: Don't worry about her expenses—or the rent here. We'll take care of it."

Norman had been listening attentively, and apparently had caught a few key words like hospital and Mary. He said in English: "Please tell mother we will come to the hospital to see her, soon."

They were all astounded, including Hope. When they were leaving the apartment, he said: "How come Chinese kids are so fiendishly bright?"

"I guess because they have to be, in a free society. But they don't seem to be so bright up North—like the Red Guards. They can't seem to figure their way out of Communism."

"That's not so easy," Hope said, "It's tough to reason with a machine gun. Except when you have more and better guns."

7

SENATOR SAMUEL SMYTHE'S MOUSE-COLORED FALCON
rolled up to the sentry post at the main entrance to the White House,
and the guard waved it on. Everyone in Washington knew the
Senator's austerity-model sedan, and most everyone was aware that it
was a fetish with him to drive one of the lowest-priced American cars,
part of his much-publicized campaign to balance the budget and "cut
out Federal rat-holing abroad."

It was a cold, overcast night with a leaden sky overhead and driz-
zle of rain falling. But the coatless, stubby figure of a man stood on the
steps waiting for Senator Smythe. It was Soloretha. He hurried down
the steps to meet the car.

Senator Smythe swung his vehicle into the first available spot on
the right side of the driveway and jumped out. He was short, slightly built, puffed with sedentary fat, and there were only a few wisps of
black hair on top of his head. He didn't wear a hat.

Soloretha extended his hand cordially. "Senator Smythe! It's good to see you." The Senator didn't smile.

"Am I late? You know you shouldn't be outdoors without a coat in this weather."

"No sacrifice is too great for my country," Soloretha joked, and regretted it instantly, reflecting that any but the most obvious humor would be lost on the Senator from Oklahoma. Sure enough, the Senator shot a frigid look in his direction.

Soloretha tried again. "The President is waiting for you in his favorite office. You're right on time."

The Senator was pleased. "I always say punctuality is the soul of business," he said.

The President had come out to the head of the stairs to meet them. "I saw your notorious jalopy coming up the drive, Sam. It's more famous than any Presidential limousine, even the bullet-proof one."

Senator Smythe reacted to the Presidential flattery with a broad smile, and a streak of suspicion. "You're too kind to me, Mr. President, like a Choctaw Indian said to me on the reservation: 'It's kindly of you to come, what will it cost?'"

The President remarked: "Why, that observation isn't very kindly of *you*, Senator. To question my motives—my bit of genuine hospitality. I thought you Oklahomans appreciated hospitality."

"You're right, sir. But you haven't even made your proposition to me, yet, Mr. President."

"Well, I will," the President said.

Over coffee, the President came to his proposition. "Sam, I want to talk to you about an operation—military operation. It's so secret that no other member of Congress knows about it. I have made sure that only the absolute top echelon of the military are aware of it, and they have been buttoned up tight against any leaks."

"Sounds right interesting, Mr. President. But it doesn't exactly sound like open military budgets openly arrived at."

The President fenced expertly. "I know if you had your way, Sam, there wouldn't be *any* military budget. And you know, I would like that, too. I'd like nothing better than to be known as the President who brought peace to the world, and reduced our armament expense to zero. But unfortunately, we don't live in that kind of world, yet."

While Senator Smythe sipped his coffee, President Landers went on: "Sam, I'm going to give it to you right out. If this were not the most important emergency in the world today, I wouldn't object to or try to interfere with your campaign for open military budgets openly arrived at, and whatever related issues you might want to bring up, like the supposed management of the news. But it happens that right now, in the next week, something is happening in Southeast Asia which can be handled only with complete secrecy, and a completely secret military budget. I'm telling you this because the future of the country and probably of the world will depend on the fact that this mission is completely secret."

Landers had always benefited from a superb sense of timing. He followed an old formula: The broad generality, prolonged to the point of boredom, and then the undeniable, sensational fact. Thus: "The Communist Chinese have an H-bomb. Only *one*, and it is in position in an airfield on the island of Hainan, near Vietnam!"

President Landers was gratified to see that he had shocked the Oklahoma senator into silence—a nearly incredible feat.

From then on, for a few minutes more than half an hour, he wound through the complicated exposition of the intelligence which precipitated the plan (actually, he made it sound a good deal more complicated and much more substantial than it had been) and then he detailed the preparations for the take-out operation. "In terms of budget, Sam, a clandestine operation by our Special Forces will be infinitely cheaper than an old-fashioned war to settle this issue— that's the final size of it."

He concluded: "Senator, I know that the elections are coming up, I know the value of public relations—good, big-bore, high-powered public relations—at a time like this. I can see how your campaign for re-election could be based very cunningly on national publicity about your campaign for economy and against secret military budgets. But, will you delay any attention to this one vitally important mission in Southeast Asia, please?"

The President pushed back his chair, leaned back, and grinned his famous broad smile. "Of course, the size and importance, and the details of this mission can never be disclosed, at least not for a year or two. Right now, not a word should be breathed about it."

Senator Smythe extracted a cigar from his pocket and lit it. He was taking his time, knowing that for the moment he had the starring role. "Mr. President, I know that you will concede that I am as patriotic as most Americans, that I'm as willing to line up and be counted when it comes to any enemy of the United States. But I want to suggest to you one thought: Isn't it better for the public to know about the military expenditures, like the CIA, and to calc'late it out, to make up their own minds whether it's better to spend the money or not? It seems to me that the basic error that many of us in high places make is that we think our judgment is so much better than the judgment of the people. I'm sure that if the whole barnyard was dragged out clean, the judgment of the people would be backed up."

The President's face grew dark. He banged hard on the table. "Surely, Senator, you're not going to tell me that you believe that our war plans can be pulled out into the open in detail so that the public can make up its mind whether we're going to choose Phoenix or Falcon missiles for our Air Force, and how many infra-red snip-er-scopes are bought for the Army. Surely you're not going to contend that every operational plan has to be exposed for the delectation of the public, and particularly the delectation of the enemy, before it can be put into effect. Surely, you know the value of the most potent military weapon in anybody's arsenal—surprise. In this sort of case, the application of democratic principles just doesn't apply."

Then the dark color left the President's face and he smiled again. "You know I've taken you into our confidence on a very dangerous mission of the absolute top importance. I must expect of you that you will not do anything to betray that mission, or to rob it of its effect by exposing it the week before it is to happen. Whatever steps you may take in this political campaign, I must ask you to regard this information as privileged. And also, I want to bring up one other matter—since I, too, realize that politics is our life blood, and that on the political shooting range, every politician has to have ammunition for his guns. So I want to give you some of that ammunition. First of all, I know the Byron Dam project is stymied. I know that Senator Long of Louisiana has been opposing it since he, too, has a large Federal project he wants to get going with: the Gulf Highway. I can promise you that I will help both of these projects get off the ground, first by getting Senator Long off your back, second by helping you with the Oklahoma Irrigation project."

Senator Smythe was puffing furiously, the clouds of smoke rolling out in front of him. President Landers saw his opportunity increasing. He fired his clincher argument: "Furthermore, Sam, when your campaign is in full swing—as soon as this endless Congress session is over and you can get back to campaign, I will just happen to make a trip to Oklahoma City, and I will speak for your re-election. I will say things about you which will constitute in effect a Presidential endorsement."

Sam Smythe leaned back in his chair, studying the brass eagle on top of the Presidential standard in one corner of the room. At last, he cleared his throat with something between a guffaw and a cheer. "Mr. President, you're rightly generous. And you are absolutely correct about the importance of ammunition in the politician's gun. I think maybe you've tagged me out, trying to sneak between second and third base. Because you're one hell of a sharp pitcher.

"But there's always the matter of principle—I find that principles are important, as well as useful. May I say that I should think over those principles, and their value, and go over the whole issue thoroughly in my mind. I must consult with my God and myself."

Bascombe Landers saw that he had nearly won and he smiled almost graciously. "Of course, Sam. You're a man of conscience and I know you must do what's right for everyone, yourself included. Why don't you come by and see me say tomorrow afternoon, late, and we'll see if we can square it up with your—conscience? And meanwhile, drag out whatever old CIA project you may choose for your purposes. But not this one."

Senator Smythe stood up, smiling faintly. "Yes, Bascombe,"—he dared the first name. "We must keep our political skirts clean as well as maintain our principles. It wouldn't do, either, for it to appear that the President of the U.S. had taken great risks with the public weal, in choosing improper secret methods to reduce the risk of an atomic war."

The President, too, stood up and he shook Senator Smythe's hand. "Sam, I'm sure that in the long judgment of history—as contrasted with the moment's expediency—the world will find that my method and my estimations were the wisest and most effective of the available methods of protecting world peace. Besides being by far the most economical. And after all, peace and sound economics are your two most important principles—isn't that so?"

"You're absolutely right, Mr. President. And I will keep your confidence. See you tomorrow, then."

When he had gone, the President confided in Soloretha: "Well, we've got him off our backs for another day or so, anyhow."

"Mr. President," Soloretha mused. "I am worried about a possibility which I don't think he's yet thought of. But he probably will."

The President waited. Soloretha went on: "The probably inevitable idea that the whole Chinese H-bomb plot could be exposed to the world."

"You mean—we would throw ourselves on the mercy of the U.N. General Assembly, and world opinion? By the time we had made the first appeal, the Chinese would have dropped the bomb and destroyed the Seventh Fleet."

"Yes, sir," Soloretha said sadly. "I would estimate that. But I don't think Senator Smythe would."

"I don't think he would either. That's why I'm worried. He might just think he could get away with this kind of game. He might see in it a chance to go a lot farther politically. He might see it as a major step on the way to the presidency. Anyhow, we do have another day's grace before anything happens."

*

Behind the heavy-gauge wire of the inner rectangle at Ching Tu Airfield on the island of Hainan, South China, and outside the tin-roofed concrete building at the center, Technician Chau squinted into the tropical sun. He watched the slightly inclined runway that rose into the foothills to the south. Out there, with a screeching sound that carried over still air, a wide-winged Tupolev-16 bomber was swinging into position for take-off at the end of the concrete. The sound Chau heard was the screech of the jet engines as the pilot applied full throttle to swing the plane around.

There, on the near end of the white airplane highway that led up into the jungle-covered foothills of the mountains, Chau knew, the chosen pilot and co-pilot, and the stand-by pilot sent along to make sure there would always be someone to fly the airplane, were ready to make their first flight out of the new Ching Tu airfield. Here it was only six days from the big drop, and Pilot Officer Ding was just getting to his first instrument familiarization sortie.

It was just like the People's Central government out of Shanghai to wait until the last minute, and then hurry up so that everybody would be pinched. Why should there be such a rush now? If the bomb was to be dropped on October 16, why? There was no national holiday on that day. Revolution Day, October 1, that would be different. But October 1 was long behind. Maybe the head men had been trying for October 1, and missed it the way they did way back on October 16, 1964, when Chau had seen the first Chinese atomic device detonated in the Sinkiang testing ground. But at least they were planning to drop it on the provocative American Seventh Fleet, which would be offshore that day. That was good.

The TU-16 had come in two days ago. There had been just about time enough to have it checked over and fueled up, and the simulated bomb load of 13,200 pounds—in this case stacks of cement totalling 6,000 kilos in weight—loaded into the bomb bay. Fortunately, the modifications in the bomb bay had already been made before the plane was flown in from Shanghai, so that the bomb would fit. Chau and his fellow-technicians and engineers wouldn't be bothered with this extra bit of work. It was enough to have to improvise the wiring and the batteries.

Technician Chau turned to go into the laboratory house. He was bleary-eyed; too much night work. As he entered, he saw a green work-truck in the guard station inside the heavy steel fence. Maybe this would be the shipment of neutron counters out of Canton. So many emission counters had been brought in—alpha, beta, gamma. This time the head men were really doing it right. Not like the first A-bomb explosions in Sinkiang. And the fourth one which fortunately the American listening stations had missed altogether—catastrophe!

He looked at the truck and saw that Driver Pung was at the wheel, with Assistant Chang beside him. He had his doubts about Driver Pung. During the last few days, when Pung had come up from Hoihow with a shipment, he had asked too many questions—especially about what was to be done with the bomb, exactly what kind it was, and when it was to be dropped. He had rebuffed the man with a joking remark about his curiosity: A good-natured insult to the effect that in matters like this it was unpatriotic to be too curious. But he knew that Pung had asked some of the other technicians, like Ching-Kuo, about the date. Ching had told him. Pung was probably an undisciplined deviationist, potentially hostile to the state, and should be watched.

Chau pulled out his identification card before going into the central laboratory building. The blue-uniformed Chek-koh guard didn't even look—he knew Chau very well by this time—and he stood aside, holding his machine pistol across his chest.

Inside, the newly installed fluorescent lights dispensed a garish brilliance. The extra lights had been put in during the last three days. If this project went on long enough, pretty soon the camp here at Ching Tu would be nearly habitable.

Chau saw his friend Cho bending over the big silvery ball at one end of the girder structure which was the body of the bomb. Now, the nose and the tail sections were being bolted over the girders in a pre-test, and the shape at last began to look like the convention-al streamlined curve of a bomb. Chau was startled to see how large it loomed: Maybe nine meters long—the size of a heavy truck, and six thousand kilos in weight.

They would have a hard time moving such a brute into position in the bomb bay. Fortunately, there was a heavy American-made hydrau-lic hoist which they were planning to use. First, they would use the lift to transfer the bomb to the underground vault, then again on the big day. That lift was a marvelous bit of engineering. The Yankee aggres-sors were great engineers, you would have to give them that. The lift was another capitalistic product brought in from unmentionable Hong Kong.

Chau wondered how it was that the capitalists of Hong Kong hadn't been able to trace these shipments brought into China. But then again, there was nothing incriminating about importing a heavy-duty hoist.

The solid electrolyte batteries, of course, would be another mat-ter. They would have very few uses except in elevator emergency kits, or the emergency powering of nuclear bomb components—they were clearly suspicious items.

Chau's friend looked up and saw him. "Comrade Chau. How does the battle go today?"

"My daily struggle progresses well enough," Chau answered, mak-ing a word-play with *Ta Kung Pao*, the name of a Communist newspa-per. Then he added, lest his levity might be misinterpreted by some party-minded outsider listening in, "It is a pleasure to serve the just cause of the People's Republic and world peace." Let them fashion some treasonable context out of that remark. He wondered why he was so jaundiced in temperament. Probably simple fatigue.

His friend stepped back a couple of paces and admired the bomb. "Now she really looks effective, doesn't she? Think of it! Soon we will be loading her, the TU-16 will be screeching like a wild goose down the runway, and soon after that, the bomb will be falling down from the TU-16 to bring thunderous destruction to the entire American Seventh Fleet. It will indeed be a resounding blow for world peace and a triumph of the sheer will of the Chinese people." He looked at his fellow scientist with an enigmatic smile. Chau knew, too, that it would be a devious construction to justify the dropping of the bomb, even when dropped on the warlike American Seventh Fleet, as the work of allegedly peaceful minds. But the military men who ran China, he knew in his heart, were illogical—profoundly illogical.

"With the delivery of this weapon, Great China will establish her place among the world's leading nations," he said, wondering whether his great contortion of a philosophic point would seem too extreme to be anything but disrespectful irony.

At that moment one of the Chek-koh guards came in and sought out Chau. "A truckload has arrived from the Hoihow docks, Technician Chau," he began. "It is Driver Pung. He says it is a load of nuclear testing devices. He calls them neutron counters. Is this correct?"

Chau said: "Correct—absolutely. Have them brought in." He picked up the phone on a work-table and asked for the military headquarters exchange: "Trademark. Give me Trademark." The phone buzzed. Blasted thing was busy as usual. "Why don't the turtles in the Army Engineers get in some more phones," he mumbled.

He hung up and said to his friend: "We'll have to keep an eye on this Driver Pung. He asks too many questions, and he knows too much, for a simple truckdriver."

✳

It was less than one hour later that Driver Pung trudged into the kitchen shack behind the apartment building where he and his wife and five children lived in the port city of Hoihow. The smell of stewing chicken descended as he climbed up the outside steps to the cookshack which served the ten technicians' apartments in the building.

Pung had been up since three this morning. He and co-driver Chang had picked up three loads at the Hoihow docks, waited nearly an hour for a traffic jam at the entrance to the waterfront area, where a police checkpoint created a lengthy bottleneck, and just now, at ten fifteen A.M. he was limp as a rag with fatigue. But he called out cheerfully: "Is that my little sweetheart above, preparing a delightful soup for her hungry husband?"

There was no answer for a moment, and then a slim, black-clad torso of a female appeared over the banister. "Yes, we *ah chee*—" She joked, using the Mandarin word for chickens since that was her native tongue— "we chickens are waiting for you." Mei was a Shanghaiese, and she would occasionally slip into these northern words which were so distasteful to the more local-minded people of the Hainan community.

He shuddered a little internally, because at this moment he didn't want anything to call attention to the fact that he and his wife might be different from anyone else. It was enough that they had managed to get into an apartment building separate from the commune housing in downtown Hoihow. And it was enough that through some local friend—after all, Pung had been born here and knew nearly everyone in the town—they had been able to get hold of occasional non-regulation rations like the chicken that smelled so delightful. A certain amount of private-profit trade was tolerated in Hoihow. But any reference that might call attention to it would be extremely unwise.

Mei was alone in the kitchen, her head in a cloud of steam issuing from the pot on the stove. When he came in, she turned and took his hand. He put his arm around her, and drew her to him. "Mei, my little darling," he said. "How could I get five such beautiful children from such a slim little package?"

She held herself against him, then broke away, her face suddenly serious. She whispered to him: "The cordier from the village sent the boy to bring a message. He wants you to come by this morning. He has some money for you—some chicken money."

He bent over the pleasant-smelling chicken pot. "Mmmmmm— that smells good," He bent close to her to whisper: "I'll go over later this morning. I'll get some more chicken-money—I have some more information—information they'll be glad to have in Hong Kong."

8

WHEN MUSGRAVE AND HOPE REACHED THE HOSPITAL, Hank was glad to see that a Chinese orderly in white was hovering near the door of Mary's room. He barred their way: "Patient on critical list."

They gave him the password: "Foxtrot."

Again Hank was impressed with the efficiency of Lowery and Company. He could also see that the posting of stake-outs around Mary and her sister was more than a humanitarian move. Lowery could check to see if Mary and family might be double-dealing. The secret agent—ever suspicious, and of course, properly so!

They found the intern still with Mary. Now, she was in a room with one other patient. Her roommate was a wizened little Chinese lady of advanced years.

The doctor was bending over the large knob of bandage which would be Mary's face and head. The shape of the head, rendered in bandages, was an almost formless child's sculpture. Black holes marked the spots of eyes, nostrils and mouth—a kid's drawing. Now, in daylight, Hank could recognize the figure as hers—the ample bulge of the bosom, the smooth golden arms, especially smooth and voluptuous by contrast with the awkward and angular needle-apparatus of the intravenous feeding gadget standing beside the bed. Fortunately, the doctors had evidently finished with the feeding. At the crook of Mary's arm, Hank could see a tape marking the spot where the tube had been inserted.

The doctor was a cherubic young Chinese with a bright smile. Hank introduced Hope and himself as friends of Mary. The older lady had turned her back, as if to shut the annoying outside world from the chamber. As he turned to meet the Americans, the doctor trailed a powerful scent of ether.

Hank stood over the bandage which was Mary's face. "Mary, can you hear me?" The specter nodded its head silently. He touched Mary's hand and she squeezed back. He asked the doctor:

"How does she seem?"

The doctor smiled more brightly than ever when Hank spoke to him in Cantonese. "You speak the language! Remarkable in a—" he left it unfinished, but added: "She'll be all right."

He was leaving, but Hank detained him once more: "Was she hurt anywhere except—her face?"

"No, sir." He used the respectful, *Sinshang*, "sir teacher."

"And will she have any—bad scars?"

Hank knew he should ask this, because Mary must be dreadfully concerned about the continuance of one of her greatest assets: good looks.

"I should think not. My personal opinion." He used the Cantonese word *Chak tok*—meaning measurement. A firm enough judgment.

Hank knew he had to arrange a little cumshaw for this smiling young doctor, to make sure his girl would get the best available local medical treatment.

"This woman is as a wife to me," he told Smiley, using the word *"fu-ren"* which suddenly seemed very satisfying in sound. "I must know how much she will be scarred. Her beauty is very precious to me."

The doctor momentarily stopped smiling, and looked at him quizzically: "Even though she is a different color?" he asked, tentatively.

Hank had chanced on another individual over-conscious of color differences. "If she'll have my color, I'd be glad to have hers," he said.

Suddenly, the doctor broke into a wide grin once more: *"You mei!"* he said. "Excellent. And no need to concern yourself about her beauty. Nose fracture is not compounded. Practically sets itself. Needs only not to be disturbed after careful molding. This I did."

Now Hank gave thanks for the man's medical competence, and in the same moment, he was aware that the doctor all along had been thinking of commission, squeeze money, on the side. He pulled out five American twenty-dollar bills and the doctor was ready.

"Doctor—what is your name?"

"Siu Yung."

"Dr. Siu Yung. I want you to make sure that X-rays are made to check the set of her bones—within a week. Please do this for me as a special favor. And if any further surgery might be needed, you must let me know."

"Very well," Siu said. He added: "We will do what is needed. A brave woman."

"When will she be able to get out of the hospital?"

"I think, if things go well, she should be able to go home in about a week—if she can get some care at home." He left.

Hank sat on the bed and Hope took the one available chair. Musgrave addressed the mute child's sculpture of a head: "Mary, I'm sorry. Can you talk at all?"

The knob of bandage lifted and moved slightly to one side. He tried to see her eyes: black blobs. He pulled out a notebook and pen. "Can you write?"

She hesitated, the knob of bandage inclined in Hope's direction asking wordlessly whether it was okay to write answers in Hope's presence.

Hank told her: "This is my friend Eric Hope." The head nodded again and she picked up the pen and wrote in a flowing, clear hand:

"Thanks for the cumshaw for Doctor Smiling-Face." That was like her, the bright remark even in a very desperate personal extremity, a common situation with the Chinese.

Her mind was perking there, within the knob of white bandages. Hank knew he must ask her a question. "Mary—my *Fu-ren*— before this—happened—did you find out anything more about—about the thing we are interested in on Hainan?"

She took up the pen, and wrote in the same firm hand: "I think so. I found a letter, from one of the scientist types to Chen. It referred to the Ball-within-Ball—and he meant the bomb. In Cantonese: *kau lin kau.* Does that mean anything? Also, he called the bomb 'the biggest,' again."

Hank passed the note on to Hope and noted he began to look happy: "I think—that sounds very important," Hope said. "I'll have to leave it to the experts."

Hope looked toward the door. "And Hank—let's go as soon as we can."

Hank asked Mary: "Anything more?"

The bandage wagged in a negative gesture. Then Hank said: "Wait, Eric—one more thing—which is important. Mary, did your head-man find out what you were doing?"

She wrote: "Don't know. And I don't know who beat me up. Didn't recognize them. But Chen must be told I had accident. My sister will tell him."

There was nothing sluggish about the functioning of this mind, despite the recent grievous physical traumas. She was penning another note: "Have you seen Norman and Liang?"

Hank told her, yes, that Norman knew about the accident. Furthermore, Hank said, he'd have Liang call Chen.

"Mary, my *Fu-ren*, I've worn you out. Sorry. I have given the hospital enough money to carry you for another two weeks or so. I have another five hundred American dollars set aside and that should take care of the hospital stay and a little left over. And the doc, Siu Yung, says you won't be scarred—he'll make more X-rays to make sure."

Mary wrote an answer: "Thanks for new gumshoe boy in white coat outside door. I'll sleep better." And she added: "You are No. 1 Boy and a sweet tangerine!"

Hope was in a hurry. Hank squeezed Mary's hand and told her he'd be coming back to see her tomorrow. They took a cab but Hope suggested, "I want to get you to the big cheese fast. So let's drive my car the rest of the way and we'll take the auto ferry to the island. Then we can get where we're going fast."

He smiled. "Besides, it'll be fun. After all, my car is a Porsche 911."

They found the little marvel at the cavernous concrete parking building near Hope's hotel.

It was a shovel-nosed wonder, a steel curve of power, with the muscles of her engine hidden behind the slick, low dome of her cockpit. The wide eyes of her head-lamps were staring, innocent, wide-set—their very innocence in such a lithe beast gave malevolent promise. She looked beautifully lethal, and her color was a light powder-blue.

They ducked into the cockpit, and Hope's key finger flipped the engine into purring life. The red tachometer needle flicked up and bass vibraharp-tones resounded from the exhausts, the barrage of rhythm rolling around the bare concrete walls of the garage. Hope took her up the steep ramp leading to the street, and in the open, under a cloudy gray sky, the car rolled smoothly, the roar of her power trailing her.

Hope's tired face seemed younger in the glow of excitement over the motorcar. He swung it sharply into the intersection of Chatham Road. It rolled around the corner flat as if it had been on the straight, without a squeal of protest from the tires. And he was enraptured.

He said: "Not much plainclothes coloring in this brute. I guess I'll have to give it up in a day or two. The chief just can't swallow it. But you have to get some kicks out of life, somehow; even when everything is about to hit the fan in a few days. This is my idea of living it up. I rented it for a month."

They swung along the waterfront artery toward the homely, squarish shape of the Peninsula Hotel and the rushing traffic of Nathan Road. They passed the line of red buses jamming the entrance of the Star Ferry, and the racks of European taxis and high-wheeled rickshaws waiting for fares. They turned inland toward the auto ferry. The engine grumbled softly behind them, humming a promise of power.

Hope flipped on the radio and two speakers boomed out. It was Cantonese ying-yang and a lovesick swain was complaining. Hank translated:

✻

"'Your eyes-like-stars shine for somebody else. Why did you change your orbit and swing around another sun?'

"Even the Cantonese tunesmiths are getting space-minded."

The blue beast was rumbling along Canton Road past the blank faces of the go-down warehouses, then past the high jutting bows of the European cruise ships.

Hope said: "I've got to keep checking this car for bugs. Pretty soon we'll be on the car ferry, and while we're making the trip across the harbor, we can check all over to see if we're being spied on."

So they were silent until Hope turned the beautiful beast into the vehicle ferry entrance, and found a place near the front in the commodious floating garage. Hank began to comb through the cockpit of the low-slung car while Hope investigated the baggage compartment under the hood. Soon he gave a low whistle, and beckoned.

He pointed to a black gadget, a small tape recorder held by adhesive to one wall of the luggage compartment. The plastic box of the recorder was stamped with Chinese characters, it could very well have been a Chinese Communist import, perfectly legitimate in Hong Kong. A clumsy solenoid switch had been attached to the side of the box. Hank trailed the wire up to the starter key switch. Hope ripped out the connection. "You better check, the next time you come down in your garage and turn the starter key," Hank said. "That thing could be attached to something much less pleasant than a tape recorder. Like, say, a brick of C-4 with a detonator. You should have known better, from Vietnam. So should I."

On the island side, Hope headed the blue beast up the slope of Hong Kong into Connaught Road Central. He looked at his watch. "It's eleven-thirty," he said. "I'm supposed to have delivered you to the chief's house half an hour ago."

The car turned south toward the center of the town, worming through the thick traffic, the European-made cars, the streams of slim Chinese pedestrians pouring across the streets, jammed into the arcades, the arcades also jammed with goods—clothes, shoes, cameras, luggage, TV sets, stationery, office machines—everything the outside, American-oriented world can supply, everything wanted by the world's most populous nation. There were the movie theatres, wide marquees with patient throngs waiting, close-spaced restaurants with neon signs burning in the daylight—a plethora of riches. In the stone terraces of the side streets leading up the slope of Hong Kong mountain, the same streams of black-clad Chinese moving, the same incredible profusion of shops by the hundreds and thousands.

While they sat and waited in the traffic, Hank could ask: "What about this Ball-within-Ball business Mary told us about? Why does that seem important?"

"Like I said, I'm not sure and I'll have to check it out with the experts. But I think that's good confirmation that it's a hydrogen bomb: the first American H-bomb, at Eniwetok in 1952 was like that, a ball within a ball—an A-bomb used to detonate the H-bomb." That seemed clear enough. Hank also was immensely curious about the raiding party.

"What's the latest in your effort? Are your people coming in the way you want?"

Hope grimaced. "Maybe faster than I want. But we're not exactly long on time."

They were sitting in the busiest traffic of downtown Hong Kong, on Pedder Street turning into Chater Road and Des Voeux, and at the moment the car was stopped, with pedestrians crossing in front of them in a copious stream. Hank cranked up his side window. The day was cool, anyhow. "Now that we're completely unbugged, what's the plan with your raiding party?"

Hope rolled the window on his side all the way up, as well. "Of course it's strictly top secret," he began. "But we're all in the same compartment together, I guess. I've got just an A-detachment in numbers—like the A-forces from Vietnam, the Special Force groups of two officers and ten or eleven men. A few more than that. But there's a lot of rank in this one, and these boys are kind of specialized: four demo men, who know everything there is to know about C-3, C-4, grenades, satchel charges, Bangalore torpedoes, everything explosive. All my people are expert on weapons, and we've got a big bag of weapons; M-79 Elephant Guns, Bazooks, recoilless rifles, Armalites—and, we hope, Stens with silencers and sniper-scopes. Then there's a communications section, a couple of medics. And some extra special technical people, heavy on rank—officially they could command me, but I'm about to get my majority pretty soon, anyhow. There's an Air Force major, who's supposed to know about The Bomb with a capital B, and a last-minute guy, a Marine major, whose family were missionaries in Hainan—I think.

"We've had big *pilikia* about how it's all to be done. I'd like to drop in by chute. After all, that's the favorite way of the Green Berets, the bent-legs. But right now, the plan is, we go into Hainan by submarine, take a small boat into shore, stay around with some friends of Ming's—the millionaire businessman Lowery was talking about last night, just before you conked out, remember?

"Ming showed up this morning at Lowery's, and he's getting things set up in Hainan. You know we've only got a couple of days before we start from here to get on board the sub. We need some running time to get to Hainan, get ashore and under cover there. Then maybe a day to get ready."

Hank wondered: "Couldn't they send over some bombers and hit the airfield? There can't be too many airfields around Hoihow. They could all be taken out, and at least no plane could take off for a little while if they bombed 'em."

Hope laughed. "Well, I'm not supposed to rearrange their strategy. I'm sure the Washington big shots have been over every possibility, or so they say: using B-52 and H-bombs, Polaris missiles from subs—everything. Also, I'll bet some members of the Security Council wanted to go to the U.N. and lay it out for them. And the President had trouble with that senator—what's his name, Smythe? —and his investigation of the CIA.

"The plan to send in a raiding party does make sense, considering that we don't know which building, or even which airfield, yet. Even if we did know what airfield, right now, we couldn't be sure, after any kind of bombing raid, that the bomb would be destroyed. You know how the nukes are. You can drop all kinds of bombs around them and you can't damage 'em—unless you do it *the* way. By hand-set charges.

"Mr. Big—I mean Mr. Really Big, the President—wants it done precisely, by people on the ground. Clandestine and real sneaky-peepy. Nobody should know. I guess the theory is the Chinese Commies would yell bloody murder if we used nuclear bombs or Polaris subs. But if we do a sneaky-peepy raid, they won't let out a word— especially if we succeed.

"The main thing is, we're really short of time. We should be getting on board that sub in two days. That is, no later than tomorrow, the eleventh, and getting over to Hainan so we can get our stuff ashore and into position."

Hank asked: "Is the sixteenth still a firm date for the Commies to deliver the bomb?"

"It keeps checking out with all the intelligence sources. It's some kind of anniversary for them. You know how the Commies are about anniversaries—like May Day. It seems like this one is the anniversary of the Chinese joining the bomb club, October sixteenth, 1964, when they set off their first little A-bomb.

"So, we've got to get to that bomb and ruin it properly before that day. Especially if it's a hydrogen bomb, and it's the only one they've got. If we can really rook it, probably it'll be a long time before they'll get another one together.

"Lowery had been getting the stuff together that we need, some of it. The ship that's supposed to take us out to the rendezvous with the submarine has already got a lot of our equipment on board. You were right about it. It's the destroyer *Edson*."

Hope gunned his properly resonant engine, swung out into the traffic of Queen's Road, and headed for the waterfront once more. They could make time this way, scooting through the easier traffic along the wharves. The pedestrians of Hong Kong, even in the less-trafficked waterfront streets, were used to fast-moving autos and would clear the way. Hope swung the car back to Connaught Road, bowled past the bustling display of walla-wallas, ferries, and beyond the buses and autos jammed up at the gates of the car ferry, the incredibly endless line of junks, with sails hung out to dry like bats' wings. Each junk was a decrepit miniature Santa Maria with high stern, low bow, and the sails a cockeyed version of a sixteenth century square-rig. Hope was driving fast and jumping his traffic opportunities, rowing his five-speed transmission like a sculling oar, dodging pedestrians with expert flicks of the wheel, riding heavily on the fade-proof disc brakes.

He had a way of biting his tongue in concentration, but he managed to spit out some information between street-side crises. Just after they passed the thickest knot of cars assembled at the auto ferry, and were accelerating through the first unencumbered straight block of Connaught Road, he said: "It's been hot and heavy at Croy's house since we were there. I don't think he's slept a wink. Right now, there should be some Navy types making the shipping plans for our little commando mission. And probably Ming is still there, too, figuring out how he's going to set up our temporary base on Hainan. It's going to be a real Grand Central Station in that communications room."

They sped through the lesser shopping sections stretching out towards Kennedy Town at the west end of the island. The automobile traffic was lighter here, but in the narrow street, they barely skinned around a teetering, ancient truck which appeared suddenly, barrelling around a curve towards them. A few minutes later, a peddler pushing a top-heavy fruit cart showed up on another curve. Hope whipped one flank of the blue beast onto the sidewalk, skimmed past a panel of narrow storefronts and startled Chinese faces stuck on sharkskin suits, and squeaked by three urchins playing penny-pitch on the far end of the sidewalk. It was a matter of inches.

"You drive fine," Hank said. "But we don't want to get held up by a smash—or get pinched by the cops."

"You're right," Hope said. "After all, the difference between thirty and fifty in these streets is only about twelve minutes between here and Croy's house."

He drove more slowly, and peered into the rear-view mirror. "You didn't see anybody following us, did you?"

Hank grimaced. "You think anyone could have followed us for the last seven minutes?"

✳

It was only twenty-one minutes later when the shovel-nosed car whipped past the barnacle-like cluster of junks in the floating village of Aberdeen, vaulted the rise beyond, and dropped into the winding narrow road on the southern cliffs of Hong Kong, near Deepwater Bay. The Bay broke below them, a huge deep sapphire in a ladle of granite, and a few yards into the slope, they turned into the driveway marked "Croy." Another Sikh, tall as the last one, with the same kind of long-barrelled shotgun, stood guard at the inner gate. The courtyard outside the house was jammed with a miscellany of autos—two Mercedes taxicabs, the Hong Kong standard model, and an assortment of British potato-shaped cars of the conservative saloon mold, as unesthetic as old-fashioned mantel clocks.

Inside, the Croy house was exactly as Hope had prophesied— it was like the five-o'clock crush at Grand Central Station.

They were checked and recognized by two alert young men in tweed coats at the door—good, fit-looking Spook types. No Chinese servants were visible in the house. Hank imagined the servant corps by now were confined to the servants' wing. They would be whispering up a storm—but separated from any of the vital meetings of the house.

They had no sooner entered the front door than they saw Lowery huddled with a group of six or eight—all in civilian clothes—in the living room. Amazingly, he seemed as tidy as he had been before, his shirt spotless white, his beaver tie still flawlessly aligned. He peered at them through the top of his glasses, excused himself from the group and came to meet them.

"You're pretty damned late," he said to Hope.

"Yes, sir, Musgrave has something very important for our pot."

Hank looked into the light greenish-blue eyes. This close, he could see how tired the face was. The mouth seemed to turn down, now, deeply at the corners. But Lowery was as bright and dynamic in manner as ever. "Was it the girl? You get it from her?"

Hank said: "Right. A good source."

Lowery said: "Okay. Will you sit down for a few minutes, and we'll get to it? And Hope, I want you to come with me here—" he indicated the group around the sofa in the living room, "—and meet with the Navy people—more destroyer people, people from the submarine service, all of them."

Lowery beckoned Hank to follow him into the code room and Hank told him quickly about the "Ball-within-Ball" and offered the explanation Hope had made.

Lowery said quickly: "I think you're right. But I'll check it out with the 'Nuke' people."

It was four minutes later when Lowery and Hank came out of the code room, and Lowery said: "Fine. You can wait there. I'll make sure you get some more money for your friend if you need it."

Hank held him one minute longer. "I want to ask about one more item: Freeman Blake. Is he around here somewhere? At least, I should say hello."

The glimmer of a smile, actually a slight elevation of the corners of the wafer-thin lips, marked Lowery's face. "He's here all right," he said. "You can go on up and see him. The upstairs study. He's up there with Ming, the Chinese millionaire I mentioned last night." He started back towards the group around the couch. He motioned to Hope: "Come on, Hope, let's get at this." And he signed off to Hank: "Hope will fill you in on what's next."

The upstairs study was also lined with books, with floor-to-ceiling shelves against one wall, and a wide panoramic window looking over Deepwater Bay. A cluster of junks moved slowly across the mouth of the Bay, some under sail, a smaller number of dismasted motor craft. Freeman sat next to the window, talking earnestly with three other men. One of them was plump and smooth-faced, impeccably tailored in a Hong Kong silk suit. He was young, probably in his middle thirties, and Hank surmised he would be the Chinese millionaire Lowery had mentioned. The other two men were shirt-sleeved, and he guessed they would be part of Lowery's working pool, technicians who worked perhaps in communications.

Freeman stood up and extended his hand. His heavy-lidded eyes surveyed Hank without any apparent emotion: "Sorry we couldn't make a deal before." If there was any impetus of ill will because he had gone over to a higher compartment, Freeman betrayed no evidence of it.

Freeman introduced the other three men. As Hank had surmised, the round-faced Chinese was Ming, with the Westernized first name of Eddie. The other two men were named Peterson and Taylor.

Eddie Ming had been looking at a large map. He started to fold it up, and Freeman Blake stopped him. "Please, Mr. Ming, show Mr. Musgrave the marvelous extent of your knowledge of the Chinese installation on Hainan." Ming hesitated and Blake reassured him: "He is properly privileged to this knowledge. He is within the fold."

Ming unfolded the map again. Smiling pleasantly, he spoke flawless English in the American idiom. "I've had good on-the-spot reports from my people at several key places in there. The Chi-Coms have been building a brand new airfield here at this little village, seven miles from Hoihow." The map covered the northern portion of the island and the adjoining little peninsula protruding into Hainan Strait from the mainland of China. "They've been rushing to build a tremendous base, protected with layers of barbed wire, sentries, watchtowers, cyclone fences.

"The airfield is finished—a runway eleven thousand feet long, and the first planes have just landed. The Chi-Coms have had four or five thousand locals there working on the runway and the buildings, and it's really built to repel boarders. They've got belts of barbed wire and one layer of cyclone fence, guard towers, and searchlights. It's going to be a tough one to crack—if that's the intention."

The two shirt-sleeved FBI types excused themselves. "I must get to Mr. Lowery downstairs," Peterson said. And Taylor got up, too. Apparently they had both heard Eddie's spiel before and they weren't about to tell him the American plan.

Eddie acknowledged their departure and went on, his wide face pleasant, still smiling. "The planes that have come in so far have been MIG-21s—God knows where they got them. And one larger aircraft, a Tupolev-16 or 'Badger' bomber as you Americans have nicknamed them, has also arrived."

Hank was startled at the extent of Eddie's G-2: "Excuse me, Mr. Ming—"

"Eddie," Ming corrected him.

"Excuse me, Eddie—but where did you get all this detailed dope? That's pretty astonishing."

Eddie looked happier than ever. "I was born in Hainan thirty-six years ago. And I spent a happy boyhood there until the Chi-Coms came down and drove us out in 1949. I was a kid. But I'm still loaded with friends on the island. And I have access to them."

His face suddenly looked sullen. "I had tried a few times to convince Mr. Lowery of my genuineness, but until recently my evidence was apparently inadmissible.

"I have been prepared, and made the offer many times, to provide my own finances for an operational mission into Hainan, as well as to offer my assistance in intelligence. But until now—" He shrugged bis plump shoulders, raised his hands in a gesture of futility.

Suddenly Hank could see why Freeman was cultivating Eddie Ming. In the never-ending struggle between intelligence compartments, Freeman perhaps was losing his grip, and Lowery was in the ascendent; Freeman was looking for all the powerful support and every bit of information that Lowery might not have. Evidently Lowery had been disinclined, at least until the last few hours, to take advantage of the Chinese pipelines. Freeman, with family links to Asia, had a greater instinctive faith in "indigenous sources."

Eddie went on earnestly: "I should explain quickly that my father did very well in the capitalistic system in Malaya and here— and that he was killed by the Communists on one of his rubber plantations during the 'Emergency,' between the British and the Communists in what used to be called the Malay States. I think this will explain my interest in the anti-Communist campaign."

Freeman said: "Eddie—we'll maybe meet later on this afternoon before I go back to Bangkok. Your ideas are most interesting, and should be most valuable to the United States."

Ming bowed, his face bright but deliberately expressionless; evidently he had been burned by American lost-promises and apparent lack of central authority but he was still willing to help.

Freeman stayed with Hank a moment. He looked around. No one could hear. "I don't know how bug-proof this place is," he said. "I have my doubts about the servants, the bookcases, and so on. Lowery seems to have a slightly different conception of security from mine."

Hank sensed that Freeman's joviality was leading to a major disclosure or proposal. Now Freeman said: "I know you've been following the preparations for the mission into Hainan, and you're probably better posted on them than I am. But did you know about the latest trouble in Washington?"

"No."

"The Big Chief back there is running into a lot of trouble from Senator Smythe, about the CIA budget."

"I knew that much."

"Well, did you know that if things get too hot there, the President will probably have to stall a little, maybe too much to carry out this job. He's really being pole-axed.

"So, being the thorough-going type, and possibly the old school inclined to economic methods, I am very interested in what Ming is talking about. Besides being very well posted on what's going on in Hainan, he also has a plan.

"Lowery hasn't told him much, he has offered to make use of Ming's friends on Hainan as a CP of our force. It apparently hasn't yet occurred to Lowery that if the President gets held up and the operation stalls, we may have to turn to an amateur kind of operation like that which Ming proposes. That's one reason I'm anxious to talk to him further."

Hank said: "Oh my gosh!" and Freeman evidently approved.

He said: "I'll call you later in the afternoon at the hotel, right?"

As Hank went down the grand staircase, he heard the sounds of many car engines outside—starting, revving up, starting off in gears, others coming in and braking. He was already looking forward to the ride home in Hope's Porsche 911.

Hope was still talking with Lowery and the Navy types in the conversational group around the couch in the living room. He saw Hank looking for him, and advised: "Hank, I'll be ready in a minute. I'll drive you back to town. I'll give you the latest word."

And Lowery turned away from the Navy types momentarily. He came right to Hank: "Musgrave. Consider yourself one of us. Hope will take care of the money you need." He didn't wait for an answer. Like a machine, he snapped back to his Navy consultation.

9

October 10 (continued)

WHEN HOPE AND MUSGRAVE WENT DOWN TO THE COURT yardpast the young tweed-coated Agency sentries, Hope was as tense as if he were that moment setting out on the great raid.

When they reached the Porsche, he suggested: "How about some debugging procedure this time? This courtyard is allegedly under strict surveillance, but from now on, I'm going to double-check everything. You want to go over the cockpit and I'll do the hood?"

They started the check-up, and Hank asked: "Did you take the bug in to Lowery's experts for identification?"

"Yeah—and it was as you suspected—the trademark was from a 'People's Factory' in Shanghai. The experts said this make of bug was a favorite of the local Commies. It doesn't mean much—except maybe the Commies are trying to watch a lot of Americans in Hong Kong. And there was nothing on the tape except a lot of car-noises."

"I'm glad their organization is at least as bad as ours."

On the way up the narrow driveway to the intersection of Stanley Road, Hope gave Hank a fill-in about the latest developments in plans.

While the car zoomed up the slope, he said above the roar of engine and gears: ". . . unless things change—and Lowery says they might very well, considering that the emotional climate of Washington is about the most whimsical in the world—we're going to get on board the destroyer tomorrow at eight in the morning, and go.

"I'll have to get back aboard that tin can, the *Edson*, tonight to check over all the supplies. Then there'll be all my people in Hong Kong. The main thing I have to do is to keep them out of trouble, and keep them away from Lowery's headquarters, because he says he doesn't want any more traffic than absolutely necessary into Croy's house. He's already worried about the British Special Bureau getting suspicious. He plans to tell the Bureau about the mission later, when the job's done."

They had reached the intersection of Stanley Road, and Hope hesitated momentarily before plunging into the traffic stream.

"Goddamn," he breathed, "you'd think this was the Washington Turnpike. It's about time the Commies took over Hong Kong— there's too much traffic."

Then he saw a break in the stream of cars and darted into it. In that moment, Hank spotted a long black car streaking out of a driveway from the direction of Repulse Bay and Stanleytown.

Looking through the fastback rear window, Hank watched the car, squeezing through traffic gaps along the narrow road, and picking up distance between them.

"You notice the black car, Eric?" Hank asked.

"You mean that Bentley? Seems to be in a helluva hurry."

Hank suggested: "When we get to the Aberdeen turnoff up here, most of the traffic will be making the other turn into Little Hong Kong Road. The traffic will be a lot thinner and we can see."

It was true that most of the traffic turned off into Little Hong Kong Road. Hope made the left-turning into the road toward Aberdeen. Hope and Musgrave both watched the rear very carefully. Sure enough, the black car, still gaining on them, turned in the same direction.

Hope estimated professionally: "In third and fourth, with my six Solex carbs, and my suspension advantage on these winding roads, I should be able to put some distance between them and us. I've got a plan for a place where I think I can shake 'em. We'd better. They might force us off a cliff, or throw a grenade."

Hank looked down the grade and at the bottom, he could see the Bentley burning rubber as it followed up the slope.

Hope swung the Porsche into a sharp hairpin turn at the top of the grade, braking and down-shifting into third, and swinging to the far side of the turn to hit it with maximum workable velocity. He shot out of the bend in third gear and exclaimed: "That turn will take a couple of years off their lives in the Bentley."

The last words were bitten off as they hit hard into another sharp road bend. Hope set up a good line on the road skirt at the entrance to the curve, and barrelled expertly into the opposite skirt at the far end.

"Nice driving," Hank said in admiration. "You're as hot with this thing as you are with Special Force warfare. You must have—" He was going to ask if Hope had driven professionally, but left it unfinished, because at that moment, finishing its line across the curve, the Porsche was well into the wrong side of the road, and ahead of them a bus, rumbled toward them down the slope of the next hill.

Hope whipped the wheel to the left, the tires screeched, the rear end of the car swung outward, as if beginning a spin. Hope lifted his foot from the accelerator, so that the bit of oversteer subsided and the tail of the car swung back into position as the bus charged by, its windows a blur of people.

The car charged up the next hill with undiminished vigor, and they recovered their breath.

"You were saying?" Hope asked.

"I was saying you must have had some sports car racing experience," Hank answered. "Now I know it."

Hope said through clenched teeth: "There's another bend at the top of this hill. Got to get ready." He down-shifted, and continued: "Hank, take a good look back, that Bentley might have some trouble with the bus, in the hairpin."

Hank turned to look back, and saw the bus rocketing into the curve, and just beyond it, the long black shape of the Bentley on the wrong side of the road.

The Bentley driver was trying what Hope had brought off, he swung his wheel to the left, but he wasn't as skillful, nor his car as adroit. Hank heard the screeching of the tires and brakes, the rear end of the big car swung out into the path of the bus, swept past the big vehicle, so close that he couldn't tell whether there was an impact. The black car spun off the road to the right, bashing into a couple of the marker stones at the edge of the road, bounding back in the opposite direction in a wrenching slide. The sound of the impact with the marker stones, a tin-kettle chorus, reached the Americans as they swept over the brow of the hill, and the last Hank saw from there was the car teetering to a stop in the middle of the road, amid the smoke of tires and brakes.

Ahead was another bend, but not so sharp as the last, and as Hope lined up for it, Hank reported: "We'll have a couple of minutes lead out of that. He spun out, and maybe he bashed a fender and blew a tire."

"And maybe not. We can't afford to take a chance. There's a straightaway ahead, and they might be able to catch up there." Hope whizzed the car into the next bend, and ahead of them, the straight strip unfolded, a belt of nearly a mile. Hope got up into fifth and the speedometer needle flipped to eighty-five, ninety. Then they saw a police car, a Morris with a tall whip aerial, coming from the other end. Hope down-shifted and braked, and the needle declined rapidly to seventy, sixty, forty-five.

The police car, and the line of regular cars which always follow a police car in any country, moseyed down the road, and the police didn't seem to notice the Porsche. At the same moment, the long black Bentley came over the brow of the last hill, lurched through the turn, and obviously saw the police car and tried to slow down. It wavered unsteadily, and the brakes squawked as it fishtailed down the straightaway.

As they rolled along at a mere forty miles an hour, Hank noticed that the two cops in the police car were watching the erratic behavior of the Bentley. "Maybe they'll pinch him."

"But we can't count on it."

"We can count on his blowing a tire pretty soon. He's on a junior license. He'd never last out one lap at LeMans."

The blue beast mounted another hill, still at the same careful speed. Beyond the hill top, Hope swept through the next curve at accelerating speed, then braked as another hairpin appeared ahead, threaded through it into one more straightaway.

"Now, we should be gaining some time on them," Hope said. Then the car was sloping up another hill, with a sharp bend edged by a stone cliff at the top of it.

"Here's the place," he said, and roared up the slope towards the curve. "Now." Near the top, Hank saw an access road off to the left. It was a private driveway leading to the house far below through a series of hairpin turns, on the slope somewhere between the road and the water's edge below. It was familiar geography. Hank remembered it belonged to the *Time-Asia* chief, Frank McCulloch.

Hope jammed the car into second, and spun the wheel. The rear end swung wide, the low gear gripped the road, he flung the car nearly sideways into the driveway, flipped the wheel back and forth on the far side and straightened into the narrow driveway leading down the grade. He turned up high revs in the straightaway and jammed his way through the hairpin at the far end, and charged down the last strip of straightaway. He brought the car to a stop just beyond the next U-turn.

Through the thick woods on the slope, Hank and Hope watched the curve of the highway above. They heard the roaring of an automobile engine, a screeching of brakes as a car charged into the bend at the top of the hill. The Bentley thudded to a teetering stop. They could make out four men hunched in it, the flat face of the driver as he peered down the road. They saw the men moving in the car. "It looks as if they're arguing," Hank said. "They know they've lost us—and somebody's lost *face*—the driver no doubt." As if to confirm the point, the Bentley started with a roar again, and a screech of tires. The thin smoke of burnt rubber swirled behind the car.

"That guy'll kill himself yet," Hope said.

"Maybe right now," Hank said. "I know this road, and at the top of the next rise is a turn that's a bitch."

A thick clump of woods cut off the view for a moment, but they heard the roaring of an engine pushed too far and the squealing of tires as the car hit a bend.

Hank said: "Watch!" The black car popped into view, wobbling through a bend. It roared into the bottom of a dip and up the far slope without slowing. "That's the bad turn, at the top of the hill."

The car charged up the hill, the driver saw the turn suddenly and the vehicle began to sway and roll like a drunk. Then came the bang, like a pistol shot—a tire.

They watched fascinated as the car fishtailed, and in one of the swings saw the driver moving frantically. It skidded more wildly, canted up on its outer wheels and began to turn over. A couple of black parts flew loose—and the sounds of brakes, and a tin-pan smashing of metal reached them.

Then, with all the leisure and inexorability of an accident viewed from afar, they could see the car rolling—rolling up toward the top of the hill, with the loud, catastrophic sounds of a saucepan Götterdämmerung. The car turned end for end, a door flew open, and the Americans saw the rolling vehicle flip off the visible end of the road.

Hope was cool. "There they go—over the top."

"The Chinese never were any good with mechanical gadgets," said Hank. "Despite their slogans about the Communist will to win."

Hope quickly backed, made a few cuts, and headed the car up the road. "Score another win for matter over willpower."

The Porsche scooted up the slope and Hope didn't slow as he roared around the tight bend in third. They saw the car down below them among tan-colored rocks, wheels up to the sky, dust rising like thin smoke around it. No one was moving down there yet.

"That one's for Mary," Hope said as he accelerated.

He took the turn which leads to the Kennedy Town waterfront—it was the road they had followed on their way out. And Hank had a chance to ask Hope the belated question: "Where did you drive professionally?"

Hope smiled. "One of my indiscretions. I drove the Targa Florio, and I was kind of a substitute at LeMans in summer—between semesters at West Point. But I didn't drive this one very well today. We were just lucky." At that moment, they heard the siren of a police car coming, from the Repulse Bay section.

They made it to the waterfront easily, and now, as the sundown gold was glinting on the tower-windows of Hong Kong, Hope swung the car sharply into the auto ferry terminal. A boat was waiting.

At his hotel Hank called the desk for messages and found one from Freeman Blake. It was signed with the Mandarin Hotel number. It was a recent message, received only half an hour before.

Hank called the number and Freeman answered.

"What are you doing tonight?" Freeman asked.

Hank said: "Going to see my friend in the hospital."

"Okay," Freeman said. "I want to see you later. Big doings in the head office. Call me when you get back."

When Hank Musgrave reached Mary's hospital room that night, she had changed, and much for the better. The mountain of bandage on her head had been chopped down, and now it seemed that only about half of the white gauze structure remained.

When he came in, Mary's elderly roommate turned away in her usual anti-social way, and faced the wall.

Then he heard a sound which shook him. First it seemed to be outside the roof—a floating, faint sound. It was Mary's voice! It had a new timbre, a hollow impersonal sound because she was unable to open her jaws.

But, quite clearly, he could hear her muttered words: *"Jong-fu!* Hank, you came back."

He sat on the bed, shaken, but marvelling at her sudden return to life. Her eyes were both discolored, the tissue around them was puffy and black-and-blue, but recognizable at last. No longer a child's scrawls on an egg of white bandage. Her mouth looked like Mary, too: upper lip puffy and bruised but the basic voluptuous curve visible below. He squeezed her hand, gently, and told her: "I may be going on a trip in connection with the current writing job. If I leave, I'll be sure to let you know. I'll leave you some money, and I'll make sure there's always somebody at the door outside who will watch over you, night and day."

The thin, disembodied voice: "You're my sweet boy, Hank."

He went on: "I don't know whether I mentioned it—things were so mixed up this morning—but your friend or somebody sent a thug, a strong-arm man to go through my hotel room. I surprised him there."

Mary said: "I see the damage to your head. You should go see the doctor about it. Like getting a tetanus shot. Don't forget."

He fancied he could see her eyes smiling. He touched her golden shoulder in the rough cotton hospital gown. She took his hand deliberately and placed it on the softness of her breast. Through the starched fabric, he knew the smoothness of her, the perfect shape of her rising under his touch, even the beating of her heart.

Then she did one of those things which he would always remember. She reached up with her right hand, untied the bow that fastened the gown, and placed his hand softly on the golden shape, the taut, bold, mauve-colored promontory tipping it, the whole perfect globe which had always set his pulse racing.

He bent and kissed her, and she held him to her, his heart throbbing wildly. He bent to kiss her body again, and her hand held the back of his neck gently.

This time the ventriloquated voice was hoarse, like a sob. "Hank — you were the only one who came to me when I needed it."

"Yeah, and I was the one that got you in trouble in the first place. But I was thinking—" He rushed on: "If we got married and I kept on as a correspondent here, or in India, it could be good."

"Married?" The word was only a sigh of disbelief. Her arms tightened around his back.

He reached to touch the satiny, perfectly-molded tissue of her thigh, the firm, healthy, athletic flesh and he found those fascinatingly deep hips with his fingertips. He felt the flood of warmth of their being close, something never to be ended. That moment the remembrance came rushing back, the full force of a dozen times he had known before with her, and yet this time the force was blindingly stronger. It startled him that it should be so much more. Why was it? The critical part of him was asking—and protesting. This is insanity. But in a moment the other part of him came boiling up in an explosive cloud of roiling emotion and swept away all his critical faculty—and he was glad to see it go.

He held her to him as if they were one new being, not caring now about the old Chinese woman on the other side of the room, not caring about Chen, or the job, anything except that moment, as long as it could be prolonged and made permanent.

Now he didn't care if the nurse came in, it didn't matter: It was the meaning of the two smooth skins, the yang and yin as yang and yin is never found in any other part of life except man-and-woman closeness, but it was more than that now, more than it had ever been. She was giving herself to him here as she had before, but never had it seemed like this, on this precipice of life and this edge of dying— a shameless love and a shameless woman, but shameless about the fact that she loved him, however impossible the circumstances. He loved her wildly and desperately, not minding the blind passion-cries that came from him as if from some other person, and not minding her sounds either, even with the ancient Chinese woman in the room, her back still turned or not turned, it didn't matter. There was nothing for Mary and him here but this blending of wanting and the need for each other, and they for once were all there was or needed to be, and still they clutched each other and it would not stop nor did they want it to.

No one came into the room, the old lady roommate didn't turn over, it was blissfully done and done. He was mystified that they should be consumed so completely with each other, and he told her: "It was never like that. Never. Never before."

October 11

He took a cab to the Empress and phoned Hope from the lobby. It was one-fifteen A.M.

"Come on up," said the cheery voice. "I'll buy you a drink."

Hope opened the door in shirt-sleeves, his sandy hair tousled. His face was lined and tired, his eyes bloodshot. Behind him, a towering pile of papers on the desk was the only sign of his work in the otherwise spotless room.

He noticed Hank's glance toward the desk. "This paperwork is a pain," he said. "But at least, it's probably better than splashing around in the rice paddies."

He extended a drink. "Looks like you need this libation as much as I do. Got a fever?"

"Practically," Hank admitted.

Hope didn't pursue it. He turned up the volume of the hotel speaker system—by now, a conditioned reflex. "Some of the boys are coming up in a few minutes. You might as well meet them." He looked into Hank's face: "You *are* coming on the raiding party, aren't you?"

When Hank hesitated a moment, Hope said: "We'll be needing you. And I've cleared it with *Mr.* Lowery."

Hank told him: "Sure. I hesitated a couple of seconds because—" He left it unfinished and Hope supplied it:

"Because of Mary, right?"

"The thing I've been worried about," Hank said, "is will Lowery keep an eye on her while we're away? And longer than that if we don't get back at all?"

"If Lowery says he will, he will," Hope said. "He's a lot different from—Freeman Blake."

Hank was reminded that he'd promised to phone Blake, and asked if he could make the call from there.

"Sure," Hope said. And he added: "Incidentally, what do you figure he's up to?"

"My guess is he wants to get the No. 1 spot away from Lowery in this operation. That is, if things go his way in Washington. I don't know what's happening back there except the President is in trouble with Senator Smythe.

"But I figure Blake is a born politician. He estimates that if the President runs into a road block in Congress, he'll somehow offer the President a real sub-rosa deal using that local millionaire—Eddie Ming. Blake figures he can run the operation through for practically nothing—and come out a hero. You agree?"

Hope nodded. "Sounds right. I know the President's been backed into a corner. Judging from the stuff on the teletype) Smythe is threatening to rip the cover off everything. Fortunately, he doesn't know *everything*."

Hank said: "I think we'd miss out if Blake was running the show with local talent. If we'd been preparing for years—or even months — for this kind of operation, it'd be different. He might have a chance.

"But imagine trying it with Chinese we haven't checked out—Chinese who aren't even trained, who might slip over to the other side, given enough cumshaw. The time is years too short—months too short, anyhow."

Hope said: "You're right, what we need is Special Forces teams, Chinese irregulars trained by us—all over China with good indoctrination and plenty of public relations—radio broadcasting stations and printing presses and plenty of arms—and always on the move.

"But we don't have it. We just haven't been aggressive enough: about the principle of one man, one vote—in every language. And freedom to talk about it, and fight for it—and no apologies. A religious faith in our politics, and our revolution. A stronger faith than the other side has and better preparation than we had in Vietnam, and than we have now. That will have to be the next time."

He stared at the high-flying lights of the destroyer *U.S.S. Edson,* straight across the harbor. Besides the graceful curve of lights outlining the rigging above, there were yellowish lights on deck—and a freight lighter lay alongside. "So we've got to do this job with what we have—the President willing."

Hank phoned the Hilton. No answer in Freeman's room, and he left word for him to call Hope's room at the Empress.

Hope looked at his watch. "If you'll bear with me, Hank, I'll be getting back to some of this paperwork, until the boys come."

He started for the desk, but stopped to ask: "How come you're willing to do this kind of job? The pay isn't very good—and the risks are only the highest. Besides, it isn't even newspaper work."

"It's the hambone in me," Hank answered. "It's the most important story around. And besides—once in a while it's good to *do* something instead of just writing about other people doing things."

"It seems to me you've always been able to *do* quite a few things. Like in Vietnam."

"That takes care of me. Why are *you* involved in this? After Vietnam, you could have spent a couple of years in an Army training school, married an Asian beauty and had golden kids. Maybe go to the War College. And had the good life at home."

Hope laughed. "Must be the hambone in me, too. I like to do things. And my poppa is an Army type—he always encouraged me."

"How about your momma? How did you sell her on the military career?"

"Well, she's been pretty thoroughly subjugated on the issue— brainwashed by my father, my brother, and me. My younger brother is a lieutenant (j.g.)—a jet jockey. Flies an F-4 on the carrier *Enterprise*. You know, my father was a straight-leg—artillery, yet, in the Reserves in World War II. But he's even more full of fight than my brother or me. He says he's not worried about us two. Only that there aren't a million more like us." He smiled uneasily. "A pretty good Pops."

Three of Hope's "boys" were coming in: The first was the Marine— massive, red-headed and blue-eyed, with a childish eagerness beaming through his freckly complexion, the skin as frail-looking as the mist on an Irish bog. He was about thirty-three, the proper age for a rising new major.

Behind him, another tweed-coated officer of about the same age, but with a totally different physiognomy: dark, shut-in, sober-faced, a man you might guess would never reveal secrets—or offer much else in the way of conversation. The third man was younger, perhaps in his mid-twenties, and he seemed more resilient and athletic than the other two. He was tall and rangy and had the same sort of lean, race-horse look which characterized Hope.

Hank could sort them out even before Hope made the introductions. The red-haired major would be the Marine expert on Hainan, who had been born there, the son of the missionary family: the tight-lipped dark one would turn out to be the Air Force authority on nuclear bombs. The third man, tallest of the group, with close-cropped flaxen hair, must be the young lieutenant in charge of Hope's communications section.

The redhead was Mike Nooley and Mike admitted he didn't mind being called Red, "since it's a pretty fair description." The Air Force type was Paul Gresham, and he still didn't smile, and the youngest of the three, with a very martial-sounding name, Kurt Helmantholer, belied his Prussian looks with a very soft Arkansas drawl.

Hope said as they sat down: "I've got a big dose of ying-yang music on to cover our conversation, but we must still be circumspect here. When we get on the ship—and that'll probably be tomorrow— it'll be different. But even there, the job is absolutely top in classification. I'm sure you've already been told this a thousand times."

He got a bottle of Scotch from a cabinet, accumulated three more glasses of different shapes and sizes, and set them out on the table.

"You know, gentlemen, this is not a briefing. I only want to warn you to be ready to go, packed and ready to go, practically from this moment on."

Red Nooley poured three whiskey shots and pushed two across the cocktail table. He lifted his glass and looked at the light through it. "Here's to our mission—or should I say fission."

"Except that it's fusion, not fission." Hope grinned. "A bigger job by far. About a thousand times bigger, since the H-bomb is at least a thousand times bigger bang." And Gresham seemed disturbed about this light approach to the project.

"Anyhow," Hope went on, "we're all to be on stand-by from now on. You all know the general shape of what we're going to do. You'll have a much better briefing on the ship, after I talk to the big chief here tonight. Right now, big things are coming across the air from Washington. The main thing, as of this moment, is do you all have, for practical purposes anyhow, most of the things you will be needing?"

Helmantholer answered: "If everything we've talked about is on the ship, I'm in fine shape."

"Me, too," said Nooley. And Major Gresham only nodded.

Hope went on: "I want to go over something very important to all of us. It's new, and as Hank here has indicated, it's the hottest news. He has some recent confirmation. It's that our objective is not the smaller of the two kinds, but the biggest—you understand?" A murmur of excitement rose in the room. "Hank has good evidence confirming that our target is a gimmick within a gimmick, one being used to light off the other, if you understand me." Expressions confirmed that they did. Even poker-faced Paul Gresham came alive and exclaimed: "Man! It really *is* the H!"

In the White House at that same moment, one-forty P.M. Washington time, the President was conscious of the basic feeling of nervousness about Senator Smythe and the Operation Typhoon trouble that had been riding him all night. Four times in the night he had risen and sat in his robe at the desk in his little office, and tried to sort out the tangle of idea, plans, and accidents which were the convolutions of this crisis.

The central problem of the night, and this moment, was unmistakable, and unavoidable: to stick by a decision which is right— but unpopular—and not be dissuaded by a demagogue who follows a popular line, which even the demagogue knows is false. The President's father had always shown this kind of certainty, the hard, flinty sense of rectitude of some Presbyterian ministers.

President Bascombe Landers had developed beyond the Rev. Landers' simple conception of sharp-edged right and wrong, because his life had exposed him to a much wider world than the Presbyterian parsonage in West Union, New Jersey, where he had grown up. World War II had taken him to the CBI, to India and China, and he had come to realize that the white man and his religion, far from being incontrovertible and correct, didn't even have the justification of majority support in the world. If one believed that the will of the majority should prevail, he had frequently said in private, then one must agree that people with colored skins, brown, black, and yellow, must eventually rule the world community.

After the war, a long career as Representative and then Senator had showed him the shape of the power struggle which drives the western world. He had a good education in the cynicism, the utter lack of principle, the hypocritical self-righteousness and selfishness which guide most politicians and the legal profession from which they generally come. He, too, had occasionally shared some of the oddly colored benefits which flourish in the public trough.

But he also knew the people of the country, the electorate, could not run the country directly—they had to have faith in their elected representatives. If the decisions of the politicians were too outrageous, the politicians could always be thrown out in the next election.

But the job was much too complex, and required too high a level of experience and skill, to admit of amateur intervention in the middle of the act.

That's the way he felt about Operation Typhoon: An attempt to throw this issue into public debate, or to leave the settlement to the United Nations, could only be disastrous.

The real question remained: Was he willing to risk his political future, or even to *give up* his political future, for the sake of the country—and the world? Was he actually going to endorse Senator Smythe for re-election? And by inference, recommend him for still further political advancement? Backing Smythe was the last of the blandishments he could offer to get the Senator off the back of Operation Typhoon. Would he risk his whole future for it?

His mind flicked back to the South China campaign in World War II, near Kunming, during the American retreat, the "scorched earth" withdrawal, there had been the bridge to blow—under Japanese machine gun fire in enfilade. His sergeant, the leader of the squad which would destroy the bridge, had been hit, killed, a bullet through his head. The squad were frozen in fright, and a Jap light tank was almost to the bridge. He had run across the open space to the dead sergeant's side to push the plunger. He remembered that dash now—the snapping of the Japanese bullets—as if it had been yesterday. He had blown that bridge and survived that moment. He would take his chances now and survive this one, too.

He phoned Charles Hudibras at the Plastics Factory.

"David Soloretha is going to bring Senator Smythe around to see me about four o'clock. David has been watchdogging him all day at the Ways and Means Committee hearing. I want to make sure I understand your suggestions for handling him. All those suggestions from Southeast Asia for carrying out the operation. Could you come over?"

"Yes, sir." Hudibras sounded breathless. "I'll be right there." He hesitated. "You know, sir, if we are going to carry out the main suggestion, we're going to have to start it right now."

"All right, Charlie. Keep your pants on. I'll be waiting for you."

*

That same moment was two-ten A.M. in Hong Kong, and Arthur Lowery was leading the way from the code room of the Croy house. When he opened the door it marked a sharp-edged rectangle of yellow illumination on the floor of the darkened living room. Hank Musgrave, Eddie Ming, Eric Hope, and Freeman Blake followed him, and Blake was saying: "I guess that hacks it. We've got to get going right now—if not sooner."

Lowery said to Hope: "Better alert your three leading people—Nooley, Gresham and Helmantholer—and tell 'em to get packed. We'll be leaving in the morning at eight o'clock—by junk, via Macau." He turned to Ming: "Eddie, we'll have to get some people to work unloading that small bit of stuff from the destroyer and putting it onto a lighter, We can get our own Navy work parties to do this during the night—but you'll have to get some people to shift it onto a junk before the night's over. It'll take some sharp operating to do it between now and daylight, and not be noticed by the British Special Branch."

Eddie said, with his usual wide smile: "Don't worry, it'll be done — if your Navy work parties will get the load into the typhoon anchorage at Kowloon in the next couple of hours."

Lowery said: "I'll take care of that through my Navy friends."

Freeman Blake spoke to Hank. "We can get one of the cars here to run us into town. We can take Hope back to the pier." He turned to Lowery, "Is that right, Arthur, can we get a car?"

"All right," Lowery agreed. Hope's expression showed shock at the sudden familiarity shown by Blake for the boss. He still couldn't believe what he had just seen in the encoding room. In the handling of messages between here and Washington, Blake had taken over the show.

Blake was still directing: "Eddie—I will bring Musgrave and Hope and the other three over to Macau on the early morning hydrofoil. From then on, it'll be your show. We'll be at your disposal. And you'll supply the muscle-power—the enlisted men, you might say— from Macau on, okay?"

Eddie Ming nodded. "That's right."

Freeman Blake used Hank as a catalyst to issue an order to Arthur Lowery. He said: "Hank, Arthur Lowery will be staying here to watch over everything, and hell make sure that somebody keeps an eye on your friend in the hospital, night and day. Is that right, Arthur?"

"Yes."

Blake had still more orders: "Hank, why don't you and Hope go on down and get a car, and I'll wind up a couple of words with Arthur." He turned to Eddie Ming: "Eddie, can we take you downtown? Do you have transportation?"

Eddie still smiled. "Got plenty of transport, thanks."

On the way downstairs, Hope voiced the wonderment he felt about the sudden turnabout in the command of Operation Typhoon. "How did Freeman do it?" he asked, speaking softly.

"Planning," Hank said. "He had it all figured out as soon as he knew the President was having trouble—and he saw how he could get the heat off the President, use Eddie Ming, and get the command away from Arthur Lowery. He's a master." Hank added with a quick grin: "But Lowery told me quite firmly it can all change, hour by hour."

*

In Washington, Senator Smythe, Chairman of the Senate Committee on Ways and Means, was driving his earth-colored Falcon up the oval driveway in front of the White House. Beside him sat David Soloretha, and Smythe was exploding in triumph: "I haven't tipped anything in the Committee, you can see that, Mr. Soloretha. I kept my promise. But tomorrow will be the day."

Soloretha turned towards Smythe: "I think the President will have a few things to say which might alter your thinking on that," he said, mildly enough.

Smythe pulled the little car up directly in front of the circular front steps of the White House. "In the chronicles of modern times, this day will go down as one of the most important of all," he said. "This is the day on which Sam Smythe, the humble Senator from Oklahoma, the Southwestern demiurge spoke up for the people and forced his and the people's will on the President of the United States. That will be a great day in the history of Senator Smythe as he made his way upwards, perhaps towards the presidency."

Soloretha followed Smythe up the steps grinning. He knew that the Senator from Oklahoma was underestimating the dialectic skill of the President, one of the great political tacticians of the time.

When they were seated the President swung on the Senator and directed at him a scowl as dark as a thunderhead. "Sam," he said. "Today you've made me do something I'll always be ashamed of— and you *should* be. I hope you realize that because of the pressure you've brought, some good Americans might be about to pay with their lives for your unwise decisions." Senator Smythe's confident face seemed to draw tight.

"Mr. President, I don't have to take this."

The President turned and faced him. "Yes, you do, Sam. There's no other way. I know what your plan is and I'm going to tell you what I have done, and you're going to have to act accordingly."

Smythe took a mouthful of tea and put his cup down unsteadily in the saucer. "Mr. President," he said, somewhat too loudly, "you haven't given me a chance to tell you about my decision—the blow I will be striking tomorrow morning, at the Ways and Means Committee hearing—a great blow for representative government in the most critical area of the machinery of government—in the budgets of the secret wars. I intend to tell the American people about your current secret war, and to expose the entire effort your people are engaged in, at great expense and risk of life and limb, and national security, in Southeast Asia."

The President riveted him with a freezing stare. "No, you won't, Senator, because of this fact. Since you have been bringing pressure, I have called off our 'secret' effort to stop the Communists in their plan to drop an H-bomb! You have forced me to cancel out our principal preparations for nullifying this bomb."

An uneasy smile began to appear around Senator Smythe's mouth. But the President bore down on him: "I'm going to tell you what havoc your threats have wreaked down there in Southeast Asia. I want you to remember this, and I also want to tell you why you can't say a thing about it, not a word."

The Senator said: "I don't see that anyone can get in my way when I start telling the public about the secret war you have underway out of Hong Kong—a great chunk of unaccounted American budgetary funds, a great risk of American lives and equipment—and a great threat to the entire future of our nation."

The President said: "Now I'm going to tell you something, Sam—something you haven't yet heard. Now, because of pressure that you've been threatening, I have called off the American expenditure in what you call my 'secret war.' American money and equipment is *not* being used. Because of your fuss about the cost of American military budgets in the clandestine kind of war which is the way war is run nowadays, my 'private war' as I'm sure you would like to see it labelled, has been cut off. That war has been taken over by a volunteer group of Chinese, supported by a Chinese anti-Communist patriot who should put us all to shame for our niggardliness in not wanting to risk anything in our world-wide war against a deadly and relentless foe.

"Because of the threats which you have been making, the Americans whom I was about to send into this mission have been released from it. Some of them have taken leaves, lest you find that they were somehow involved in this effort on government time and at government expense, and they have volunteered their services to assist the Chinese anti-Communist effort. This is what you have forced me to do—to send American boys into an engagement without the support of the American military which they should have, to the hilt. Instead, they are going in a private Chinese army—which incidentally has no United States Government military support, and is being supported entirely by this anti-Communist Chinese—and if they die in the course of this mission because they don't have sufficient support in the military sense, their blood will be on your hands, even more than on mine.

"Furthermore, this volunteer effort has already moved into action. You have forced me to let them do this without American assistance. I'm going to insist that not a word be breathed about this publicly. Not a word about the Chinese plans for the use of their H-bomb, or the mission which is now enroute to destroy it. Americans are involved in that mission now, but not under American instructions, and without American support. Certainly you would not jeopardize their position, which is now beyond American control, by mentioning that they are on their way to do this job." He banged a fist on the table. "And I want you to be aware that because of your campaign for 'open defense budgets openly arrived at' these people are going into the action insufficiently prepared."

He hit the table, even harder, and shouted: "One thing is certain, the mission to take out the H-bomb is on its way, it includes American personnel, but without American budgetary involvement—and if you let out one word about it, in effect you will be signing their death warrant."

He got up and walked to the window, looked down at the sparse cloud of dried autumn leaves whirling in the wind below. "You're not going to get any leg-up from signing the death warrant of those people making this expedition. As I mentioned to you before, I don't care if you go over the past and drag out all kinds of embarrassing stories about the CIA operations in our previous wars. But you're just not going to do what you've indicated you want to do. In view of the circumstances, you simply aren't going to be able to do it."

The Senator shouted: "You can turn these things all around so they sound completely innocent. You can turn a knuckle ball into an outside drop curve in a second. But I'm wise to what you're doing."

While Senator Smythe ranted, the President's black mood vanished, and he watched Smythe with benign good nature.

When Smythe finished, the President said: "Sam, you can raise all the hell you want with our past 'secret military budget.' But please, leave this one alone—at least until later, maybe six months or a year from now."

Smythe snapped back: "Yes, in time to give you credit for a secret war well done, in the next presidential campaign. Is that right?"

The President smiled benignly. "I hope so, though I doubt it. I've been thinking a good deal about it—and I've decided I may not even be running."

"Incidentally, I still intend to come through Oklahoma in the next few weeks, and I also intend to make speeches—in one of which I will in effect endorse you for re-election in the Senate race."

"Furthermore, you can count on me for support in the matter of the dam—and the other section of that package—Senator Long's Louisiana project which is part of the deal." The President's confidence seemed unassailable.

Senator Smythe's own confidence seemed to be wavering. "Bascombe—you sure are the most convincing—"

He left it unfinished, and President Landers went charging on. "You see, Sam—even if you wanted to go after this 'secret war' and make it seem like the most nefarious conspiracy to spend the people's money that you ever heard of, you couldn't make it stick."

"The fact is that American money is not involved." He added: "Only a few American lives. And as long as American lives are involved, you can't compromise 'em."

Senator Smythe seemed to be converted. The President turned to Soloretha. "David, tell the Senator about the order I just now issued to our man Lowery in Hong Kong. Do you have notes on that?"

Soloretha nodded, and pulled a spiral notebook from his side pocket, and flipped through the pages. "Here it is," he said, and read: "'B'—that's Blake, in the effort with Lowery in Hong Kong— 'suggested to P'—the President— 'that if American military and naval backing had to be withdrawn, the Chinese group under M'— Eddie Ming, the independent organizer of the volunteer group— 'would lead the mission in'—*and Ming was willing to pay for the effort.* 'B'—Blake— 'suggested that the American experts, H, N and G—since they couldn't go with any government support at all—might go along with the Ming expedition as volunteers, on leave from their government duties. Operation Typhoon is cancelled.'"

Smythe was listening intently, and nodding his head. President Landers hammered home the moment: "So—if you'll excuse the expression—it was because of your bastardly investigation that we had to pull government support out of the 'secret war,' if you like."

The President stood up, dismissing his visitor with a pleasant final word. "But all I told you about supporting you in the senatorial race—and the Oklahoma and Louisiana projects—all that remains as a promise. It's all a deal for not mentioning this whole ghastly business."

The Senator smiled. "All right, chief—I'm convinced." He stood up and shook hands.

The moment he had gone, President Landers moved quickly. "David—I want you to bring the Chairman of the Joint Chiefs of Staff here right away. I want the Chief of Naval Operations, the Secretary of Defense, too. I'll call Hudibras myself. I want them all in the big office in the West Wing—let's say in half an hour."

He saw a strange expression come over Soloretha's face. "Go ahead, David, make those calls."

Soloretha still seemed incapable of action. "Sir, you're not planning to restore our original basis to Operation Typhoon are you?"

"I certainly am—and without untruth. I told Smythe I had cancelled Operation Typhoon—and I did that—temporarily at least. But now that I have taken care of this danger of a leak by making some terrific political promises, we can go ahead with our secret war. That's what Senator Smythe calls it, and that's what it shall be, with him off our back. Maybe later on—maybe even two weeks from now, he may get wise and haul it out into the open. But by that time, the Chinese

H-bomb will have been destroyed. It'll probably be a long while before she can muster the raw materials and equipment to build another.

"I don't intend to let our people down there go into the world's most important operation with only the support of a Chinese amateur. Now get on the phone and bring my Rump National Security Council over." He picked up the red phone and pushed one of the buttons on the base:

"Charlie, I want you to come over to the West Wing office—yes, right now. Big changes to be made."

He scratched his chin. "I only hope that our political shenanigans haven't fouled up their preparations too much, down there."

10

HANK MUSGRAVE DIDN'T SLEEP THAT EARLY MORNING. HE was up sorting his belongings, deciding which he was going to leave behind in the hotel storage, and there were multiple telephone calls from Freeman Blake, with veiled instructions. The last word was to be at the hydrofoil terminal near the Star Ferry, to meet the other "tourists" from Blake's party going to Macau.

Before he went down to the dock, Hank made a quick trip to the hospital, and bribed his way in to see Mary. He was gratified to see that a hospital orderly in a white coat still hovered near the door.

The time was six A.M., and the nurse was making up the bed of Mary's aged Chinese roommate. The nurse was a moon-faced, plump Chinese gone too much to fat, who regarded Hank with outright hostility.

Hank explained in Cantonese—thinking he would get a more sympathetic reception if he did so—that he was sorry, but he had only a few minutes before leaving town, and he had to see his *Tsing yan*. He hoped that the nurse would forgive him.

To cement the plea, he offered her a twenty-dollar Hong Kong bill —four dollars in American money—and she turned back to her work without a smile or a thank you.

Mary had been watching him, and had evidently heard what he said about leaving town. The first words that floated to him from the disembodied voice behind the wired jaws showed that she had heard. "Hank, my *Jong-fu*, are you really leaving?"

He kissed her hand, the healthy, yellow-gold flesh, so miraculously and perfectly formed, with two dimples where the curve of her wrist began.

He shifted into Mandarin, and spoke softly: "It will be for about a week or ten days. I can't tell you much about it, I don't have any time. But I wanted to see you. I've got to go and rob a bank—so I can buy you those nice dresses. I wanted to give you what is probably the best security—the *Lu-duh*, the good green.

"I am sure that there will always be somebody watching your door night and day, even when you get out and go to your apartment to recuperate. Ill make sure of it before I leave."

He reached into his pocket for the notes he had folded, 700 American dollars, in a hotel envelope. "You know how to take care of this stuff. It should be enough for anything that happens until I get back, pay for Norman's tuition, and to get your brother into Hong Kong."

She looked into the envelope and he saw her eyes light up, even in her bruised and discolored face. "Hank—you are a dear—I mean *chin ai, kuei*." Her mind was always amazing, in this word play, which differentiated between *kuei*, meaning dear in the sense of high-priced, and *chin ai*, dear in the sense of beloved. No matter what happened,

Mary's sense of humor never seemed to desert her. "I see you've already robbed the bank."

Hank kissed her hand again. "My little Fu, how are you feeling? Obviously, you haven't lost your sense of humor."

No smile could cross her face but something between a laugh and a sigh reached his ears. "I've been thinking. Maybe you won't even want me, with my face all smashed, when they take off the bandages."

He stroked her golden hand, the molded perfection of the wrist. "I want you now," he said, "even with your face in bandages, I want you. Remember when we talked about Socrates and Mo Tzu? And about the 'Stair of Love,' about the way love builds up or down from the physical? Besides, you have courage, and a brain, and a strength I never knew in a female. Also, I still want you the other way, more than ever, like the last time I saw you."

Again, the sound as of a sigh and a sob floated from her clamped lips. "Hank, I want you—that way, too. And I speak with the voice of experience. I want you to make love to me more than any other man.

"If a girl has known no lovers, or maybe only two or three, and chooses a man to be her lover, that isn't so much of a compliment. But when someone who has known many chooses a man, that is something special. Am I wicked?"

Hank laughed. "That's my Mary. The wit I admire, the courage that astounds me, the body I love. And one more thing, Mary, my *Fu-ren*. When I come back—the doctors tell me you may be out in a week or so, and go home to rest—I want you to live with me. And maybe, if I can persuade you, be my *Fu-ren* in law as well as in fact."

"*Ai ren*—" It was a word which he had heard mostly before he knew Mary, meaning sweetheart, rather than "Fu", married person. "I will listen to you and I will learn from you, you have your whole world to teach me about. And—remember, this is the voice of experience talking—I will never want another man for my bed. I've had enough of others. Will you believe me? Only you." She took his hand and placed it inside her gown, on the divine smoothness and roundness of her breast. Warmth flooded through his brain, filling him with quick imaginings of the rest of her loveliness, the dimples of her lower back, the firm texture of her thighs, their perfect movement. Now, he might not know this loveliness ever again if the mission should go agley on Hainan. He moved towards her, and in that second he heard a loud clearing of the throat, a feminine throat, from across the room. The plump Chinese nurse was still bending over the bed, and her face was averted as she harrumphed.

Hank looked at his watch. He stood up, bent over, and kissed Mary's hand once more.

Mary said: "Hank, when you go to rob the bank, don't get shot."

He turned to go. As he did the Chinese nurse with a face like a mooncake came toward him smiling. Then, without a word, she kissed him on the cheek. "I speak Mandarin, too. Good luck on your trip."

Outside, climbing into a taxi, Hank watched the heavy early-morning traffic on Chatham Road, the coolies with their cargo poles, the vendors shouting their wares—and the heavy trucks with Chinese markings. Now, he thought, he had committed himself to Asia—to those pale-gold children—if and when he was lucky enough to get back. He had made a kind of promise—and, he thought with a smile, paid a healthy deposit. But he had no regrets. With her usual lightning instinct, Mary had said exactly the right things to warm his heart and his superego. Now, on the eve of the most dangerous job of his life, he floated on a solid golden cloud—the happiness of a cloud he could easily identify as love.

Eric Hope was in his room with Nooley, Gresham, and Helmantholer when the latest ruckus hit the Hong Kong group. It was a call from Arthur Lowery at six-thirty-five A.M., and the voice was more weary than ever, but a note of elation was detectable in it. "Signals changed," Lowery began.

"Going back to the old plan. A lot of the merchandise was shuttled back and forth; we might have lost some of it in the process. We hope not too much.

"We just got the new instructions from the Big Chief."

"So we go back to the first ship after all. All of us?"

"Yes. I've told them you'd be on board by eight o'clock. There'll be a walla-walla at the old landing. I may see you later, but not now."

Hope exploded to the others: "Jesus! These signals are like a code-exercise. Another flip-flop. I don't know what's happened, but everything is upside down. The Macau trip is off, we have to be at the dock east of the Star Ferry to get picked up; they'll take us to the destroyer. I guess approximately the same gear as we were going to take to Macau. I haven't checked on the stuff we already had loaded on the tin can, we'll have to wait till we get aboard. Better get going. Wear civvies, of course."

While the others took off, he asked for Hank Musgrave's phone number. Hank's voice was bolt awake and full of questions. "Hope! I just got a call from Freeman. Everything's gone crazy."

"Not crazy—just where we were before."

"Yeah, but maybe crazy from Freeman's point of view. He sounded really down. Your Big Chief is back in the saddle again, huh?"

"Yeah, I guess, but I don't know the story, yet."

"This deal has more changes of command than Vietnam in 1965. Anyhow, I'm packed. I'll see you on the dock."

Hank called Freeman, and the rolling voice seemed to have regained confidence: "All right, Hank—so I gather you're shoving off, is that correct?" He didn't wait for an answer. "I'll be staying around these parts for awhile. Maybe I'll just happen to see you where you're going."

Hank took the chance: "By the way, will you check with Mary, at the hospital while I'm away? I'm a little concerned. She is valuable to us." Hank knew it sounded lame.

There was a palpable pause on the line. "All right, Hank. You don't have to justify it. I'll look out for her."

Hank also called George Yerby. It was twenty minutes to seven, and George was shaking the sleep out of his voice when he answered the phone. Hank told him quickly: "George, I'll be leaving town for a few days, but I'll be back—before the end of my vacation. If I get any messages from AMS headquarters in New York, please keep them for me."

"Right, Hank. Going back to Bangkok, eh? Take it easy on those Khmer damsels." Hank thought thanks for giving me a good cover story.

Hank checked over his bags. He was all set to go. Except for one thing. He took a postcard from the desk blotter, addressed it to his parents in Costa Mesa, California, USA, and scribbled the short message:

"Everything okay. Not sure what my next assignment will be. Much love. Hank."

Hank knew that his father, a copy editor on the Orange County News, would read between the lines, and get the signal that he would be involved in some nefarious cloak and dagger business for a couple of weeks—and knew that his old man would be proud of him. He was one of the few people back there who knew how modern wars work.

✻

At the Queen's Pier on the dot of eight, Hank saw a Navy liberty boat tied up, a group of civilians climbing aboard. Hope stood on the dock and Hank saw that the civilians were his team.

Hope loped over and told him: "Get aboard. We're shoving off for the tin can in five minutes." He added softly: "We're going to need your language ability. Nooley—well, he's a good soldier—I mean Marine—but no linguist." He glanced at Hank's airline bag: "That's your baggage?"

"You know—the Vietnam essentials: Go and No-Go pills, a spoon, toilet paper, can opener, and soap. All you need for the expeditionary diet of dysentery bugs and Polymagma. And the mark of my profession: a pencil."

Hope smiled and led the way toward the boat. "And, I hope—a good Cantonese dictionary."

Three sailors in worn dungarees were lowering a wooden packing case into the boat.

"Armalites," he said. "We should have plenty of 'em. You can run an M-16, right?"

"Sure," Hank said, not feeling very sure of it. It had been a couple of years since he had fired an Armalite.

"If I remember, you were pretty good with it—up there on the Ho Chi Minh Trail."

They climbed into the Liberty boat and Hank found a place on a board bench next to Helmantholer and Hope. The group was lost in the fifty-foot open launch, which could carry one hundred people. Hank counted the passengers: eighteen, including himself.

"Is this your Task Force?" he asked Hope.

"Yes," he said, as the boat began to move away from the pier, and roll in the harbor waves. "Eighteen men, but each has the strength of ten. That gives me approximately an under-strength company."

Hank asked Helmantholer: "How did the arms and ammo survive all the trans-shipment—from the junks to the tin can, to the junks, and back to the tin can?"

Helmantholer had a handsome, wide white grin. "Beats hell out of me," he said. "Been up all night. I'm so groggy I wouldn't know a condenser from a diode—and I'm supposed to be the communicator for this lash-up."

Hope stood up to call the roll: "First, our officers. Major Nooley?"

"Here."

"Major Gresham?"

"Here."

He went through the list, while the boat rolled through the harbor chop toward the lean, low, greyhound shape of the destroyer, the morning light etching her sharply against the Hong Kong mountains.

Hank listened to the names: Veracruze, Sergeant Polk, Sergeant Espinoza, Sergeants Hildebrand, Hanson, O'Connor, Hing. He looked for Hing, a muscular, dark-faced American undoubtedly from California or Hawaii; Roberts, Wohl, Bissell, Jones—all the American cross section all in top physical shape. There was a saying in Vietnam, "The Best Go West," meaning to Southeast Asia or farther, and these, thought Hank, were the best of the best.

There were two PFCs, Muhlbach and Trotter. Kids—teen-agers with faces right out of junior-high school—both trying hard to look very responsible and serious, aware of being much under age, compared to the hoary sergeants and officers of Operation Typhoon.

It was good, Hank thought, to climb aboard a Navy ship again— to walk a scrubbed deck and know that for a while they were going to live in an aseptic steel home at sea, with a family restricted to strong, healthy males, and discipline to keep it livable.

They stowed their B-bags and Valpacks in the ship's open fantail —
where their gear had been lashed in a mountain of packing crates.

"We'll be on the ship for only a few hours," Hope said. "Not long
enough to rate as passengers."

They cleared the harbor to the east, through the narrow Tathong
channel, passing close to one of the big rock islands. Hope warned
them to stay below, in the miniature ward room and the mess hall:
"Not good to have too many civilians on deck."

Hank was talking to Veracruze in the messing compartment, and
the majority of the group was lo_unging there, drinking coffee and
smoking. A few ship's sailors in dungarees and T-shirts had joined
them, and they felt the heaving of the deep sea. Hank saw Veracruze
growing slightly green around the gills. The bo'sun's pipe called attention to a PA transmission:

"To all hands—this is Captain Bowles speaking. We welcome
aboard Captain Hope and his detachment. His detachment are wearing civilian clothes. You are familiar with their gear, which you have
loaded and unloaded too many times in the last few days.

"There's been a lot of scuttlebutt about their mission—but I have
said before and I repeat: It is highly classified, Top Secret. Remember:
any grade of secret is not to be repeated, to *anyone*.

"About thirty minutes from now, we will have a rendezvous with a
U.S. submarine, the *U.S.S. Mako*. We will make a transfer of personnel
and gear to the *Mako* at sea."

There was a pause: "I want the fantail cleared of all ship's personnel. Captain Hope's detachment will report there immediately for a
briefing."

Hope was the first on the fantail. The others came to stand before
him. A following sea lifted the stern platform in a heavy lurching pattern which terminated each time in an unpredictable sideways yaw.

Veracruze and Helmantholer set a bad example by hanging over the rail and retching before Hope could begin to speak.

Hope was disturbed but Hank reminded him of the fact: "Motion sickness isn't interchangeable from place to place. An airman who can ride out the worst turbulence in the tail of a KC-135 would throw up in a Central Park rowboat. You've just got to get used to the new kind of motion." At that point, Hank had to cease his advice because a few greenish qualms were hitting him.

Hope was speaking: "Gentlemen, we almost lost you in that last change, in Hong Kong. And I hope we didn't lose too much gear in the process. There were many alterations of orders. But now, it looks as if there won't be any further changes until we get to our objective —we hope.

"The plan of action is that we are going to transfer about a half-hour from now, to a submarine. One of our first jobs on the sub will be to check over all the gear and see what, if anything, got lost in Hong Kong.

"The sub will be the *Mako*, an attack submarine, and she will take us across the South China Sea and land us on the northeastern shore of the island of Hainan. We hope within walking distance of the farm where we will be hiding out and preparing for our operation.

"It'll take us nearly three days to get there. If the plan goes as scheduled, we will have three days maximum in which to prepare for the big job. The big job is really the biggest in the world today. Strict secrecy has been kept about the mission until this moment. But now I can tell you what it will be: To take out China's first and only H-bomb which is in position at an airfield near Hoihow on the northeast shore of Hainan." Even in the wind, you could hear the gasp of excitement after that.

Hope went on: "The mission is still the most highly classified in the world, although of course the crew of this destroyer are aware that we are departing on a secret mission. That much: nothing much more. They will also be aware of the identity of the *Mako* when she keeps her rendezvous with us in a few minutes. But it is better that we do not discuss the details of our assault mission with them. Later on, when we are aboard the submarine, everyone on that boat will know the intimate details of our operation. Therefore, there will be no security factor with that crew."

He was interrupted by the PA system of the ship: "Now hear this. Boat crew fall in at the after davit. Work party Alpha report to the fantail."

The submarine had been spotted.

They saw the tall dark fin of the submarine gliding obliquely toward them on the horizon. Hank was surprised at its size. The submarines he had seen before were long and rakish—and the promontories of hull which extended fore and aft of the fin in this pig boat were, like them, long and low—but the part which used to be the conning tower, a little steel sliver, was now a huge streamlined slab rising 35 feet above the water.

The submarine commander, the collar of his uniform jacket turned up around his neck, held a powered "bull-horn" at the ready, the round metal speaker in front of his chest. Hank caught the glint of gold on his cap; the skipper of a ship of this size would be at least a full commander, possibly even a captain.

The B-bags and C-bags of the raiding party were being hauled to one side of the destroyer's fantail by this time, and crates of supplies beside them.

Eric Hope, standing beside Hank, looked up awe-struck at the looming tower of the submarine as it moved in beside the destroyer. "She's a giant!"

The two ships were moving slowly side by side, and it was clear that they were almost equal in length, the *Mako* an iceberg of power, with her long wedge-nosed hull barely out from the water, the lean black command post of the "sail" rising above it like a fort.

The submarine skipper, a large, heavy-shouldered figure, was bellowing through the bull-horn: "We're ready to receive your passengers." A force of sailors, bulky in life jackets, had popped out on the slatted wet decks of the pig boat below the structure of the fin. Midships in the *Edson*, crewmen were swinging the ship's motor launch on its davits, the boat pitching and swaying as it was lowered. Hope said: "Well, here we go."

"That's better than saying, 'here goes nothing,'" Hank suggested.

Twenty-one minutes later, on top of the tall sail structure of the submarine, Hope, Gresham, and Musgrave stood at the rail, while Commander Wilson, the submarine skipper, watched the slim gray shape of the *Edson* turning and steaming away, bucking against the windy seas. All the rest of the Hope force had gone below to the congested steel intestines of the sub.

Wilson said: "Captain Hope—you and your people should know that we have a special problem. As you can see—or perhaps you don't yet know—this is not the latest model submarine, by a long shot. It's not even nuclear-powered. Our assignment to this job follows the usual pattern of war necessity. In the pinch, they call on the standard ship in the war navy: *U.S.S. Make-Do*, sister ship of the *U.S.S. Can-Do*. In this case it's the *Mako*. Unfortunately, there's no such thing as James

Bond or The Man From Uncle to solve our problems. I mean, unfortunately all those miracle gadgets are fiction.

"We *do* have a situation. We have to deliver you through well-patrolled waters onto a hostile shore, so we will have to travel much of the time submerged. But our actual maximum speed submerged is ten knots, not twenty or twenty-five as in the latest nuclear submarines. We will have to choose between the greater risk of being spotted, and travel on the surface, where we can make as high as eighteen or nineteen knots, or to creep along at eight or nine underneath the water. Later on, in the chart room, we will go over our route, and you can pass on the briefing to your men. Has the First Lieutenant shown your people to quarters?"

"Yes, sir," Hope answered. "Considering the outside size, there's not too much room below in these boats."

Commander Wilson laughed. He had a battered face, with a fighter's nose and scar tissue on his brows. When he smiled, his face lit, a very successful smile even though his teeth showed much gold construction work. "Yes," he said. "They're big enough on the outside, but by the time you put engines, batteries, torpedoes, pumps, ballast tanks, radar, and radio in them—there's not much room for men inside."

The *Mako* was travelling on the surface, running south, now, with a following sea. "We're making about eighteen knots," Wilson said, "just about flat out. If we can travel on the surface, we can get to the other side of Hong Kong by tonight. Then we're going to have to be careful. We're going to have to take our chances and run on the surface as much as we can. But we can't afford to be spotted by any Chinese ship. If we get a blip on our radar, we'll have to submerge. Any blips we're apt to pick up from tomorrow on will be Chinese, more than likely junks—but we can't afford to take a chance that they might send a radio contact report to the Reds."

Commander Wilson turned back to his position next to one of the lookouts: "Another problem we will have is our draft. In the shallow water around Hainan, our size is going to be a problem. Even when she's on the surface, she draws seventeen feet of water."

*

In Hong Kong, Freeman Blake had phoned Arthur Lowery at Croy's house in Deepwater Bay.

"Chief—" He had adjusted rapidly to the change in the command situation—" I have a feeling I should be checking on Hank's friend across the harbor. You know how the opposition is: they might just make a grab. And she might help us to find out where the Number One guy has faded to. There's no new word on that, is there?"

"No. And you're right. Are you going over soon? Let me know when you get through."

"Fine. We'll see you later in the afternoon."

*

When he reached Mary's room, Freeman was aghast to see what had happened to her. He saw a female form sitting up in bed, in a gray hospital dickey; something very familiar about the feminine delicacy of her shoulders, the mound of black hair—and where the face should have been, a band of white bandage across the middle, a cage of white around the jaw, and when he looked for eyes, bruised tissue with only the faintest gleam of life visible.

But she was her usual alert self. He saw a twinkle in her eyes: "Mr. Blake! I apologize for what I may laughingly call my appearance!" The hemmed-in voice struck him as eerie, other-worldish. The jaw hadn't moved perceptibly.

Blake remembered her from the time when she had been Hank's girl friend: the small, delicately modelled nose which curved up, the graceful arch of her jaw curving to a lovely throat, an amazing blend of femininity with the implicit strength of great good health. He had admired her from afar, with proper respect, when he had first met her. Now, what would be left behind those bandages? Her body in the rough hospital gown seemed as fascinatingly attractive as before—the golden arms as smooth as bronze, the modelled swell of her bosom. And even now, the way she held her head with such poised femininity. That such beauty, with such a quick brain, such a bright personality, should have been a struggling taxi-dancer and prostitute—that was one of the social ironies of Hong Kong, the most competitive labor market in the world. Or rather, she *had been* a beauty, until the power politics of the world swept down to smash her.

He answered with his usual caution: "Don't apologize—too bad about the—accident. Hmm—well, Hank wanted me to keep an eye on you while he's away. That can be done all right."

He looked across the room towards the ancient Chinese lady, the roommate. Now, she was lying flat on her back, eyes closed, evidently asleep. Mary noted Freeman's searching glance.

"I don't think she speaks English."

Freeman said nothing. He pulled a small, leather-covered radio from his pocket and snapped it on. A stream of Cantonese ying-yang music blared out. The Chinese roommate stirred, but her eyes stayed closed.

The half-sob, half-sigh of Mary's peculiar constrained laugh floated on the air. "Mr. Blake," she said. "I want to ask you—will you get me a transistor radio like that?" She had quickly found a U.S. $20 bill from some secret hiding place, and she extended it towards him.

He took it. "All right," he said. She had certainly estimated him correctly, her intuitive faculties serving her well.

"Or," she added, "would you like to leave that one and you could get another to take its place?"

Freeman thought about it. "Okay," he said.

And she pursued her sensitive estimates. "Hank thinks highly of you, Mr. Blake."

"And I respect him, too—a very smart boy."

She pursued a hunch. "I know you work with him."

She watched him carefully, but his eyes were illegible. The hoods of the heavy eyelids seemed lower than ever: "He's a good friend of mine." He laughed, and added: "Yeah, we go around sticking up banks together."

"Yes, he said he was going to go out and rob a bank on this trip," Mary agreed. "He said he would get some money so we could be married when he got back. I told him he should be careful not to get shot."

"Sound idea," Freeman agreed, noncommittally. "Bank robbing—that's a dangerous job." He took out his mahogany-hued meerschaum and made a large show of lighting it. By now, both he and Mary had established contact about their special needs. Each had made clear that he had a grasp of the other's game, without a single explicit word.

Freeman stood up. "Well, Mary, I'll be looking in on you from time to time, to see that you're all right."

She said: "And if you can do anything to help my wandering boy Hank in his bank-robbing career—please do."

She paused so that he would understand that what followed was to be emphasized. "And if I can help him or you in any way, will you please let me know?"

Freeman stuck out his hand. "We'll shake on that, pardner."

✻

At Colonel Croy's hilltop house overlooking Deepwater Bay, the clatter of the coding machines had dimmed. In the room off the parlor, where there were no windows and the lights were always on, only one decoder was going now, but until this morning, all the machines had been running nearly constantly. Arthur Lowery came out of the coding room into the bright sunlight of the parlor and the wide span of the window overlooking Deepwater Bay, a clear deep blue with a background of piney woods.

Lowery was impeccably dressed, as always, with a clean white shirt and a perfectly adjusted, hand-tied bow.

"Well, did you make any progress with our friend at the hospital?" Lowery wanted to know.

"I made contact," Freeman said. "But I didn't make any arrangements with her, or set up anything."

Lowery seemed annoyed. "Pretty cautious. Did you mention that she might benefit by helping us—benefit financially?"

"No. I've been chary about that. I don't think Hank has told her why he wanted to know about Chen Yu. He has apparently given her money and paid her hospital expenses. He hasn't tipped off anything about us—or even about himself. But she's a smart girl. She seems to have guessed what kind of operation Hank's involved in. But she doesn't *know*. And I would hesitate to indicate anything more."

"You could at least give her some more money to soften her up a little. Without tipping off anything."

Lowery sat by the wide window and watched a fleet of junks moving west. "You and I seem to operate on somewhat different principles when it comes to money. One reason Hank crossed over, got into a larger compartment, was this matter of money—wasn't it?"

Blake snorted. "Yes, he was marked as *my* man—when you moved into the picture."

Lowery said: "Anyway, things have cooled off here. We're subsiding into an intelligence-collecting agency, now that the mission is gone. But we can still pass on intelligence to them and to Washington, Whatever we can collect, from all sources—and that includes Eddie and Mary.

"So you can pursue the matter with Mary. She should be able to get us a lead to where Chen Yu has gone. He's just evaporated. The Tiger office is closed up tight. And we can't get a tracer on him."

Freeman got up to go. "Okay. So what's the latest from Washington, and from the Typhoon mission?"

"Zero from the mission as of now—though I'm sure they want anything we can dig up about their target area. And about the friendlies they're supposed to contact there. They've got precious little to go on now, You know what we gave them so far. All we had, but not much."

Blake nodded. "And what about Washington?"

"Nothing. Apparently the Big Chief is having smooth sailing for the moment."

Lowery added fast instructions as Blake was leaving:

"About Mary: I don't think her friend in the smuggling business has any idealistic connection with the big boys on the other side. For him, it's strictly a monetary affiliation: He's doing some smuggling and some shadowing for them, for money. He's not very important— I guess your sense of caution was right—but don't be afraid to spend money."

Freeman left steaming—and trying hard not to let his temper show in his face. He was being assigned to a job which even Lowery said was minor, "not very important." Mary was a source which had been pretty fully exploited, if not actually drained. Lowery was holding onto the main source of information about Hainan—Eddie Ming— for himself. But Lowery didn't know that Ming was by now a good friend of Blake. Blake might be the old model Agency man, but at least he was closer to Asia, and Asians—and most important, knew one or two of their languages.

But now he said tactfully: "About Chen and Mary—She can help us to locate Chen—his hideout. I'd estimate he's obviously enamored of her. There are lots of indications: viz, his apparent limitation of the beating-up, his sparing of her 'vital parts.' He's probably wanting to come back to her, even in her present damaged condition. A very attractive female. He might even want to apologize. If 'human' means sexy, Asians are generally more human than we are."

Lowery nodded. "Why don't you try it? Work up the mousetrap: she should at least be able to find out where he is."

"Okay. I'll tell the orderly to let Chinese in to see her—whoever they are. But I'll tell him to watch them carefully."

"Yes, and you'd better give her a weapon, too. Could be an emergency before help can get to her. Maybe a knife."

One of the bright young lads came out of the code room as Freeman left. The sound of the clattering machine burst out after him. "Message from the *Mako*," the young man told Lowery. "They want any extra dope they can get about the target vicinity, any intelligence available at all."

Lowery nodded: "Delay the answer for an hour until we see what's in from Home Plate."

11

WEST OF HONG KONG, THE U.S. SUBMARINE *MAKO* RAN smoothly on the surface. Captain Eric Hope had climbed into the conning tower level, the crowded command compartment one deck above the Control Room. Here, amid a jungle of piping, tubing, and electronic instruments, the skipper and his exec held forth in the after section, near the two oiled steel pillars of the periscopes.

Hope had changed to a camouflage "Tiger Suit" of spotted green and brown, and wore a dark-green beret at a rakish angle. The transformation wrought by the uniform was miraculous. He seemed ten years younger, his physical trimness much more apparent.

Commander Wilson stood beside one of the radar operators who scanned a radar scope, a mound of "black-box" dials and switches.

Hope saluted, and it was returned with a wave. Then Wilson did a double-take. "Uniforms?" he asked. "You people going to wear uniforms?"

Hope said: "We did in Vietnam, with the Special Force detachment. It's better, if we should get captured. There is some rudimentary chance of not being executed, if it should all go bad."

Wilson said: "It's not my field, Captain—but won't you be kind of obvious in this Hainanese town?"

Hope laughed. "I hope not. We'd be obvious in any kind of clothes in that locale, because of our size. No—this kind of operation is usually in uniform. You are in hiding, the people you are staying with provide your cover. After all, we might change our skin color with paint— but not our size, Of course, if we make any daylight patrols, we'll probably wear the basic black: Chinese peasant suits."

"Apologies," said Wilson. "Thanks for the short course."

Hope nodded. He unfolded a sheet with a long assemblage of items. "We seem to have most of what we need, Commander," he said, suddenly urgent. "But we've lost some very important stuff in all the trans-shipping in Hong Kong. We seem to be short of some vital items, like infra-red sniperscopes, and automatic weapons with silencers. I know an airdrop would be risky. It might tip off our mission—a junk might spot us, and report to a Commie patrol boat."

Wilson scanned the list. "Lot of radio equipment here. You can meet with our communicator, Lieutenant Bosworth. He would know exactly what we have. I don't see anything in the nuclear line. Did your nuke man—what's his name, Gresham?—did he get what's needed, from our nuke expert—Lieut. Harrison?"

"I think so. I know Gresham needed some gamma and neutron counters—we didn't have a one. But—Commander, our worst needs are for silent automatic weapons and infra-red 'scopes—and some extra C-3 or C-4 plastic explosive. Those are the things that I, as a Special Force man, would notice first. You wouldn't by any chance have any infra-red sniperscopes? For night action. We couldn't locate one!"

Wilson was grave. "Sorry. But we do have a few Armalites we can spare. And plenty of plastic—I guess it's C-3—is that the old-model stuff that smells so bad, like an old cheese?"

Hope went on listing what was missing: "I had four Sten guns with silencers. Three sniperscopes and a couple of metascopes for night operations. And a couple of APQ-14 portable radars. But they're gone now.

"I'm going to really hurt if I don't have any silent killers. I can see they'd be a high-priority item among the smuggling gentry of Hong Kong so they apparently just disappeared on the dock."

Commander Wilson whistled. "Pretty exotic for what we've got on board. I'll request an air drop of the things you need. But we could have trouble coordinating with the drop. You know how those things go—especially when we might have to crash dive any moment.

"You'd better check with the Exec, Lieutenant Commander Joe Battersby. In case the air drop doesn't work out, we should have an alternate. Battersby might know some crew-member—some commando-type, some ex-thug, who might help to improvise the weapons. I don't mean that personally. Matter of fact, I was a kind of thug—light-heavyweight, at the Academy."

Hope laughed. "That's all right. We're supposed to be good at the civilized thug kind of thing. That's why we're on it."

Wilson shot a curious sideways glance in Hope's direction. "You seem to enjoy this stuff."

"Damn right, sir. A damn good job, the best one I can think of. I'm glad I've got the necessary skill." His wide grin beamed: "I'm glad right now anyhow, while nobody's shooting at us."

Commander Wilson grunted. "If you'd try to sell that idea to the average American back home—especially a female—they'd give you a horse laugh and tell you you're crazy. But I know what you mean." He lit a cigarette.

"Anyhow, I'll connect you up with the Exec. You need the tools for your job. Maybe, as a back-up, the Exec can dig up some bows and arrows from our Special Service stores."

Hope chuckled: "You may think that's a joke, sir. But it wouldn't be the first time. In Ban Methuot we used the Montagnard crossbows a couple of times. A good silent weapon."

Wilson signalled a crewman standing near the public address system.

"Get Commander Battersby." The call boomed out of the ship's loud-speakers. "Commander Battersby, report to the Conn."

Wilson squinted into the periscope binocular, looked ahead to the rolling green backs of the waves in the glinting sun. The endless field of motion was strangely empty of ships. He addressed a question to the back of the radar operator's head, bent over a tall, cone-shaped hood: "Johnson, you see any likely blips on your screen?"

"No, sir. Nary a thing."

"Okay." He spoke to Hope. "We're running with good luck. Forty miles southwest of Hong Kong and not a single contact yet." He drummed on his crew-cut head: "Knock wood it'll keep on. Incredible. It *can't* keep on."

He continued: "Captain, by the way, we sent your request for further info from the friendly contacts on Hainan, back to Hong Kong. No answer yet."

The radar scanner called out, clearly: "A blip bearing 72 degrees true, sir! Looks like a good-sized craft: About the size of a PT boat. About 9,000 yards."

Commander Wilson called out: "SUBRAD! Any contact?"

Another dungaree-clad figure, forward in the Conn, his face buried in a tall scanning-hood, sang out: "Negative, sir."

Commander Wilson mumbled a curse: "Damn SUBRAD!" He rushed to one of the phone receivers at the center of the compartment: "Bridge lookout—radar contact at 9,000 yards, bearing seventy-two degrees. Can't you see them? Take a quick look before we submerge." He switched to another phone channel and the ship's PA system boomed: "Prepare to dive, prepare to dive. Clear the bridge." In another phone receiver, Wilson said: "Diving officer— take her down!" He swung toward the SUBRAD desk.

"Just got them that minute, sir. I was just changing scopes— maybe that was it. A mistake, sir."

Hatches banged topside, the two lookouts thudded down the ladders from the bridge. The *Mako* began to shiver. There was a sudden silence as the thrumming of the big diesel engines stopped. Whishing and thumping sounds—far off. They were diving. The klaxon sounded twice: "Oo-ooga! Oo-ooga!" And the PA system warned, "Dive, Dive, Dive!" The steel deck tilted downward.

"I don't think they saw us," the Skipper spoke with tight calm. "But I don't like the possibility of their reporting an American undersea boat in these waters. We'll have to travel submerged for a while."

✳

The second radio was suddenly very busy, da-dit-ting angrily at a rapid pace. "What is it, Dawson?" The radio operator flipped through a message book, and the automated teleprinter in front of him began to clatter.

"Sir, it sounds like the Seventh Fleet. They seem to be a little early. Weren't they supposed to be showing up for maneuvers off Singapore tomorrow?" Wilson nodded.

Captain Hope said: "I gather from the traffic that the people in Washington were very much aware of the passage of the Seventh Fleet. But I didn't know they'd actually go ahead with the scheduled maneuvers."

"Come again?" Bosworth asked.

"I mean that apparently the Seventh Fleet is going ahead with the maneuver on schedule, so the Commies won't suspect anything."

"Well," said Bosworth. "I hope they turn away before they come in too close—just in case we don't make it to the target."

Hope laughed. "My personal feeling is, we better make it." He watched the clattering printer. "What's the bearing and distance on the Seventh Fleet radio contacts?" he asked the radio man in front of the machine.

"About 1100 miles, sir," the operator answered. "That would put them somewhere off Singapore, right now."

*

One hundred miles off Singapore the great flattop *Enterprise*, the biggest moving object ever built by man, charged into a freshening gale. It was nearly five o'clock and the floating city of 5,000 Navy fighting men was securing her brood of jets for the day. The huge flaring bow flung the low seas aside like dust, the thousand-foot-long deck glided over the chop, riding steady as a gyro.

On the next-to-the-top level of glass-windowed bridge in the island structure rising above the landing deck, Admiral Andrew Kerr squinted through the broad window into the flickering light on deck.

He mumbled to the slight man in a long-billed salmon fisherman's cap next to him, the ship's commander, Captain Morheim. They were watching a jag-winged F-4 scream low over the white, boiling comb of the ship's wake. The F-4 came rocketing across the stern with a final screech of power, hovered unsteadily, and descended with a pronounced thud to the deck, where the spindles of the arresting wires ripped forward with it, then stopped it dead in the rear quarter of the canted landing deck. Admiral Kerr's mumbled message was lost in the screech as red-shirted crewmen flipped the wire clear of the huge fighter-bird.

The Captain in the long-billed cap leaned toward the sturdy man with three silver stars on his collar. "I'm sorry, sir, I didn't hear what you said. Say it again, please."

The Admiral said: "What do you make of those peculiar orders? That language is—incredible."

The Captain answered: "It *was* weird. 'You will not leave the South China Maneuver area without specific instructions from Cominch'— I think that was the verbiage."

The Admiral went on: "I haven't hit this kind of nonsense since the early days of the Vietnam campaign when President Johnson had to tell the A6 pilots how to drop their bombs."

Admiral Kerr continued: "At least, there is nothing else in the orders to indicate any special monkeyshines. Nothing about launching any presidentially guided strikes into Canton or anything like that."

"They did say something about maintaining the maneuver dates. What's so special about those dates?"

"It seems to me that October 16 was the date of the first Chinese atom test, in 1964. You know how the Commies are—they always love to do things on glorious anniversaries. A great day for them to pull a fast caper. Like right now, the bastards!" The jet which had landed blasted its engines to gun it away from the landing spot, toward the elevator.

In the sudden silence afterward, the Captain asked the Admiral: "You don't suppose, sir, that they have built some kind of super bomb they can load onto some kind of decrepit old Soviet bomber, do you?"

"Goddam'f I know. But I'm going to keep my anti-nuclear attack defenses up night and day, whether Cominch's giving me my running orders or not." He looked across the glinting sea, as the low cloud cover suddenly ripped away. The ocean was bright and the task force of knife-sharp little destroyers and huge shoe-box carriers spread like cardboard silhouettes against sun and waves.

Another shadow-shape of a fighter, spread out in her awkward landing stance, gunned in towards the *Enterprise* angle-deck. She was too low, the automatic meat-ball signal on deck dropped out of sight, the orange ball in the mirror disappearing. The canvas-helmeted landing signal officer tried to lift the staggering shape by waving his paddles upward. The pilot behind his shining plexiglass jammed throttles forward, the engines roared, the plane rose like a wind-wracked kite, and then since there was no criss-crossing of the signal paddles from the landing officer, (a millisecond's lag in decision) the dark head of the pilot behind the canopy pulled back his control yolk too late.

The Admiral, peering out of the flag bridge window, saw what was happening. "Here comes one!" he shouted, and that second the crash warning was sounded, a hee-haw sound, the donkey bray everyone dreaded. Then a rending impact. The plane's long tail flipped skyward, the nose angled sharply into the deck, there was an awful smashing of airplane substance as the bird flipped upside down.

The Admiral watched as the next jet, making its landing approach, was waved off. The roar of its engine rattled the tower windows and it banked away to the port side. Kerr watched the comical small-sized fire dolly charge up to the shimmering wreckage on the deck, and the great heavy-girdered rescue crane known on the ship as the Deacon charged out to the topsy-turvy plane. Four blue-helmeted and sweatered crane-men dashed to the plane to hook it, and on the far side, a big-wheeled ambulance-truck charged up to the cockpit. The crane arm took hold and lifted the groaning bulk of the fuselage like a toy, and held it two feet from the deck, while a cascade of broken glass and metal poured from it. Men in white freed the pilot and laid him on a stretcher. He sat up as two bearers carried him towards the ambulance.

"He's all right," the Captain said. "That's the first one for today. Better than the usual attrition rate."

"Goddamn," the Admiral swore. "I hope we keep on so lucky for the next four days."

The crane was hauling the wrecked F-4 like a broken toy towards the flight-deck elevator. The ambulance darted for the island structure. Crewmen in red sweaters were sweeping up the bits of wreckage with high-powered air hoses, funnelling them towards the edge of the deck. Another F-4 was screeching up the roaring foam carpet of the ship's wake, the landing signal officer had jumped up to his position on one side of the catwalk. Up on the flag bridge, the Captain was saying to Admiral Kerr: "I have a feeling that I'm going to be spending the next four days in my emergency cabin, up here on the island—and not because of crashes!"

✻

Two hours later, another man in naval uniform, his uniform practically solid gold from forearm to cuff, sat by the window of the President's office in the White House. "Mr. President," said Admiral

Bloomfield, the Chief of Naval Operations, "I'm leaving in my personal car, as you suggested, without a driver."

"I'm sorry, Joe," the President said. "But right now, the heat is on, and I am building a new set of Pavlovian reflexes every time I have to arrange a meeting with any member of the Joint Chiefs. It's because of the affair with Smythe. Operation Typhoon has become more secret than the Manhattan Project ever was, back in World War II."

"Yes, sir, I understand that. So I'm practically a plain clothesman."

"Correct," the President said. "And for the next five days you're going to be doing a lot of driving from your home to the White House—at very odd hours."

Admiral Bloomfield stood up to go. Then he swung back to face his Commander-in-Chief. "Mr. President, you said five days. Has the date of delivery of the bomb been confirmed?"

"This illustrates one of the curses of compartmentation in Intelligence," said the President. "But Hudibras finally got confirmation —out of India—from a Third Secretary of the Chinese Embassy— for a handsome fee. The Chinese Ambassador didn't live long enough to defect, but his assistant went for the same kind of reward without defecting. It's from the horse's mouth: October 16, at dawn, the Chinese are planning to drop the bomb on the Seventh Fleet."

"I like your plans for the Commies much better," said the Admiral as he left.

12

ONLY 110 MILES WEST OF HONG KONG IN THE SOUTH CHINA sea, the U.S. submarine *Mako* was travelling on the surface, making eighteen knots with a following sea. Commander Wilson had said he would run all through the hours of darkness and make up for the slow progress the *Mako* had made during the afternoon submerged.

The control room was bustling with life. Amid interminable banks of metal switches and navigation instruments as archaic-looking as Jules Verne's *Nautilus*, the dungaree-clad work-crew slaved. The oily thumping of the diesels vibrated from the companionway aft and shook its way into this center of activity. The skipper had come down from the Conn. He now stood next to the helmsman. The helmsman, holding a wide steel wheel next to the binnacle, was maintaining a course of 182 degrees, approximately the direct route from Hong Kong to the southern reach of Hainan island.

Down the companionway a short distance, two radiomen watched the two decoders chattering:

HOPE FORCE FROM LOWERY CONTACT TIME CHANGED RO 230 RPT 0230 SAME COORDINATES WILL ARRANGE AIRDROP TIME TO BE SPECIFIED STOP FURTHER INTELLIGENCE REPORTS ON TARGET AREA POSITION EXPECTED ACKNOWLEDGE LOWERY MMXX

✳

Wilson squinted at the yellow teleprinter: "Not much—but at least they're responding. Better take it right down to Captain Hope."

Bosworth leaned over and tore the top section from the machine. "Aye, sir."

Bosworth dodged aft through the crowded corridor into the ship's messing compartment. He estimated Hope would be briefing the troops there and the guess was correct. Hope was saying:

"This point, called Meng Wan, is where we're going to make our contact. Our friendlies, that's Wing On, live near this area. It's a kind of suburb of the port area called Hoihow, where the ChiComs have been shipping in stuff for the construction of the base. As far as we can find out, the base is near this little town of Meng Wan.

"But you know how assault intelligence is, especially when an assault is put together in a crashing great hurry like this one. It's usually upside-down, cockeyed, stewed, screwed, and tattooed." There was an appreciative grunt and he went on: "So we're going to have to get some fresh, on-the-spot intelligence ourselves and get the true lay of the land when we get there."

He paused, asked: "Any questions so far?" And Paisan Veracruze stood up. Articulating carefully—it was always difficult for him to talk—he said: "Sir—like what do they—people—know about the airfield? And their security—what security?—do they have? I'd like to know. I want to know what we'll need, like equipment." Veracruze was a great top sergeant and expert in demolition, but like many a man of action, he couldn't say it.

Hope said: "Yeah, the dope we have isn't very much. We know it's a good long concrete runway—about 12,000 feet and brand new, And our target is in a shack near one end of the runway.

"I'll draw a map with the geography as I understand it now. I'll get some help with it from Mr. Musgrave here, and we'll all go over it tomorrow."

Veracruze was still standing. "I'd like to know—sir—what kind of wire they got out. Whether they have double A-frame barbed-wire or cyclone fence. I'd like to know if we're gonna need bolt-cutters to get through the wire or maybe we can hack it with just plain wire-cutters. Maybe we have to dig under it. Could save us a lot of luggin' if we don't have to haul no bolt-cutters. Save us some weight. Size, too." He sat down, exhausted with the super-effort of expressing himself publicly.

Looking around at the taut, trim faces, Hope sensed that there were many questions unasked. Notably, none from Major Gresham, the nuclear expert who would have the most ticklish job of all when they got to the bomb. The intelligence at the point was just barely hearsay, and probably Gresham's educated guess about exactly how the heart of the bomb was layered—whether the hydrogen works was inside the A-bomb which would trigger it, or outside, and its size and power—his guess would probably be better even now than the intelligence passed on by laymen who might actually have seen it.

Hope said: "We don't have sufficient G-2 on this job yet—there's no doubt about it. I don't think it can be helped because the whole deal was put together in such a God-awful rush. But we may have some more info reaching us before we get to the target area, and we'll have to pick up a lot of intelligence for ourselves when we get there—and that'll have to be in a big hurry, too."

He paused, feeling that there had been no statement from him about the importance of the job.

"This is probably the most important military mission anywhere in the world, really a Presidential mission. Some of you remember how it was back there in Vietnam when President Johnson was on the direct bull-horn to the F-10S and F-4 pilots when they took off to drop bombs on North Vietnam. If you think President Johnson was riding on the toggle arm of the pilots on those raids I should tell you that President Landers has been practically sitting on the mike in Washington all during the arrangements we went through in Hong Kong. He was watching over every piece of information coming and going and I know he must have had some pretty terrible nights cudgeling over the decisions. And it's a pretty safe bet that this very moment in the White House, he is devoting about ninety-nine percent of his thought to this particular mission and all its ramifications.

"He has decided that the safe way to do this job is to send in a secret, commando-type force—that's us—to take out this bomb with precision, by hand. He knows that he could send over a strike of fighter-bombers and shoot up the airfield and knock a hole in the ChiCom runway. But any pilot dropping a bomb would just be damned lucky if he could take out the H-bomb itself. You could drop a bomb practically next to it, and chances are the H-bomb would never go off, unless the critical masses were jammed together forcibly and held there long enough for the proper kind of milliseconds of heat generation.

"And besides, even if it could do the job, an air strike by our people would raise too much commotion. So the President decided that the thing has to be silent, sure—that's why he is sending us." There was a polite laugh, and he went on: "In most military efforts, you know, there is usually a back-up plan, maybe even five or six back-up plans in case the first one doesn't work. But as far as I know, there's no back-up plan for this job. We've just *got to do it.*

"You know that in any battlefield situation you've got to get the result with whatever you can lay your hands on. But in this situation, that's ten times truer. Churchill thought, way back in World War II, that a lot of people owed a lot to 'so few,' namely the RAF pilots who fought off the Luftwaffe in the skies over England. He also thought that there was very little time to carry out the critical mission of defending England and beating Hitler. But consider how few of us there are here, how much less time we have, and how much more depends on what we do. We can't afford to miss. And when we succeed, we will have done a great job for—excuse the expression—the country and for the world. I'm sure you all have learned the reason already: there seems to be only *one* hydrogen bomb and this is it. The ChiComs found it was pretty easy to make atom bombs—although they still don't have any sophisticated systems to deliver them, except a few little short-range rockets.

"They've found out what a superhuman effort it is to make an H-bomb, when you're so short of resources and technical skills. But now they've got it, they're going to deliver it, they think, aboard an old Tupolev 'Badger'. It's the only way they can deliver this giant of a bomb, and their projected target is the Seventh Fleet, which is coming in to South China waters right now in maneuvers.

"As far as we know, their target date is going to be the 16th of October, which happens to be the anniversary of their entry into the nuclear club in 1964, when they set off their first little atomic firecracker device in the Sinkiang Desert. Apparently they've decided to take the risk and drop the bomb on this big day, and hope that in the fuss and foray of the aftermath, the whole issue will get lost in negotiations and United Nations hearings, and that they will have struck a great blow for Asian self-dependence, or some such kind of bush-wah. They'll plan to come out with some kind of white paper to prove that the Seventh Fleet was planning to drop nuclear bombs on South China, and this was a defense measure to fight off the imperialist provocation—you all know that line. And you all know also that we're going to prevent the whole deal.

"Commander Wilson and I have decided that the *Mako* will be back to pick us up in the early morning of the 15th, that is, provided we get there and do our job. That night of the 14th–15th will be the last chance well have to take out the bomb. The following night, the 15th–16th, will be too late.

"Tomorrow we'll go over the whole thing again, and well have in-dividual briefings about every section—demolition, communications, medics. As of right now, our H-hour for our landing at Point Meng Wan is 0330, day after tomorrow."

Lieutenant Bosworth stepped forward toward the table. "Captain Hope, I have a message which may have some bearing on this last information." He extended the message from the decoding machine. Hope scanned it and announced: "That should read 0230 Thursday morning."

And he added: "I want to see Major Gresham and Major Nooley right now. Commander Wilson has let us use the mess compartment for an hour. The crew will come down for their 'soup down'. We'll just have to fit in—and hope they won't cuss us out too much later on. He's let us use the officer's ward room, which as you know is smaller, for our section work."

Wilson had appeared in the mess compartment; "There hasn't been such a very important party aboard since Mrs. Eisenhower christened this pigboat back in 1958," he said. "And you gentlemen are fixing up the biggest social occasion in *Mako's* history. May the Reds never rattle your teeth—or ours."

*

Driver Fung, foremost of the Friendlies in the target area on Hainan, was at that moment reporting to his intelligence contact, a middle-aged shopkeeper who ran one of the few free-enterprise businesses tolerated by the Communists in the Hoihow area. Wing On and his family, his wife and four sons, lived behind the cordage shop in the Hoihow section called Man Cheung. He was one of the few 'tigers'—meaning bourgeoisie, whom the People's Republic had missed in their previous campaigns against these anachronisms surviving from the age of capitalism and imperialism. The local village chief, or *Tau Muk*, had permitted him to exist and manufacture and sell his particular product, fisherman's cordage, because he continued to be able to provide good cordage at a low price, and also because incidentally he managed to supply cordage for the individual needs of the Village Chief *Nhap Dat* in Ling's home, and Ling's brother, Kung, a fisherman.

Wing On, a shaven-headed, stumpy man of about forty-five, received Driver Pung in the little living room on the second story behind the cordage shop. Pung, for all his ox-like slowness and crudity, seemed very nervous. Wing On wondered how much of this tenseness was genuine and how much was put on in the hope of eliciting further financial reward tonight. The blue-uniformed Pung paced restlessly up and down.

"Comrade Wing," he was saying, "you have no idea how closely the people at the base watch over me. I think that several of them are much inclined to think ill of me."

Wing On held up a restraining palm like the traditional Buddha telling the sea to subside. "Please, Driver Pung, remember our habit of speech. Even mere walls these days can hear." With that, he walked from the room, and came back bearing a small transistor radio. He switched it on, and soon a thunderous propaganda speech from Kiungchow political headquarters was blasting forth.

"Comrades," the announcer boomed. "You should know about the provocations of the imperialistic American war mongers, the *fei-to*. The ships of the American Seventh Fleet, loaded with aggressive air pirates in their rat-like swarms, again are approaching our shores. They must know that the People's Republic will not lie supine and suffer the continued insult of American provocation carried out by the air pirates, the running dogs of capitalism and the scrufulous *fei-to*, their bandit allies . . ."

Wing On motioned Driver Pung to sit beside him, and set the blasting radio on the table between them. "Now, Comrade Driver, what is the news?"

Pung wet his lips. "Everything is changing at the airfield, many new things have happened. They are growing immensely suspicious at the base. There are many more security police. We have to be checked four times now to make our way from the main gate to the bomb operations house."

Wing's expression remained as benign as ever. "You are absolutely right, Driver Pung. And it is very taxing to your nerves to work amid such tight precautions, I'm sure. Your work is very valuable, and I want you to know that we are very grateful for it. We have thought that some final present, such as valuable diamonds brought in from Hong Kong, must be given you. But that will be later, when all of the work is done. For the present, it would be more considerate to give you money, good and valuable currency of the People's Republic, because it is difficult to sell valuable objects such as diamonds—the block wardens and Chek-koh—Big Brother, the People's Police, are much too inquisitive. You must not make too much of a display with the money. But I have brought along for you one hundred Yuan, enough to support your whole family on the Hoihow open food market for the next three months."

That sum, 100 Yuan, would pay the rent for half a year. Wing, still smiling, extended the 100 notes in a folded wad. Driver Pung laboriously counted them, nodded approval that the amount was correct, and went on with his story: "So, Comrade, let me tell you what has happened at the airfield."

Wing interrupted again: "Excuse me, Comrade Pung, but I must summon my son, Wing Run. He is also very interested in knowing what is happening at the airfield."

A slender Chinese youth came into the room. He was about twenty-three or twenty-four years old, taller than his father, with the same calm, wide-set eyes, and bony shoulders. Wing explained to the driver: "My son Run will make notes on this important information." Run extracted a student's notebook and pencil from his pocket and pulled a chair up to the table.

"And now, Driver Pung, what were you saying about the changes at the airfield?"

"Never has so much happened at the airfield in one day," Pung answered, "This afternoon I took a load of ammunition out from Hoihow—ammunition of forty-millimeter size. A sky of cloth—made by man of pieces of cloth—was being stretched over the houses where the technicians work. It is colored like the woods, and it extends to the outer towers. It is to fool the American warbirds who might fly over, is it not?—to make them think that it is all jungle when seen from above?"

Wing On knew an answer was expected. "Yes, that is the purpose. And the forty-millimeter ammunition, did you deliver it? Are there many forty-millimeter guns aimed towards the sky to frighten away the American aircraft?"

"Yes, Comrade Wing. The canvas net is stretched low over them, and the gun-barrels protrude through the make-believe forest."

"And how many guns-against-airplanes would you say there are underneath the artificial sky?" Wing wanted to know.

"Only a few underneath the artificial sky around the bomb buildings. But there are other guns-against-aircraft in all directions. Each family of guns has its own sky of canvas painted green, in strips, over it."

"And how many guns-against-aircraft would you say there are underneath the main net, and how many outside? Try to think of them as if you were counting children."

"I should have the misfortune to count so many girl-children." Pung guffawed. "Possibly a family of fifteen children under the main net, and five or six families scattered out towards the road coming out from Hoihow. My own load of forty-millimeter shells was taken to the main buildings, where the bomb is."

Wing spoke to his son: "Are we proceeding too fast for your pen, Run?" The break gave the scribbling Run a chance to catch up. Wing turned back to Pung: "And are there any changes, as well, in the area where the bomb is housed? Are there any new buildings? And many new people?"

"Many new people—many more detachments of Chek-koh secret police. The camp is crawling with them like an anthill. And many more workers. A whole city of workers are digging a large cellar in the ground next to the bomb house."

"And do they have bins for mixing cement?"

"Cement, Comrade Wing? Is that the powder from which they fashion walls? And what are 'bins'? I know that there is a large mixer of paving material, a giant cylinder on a truck with a separate engine driving it, such as they used for making the concrete road for airplanes at the airfield."

"Oh, yes, I had forgotten that you are familiar with the concrete mixers from the airfield. And are the technicians pouring this concrete?"

"No, Comrade Wing, but they are getting ready. The workers are digging the cellar next to the bomb building. It would seem that they are waiting for the digging to finish."

"They are preparing an underground room in which to store the bomb and the bomb mechanism, is that correct? No, never mind—how would you know that?"

"On the contrary, Comrade Wing," Pung said proudly. "I overheard one of the technicians talking about fashioning a room for the bomb underground." Concern disturbed the placid face of Wing at last.

"You did not ask the technician anything about it directly, did you, Comrade Pung? You know, one must be very careful that no one should be aware of any investigating. You were saying before that they are very suspicious, in the vicinity of the bomb."

"No, Comrade, I asked no questions this time—because you are right, they are very suspicious."

"Very good, Comrade Pung. You have done very well with your job, and you must continue. Each time you drive into the camp with another truck-load, you must be observant, and watch everything around you. But do not ask too many questions. And we will reward you well for all information."

Wing On dismissed Pung with a nod of the head: "Thank you, Comrade Driver. Now you had better go home—it would not be well to appear to be spending too much time in the house of the cordier."

The driver stood up. Wing reached in a drawer and extracted a coil of rope. "A present for your brother-in-law, the fisherman. This will account for your visit to my shop—that you came to fetch some rope for the fisherman. And by the way, you should not mention this information in any way to him or to your wife—remember that. If you mention it incautiously, you will bring death to both of us, and to your wife and my children. And—" He paused significantly and looked Pung straight in the eye. "If you mention this matter to anyone in authority, you will die first—before we do. We will make sure of that, and you must remember it."

"Yes, Comrade Wing," the driver said nervously, holding his hat before him in a posture of subservience. "Yes, I will remember that." He bowed and left.

Wing turned to his son. "I want you to prepare all that in the form of a message. I am not yet sure whether we should send it by radio—it is extremely dangerous and growing more so. I will have to think whether to send it or wait for the arrival of our friends."

He walked toward the table, where Run was pencilling a message in code.

"Some of us have longer-range goals—like the Wing family—and their objective is quite correct—that the whole family should be moved to Hong Kong—and live happily with the people whom Peking calls 'Bandits, Pirates and Running Dogs of Capitalism.'"

Wing looked at his son's pencilled message, folded the message, pulled up one black pantleg and fastened the paper behind his knee with a rubber band. Then he carefully dropped his trouser leg in proper position. "We must be exceptionally cautious at this point," he said. "Because there is a most important job to be done in the next three days."

13

THAT NIGHT, AMID THE COTS SET UP IN THE MAIN CREW compartment of the *Mako*, some of the Special Force sergeants were playing poker under the dim night light. Around them, a knot of dungaree-clad submarine crewmen kibbitzed and applauded. Other less-interested crewmen snoozed on the nearby four-tier bunks.

Paisan Veracruze had the largest pile of greenbacks on his section of the folding card table. In the game with him were Sergeant Billy Bissell, whose stock of bills on the table was minimal; Sergeant Stanley Hing, Sergeants Jack O'Connor, Bull Wohl, and Bob Roberts, the medical section; two sergeants from the Communications section, Hildebrand and Hanson, and PFC Muley Muhlbach.

"Okay, okay, you fuckers," Bissell said, throwing down his hand. "You cleaned me and I want out. Your lousy winnings won't do you any good where we're going—besides, I'll win it back tomorrow if I can negotiate a loan."

PFC Muhlbach followed suit. He stood up. "I say the same, Sergeant Bissell. And I want out, too." He picked up the remnants of his bankroll. "But I would call them non-fuckers, Leastways, they ain't going to be doing any of that jazz for a week or two, if at all."

Sergeant Veracruze studied his hand with evident satisfaction. "You guys—sinful types," he said. "Usin' them foul words. Just because you're losin'."

Stanley Hing slouched further down on the Army cot, where he was using his big Special Force haversack as a backrest. "Now we've got rid of the amateurs, we can have a real serious-type poker game," he said.

Sergeant Bissell motioned to Muhlbach. "C'm on, Muley," he said- "Let's get away from this mob of pagan sinners and non-fuckers. They're undermining my morale. Let's go and do some more checking with our lists. These non-fuckers can waste the whole night, but we've got some business to do." Sergeant Veracruze, chewing on a cigar, took the stogie out of his mouth to make a loud, disrespectful sound.

At the edge of the crew compartment, Bissell told Muhlbach: "One thing we ain't checked into yet, Muley, is how we're fixed for bolt-cutters and wire-cutters. We also gotta get a rundown on the number of grenades we got, and what kind. Did we get all the Armalites we wanted?"

"Yup," Muhlbach said. "And the redhead major—what's his name, Doolan or somethin'—if we don't get no silencers or sniperscopes, he's going to do it all with a bow 'n arrow. How about that?"

At the after-storage room where the torpedoes were racked, they found Captain Hope, Musgrave, and Major Nooley bending over an open packing case. They were deep in discussion over an oil-spotted smelly package of C-3. Bissell said: "Captain Hope, we came to look after the grenades and the Armalites."

"Good," said Hope. "We were just going over some of the assault stuff."

"It seemed like to me we hadn't checked over the number of grenades we're gonna be carrying," Bissell said.

Hope agreed. "And right now all of that's getting to be damned important, because it looks as if we're going to have less time than ever to load up and get to the beach. The last message from Hong Kong: We are to make our rendezvous with the boat at 0230 instead of 0330 and that doesn't give us much time to horse around loading our gear on a boat—and getting to the beach before we get caught by sun-up. What time is sunrise this time of year in Hainan?"

Nooley answered: "I checked out my own memory on that with the Almanac, and I reach a figure of somewhere around 0600."

"Better than 0500," said Hope. "But it sure doesn't give us any time to spare." He put down the package of C-3 he was holding. "About your question on the grenades, Bissell. I figure if each man's got two, and maybe six or eight more in our gear, we'll be all right.

"Of course, the C-3 is going to be the heart of our expedition. Without plenty of explosives, and plenty of blasting caps, we might as well not go ashore. So we'll probably have more than enough of that."

Commander Wilson appeared in the doorway. "Doing your homework, boys? I've come down to tell you that we're going to be submerging for a little while, the lookouts spotted some lights on the horizon, and the radar contacts show three blips, evidently small fishing boats, or junks. So when you hear the Submerge Alarm, you'll know what it is." Just then, the Submerge Klaxon sounded over the ship's intercom, a duck-like honking. Commander Wilson started for the doorway. "I'll pass the word about the submerging," he said. "So your people won't think it's the end of the world." He passed on through the compartment and into the companionway outside, and Al Muhlbach followed him. "I'll be back in a minute," he said to Bissell. "There's something I wanted to ask the Commander about."

Out in the companionway, he hailed the Skipper. "Excuse me, Commander Wilson," he began, "could I ask you a question, sir?"

The Commander halted. "Certainly."

"Well, sir, I was wondering if there might be any kind of chaplain or something like that, on the boat. I don't need it, but if there was somebody like that, I'd like to see him. We only got a little more time before we go ashore, and it might get pretty hairy in there—sir."

"A good idea. Wait, I'll pass the word about it, when I get on the bull-horn. I'm going to pass out the word on the PA system from the Communications Room here. What's your name?"

"Muhlbach, sir."

"Okay, Muhlbach, we'll pass the word. We don't have any chaplain, but we do have a lay-reader, Lieutenant Frisbee—who has the collateral duty. He'll talk to any one of the landing party who wants it."

"That'd be great, sir."

Commander Wilson turned into the Communications Room, and in a few minutes the PA system crackled: "This is the Captain speaking. For the benefit of our passengers who may be unfamiliar with the submarine routine, the ooga-ooga, or two-klaxon signal you heard is the Submerge warning. We are taking the precaution of running submerged, because radar contact showed three unidentified surface craft, probably junks, nine miles away, and we do not wish any sighting of us reported to the enemy." He paused, and went on: "In response to questions from some of the members of the landing party group, there is a lay-reader—chaplain type—on board, Lieutenant Frisbee. For any of you who want to speak with him, his room is 12-B, and unless some emergency situation develops, he will be available for consultation. Lieutenant Frisbee's roommates in his compartment will be clear of the room so that individuals may see him alone."

When Muhlbach got to Lieutenant Frisbee's cabin, two others of the Typhoon Force were lined up outside. They were Sergeant Espinoza, and Sergeant O'Connor. Muhlbach said: "You guys sure got here fast. There must be some bad consciences in this crowd."

Freckle-faced Sergeant O'Connor, one of the communications section, smiled. "You and me both, Muley," he said. "Like the man said, it's who you know that counts."

Back in the torpedo storeroom, Captain Hope was going over his endless preparations with the heart of his assault group: ". . .So well get everything combat-loaded tomorrow morning, and we'll go through a dry run with the loading process in the afternoon. And maybe, if we're on the surface any of the time tomorrow afternoon, maybe you could try out the bow and arrow, Major Nooley. Just in case."

In the little cabin which he shared with Lieutenant Bosworth and Ensign Grundler, Hank Musgrave lay on the upper bunk, with the lights out, and studied the heavy girders of the overhead a couple of feet above him. Up there, in the shadows, he was seeing the golden skin and perfect soft shoulders of Mary Wu, and wondering if she might be thinking of him and his career of mayhem. Was he undertaking it primarily for her? He decided no, it was for its own sake.

How about the damage to her face, the dreadful shock the beating had been to her? And what would her nose look like when they took off the bandages? The intern, Smiley, who had set it seemed to be an able man and he had said the scars would be barely visible, and Hank had reassured her that her beauty would be unmarked.

The main thing was that she still had her flashing wit and quick apprehension, her aptitude for affection and little kindnesses, and of course, that magnificent body. It had sounded for a moment, he reflected, as if he had really climbed the Socratic stair of love from the physical to the spiritual, but that golden body, the perfect masses and textures, the incredibly affecting geometry, that was still, truthfully, the clincher.

That beauty was perishable, those few millimeters of difference between perfection and grossness were apt to become smeared with age. Maybe. But there was comfort in the fact that she was supremely aware of her femininity and the importance of each of those curves and its blending properly into its neighboring shape. So he *did* love her, too, for a mental quality higher up on the stair of love than the pure physical. Her quick, ambitious brain, and the simple mental determination that she would work hard to hold onto her beauty—her greatest resource to keep her and her son, and her family, afloat in the jungle of Hong Kong. She had, in effect, the will to beauty and feminine attractiveness which characterized a cinema actress. With them as with her, that will was an economic necessity, it also became a spiritual quality.

But Hank was thinking: It was possible he might never again have a chance to know her beautiful body or her will to beauty, her wit, her clear-eyed feminine bravery, or her instinctive generosity. That might all be gone from him in a day or two. It hit him hard now—suppose he was lying in a Hainan rice paddy, with Communist bullets in his body, in the muck, like the muck of Vietnam.

Since he had twice been wounded in action, he knew the chances were five or ten to one that initially he would be hurt rather than killed in the average battlefield situation. But in this kind of raid, a bad wound would be death.

If the Typhoon Force failed, they would probably have on their consciences not only the end of the Seventh Fleet, but the deaths of millions upon millions of Chinese, Americans, and Russians. And if that happened, it might include his own parents and his blood relatives in Costa Mesa, California, and Nahant, Massachusetts.

Lieutenant Bosworth came into the room, saw his temporary roommate lying in the shadows of the upper bunk, and did not switch on the light. Instead, he fiddled with a desk drawer and pulled out a flashlight.

"It's all right, Bos," Hank said. "I'm awake. Go ahead and turn on the light."

Bosworth flicked the switch. "You got the heebies?" he asked. "I've had 'em—a couple of times myself on other missions—but bad."

He was digging into the cabinet drawer trying to find some mysterious object.

Hank said: "Not bad. Just thinking about all the things that could go wrong, and hoping only the minor ones do."

Bosworth said: "You ought to come up to the Conn and see what's already going wrong—make you feel better. What is it the Bard said— 'Present fears are less than horrible imaginings'?"

He found what he wanted in the drawer and turned the light off. "So," Hank said, "what's so bad up on the Conn? I want to be cheered up."

Lieutenant Bosworth went on: "Commander Wilson is really sweating blood. SUBRAD has a contact which looks like an enemy pigboat. He's so worried about it that I can't even run the sending radios for a while—he's afraid they'd somehow triangulate and get a fix on us.

"We're running submerged because they'd be less apt to get a blip on us, if they should be lucky enough to have something like our SUBRAD locators. I told him I didn't think there was a chance of that if it was a Chinese sub. As far as we know, even the Russians don't have SUBRAD.

"Still, he's following evasive tactics and we're already three or four hours behind the schedule. We should be fifty knots closer in to Hainan, by now. Imagine where we could be if we could start running on the surface!"

Hank stirred and jumped down from his bunk. "I can't sleep anyhow," he said. "Might as well go on up and take a look."

He pulled on his camouflage suit and shoes and followed Bosworth from the compartment. "It's better than lying there thinking about my girl friend," he said. "Or is it?"

"Probably not," said Bosworth cautiously.

*

Mary Wu was also awake, in her darkened hospital room in Hong Kong, thinking of Hank, the money, and the pain. The pain was knifing like a huge toothache into nerves that ran through her jaw.

Then she dreamed brightly of the life in America she had seen in the American movies and TV—far brighter and more splendid than even the life of the British functionaries in Hong Kong, That of an American *Fu-ren* would be incredibly rich. She had seen them in the Hilton and the Mandarin, especially the older ones, no longer offering much personal wealth in the form of beauty in return for the riches their men bestowed on them—their men remaining kind to them, and turning secretly to other women. She must remember to avoid that mistake with Hank, to keep her looks for him.

She remembered one time—the first night Hank had spent with her on a visit to Hong Kong, when he had told her—that was before he grew so serious as he did later: "Mary, always keep that beautiful sleek shape and that smooth golden skin. Fight for it and keep it and you will never have to worry." He was absolutely correct. She had agreed and told him: "My professional assets, Hank," and even then, at that early date before she had given up the dancehall, he had looked slightly shocked and hurt.

Dance hostessing had been her business, she had learned the dodges necessary to keep men in line, she could choose the ones she liked, a luxury rare in the jungle of Hong Kong; and just about impossible in the hunger-stricken and police-ridden China, Tonight, thinking back over it, Mary felt a surge of optimism despite the aching hurts, because she could see that as Hong Kong was for her a great leap upward from China, so being a *Fu-ren* for an American like Hank was going to be an incredible vaulting jump out of Hong Kong and practically into heaven.

And then, there had been the strange visit from Freeman Blake before lunch. Blake had been much more smiling toward her than ever before. But he hadn't wanted what patrons at the Asia Ballroom had wanted. That fever wasn't in Freeman's eyes, only a lavishness, a kind of generosity which seemed so out of joint for him. He had brought her a much better, three-band transistor radio, and had exchanged it for the one he had left with her before, such a strange, unexpected kindness. She was sure she had analyzed him correctly before when she had offered him the $20 American and he had left her the small transistor. Now, something had happened, something had changed, and not only had he brought her the three-band Sony, twice the size of his own radio, but he had offered her a gift of money, and for no favor in return, except a strange one which came as a great shock to her.

He had said: "I am going to do you a small favor—and ask one of you." And he had looked across the room towards the roommate, and Mary had reassured him, again, that the old Chinese lady did not understand English, Mary was sure of that now.

And Blake had given her another $100, American (More than $500 Hong Kong!) and told her: "We have reason to believe that your friend Chen will be coming back to see you—without any murderous intention. And we think that he will try, in fact, to be friendly. So we want to know what he says, and mainly, where he can be reached—if you can get his phone number, that would be good enough. He has disappeared: the Tiger Importing Company is closed. I am trying to help Hank Musgrave with his—story— while he's away. Understand?"

And Mary had told him: "Of course." And then, wonder of all wonders, he had given her a very strange present. He had looked across the room, again, and seen that the old grandmother was asleep, and then he had extended to her a sharp black dagger with a sinister pointed blade like the knife which that British paratrooper, in red beret, had one time shown her. A commando-type knife, and she knew that a knife like that was illegal in Hong Kong, except for such as the British commandos themselves, who had been assigned to the Malaysian War. But she had taken the knife from Freeman, as readily as the money. And she had said: "I know how to use the money, and the pig-sticker, Freeman. I have done both before."

And she had seen an expression as shocked as Hank's had sometimes been at her flings of wit.

She told him: "Don't worry, I understand that I am to help with Hank's 'story' and naturally, I must have some forcible answer like this—commando dagger to protect myself in case Chen should have some unreasonable and emotional reaction to questions I might ask him, without skill, about the story which interests Hank: a newsman's story, of course."

And she had seen that Freeman Blake was as startled as Hank had sometimes been at her perceptions, her grasp of the "central thread," the *Chang*, the *Shin*.

She lay there thinking about her face, and how the nose would look in a week or so, when, Smiley said, the swelling would have gone down. She tried to remember how it had happened, but it was all still a blur of flashing lights and explosions in her memory, the broad face of Chen and the narrow face of the other man standing out like pictures illuminated by searchlights.

She reflected that it was strange that they had hit her so hard on the face, and not hurt her anywhere else in the soft bodily places where she could be so easily damaged. Thinking about this, she knew that Chen would be back. He had deliberately not hurt her there. For a long time, at the Tiger Importing Company, she had seen that familiar look in his eyes and tried to keep her work strictly business.

And now, an hour after Blake had left, she was wondering when and if Chen Yu would come, sometime during the night, perhaps in an "unofficial" hour, because she had heard Freeman talking, softly, to the orderly whom Hank had told her was well-paid by the Americans. And she had guessed that Freeman had given some of that good American *Lu-duh*, the good green again, to let Chen Yu pass if he should come. But after what the Americans called this "build up," Chen had not come to see her so far. However, she was still ready for everything.

She reached for the knife, felt the shiny black leather sheath and the curved, hard steel handle under her pillow. Also forty-three dollars American. The American dollars were fine for *cumshaw* and she preferred them to the Hong Kong variety. Mainly it was because they were five times as valuable. She had sent the rest of her recently acquired small fortune down to the main desk storage vault in a sealed envelope, entrusting the job to the sharp-faced English floor supervisor. The English were not incorruptible, but their corruption usually involved certain rules; rifling valuables in a safe deposit envelope violated one of them.

From the jungle thinking she had learned in China, her mind drifted to a dream about Norman, who was staying now with her sister and her sister's children in the apartment in the Tak Shing section. Perhaps in a week, when they would take off the bandages and the puffing of her eyes had gone down—then she could see Norman and Liang again.

Her half-dream now was about Norman and how he could have a good schooling, in the Tau Lok preparatory, or even go to Hong Kong University—that is, if she became legally a *Fu-ren*, Mrs. Musgrave! She laughed at the thought—such a funny name. Yet Hank was a sweet boy—kind, smart—and he knew his *Kama Sutra* very well.

She was not much afraid. Men were not much to be afraid of, usually. They were very endearing, like little Norman and Hank. They were all puppies, very easily hurt, inside and outside. She smiled inwardly: How, then had she been badly damaged by two of these harmless puppies? It was because of the surprise. She had not been aware. The other man must have hit her from behind, very hard, and dazed her very badly. From then on, she had not been able to resist. She must not ever be taken by surprise, again.

Once before, she had been set upon that way, taken by surprise. It was the time in Hong Kong when three worthless youths—what did Hank call such people? "Punks," that was it. Those punks had waylaid her as she left the Asia Ballroom one night with another date, and swarmed all over her and the date. Fortunately, she had not been hurt, because a policeman happened to be coming by, there on the upper reaches of Nathan Road. But they had jumped her, knocked her down, taken her purse and badly beaten the boy friend. That was a time when she should have been more aware— and again, in this recent beating, she should have been more ready for the unexpected. A jungle beast mustn't forget the first rule of the jungle, which is to take the prey by surprise with superior forces.

Other women might lose sight of the man's perspective, which put the sensual enjoyment of women at the top of their lists, whether men would admit it or not, and women had a tendency to forget this, to put everything else ahead of it—the family life, children, parties, women friends. To so many women, sexual enjoyment was the last order in importance, their desire for sex was as weak as that of a sick man. She knew men never lost their love for sex, not really. Even older men never changed in this, the idea at least was there, a paramount priority.

She had often thought that she had something like a man's attitude toward sex. It could be such a beautiful adventure, such perfection—with the right man. A good man, clean and beautiful. There *were* some, like Hank.

There had been too many of the other kind when she was a dance hostess at the barroom: like the plump American tourists whose idea of heaven was to see a well-turned feminine leg, for some reason, in a silk stocking. Then men who liked this were usually older, perhaps in their sixties, and the special crowning delight for them seemed to be the sight of a woman's leg, the bare flesh above the stocking. But not the more attractive bare flesh without the stocking. They liked garter belts, too. They were the height of ugliness. But these men loved them. Why? Something in the Western culture; it was inscrutable and unaccountable.

And the Americans who had slept with her as if she were a curiosity, because of her color, and seemed to think it was very daring to make love to a person of different skin-tone—and even had bizarre curiosities about her body, and a hard-dying belief that somehow an

Asian woman would be constructed differently. What was the song they sang: "Is it true what they say about Chinese women?"

And then, the endless column of Chinese lovers. She had made love to them because that was business, it was a way to earn rice for her son and for her, and to put aside money so that her sister, mother, and one brother could come across from China, illegally. In this long column were small, thin men generally with ferocious appetites for bodily contact with the female—too often with a driving desire to make it somehow shameful and ugly when it could be breathlessly lovely. Fortunately, she could choose among them— somewhat.

And on the other side of the border, it was much worse: all the dull, boring, machine-like Communist party members with their universal phobia of being spied upon, being "reported." There were too many millions of these suspicious little tyrants in the world, persecuting and being persecuted—that was their life, to be professional bullies.

Mary found herself thinking about Hank, again. After all these men, would she be able to get along with just one? She knew that was a question high in Hank's mind. He had almost asked her that question literally, a few times. And what she had told him was perfectly true: She had tried many and she knew a good one when she saw one. Hank had the same kind of healthy attitude about the beauty and pleasure of sex that she did. He was one of the few who could bring it to her in full measure. And he had so many advantages: He was tall, good-looking, and smooth-skinned, although his body was pale—a *kwei*, which means "devil" and "ghost."

But Hank, though a "foreign devil" had a very quick, perceiving mind. And a great amount of courage. He had a big heart in the Chinese sense of the word, meaning courage, and a big heart in the sense of generosity, too. He lived as if life could end tomorrow and he was not afraid of living it fully. And he was just at the right age to enjoy and make the most of sex as well as having the right attitude toward it. With many men, *hsing yu* was really a small, rapid pleasure, and the small pleasures of the small men were not very much for the lady involved. But Hank knew how to cultivate the moments and make them bloom. And he had several times quoted an old Indian book on the subject of satisfaction for the female. What was it? "A man who leaves a woman unsatisfied is like a coward who runs away from the field of battle." That was the *Kama Sutra*, that was the name he had mentioned, and he said that was an Indian treatise on love, from the fourth century.

There was a strange shuffling noise outside the room, and Mary's senses snapped broad awake. This time, she would not be caught by surprise.

She looked across the room, where her aged Chinese roommate appeared to be sleeping soundly. No movement there. Then she saw something stir at the door, a figure moving from the light of the hall towards the shadows of the room. She was sure that it was the stumpy, wide-based figure of Chen Yu.

He was alone. She saw him moving past the bed of the elderly Chinese, as he made for the window. He had evidently checked over the sleeping form of the roommate, and now in the light of the window she saw that it *was* he. As usual, he wore the Chinese *gwa-dz*, or tunic, and slippers rather than the western style garb.

She thought coolly: I had better have a plan. If worst came to worst, if a push became a shove, she could always fall back on the classic method of reducing man to harmlessness. It would work. The business of what the dancehall girls called *Tsau Tsat*; approximately, cutting down a man with the strength of his own virility, or in less proper words, seizing the handle. She didn't want to use the knife on him, not because of any compunctions about sticking someone, but only because she knew that it would be immensely complicated with the British-trained Hong Kong police.

Now he had made out her shape on the bed and apparently identified her, He came out of the window light, a moustached face, not smiling, but a mild expression for Chen Yu, the mouth almost conciliatory beneath the dark moustache. The gleam in his small brown eyes was anything but anger.

Now she was aware that he studied her very carefully, checking over the identifying bandage in the center of her face, the wired cage of her jaw, the shape of her bosom beneath the bedclothes.

He began softly: "I see you have not attained sleep. I must talk with you."

She knew she must at least simulate a fierce revulsion. "You treat me with indignity, to come back after what you did." She could see that her unearthly voice shook him. Some of the gleam of "happen-relations" seemed to fade from his eyes.

Chen's voice was rasping as ever, but suddenly unsteady. "I've been remembering about the other night." For remembering, he used the word *sz min*, which had the connotation of reflection and contemplation. "Perhaps we were too hard on you." He gave a harsh laugh.

"You have a big nerve! With my nose broken and my jaw smashed in two places, to come here, you have a nerve! Every time they bring my food on the tray, and it is some miserable kind of gruel with a straw, the only way it can be eaten, I curse you and wish you were dead!"

"Little Tigercat! I like to see you wanting to hit out, to be fierce."

He reached out to seize her hand with a rough touch, and his grip was sinewy.

"You're hurting me," she said, wincing.

He squeezed harder. "I like that."

She spat out: "I don't! It's nothing: be a *man!*"

He grinned lasciviously. He fumbled in his pocket and extracted three Hong Kong bills—fifty dollars Hong Kong, about nine American dollars. She threw the money back at him. Then she saw the humor of what was happening. Sometimes if things were terribly wrong and couldn't be worse, the only thing to do was to laugh. "What do you think I am, a Wanchai girl?"

He responded in kind. "Your American is making you into a spoiled rich woman."

She was remembering that Freeman Blake had asked her to help out with Hank's "story." One of the jobs was to find out where Chen Yu lived, or at least his telephone number. And yet how to do it?

When she had thrown the money back to him, with the movement her hospital gown had slipped from her shoulder. She restored it, but she saw his hungry eyes following her shape as he stooped to pick up the money.

"You know your American friend is a spy, don't you?" Chen said. "Not that it matters to me. I'm in it for the money."

Abruptly he reached out for her. She pulled away. "Think of my roommate!" she warned, indicating the elderly lady across the room. Her heart was beating very fast.

"She'll wake up!" Mary said. "Shell call the nurse, and then there'll be a lot of trouble. They'll call the hospital police, and they might even question you." She could see that the possibility of being questioned by the police didn't sit pleasantly with him. But he still had that feverish, questing look in his eye, and she knew that he didn't take kindly to opposition to his wants.

She summoned her acting talent. "You! You—Turtle!" She said, "A hospital is no place."

He laughed roughly. "Any place is a place."

She knew that the main thing Freeman Blake wanted was Chen's phone number, his hideout, where he could be found. But how to do it?

"I should be out of the hospital in a week. Or perhaps even earlier. I will have to go through a long recovery period. Do you want me to phone you? I don't know where to reach you. Give me your phone number and I will call you." She was getting alarmed, and in her fright her breathing was coming hard. She saw his eyes following the movement of her breast.

"Never mind that," he rasped. "This is what I—want." He projected himself towards her, his hand reaching for her. She could scream for help from the nurse, but if she did, he probably wouldn't come back again, ever. There was one way. *Tsau Tsat*. That would be the way out, and not too much trouble, and the game wouldn't be lost.

It was a trick known to every Wanchai tramp and especially popular with young Chinese and American customers who were afraid of what the Americans called social diseases. It was one way also to make a mean and aggressive cockscomb into a meek and mild little boy, with a very immediate loss of aggressive qualities, a very successful way to reduce a rapist, and quickly.

She spoke to him kiddingly the litany which she knew as well as her name: "Come on, we can do this. The other one won't do, but this we can do. Now, come on and it will be fine and very good for you and over very soon. Very soon but very, very good and a long, long time." Not really a classic song, because each of the baggages sang her own individual song to the tune, but much the same in import and the end came out just about the same: calmness, satisfaction, and also a sense of guilt for the man—why the sense of guilt for enshrining the pleasures of virility she never knew—yet, in the Buddhist faith or the western world, sex was never enjoyed without guilt, she was thinking, and wondering why. She told Chen this would have to do for now and that later she would telephone him, perhaps tomorrow, and she would call him if he would give her that fine telephone number and he did, gasping it out—939426. She remembered it, then the temporary and pleasant insanity reached its peak, and it was a mechanical process to her, as far as *he* was concerned a—what did Hank call such a man, a *slob*—and she was remembering what Hank had said, his mention of the *Kama Sutra*, and how the man who leaves a woman unsatisfied was like a coward. This was a *big* coward, Chen. Very quickly it ended and the aggressive Chen with moustache and gray hair was a little boy, worn out, exhausted with his guilt. The old lady across the room was stirring, they could see her tiny husk of a shape moving in the shadows, and Mary took advantage of the moment to accelerate Chen's departure.

"Look out, my ward-mate is moving and you'd better go. She might wake up any minute now. The wing nurse should be coming by to check at eleven o'clock, and that's only three minutes from now."

939426, she thought, I will write that down and make sure that Freeman Blake has it tomorrow morning. And then, she thought, she could make sure that the orderly was alerted to keep out any further visitors except Freeman Blake.

Her heart was pounding very fast, and with the pulse, a heavy throbbing seemed to beat through the center of her face. When the nurse came she asked for an aspirin, and her mind went drifting back to Hank and she wondered what he would be doing now, and she decided she would ask Freeman when he came tomorrow, and her intuition told her that Freeman would tell her next to nothing.

14

October 12

IN THE PRESIDENTIAL OFFICE AT THE WHITE HOUSE, TV trays had been set up for the President, Admiral Bloomfield, and Charles Hudibras. They were drinking coffee and talking until such time as the food could be brought.

Admiral Bloomfield was speaking: ". . . So the last contact report we had from the *Mako* was two hours ago. She was approaching the island of Hainan, but was still a hundred miles off the central coast. She was running behind schedule, and forced to travel submerged because of several radar contacts on the surface. There also appeared to be a submarine contact, an unfriendly submarine, somewhere in the vicinity. So they were shutting down their radio-sending activity —the black-box deceptive device had gone haywire the way they usually do and so rather than take a chance, they had just shut down on their sending."

The President had a high-priority question: "What about the Seventh Fleet, and Admiral Kerr? Are they still steaming into the South China Sea, as if nothing untoward were happening?"

"Yes, sir, that's the total effect of it. At least, that's *approximately* the effect. There's one other item: I'm sure Kerr is beefing about the fact that there's a higher degree of CINCNAV and COMINCH control than he likes. But they're going to have to rely on our judgment as to whether they should strike or run at the last minute.

"One thing I would like to urge, Mr. President, is the consideration of an alternate plan, in case the whole *Mako* effort blows up —as well it may.

"Of course, the air group of the *Enterprise* is standing by. If I know Kerr, he won't relax a minute as long as they are that close to China. He'll have his squadrons ready to go—with all kinds of loads—nuke or non-nuke. But I believe that we should formulate a plan to back up the *Mako* effort if it should go afoul. For instance, if she should get caught and depth-charged, or run askew of some barrier nets or mine fields in the Hainan Straits. Or if our landing force should not make good on their effort to take out the bomb."

"I have nearly complete faith that they will manage the mission," the President said. "After all, they are the best men we could pick, within the limitations, and the *Mako* is the best assault submarine you could produce for the job, isn't it?"

Bloomfield smiled: "Yes, sir—within the limitations of time and geography."

"I know you're right, Joe. And I do want you to think about alternative plans, just in case everything should go wrong."

Bloomfield smiled again. "Don't forget Murphy's law, Mr. President."

The President said: "Is that the law that the space people dreamed up—that anything that *can* go wrong *will* go wrong?"

"Right. And it is the first principle of armed forces operations here on the terrestrial planet as well as in space," said the Admiral.

"You *are* a pessimist today—and I guess every day, Joe."

"I guess that's why the enemy dislikes me so much. I know the censorable secret of their operations as well as ours."

"I guess it *is* realism, not pessimism, Joe, and I'm glad we have such a genuine realist in charge of the situation."

The President turned to Charles Hudibras: "Charlie, what's the latest from your expert legions of Secret Service down there on the Hong Kong battlefront? What's the latest you're getting out of Hainan?"

"Well, Mr. President, we do have some late dope about the Chinese preparations. Apparently, they have brought in some antiaircraft defenses, and strung camouflage over the whole complex so it won't be spottable by air. Also, we hear that they are digging underground quarters and defensive ack-ack for the bomb people. Fortunately, it's a rush operation, and they don't seem to be alerted against ground attack."

"They're like us," the President said with a sidewise grin. "I wonder which is improvising more. We or they. I guess we, because we always have to move more complex matériel."

✳

It was ten minutes to one in the morning on the island of Hainan, and Driver Fung, instead of being home in bed with his wife, had found some buddies who had snared a jug of *Ko leung*. Pung had paid for the stuff, available in small quantities on the free market, and since the liquid fire was almost gone, he had announced his intention to have a different kind of fun. The group were sitting in the darkened back room of a rickety old house overlooking the foul-smelling stream that ran down towards Meng Wan Point, when Pung made the announcement to his friends. "My little wife has turned as cold as the *Kwai suet*, that fancy machine which makes ice in the *Tau Muk's* house. You, Wong. You know a place where women can be bought. What are they, commune girls who want to make some money on the side?" The others shushed him.

"All right," he went on in a whisper loud enough to wake a graveyard. "All right, I'm the one in this nest of lazy louts who has money. I will pay for all of us. And I will do it to spite my ice mountain of a wife."

But there was no assent among his cronies. Pung roared on: "So none of you wants a little *siu fa*. Has your *Tsat* fallen off, too, or been mobilized in the People's Militia? Are you afraid the block warden will turn you in for chasing after a female, other than your legal one? Or are you afraid the Chek-koh will find that your playing around is endangering the nation's security?"

Tak, who was Pung's friend, interceded; "Not so loud, Pung. You'll wake up the block warden, and the Chek-koh. If we're going to go after some *Maau*, we don't have to announce it to the whole world— our wives included."

Gong, a netsman in the fishing commune, said: "You alleycats can go out and get your *maau*, but count me out. I figure I'm taking enough of a chance going out to drink illegal *Ko leung*. Somebody in our dormitory building might report me for that, and if we get mixed up with females when we go after *maau*, and I should hope we would, that only increases our chances of being turned in. So I'm going to leave right now." He guffawed. "The *Ko leung* is just about finished anyhow."

Kong's great buddy, Wong Chu, supported him. "Me too, I'm going to leave, too. A fine party, Comrades." He bowed to Pung. "Thank you for the nice liquid dynamite." The two men stood up, and two of the others followed.

Pung whispered hoarsely: "Why is it everyone is always so afraid? You'd think that it was a crime to mention the Chek-koh." His voice rose at the dreaded word, and his friend Tak shushed him again.

"Not so loud," he warned. "I'll go with you. I know a couple of girls who work in the Rice Commune office. They live in a house on my street. But I don't think they're going to take very kindly to our waking them at this hour, unless we have something good to offer them."

Pung growled: "I told you I've got plenty of yuan. People are still influenced by money, even in the People's State."

Tak chuckled. "But not so anxious to announce it."

And so it was that Pung and Tak came to be sitting on the bed of Mei Ling, and talking to Mei and her roommate Kei Ying. Mei still wore a rough blue jumper-suit she had put on when Tak's pebbles bounced off their wooden shutter a few minutes before. She had gone down to open the back door and had led the visitors up the narrow hallway, meanwhile warning them repeatedly to be quiet.

Mei Ling had enjoyed numerous evenings with Tak, who frequently brought her small presents such as fish sauce and spices, the latter being especially hard to get in the People's State. Now Pung, who was not noted for his finesse or tact, had received careful instruction from Tak to offer Mei Ling and her friend presents of money, but to do it tactfully: To tell her that in their hurry, because they had been working

so hard for the People's State, they hadn't time to buy a suitable present for Mei Ling and her friend; so that he hoped that they would be
able to take the money and go out and buy exactly the presents they
wanted on the free market.

Pung, as clumsy as usual and still thoroughly befuddled with al-
cohol, had botched the job. The moment they got into the hallway,
Pung had burst out: "Well, my little Sweet-Fish, you are as beautiful
as Tak told me and that's what the name Mei Ling means. Your name
is beautiful and you are, right? So Tak said we should bring a present
for you and your friend. Is your friend in? Tak says the best present is
something that would let you buy anything on the free market—yuan.
So here Is twenty-five yuan for you, and we have twenty-five more for
your friend."

Mei Ling hesitated, then smiled graciously. She took the money and stuffed it in a pocket in her blue worker's jacket. "Thank you,
Comrade Pung. And please, try to speak less loudly. There are fifteen
people who also live in this house."

Driver Pung groaned. "Everything we do has to be done in public.
We must live like goldfish in a tank in the People's Museum."

Mei Ling continued to wear the pleasant smile: "We will be private
enough upstairs," she said. She turned and started to climb, a cute
Teddy-bearish figure in her rough work-suit.

Pung saw the intriguing swing of her hips even in the faint light
of the kerosene lamp she was carrying. He nudged his friend: "What
a *poon kwat!*" he exclaimed. "What a ship to paradise!" Excitement was
throbbing in his head. "I may not know much, but I know that."

Tak grinned at him. "Not so much noise," he said.

Pung led the way upstairs following the *chi-nu*. What he didn't
know was that she and her roommate were permitted to carry on their
sideline profession because occasionally they would bestow favors on

the local Tau Muk, the boss of the commune-district, and that she also managed to augment her income by supplying information on her clients where she felt it might be interesting to the Tau Muk, or others of the local commune organization. Besides being beautiful, she was a hustling businesswoman on two fronts.

Now, as she sat beside him on the bed, she put a friendly hand on Pung's shoulder. "Comrade Pung, I like you. You must tell me all about yourself." She unbuttoned her heavy blue blouse and it slipped partially open. Pung's eyes bugged out. "I would choose you, and my old friend Tak will like my girl friend." She kissed his cheek. "Shouldn't you give Mei Ling a little larger present?"

Pung could hardly swallow. Finally he blurted out: "I think I should. You are really *Mei*, most beautiful!" He extended an extra thirty-five yuan towards her. "Twenty-five yuan because you are Mei Ling, and ten more for my friend Tak." He added loudly: "*Sin kan li!*" which was properly a toast, but literally meant "Bottoms Up!" Pung laughed, thinking it was a very good joke, and his friends joined him politely. Mei Ling was reflecting that she had heard this lout's name somewhere, she thought perhaps one of the Tau Muks' companions had mentioned it at one point—something about one of the technicians at the airfield saying this boob should be watched. Perhaps there would be a special value in the intimate information he would blurt out in the course of the night's activity.

At that same moment the *Mako* was thrumming along at eight knots below black seas. The top of her fin moved some sixty feet below the waves. The time was two-fifteen.

In the sub's radio compartment, Commander Wilson bent over the shoulder of the operator as the unscrambler machine clattered:

. . . AIRDROP COORDINATED FOR 0900 OCTOBER 12 COORDINATES 76924 AND 36312.

Wilson beamed at the operator. "That will make Captain Hope very happy. Six and three-quarters hours from now he'll get his fancy weapons—provided the Communist PCs cooperate."

Wilson ducked down the corridor and climbed up the steel ladder to the conning tower compartment. There, the SUBRAD operator bent over the hooded device where he had been watching a thin line of light turning like a wheel over a black shiny surface, each sweep moving whitish clouds ahead of it. He called out: "Negative on SUBRAD contacts, sir. Nothing on the scope for the last twenty minutes."

Commander Wilson said to Jack Colvin, Chief of the Boat: "Cob, we might as well surface, and make some time. And tell Captain Hope that his airdrop is laid on for 0900."

Chief Colvin answered: "Aye, aye, sir." He picked up the phone to the Control Room below, and in a few seconds the PA speaker in the compartment emitted the three honking sounds of the klaxon, and the crackling voice: "Prepare to surface, blow all ballast." In the Control Room below, a crewman pulled a dozen shiny steel levers with all the gentle precision of a transport pilot, and the shooshing of the main ballast air vents could be heard from several directions.

Colvin dialed Hope's compartment. "Captain Hope: good news. Captain Wilson says Hong Kong laid on the airdrop—for 0900. He says 'if the Commie PCs will cooperate.'"

"We'll try positive thinking," said Hope.

Near Hope, in the two-man cabin which he shared with Lieutenant Commander Hammond, the *Mako's* navigator, Major Nooley was stirring at the sound of the klaxon and the surfacing commands.

The room was dark and he craned over the edge of the upper bunk to see if Hammond was asleep in the lower. The bunk was empty, the counterpane drum-tight in neat midshipman patterns.

Nooley jumped down, wearing only his shorts, and flipped on the light switch. He took his longbow from the corner and examined the pistol-type grip at the center. He strung the bow, slipping the heavy cord over the bone end of the bow—always a muscular feat with a bow of such heavy poundage. He twanged the weapon and it sang a bass tone.

There was a quiver of long varnished arrows in the corner of the room, with the feathered tips protruding from the fiber container. He threaded one of the arrows into the bowstring and pulled the arrow towards him, feeling the power of the flexed wood. His broad Irish face bent with evident pleasure as he tested the heft of the weapon.

It occurred to him that probably tomorrow by daylight they would be travelling mostly under the water. He might get up on the open top of the sail structure now and fire a couple of arrows, to get the feel of the bow. He wouldn't be able to recover the arrows anyhow, whether they were fired by day or night. And he should try the bow once or twice before the moment Thursday morning when they were going to be put ashore on Hainan. It was more than possible that his skill with the bow might be tested even before they hit that beach.

He slipped on his camouflage suit, buckled the heavy leather protector on his left forearm, seized the bow and quill, and went out the door. In the companionway he saw Gresham and Hank Musgrave coming from the opposite side of the hull.

"It sounds like they're flushing out this baby for a little speed-running on the surface," he said. "If they're going to get some fresh air, I thought I might try a couple of practice shots with the bow."

Hank nodded. "Good idea. But you heard about the air-drop. At 0900. We're going to get all the fancy stuff out of Hong Kong. Sniperscopes, portable radar, silencers."

They started down the corridor towards the ladder together, with Nooley leading. Nooley spoke without looking back: "I'll try out the Robin Hood business in case the drop goes bluey. They always said at the War College you should have at least one alternate plan— because of Murphy's Law."

Nooley had trouble getting his longbow through the narrow hatchways in the access tubes up to the bridge. Gresham, after nearly being stuck with the horn end of the longbow a couple of times, assisted by feeding the lengthy weapon through the last three ladders. Then they passed through the last dripping iron rungs of ladder and found themselves on the open, wet deck of the bridge.

Commander Wilson from the forward part of the deck saw the three tall shapes moving towards him. "Somewhere out there over seventy-five miles of sea is China," he said, "the pendant jewel of Hainan dangling from the biggest hunk of population on earth. But fortunately they don't seem to have any Chinese navy outposted to protect their precious lavalier. None that SUBRAD or our surface radar can pick out, anyhow."

Nooley said: "Commander, I thought I'd better come up and try out my quiet weapon while the night was still up. In the morning, we're going to be going ahead with the airdrop—I hope." Wilson nodded.

Nooley extracted the long gleaming shaft of an arrow from the quill angled over his broad back. He aimed the long wooden finger towards the horizon, his gloved right hand straining to hold the arrow notch against the bowstring. Then his fingers snapped straight, the bowstring slapped against his leather armguard, the arrow whirred against the wind of the ship's movement into the background of whitecaps.

"I'll have to do better than that, if the real thing ever happens," Nooley growled.

"We'll probably never know," Hank said. "It's too dark."

Nooley said, "No, it was just no good."

Carefully, Nooley took another long, barbed-tip arrow from his quiver and fitted it to the bowstring. Then Nooley slackened his bowstring. "Would you have any meteorological balloons?"

Commander Wilson said: "Fine," and went below. He came back shortly with a limp balloon and a cylinder of helium, and soon a three-foot silver globe was beside them on the bridge.

"It'll be a good test," Commander Wilson said to Nooley. "You'd better hit it, because we don't want too many American weather balloons floating around off the coast of Hainan. Besides, it's visible, even at night.

"Fortunately, there's not a Chinese blip in sight, I just checked with radar. Radar and SUBRAD. There's nothing within twenty miles of us."

"Okay," said Nooley. "Let 'er go!"

Gresham loosed the silver sphere and it bounded sternward, oscillating violently in the wind. Nooley aimed deliberately. Then the bow twanged, the string slapped hard against Nooley's leathered forearm, and the arrow gleamed in the starlight. They waited a long second, and there was only blackness where the balloon had been.

"I should have waited a little longer to shoot," Nooley said. "I took advantage."

"You always should," Wilson said. "The Communist Golden Rule: Take advantage of others before they do it to you."

*

In the crew compartment, Paisan Veracruze was folding up his winnings for the evening. He and Muhlbach had cleaned up and routed all the opposition, and Paisan felt very tired. He counted his money: $212. Not bad for a night's work, and besides, he thought, it took his mind off other things, the things that would be happening in the next couple of days.

The other players had all gone off to bed, there was some heavy snoring in the crowded bunkroom.

Paisan folded up his money and stuffed it into a leg pocket of his camouflage suit. He stretched and ambled over to the end of the line of bunks where his empty canvas cot was set up. Near it, on the top pole of the three-decker bunks nearest him, he had hung his canteen and pistol belt.

No pistol. Only the canteen and a first-aid kit and ammo clip container on it. He would trust his luck to the Armalite—damn good weapon. He had picked one up from the ship's store, and four clips.

Tomorrow, he would have time to go over all his personal gear, and make sure he knew who had the C-3, and also there would be the matter of rations. As First Sergeant of the unit, he would have to make sure there were enough C-rations for—what was it going to be, two-and-a-half days? Maybe they could use some 5-in-1 or 10-in-l units besides what they'd be carrying in their packs. He reached over and hauled down the big haversack he'd been using as a pillow during the poker game.

Here in the corridor between triple-decker bunks and the crew compartment of the submarine *Mako*, he had everything he needed. And what about the money? He decided he would ask one of the crewmen to send it home to his brother Joe. Joe was five years younger, which made him twenty-one, and he was a lot more deserving of everything than Paisan.

Paisan rolled himself onto his bunk in the aisle between the three-decker beds, and closed his eyes. He kept thinking about his brother Joe, and what would become of Joe. Joe was taller and better-looking than Paisan, not so beat-up, and smarter. He'd be getting that degree at Princeton next June, and then—Paisan grinned to think of it—Joe would have to go into the Army, as a lousy draftee. Joe never could understand why Paisan thought the Army, especially the Green Berets of the Special Forces, was so great. Once or twice, while he was home on furlough, Paisan had tried to tell him what the Green Berets meant to him. He had said that the Special Forces were kind of special, and Joe had laughed and said obviously. And Joe had asked him why it was so wonderful to be in the military service, and what war achieved, and Paisan had repeated what General Yarborough had said one time in a speech back at Bragg, that a man in an outfit with esprit de corps thinks that his squad is the best squad in the company, his company the best in the battalion, the battalion the best in the regiment, and the division the best division in the world.

And Joe had said: "But why do you want to be the best soldier in the best squad, etc.?"

And Paisan had said: "I dunno. Maybe for patriotism?" And Joe had guffawed and said: "So I suppose a sergeant in Napoleon's army had the same idea, when he went out to risk his neck at Jena or Waterloo, or wherever the enemy was at the time."

And Paisan had said, with a sudden flash of inspiration: "I think I do it because it's expected of me. I'm just damn glad that I'm elected to be in the best outfit there is, that's all. Doesn't that make sense to you?"

And Joe had laughed. "Yeah, maybe if the outfit was something special, like a team of doctors or architects setting out to do some good somewhere. But not to do the best job of destruction."

And the inspiration was still with Paisan, and he had said: "So supposing you're not in a good military outfit, where you're all sharp and in good training and ready for anything, like the Special Forces, what do people do instead: They get married, get kids, do a nine-to-five job and knock themselves out for the kids and die. Is that better than being in the best squad in the best outfit in the American Army, the Special Forces, and being ready to prove you're the best soldier in the world? Maybe it's not so dumb. Anyhow, it's better than getting fat and puffy."

"You have a point there," Joe said.

Paisan was reminded of a fundamental proposition he had subscribed to long ago, that it takes will and training to keep in condition, and he got up and walked down the line of bunks to a relatively open place and started doing push-ups. Pretty soon he decided he would try the hardest one of all, the one-armed push-up, and he did that laboriously, but triumphantly, five times.

On the cot nearest that end of the room, Muley Muhlbach lay on his back witnessing Paisan's display of strength, through half-closed lids. Of all the enlisted men in this detachment, Muley was the lowest in rank, and the youngest. He was a PFC, twenty years old, and he and the other PFC, Jim Trotter, were the only ones who hadn't seen combat in Vietnam. But Muley had been one of the outstanding graduates of the Special Force training school at Fort Bragg, and Muley knew his being assigned to Typhoon was a considerable recognition of his talents as a soldier.

In an army of professionals that had been trained in Vietnam, he would have been a natural for the freewheeling Special Force duty along the Laotian and Cambodian borders, but he was just too late for that. With his record of sixty parachute jumps, high scores in every branch of Special Force activity, including demolition, weapons, medical care, and communications, he would have been a splendid addition to any one of the Green Beret groups sent out to organize the Vietnamese local troops into militia bands to stop the infiltration of Communists.

Two earlier episodes when he exhibited cool-headedness were duly noted by the lieutenant, and also Muley's extra skills in all the branches of Special Force training, and in his speciality, which was demolition. When the urgent call came to the Special Force headquarters for five qualified enlisted men, Muley was one of the chosen. This once, the Army selection system, supposed to pick the best trained men for the job, had worked. Or had it? Muley wasn't so sure since he had never before been in action. Didn't they say that you could never tell until the guns went off in anger? Then, they said, people you would never expect to be heroes would come into their own. He hoped he would be one of those lucky ones.

At the same time he would have to admit that he was petrified right now. What, after all, were his chances of getting back from this one? Eighteen men—thirteen enlisted and four officers, and that one civilian, what was his name, Musgrave?

What they had to do was pretty damn near impossible. To get through the layer of barbed wire and cyclone fence, to take out the guard around the Shape, to mold the C-3 onto the bomb itself, to use exactly the right amount so it would be a low-order detonation instead of an H-bomb detonation; then, to run out the correct number of feet of time fuse, a foot for every thirty seconds—get back through whatever the Chinese could throw at them and out of the holes before the blast, and somehow get to the submarine and get away through the Hainan Straits defenses—would that be possible? Pretty near impossible, he thought. But maybe Captain Hope, and Commander Wilson, and all these officers and big shots would figure it all out so they could make it.

Muley knew one advantage he had over the older members of Operation Typhoon: that they all had wives and family. If Muley Muhlbach got killed, no grieving wife, no kids without anybody to pay for their education. Only his mama, and his brothers and sisters, aunts and uncles, in Evanston, Illinois. They could take care of themselves. But he was going to get back, anyhow. He knew that.

Muley's reverie was interrupted by two ooga-oogas of the horn on the PA system, and the hurried announcement: "Prepare to dive . . . Prepare to dive . . . DIVE! DIVE!" He sat up on the edge of the bunk and saw life stirring all around him, people jumping out of bed.

"What is it? What's going on?" he asked a submarine crewman who landed next to him after a leap from the top bunk.

The crewman, clad only in skivvy drawers, looked around him in confusion. "I dunno. They must've had a good contact or they wouldn't be diving." He mumbled something. "Can't find my pants. Too many people all over the place."

The sub was going down with the familiar rash of sounds: the banging of hatches, the muffled whoosh rushing of tons of water— then sudden silence as the diesel engines shut off, and the boat switched to battery power.

The seaman went on: "We won't know what happened for a little bit, until the officers tell us."

"That's right," said Muley. "Unless it's Captain Hope." That's the way he should talk about his outfit, which was the best anywhere. And it was true.

15

ALL NIGHT LONG THE *MAKO* HAD BEEN RUNNING SUB merged. At five o'clock in the morning, Commander Wilson was still in the conning tower. Commander Battersby, the Exec, nervously fingered the folding motorcycle-type grips on the main periscope column. Now he called out to Wilson: "Do you think we could snorkel along a little bit, and save some battery juice?"

"The snorkel top will give them a radar blip, and the snorkel makes too much of a commotion in their sonar," Wilson pointed out. "No, we'd better keep submerged. And take our chances on running the batteries out." He walked over to the navigator's desk, and peered over Lieutenant Commander Hammond's shoulder. Hammond was laying out a course and position on the chart.

"Dead Reckoning Tracer puts us right about here, sir. About sixty miles east of Lokwei. If we keep on at this speed, it'll be twelve hours before we're on the Meng Wan coast."

Commander Wilson lit a cigarette. "Then how long before we get to this initial point fifty miles east of Meng Wan, assuming we're still travelling submerged all day long?"

"Well, sir, during the last eight hours, we've averaged only eight knots, with the surfacing and the running submerged and all the contacts we've had. We'll be lucky to make the rendezvous point by six or seven o'clock tomorrow morning."

Wilson said: "We're bound to get contacts, and we've got to play it safe, and stay submerged. How about going this way?" He put a blunt finger on the chart. "If we could take the hypotenuse of this triangle, and run this way directly to Point Meng Wan, we'd be able to make it on time, wouldn't we?"

Commander Hammond said: "But Skipper, how about the screen of patrol boats up there? Pretty damn unsafe."

Wilson said: "It is. But if we're travelling submerged anyhow, it won't be too bad. Wait a minute, though, while I check with the communicator." He picked up the intercom phone and called through to the radio room on the next lower deck. "Lieutenant Bosworth there? Fine. This is the Skipper. Listen, Bosworth, I want to know everything you've had on the unscrambler about the waters north of Cape Tung Ku. Have you noticed anything recent on SR-71 surveillance out of Formosa? It seems to me I saw something to the effect that the Chinese patrol boats were trying to keep it a heavy militarized zone, and were checking over the junks coming through. Do you remember any dispatch like that?"

"Just a minute, sir. I'll check," the receiver crackled. A pause, and the voice came back: "Yes sir, here it is, out of the Operation Typhoon file: 'SR-71s from Trumpet—that's Kaoshiung—consistently reported heavy traffic patrol boats in militarized zone north of Cape Tung Ku. Apparently examining junks and all marine traffic.'

"Is that what you were looking for, sir?"

"Absolutely—Bosworth, thanks."

He hung up the phone and turned to the navigator. "Well, there *is* heavier traffic of coastal patrol boats in that area, but we're going to have to chance it. So redraft the course and we'll try the short side of the triangle, we'll head straight for Point Meng Wan."

By the time the *Mako* had travelled thirty miles closer towards Point Meng Wan, and miraculously had not one contact on her SUBRAD, Driver Pung had long since stumbled home from Mei Ling's room. Now, at seven-oh-two o'clock in the morning, Mei Ling had walked up to the town, and was patiently waiting for the Tau Muk in the ramshackle office suite he occupied in the second floor of the Communist Party headquarters. The male secretary came through the worn door to the inner office, and motioned to her: "All right, Comrade Mei Ling, the Tau Muk will see you now." She walked past the row of suppliants and, with a quick pat to see that her hair was well ordered, and a dexterous flip of the third button on her blue jumper so that an extra few inches of golden skin were visible, she marched into the room.

Tau Muk Nhap Dat was thin, tall, and severe-looking, and he wore the semi-military tunic affected by good Communists. He leaned back in his chair, when Mei Ling came in, and his eyes glittered as she walked towards him. Then he said sternly: "Comrade, you must close the door. This, I take it, is a private matter." And he warned away the male secretary who was at that moment starting to follow Mei Ling into the room. "Cao, leave us alone. It's a secret matter, the Comrade and I must talk privately."

Secretary Cao stopped and backed out of the door. He was unable to suppress a slight knowing smile and the Tau Muk duly noted this. Once the door was closed, he stood up, and came 'round the desk to stand next to Mei Ling. His face was suddenly less severe as he looked down at the golden swell of her bosom. "Very well, Comrade," he said in a voice which belied his affectionate expression. "You are going to give me an official report? Is that it?" Then he bent closer to her, and whispered: "The walls in this room may very well have unknown electronic ears."

"I understand," she said, in the same soft tone, And she went on more loudly: "I do have a very important matter to report, Comrade. It concerns a Driver Pung, who is engaged in carrying freight up to the airfield near Point Meng Wan."

"Good, Comrade," he said, in the same moment plunging his hand inside her blouse. She smiled, and went on in a steady voice:

"I have heard that Driver Pung is under some question. I understand there have been denunciations of his devotion to the common cause by other workers at the airfield." He removed his hand from the front of her dress, and firmly grasped another pleasant curve, that of her trim derriere. He went on in a businesslike voice:

"Yes, Comrade, of course I am interested in maximum performance by workers, and if there is any question about Driver Pung, you must tell me. That is the duty of a good party member."

"Yes, Comrade Commissar," she said, responding with slight pressure to the touch of his hand. "I have some doubt of the propriety of his behavior, and I believe that he should be watched. Let me tell you, Comrade, what I have discovered."

Quickly she went through the things she had learned about Pung: That Pung had a considerable and inexplicable wad of Yuan, that in the moments of amatory excitation last night, he had told her that he had plenty more money coming. She said that unaccounted-for income was alone sufficient grounds for suspicion in a well-disciplined state, and Nhap Dat agreed loudly. Pung had also said that he would bring her a beautiful diamond! That promise had been made in the moments of madness leading to his greatest delight of the evening— and there were a few fragmentary bits of intelligence which she could link together: the mention, several times during the night, of the cordier, Wing On. Pung said that since he had known the cordier, his fortunes had come up in the world. Pung said that because he knew the cordier, he could promise her, Mei Ling, plenty of beautiful presents like the chickens on the free market.

The Party Chief, trying hard to keep his voice steady in the midst of high-grade *maau* maneuvers, said these were indeed valuable bits of information, and he would certainly take the matter under advisement. He promised Mei Ling a good-sized reward of Yuan if the information proved to be valuable, and said he would deliver the reward himself. Even though it was intelligence money, to be paid for valuable information, nevertheless it would give him a special pleasure to be able to give it to her. At that moment, he was indicating his earnestness through a hand skillfully slipped inside the elastic waistband of her jumper trousers, his fingertips trying to sound her curves like a flute.

At this moment in Mei Ling's conversation with the local commissar, the cordier Wing On, and his son Wing Run had walked the four miles from his home behind the cordier shop in Hoihow to a farmhouse on the shore of Point Meng Wan. There, old Dinh, who grew the best jute anywhere on Hainan, had a farm of 120 *mo*.

Wing On and Run came upon Dinh in the jute field nearest to the dirt road. A wiry, resilient man of fifty-five, Dinh was directing two workers in the job of repairing an irrigation foot-pump.

The cordier called across the irrigation canal to Dinh. Dinh started, as if electrified, at the mention of his name, then he bounced away from the two workers and rushed to the bank of the ditch.

"Comrade Wing! I'm glad you came to see me. Do you have some important news?"

Wing called out, smoothly: "Nothing more important than that I have urgent need for a new shipment of cordage." The tension in Dinh's body seemed to ease. He smiled broadly.

"Then, Comrade Wing, come around the divider at the end of this field, and we will have a logistic conference."

Dinh hopped back to the repair work on his pump. Wing and Run walked over a narrow plank bridge across the ditch, Run pausing momentarily to survey the wide, orderly expanse of fields—jute, the rich green of rice paddies, and the heavy, nodding sugar cane. Dinh bounded over to meet Wing On and Run as they stepped down from the bridge. "One of my pumps was ailing," he explained, breathlessly. "Now it is repaired. May I invite you to a cup of tea at my abode? There is much to talk about—" He shot an appraising glance back towards the two workers at the foot-pump, saw that they were bending concentratedly over the machinery, and went on: "More than just your need for a fresh crop of rope."

"Yes, Comrade Dinh," Wing said, "there's much to be done, especially today, and tonight."

Dinh led the way back along a yellow-green rice trail, along the mud dike of a rice padi, where the rice plants of a coming crop were beginning to sprout a pale-jade sea, and then through rows of half-grown sugar cane, their tasselated heads bobbing in the brisk breeze.

"Such a kingdom as this," said Run, "a man could dream about—in a non-Communist state."

Wing On smiled. "Such dreams had better be silent ones in a nation run by Big Brother."

They crossed another rice field and came to a homely clump of buildings with bamboo walls and thatched roofs.

The house was luxurious, for South China: Instead of a dingy mud floor, it had a wooden surface which was actually clean and shiny. The visitors left their shoes in the porch alcove, following the Japanese custom. During the long Japanese occupation, from 1939 to 1945, Japanese agricultural officials had lived in the house—permitting Dinh to operate the farm—and had left unmistakable signs of Nipponese influence. Dinh would say in confidential moments with Wing, that he had survived two occupations—first the Japanese, now the Communists, and that of the two the Japanese were less cruel.

Dinh had a small plastic radio, a violent pink color, which he turned on, following the universal espionage counter-bug technique.

✳

His wife, bowing to the guests, went out to arrange the tea, and the radio blared music from the Kiungchow government station.

Wing spoke against the roar of the triumphal People's Chorus: "Did you send the message?"

Dinh nodded: "And we had a message in return. They are concerned about the lateness of the hour. They feel that they may be too close to daylight. But they don't understand the method in our thinking—that the junk is to come in with the fishermen at daybreak, that too early an arrival at our pier here at the farm would be suspicious."

Wing had a quick answer: "You'd better send them another message, when you can, in cipher code, as soon as you are able. And you had better clarify that this is to be a fishing junk apparently coming back from the previous day's work."

Dinh's wife came in carrying two earthenware cups filled with steaming green tea. She bent over and whispered in his ear.

"My wife says that a detachment of Chek-koh police in plainclothes have stopped on the road outside to talk to my workers—the same who were earlier repairing the pump in that field."

Wing moved to the open doorway so that he could see the field in question. A muddy Red Star sedan had pulled up to the wooden bridge over the irrigation ditch. He could see three men in blue workclothes talking to the workers. His face was drawn with concern. "I have had reason to worry about one of my people, one Driver Pung," he said. "I will have to talk to him today and ascertain whether he has been injudicious in his pursuit of information for us, or worse than injudicious. The man talks too much, he has the discretion of a pig."

Dinh stepped to a window to watch the Chek-koh people. "They seem to have finished their questioning, they are crossing the bridge to the car. They are turning around and heading back up the road."

"Evidently they feel no need to come up and arrest us," Wing said. "Nevertheless, I will talk to Pung and find out how much he has been talking."

Wing knew there wasn't any time to spare. He must reach Comrade Pung.

Wing was hurrying when he reached the Man Cheung section of Hoihow where he and Driver Pung both Jived. He had equipped himself with a coil of stout rope which he carried prominently in his hand, to justify the visit publicly, and to satisfy the curiosity of the block warden.

Wing spotted Mei, Pung's wife, leaning over a string of washing. She saw him, too, and he caught a glimpse of the bleak unfriendly look which crossed her face. He guessed that stupid Pung had used the money to get drunk, maybe worse, and she was blaming Wing for this—rightfully so, in part.

Wing, making a display of his business for the benefit of the neighbors, called out: "Madame Pung! I am bringing some rope for your husband. Is he at home?"

Her look of hostility was replaced by one of polite attention. "He is here, Comrade Wing. But he is asleep. He is going to work at one o'clock this afternoon. I'd better not wake him."

At that moment, Driver Pung appeared in the window beside his wife, and called out in his habitually fortissimo voice: "Come up, come up, Comrade Wing. My good baggage of a wife doesn't know how to be hospitable. Come up, come up."

By this time, the heads of a half-dozen men and women were extending from the windows of the tenement building. Wing On held out the rope at arm's length, making a display of it. "I'm bringing the rope you wanted."

Wing On said it was essential that he see Pung, and that Pung come with him immediately. The driver, in undershirt and work trousers, and still tousle-haired and hung-over from the night's dissipation, could sense the urgency of Wing's tone. Pung went out on the street with him, mumbling apologies to his "little chicken."

Pung, running true to form, blabbed out the story of his conflict with his wife before they had moved a hundred meters: "My little chicken-baggage thinks I'm a blaggard today," he said. "And she's right." He looked thoroughly miserable and repentant. "I went off with a friend and we raised inferno with two town baggages. We drank *ko leung* and the baggages took my money."

Wing On watched him sharply. "Did you tell them how you got the money?"

"No, Comrade, do you take me for a magpie? Do you think I go about blabbing my secrets?"

Wing On studied him. "Did you mention your friend Wing On?"

Wing could see Pung was disturbed anew. "Well, I told Mei Ling that you were a friend—but nothing more, nothing important. I—I spoke highly of you. I said you were a fine friend and an admirable man."

"And you said nothing about our—relationship?"

"No, Comrade Wing, do you take me for a donkey?"

Wing tried not to react to that suggestion. "And how did you explain your money to Mei Ling? Did you tell her that I gave it to you?"

There was a sharpness in his tone and Pung felt the menace. Wing saw a wave of fear cross the crude peasant face. "I told her nothing about where the money came from."

"But you did mention my name in the course of the evening, a few times?" Now Wing was beginning to understand why the Chek-koh might have been at the farmhouse—and, it occurred to him, perhaps they were checking him at the moment. He looked behind him. Two sturdy peasant types in black sharkskin were walking together, about ten meters behind. They looked suspiciously like Chek-koh detectives. They were in the correct age group, of eligible military age, they had the look of being physically fit and alert. He hurried on: "And this Mei Ling, is she the sweetheart of the village chief?"

Pung appeared more stricken than ever. "The sweetheart of the village chief? Oh, no, Comrade Wing, that wouldn't be possible. She is just a—just another baggage who takes money for favors—and causes upsets in happy households like mine. I'm sure she doesn't know the village chief. She and her roommate work in the rice commune. She is one of the office workers. They take on men as a sideline." It was clear that misgivings were swarming over Pung in visible profusion. "No, Comrade, I don't think she even *knows* the village chief."

Wing On nodded. He glanced to the rear and noted that the two men in black were keeping a fixed distance behind them. "Let's cross here." He guided Pung's arm and directed them across the muddy street. "And the roommate of Mei Ling, her name was Kei Ying?"

"Do you know something about them, Comrade Wing? If you do, please tell me."

Wing shook his head. "And so Mei Ling was your friend for the evening. And you told her nothing about me, except that you admired me as a friend, is that correct?"

Pung moved diagonally in front of Wing, so that Wing had to stop. Pung was so disturbed that he stood firmly like a tank trap. "Please, Comrade Wing, you must believe me. I have done nothing to cause any trouble. All I told you is true. I said nothing about you except that you are a friend." His eyes were pleading, the eyes of a Bassett-hound. "And remember—my four children. They must not be deprived of—parental support. Remember. Please."

Wing stepped beside him and took his arm. "Come on, Comrade Pung, we must not attract attention. Walk along with me as if we were—friends. Do not—demonstrate. Did you know that we are being followed? Don't look back."

Pung walked meekly along beside him. Wing noted that the two trailers had pursued them down the alley, and were maintaining a consistent distance behind.

Pung was talking fast: "Do not be hasty, Comrade Wing. No harm has been done. No one has been following me, until just now. You need not worry, Comrade Wing. I have said nothing, and I *will* say nothing. That is my promise, Comrade. Believe me, Comrade Wing."

Again, he began to move into Wing's path. "Was that the reason that you came to see me, Comrade? You were concerned, was that it, Comrade?"

Wing said, speaking very low: "Walk along beside me, Pung. Walk along calmly—like a friend." His voice was authoritative. "The two men following us are still there. We will go back to your house. Later on in the day, when you come back from work, you must contact me. You must tell me what is going on at the base, if you drive there today."

Pung was relieved. His face brightened. "Then, everything is all right? Thank you, Comrade Wing, you are not going to do—anything, are you? I will say nothing to anyone. You may be sure."

Wing kept looking ahead as they walked. "Do not be—animated," he said. "Simply walk along beside me. And do not talk too much." He didn't like to look at a man he was planning to kill. He had killed men before but he did not like to be reminded that they were human beings with wives and children like this loutish driver. And he must be very careful.

Now he was saying: "Remember, my friend, if they should come to you between now and tonight, remember, you must deny everything they accuse you of. And tell them nothing about me, or the information you have passed on. Understood?"

Driver Pung nodded soberly, like a schoolboy learning his lesson.

Wing On smiled, forced a laugh. "Well, Comrade Pung, let's go back to your house," he said loudly. "Let's have one more cup of tea before I go back to work." He turned them back towards the main street, and in the same moment he reached into his pocket to grasp the small red-and-black capsule of cyanide, barbiturate, and phenolphthalein.

Pung was positively expansive. "By all means, Comrade Wing. And we should do better than tea. I have still some *Ko leung*."

"Yes," said Wing absently. "And I must give you some more money to replace the funds which you—perhaps foolishly—spent on the ladies and refreshments last night. You must promise not to be so unwise with your wife in regard to these funds."

"Oh, yes, yes, I promise, Comrade." And Wing was thinking: He will have half an hour before his heart attack. That time factor is a fixed quantity. I must simply hope that the Chek-koh don't get to him before that—and I must leave well before he has the seizure.

He wondered if the Chek-koh were following *kirn*, or Pung. Either could be the case, or both. He had never before felt the breath of the Communist Secret Police this close on his neck, during the six months he had been collecting information, and relaying it to Eddie Ming in Hong Kong. It was a wonder to him that with the frequent broadcasting done by Dinh on his shortwave radio, in cipher code, none of the transmissions had been intercepted. Now, with the vast concentration of police surveillance which came with the establishment of the bomb base, things were different. He hoped that there would be room on that submarine when they came back to pick up the raiding party, for his wife, his son, Wing Run, and him. Certainly the great United States government would be able to help him.

16

THE GOOD LUCK OF THE *MAKO* IN AVOIDING CHINESE
patrol boats ended shortly, at eight-fifty-two Hong Kong-Hainan
time, eight minutes before the scheduled airdrop.

Eric Hope had assembled the Operation Typhoon detachment in
the after-torpedo room, and with a hand-drawn map of the layout of the
Chinese base, he had been going over a tentative plan for the raid, which
was predicated on the division of the force into two units—one, the
covering force, which would supply fire cover if and when needed,
and the other the attack group, which would breach the Communist
defenses.

He had been saying: "This geography is very tentative, and the
whole plan of action is subject to change. I want you to know that this
will probably be different after we look at the ground."

At that moment, the PA system sounded: The rapid-paced ding-
ding-ding-ding of the General Quarters alarm, and a tense, high-
pitched voice: "General Quarters, General Quarters, All hands man

your battle stations." There was a scurrying and thumping of feet as men jumped from their bunks. Then, Commander Wilson's voice, fast-paced but calm: "We have our first solid radar contact with an enemy PC. It's evidently a Chinese Communist patrol boat, about 3,000 yards away. Bearing 85 degrees true. We've delayed as long as possible because of the airdrop. But now we have no choice. We'll try to set up the airdrop for later in the day. We're going to submerge to 300 feet because the contact will probably be dropping depth charges."

In the conning tower, above and forward of the torpedo room, Commander Wilson hopped to the desk where Lieutenant Hammond was marking a course on the Hainan chart. "How much depth have we got right here, Stan?"

"I make it 600 feet here, sir. We haven't got to the coastal shelf yet."

Commander Wilson jumped back to the telephone near the forward periscope tube. "Sonar? What kind of a reading have you got on this vessel? Would you say three screws? . . .Thanks."

The deck tilted downwards under his feet. He moved to the PA phone and spoke for the benefit of the crew: "Our contact appears to be a Chinese patrol boat. He's closing the range. We're rigging for quiet running."

Commander Wilson hopped back to the SUBRAD operator's desk. "Have you got a better blip yet? What can you get in your tuning?"

The radar man answered without taking his eyes away from the hood. "It looks like a good-sized PC, Maybe 100—125 feet long."

The skipper said: "He's evidently got Sonar gear, because he's got a vector on us. Thank God the Chinese haven't got SUBRAD."

He jumped back to the phone and dialed the Control Room number. "Negative tanks full? . . . Good. Five degree negative bubble? Keep it there. What's your reading from Sonar on bearing and range? 1200 yards? Bearing 90? . . . Good. We'll get away. Better make it 400 feet, to be sure."

He hopped back to the navigator's table. "Do you think we've got about 500 feet here?"

Before Hammond could answer, they heard the first faint crunch of a depth charge. "He's got an itchy trigger finger," Wilson said. "We won't have any trouble with this one, he's green." Wilson's long background of submarining, stretching back through the Korean War, had made him ready for the surprises of a fight.

He jumped back to the sound-power telephone and dialed the Control Room: "Give me the Cob, please . . . Cob, make it hard right rudder, about two minutes of power, then shut down. We'll submerge to 400. I think we'll be able to lose this vessel. He's too anxious. Or maybe his Sonar is no good."

"Aye, aye, sir."

Commander Wilson jumped back to the SUBRAD operator. "What's your plot?" The operator, his face still buried in the hood, pushed a clipboard towards the Captain: "I make him out to be 1,000 yards out, still bearing ninety. He's closing."

"He's still not close enough," Wilson said. "He's on the right track, but he won't be by the time he gets here. We'll be out of the way."

The Captain hurried to the navigator's plot board. He pointed to a straight line Lieutenant Commander Hammond was placing with a protractor-ruler. "Is this our DRT?"

The navigator, busily scribbling figures on a piece of scratch paper, nodded.

Wilson said: "Chart shows only sixty-six fathoms here—that's just short of 400 feet."

Hammond turned away from his arithmetic: "You're right, sir. I wasn't watching depth. We're coming up on a bank—"

Wilson hopped back to the telephone, switched to Control Room. "Control?—Quickly—what's your Sonar depth reading? . . . 360 feet?" He hurriedly switched again: "Diving officer? We don't have any clearance. Better blow the negative tank. Quickly, and give me two degrees positive bubble." From the distance, came another 'crump' as a second depth charge went off. This time it was louder than the last.

The SUBRAD operator called out: "He's 800 yards out, Captain, bearing 135." At that moment, there was a thud underneath them, the boat shook. The Captain looked over at Hammond, saw that the navigator was puzzled. "We hit bottom," Wilson said. He looked at the steel bulkhead. "I wish I knew what was out there—if we're in mud, or rocks. We can float free, but we can't use power—he'd zero in on us."

In the after-torpedo room, Captain Hope's group had halted and were listening for sounds on the intercom. Hope had heard the two explosions—they sounded like distant mortar bursts to him—and he surmised that they were depth charges, even though they didn't follow the pattern he had seen on TV, in submarine movies, with lights flickering and the sub tilting. The third thud, which was the grounding of the metal hull on the bottom, he was at a loss to understand. "I read those two bangs as depth charges," he said, trying to carry out his policy that the troops should be informed on developments. "I don't know what the third noise was—the one that seemed to come from underneath. One thing is certain: We seem to have blown the airdrop. Maybe we can rig it for later in the day. Otherwise, it'll be M-16s, one bow-and-arrow, and some stinking C-3 for us."

They were simply sitting and waiting. When the fans shut off and the whirr of the air-conditioning stopped, he felt constrained to interpret: "I think this is the 'quiet running' the Captain was talking about. I guess he's trying to throw off the patrol vessel, And it'll probably get hot here."

*

At the same moment, in Hong Kong, Arthur Lowery and Freeman Blake were sitting in a Morris sedan outside the front gate of an estate in Big Wave Bay. The highway curved close to the entrance, and their position was seventy-five feet removed from the entrance, the skirt of the road.

After Mary Wu's ring to report Chen Yu's phone number, Lowery had used the services of Colonel Morgan, the military attache who had a contact in the British Intelligence, for the telephone check.

Now Lowery's car sat on the edge of the highway, with a clear view of the tall concrete gateposts marked G. M. Barkham. Lowery had kept the house under surveillance beginning shortly after ten when he had located the phone number. The tail had phoned him at home a few minutes ago that someone looking like Chen Yu had just driven into the Barkham driveway. Freeman and Lowery had piled into one of the Morrises and hurried over.

First, two of Lowery's bright young FBI types had gone out in two cars to stake out the house. They had seen a Chinese with Chen's distinctive physiognomy and physique drive into the Barkham's house, alone in a gray Bentley. One agent had watched the gate while the other drove to the nearest phone.

Now, the two agents had stationed themselves at vantage points half a mile in both directions along the highway, and they were standing by while Lowery and Blake continued the stake-out at the house.

"Assuming he comes out that drive in his Bentley," Blake was saying, "what do you figure will be the course of action?"

"There are only two ways he can go on the highway: either down towards Big Wave Bay or the other way, back toward Repulse Bay. Santos and Nicholson are alerted to start the minute they see us on somebody's trail, and get out in front of him. Then we can box him in when the right time comes."

"And when we box him in, what then?"

Lowery seemed pained. "Plan is to get him out of the car and into one of ours, as inconspicuously as possible. We don't want the police to be in this."

"And we take him up to the house and work him over, is that it?"

"I don't think it'll come to that. From what we know of Chen, he can be purchased once we get to talk to him."

"What if he has some strong-arms with him—like the toughs who trailed Musgrave and Hope?"

"We'll have to take our chances on that," Lowery said. "There will be four of us, that should be enough for three or four Chinamen."

Blake swallowed and his eyelids lowered, "Sounds possible." He squinted towards the tall concrete gateposts. "And I think I see the Bentley coming now."

The long, shining gray Bentley wheeled out of the gate and turned towards Lowery and Blake. The driver was alone in the car.

"That's him," Blake had seen Chen only once before but he remembered him.

Lowery started the little Morris. In his attempt to be conservative and undistinguished in Hong Kong, he had accidentally chosen a car more than a match for the Bentley on any roadability contest, the Morris 1100, which happened to have one of the sportiest of all suspensions, the so-called Hydrolastic. Lowery didn't know this, though it would have been apparent to any car bug like Eric Hope or Hank Musgrave.

When Chen gunned his big Bentley, he did it with a vengeance, as if he had seen the Morris sitting in the shadows of the road. He jammed down his accelerator so sharply that the tires screeched.

Lowery flung the steering wheel hard over and whipped the car into a U-turn at the moment the big car shot past. And since there was no secret now about his intention, he shoved his hand down hard on the horn and kept it there. Ahead, on the road toward Repulse Bay, he saw that his warning was heeded by Santos, the agent on the other end of the stake-out. On the slope heading down to the water, he saw Santos' dark-green Morris pull out into the roadway and mosey along with one wheel on the white center line.

His foot pushed hard on the accelerator, Lowery could see the other Mortis, alerted by the honking, coining up behind him. The car was charging over the crest of the hill from the east. That would be Nicholson from the opposite extreme of the trap.

Ahead, the gray Bentley was barreling towards Santos' Morris. Lowery could see the neat seersucker shoulders of Santos at the wheel. Beyond Santos' car, two autos had appeared over the next hill, and Chen was racing to get past Santos before they closed the gap, The Bentley waddled onto the right side of the road, and Lowery saw Santos edging farther over the center line.

The foremost of the two oncoming cars was an open Lotus, and he was moving with great speed. Santos saw the situation and held his position. The bulk of the Bentley swayed like a fat, angered bee, held unsteadily on the right side of the road for a moment before the on-rushing Lotus, then abandoned the project. Santos flicked the Morris back out of the way of the Lotus, held the car there because the second oncoming car, a slow sedan of ancient vintage was drawing close. Chen tried again, unwisely, pushing into the right-hand lane.

The Bentley fishtailed as Chen hesitated, then slipped back into his proper line, behind Santos. In the moment's time, Lowery had closed up and in his rear-view, he could see the green Nicholson car coming down the hill from the east.

Chen's broad yellow face flashed as he turned to survey the situation behind him. "Looks like we've got him," Blake said. "And he knows it."

Lowery said nothing; he was busy edging around the Bentley, nosing his small car toward the shining hump of the Bentley's fender. With surprising skill for a man who knew little of driving, he held the left fender of the Morris only inches away from the Bentley's mammoth metal hip, then began closing the gap.

Chen glanced in Lowery's direction, Lowery saw the moustached face, saw a surprising expression—a calm acceptance. From the corner of an eye, Lowery glimpsed what he thought might be the reason. Next to him, Blake had taken out a P-38 and was holding it at parade rest in front of him. But he wasn't looking in Chen's direction. He was watching the road ahead. However, Chen seemed to understand the message.

Chen swung his arms and the big car edged from the road.

Lowery pulled his Morris in behind the Bentley, Santos stopped in front, and in his rear-view mirror, Lowery could see the green Morris of Nicholson coming to a stop a hundred yards to the rear. Nicholson was smart: Three men could handle Chen, and the main danger would be of reinforcements who might be coming up to help him.

Lowery saw Chen sitting calmly in his car, not moving. He looked back, and there was something like a smile beneath the moustache. "Better duck the gun," he told Blake. "We don't want trouble with the police. And I think he's going to be easy to handle."

"Okay," Freeman said. "Give me a yell if you see him move. And I'll watch him from this side."

Lowery walked up on the driver's side, and Blake approached from the other. Santos was coming up from the front of the car, warily.

But their precautions were unnecessary. When they came up to the front seat, Chen was still sitting motionless behind the wheel. Now he was smiling broadly as he spoke to Lowery: "I've been waiting for you, Mr. Lowery. Believe I have information interesting to you. Perhaps we could make business arrangement."

"Of course, Mr. Chen," Lowery said.

*

On the coastal shelf of Hainan Island, twenty-four miles from Cape Tung Ku, the black cigar-shape of the *USS Mako* lay in the luxuriant bottom growth of the shallow South China Sea. Within the inner core of her hull, inside the chamber that held a thousand tons of water to anchor her in the deep, 117 Americans waited in yellow incandescent light for the attacking Communist patrol boat to continue its assault.

Since the fans and air-conditioning remained shut off, and the temperature had risen to 100 degrees, Commander Wilson, standing in the conning tower, had undone the top two buttons of his shirt and removed his cap.

The SUBRAD operator called out to Wilson, who was at the moment leaning over Commander Hammond's shoulder at the navigator's table: "Captain, I have him going away. He's on a relative bearing of 145 degrees. He's turned and is heading south." As if to punctuate the information, there was a distant thud, fainter than the previous two, from the sea to the south of the submarine.

"Maybe we're losing him," Wilson said to Hammond. Wilson stepped to the PA system phone: "To All Hands—and our guests. This is the Captain. We seem to have shaken the Communist bugger. But we're going to have to lie doggo for a few minutes longer, until we're sure. We might even be able to turn on the air-conditioning again, pretty soon."

In the after-torpedo room, the men of Captain Hope's detachment heaved an audible sigh. Hope said, voicing a thought which had probably been in all their minds during the depth bombing episode: "Damn unsafe business, this submarining."

Old Sergeant Bissell said what also was expected: "They can have this fuckin' submarine business. I'll take somethin' safe like Special Forces." The group laughed politely at the familiar joke.

Captain Hope thumped on the map which he had stuck to the bulkhead with scotch tape. "We might as well begin again." As if to substantiate his decision, the overhead fan in the compartment started to whirr, and the air-conditioning was humming once more.

The PA system crackled: "Captain speaking. We'll hold this position without turning on our power for half an hour more. Our friend upstairs will be chasing around for a while trying to find another ping. We can't take a chance of giving him another but, by way of public information, we are on schedule with our approach to Hainan. We even have a hour or two to spare, in case we run into further trouble."

*

In Driver Pung's house in Hoihow, Wing On sat at a table while Mei, Pung's wife, set out two cups, and Pung approached with the cobwebby bottle full of *Ko leung*. There were still a few ounces of the yellow sorghum liquor in the bottom of the bottle.

Pung put the bottle down and declaimed loudly. "We must drink a toast to our friendship, Comrade Wing."

"Yes," Wing said. "But first, you must take a look out the window, Comrade Pung, and see if our unwanted friends are still following us." Pung nodded and started for the window, his cup in his hand.

Wing, still sitting at the table, carefully stopped him. "Wait a minute, Comrade. Better not carry the cup, the evidence of our drink, to the window. It is very poor tactics to advertise breaking of a law—and drinking during working hours is a clear violation in this well-disciplined state. Leave the drink behind."

Pung put the cup on the table, apparently not considering that the cup would more than likely be interpreted as only tea, if anyone outside should see it.

Pung squinted into the bright sunlight of the street below. "Our two friends are not down there, Comrade Wing."

"Take a very thorough look, Pung. They may be in any corner down there. Make a thorough search with your eyes." Wing was gratified to see that Pung's wife was going out of the room.

Wing had the small capsule in the fingers of his left hand, and was taking it out of his pocket. Momentarily, he thought about Pung's children—were there five or six?—and he heard infant laughter on the stairs below. At the same time it occurred to him that if he killed Pung, he would have no source of information at the bomb storage house at the airfield, and this matter could be critical, with the Americans arriving tonight. They would need all the information they could get about the geography of that installation. Wing hesitated with the pill. Should he take a chance, and not kill Pung? Maybe Pung would not be bothered by the Chek-koh. The Communist police were usually clumsy in investigating things—heavy-handed and inefficient. They might botch up the whole investigation. They frequently did—they were human.

Mei, Pung's petite wife, burst into the room with two rollicking young sons, who were flung ahead of her as if in a projection of her movement, and they were throwing a ball at the centrifugal extremity of her line of force. She was occupied, now, with taking the ball away from them, and Wing could still perform the clandestine movement with his left hand, dropping the capsule into Pung's cup. But he didn't. He hesitated. He called out to Pung: "Comrade, why don't you see if they are in the block warden's house across the street?"

Mei had corralled the ball, and one of the boys, abruptly flung his short arms and legs around his mother's legs. There was something familiar about the gesture, which reminded Wing of Run when he was three or four. The moment passed. Wing let the capsule slip back into his pocket, and he reached into another pocket with his right hand and extracted a roll of yuan. He walked to the window and stood in the sun with Pung. It was true that there was no visible evidence of the two detectives now. Wing summoned Pung back to the table. "Come back and we will drink a *kanpei*." he said. "I have some more yuan for you, and we want to see you tonight, remember? With a visual report about the airbase house we are interested in."

Mei was wiping a smudge of dirt from the cheek of the older boy, preparing to feed the children: "Masters, I will bring you some fine chicken soup."

Pung shouted: "And don't we get some 'nice chicken,' wife? Comrade Wing and I—"

Wing interrupted him: "No, thank you, Comrade. I must hurry along to another appointment. Let us *kanpei* and I will go." They stood by the table and downed their drinks. Wing pressed a wad of fifty-yuan notes into Pung's hand. "Spend it more wisely than last time," he said. "Buy your wife a present."

Pung bounded toward his wife and seized her with a gorilla embrace. "My little chicken," he enthused. "I'm not really such an evil man, am I?"

Wing quaffed his drink and made for the door. As he left, he said: "Remember your promise, Pung. And we will be seeing you later in the day."

Wing was berating himself as he went out the door. He was really too tenderhearted. He would never make a good espionage agent, balking at the execution of a mere lout like Pung, But that was probably why he was doing right to plan escape to Hong Kong. He had too much of a soft heart to live among the Communists. Compared to him, they were Attila or at least, Ghengis Khan.

In the Mandarin Hotel room of Freeman Blake—Lowery naturally had not wanted to bring Chen Yu in to the headquarters at the Croy mansion overlooking Deepwater Bay—Chen Yu lounged in a chair. Opposite him sat Blake and Lowery, agents Nicholson and Santos overlooking, and against the background of music from the hotel radio system, Chen was telling his story.

". . . So, gentlemen, I was retained by the People's government to carry on my noble profession of smuggling—smuggling, as you know, being an honorable pursuit and even encouraged by the British Intelligence section, also by the Americans.

"I would be glad to discuss my business arrangements with the Communists, but those arrangements are indeed, for the moment at least, confidential. The People's Republic has paid me very well, and for passing their secrets to the other side, I would expect an even better reward."

To gain the point, he said, "If I am to be a merchant, I should display some samples of my wares. Is that correct?"

Lowery nodded and turned up the volume on the radio slightly. "Go ahead."

Chen continued. "As a workroom sample, would this be sufficient? A list of the items brought in from Hong Kong for the Chinese installation in Hainan, the route of delivery, the dates of delivery—" He paused, looked around deliberately at all the faces as if to signal that this was going to be his major offering: "And the construction and strength of the hydrogen bomb of the People's Republic in the airfield installation near Hoihow. You gentlemen probably didn't know it, but there have been five shipments of items into the hydrogen bomb base. I have a full list of those shipments, and on the second shipment of batteries, I was able to accompany the shipment and observe the bomb." He added as a clincher: "And confirmation that the bomb is to be dropped on October sixteenth!"

Lowery smiled his wan smile. "Very good. And you can be sure that we will make it worth your while financially."

Blake cautioned: "Of course, we will have to be given time to evaluate the information, to figure out exactly how much of it we already possess, and to check it for authenticity."

Chen glared at him, and Lowery added a palliative word: "Only standard procedure, Mr. Chen. Nothing to worry about, and the reward will be there." And Lowery was thinking: Blake's instinct for economy is always tripping him up. He called out to Santos: "Did you bring your shorthand pad?" Santos nodded, and moved in to sit beside Chen on the couch, ready to record.

One hour later, Blake and Lowery, with Santos and Nicholson following, emerged from the front entrance of the Mandarin. Freeman, cautious as usual, had a warning: "It could be this guy is full of malarkey. Maybe double-agenting, too."

Lowery thought it over: "But what he told us seems to check out with what we got from all other sources. Also there's considerable brand new stuff."

"Do you think it'll be worth eight thousand dollars, U.S.?"

"He says it's an improvement over the five thousand he got from the People's government."

"Five thousand minus about a third he added for psychological effect," Freeman said. He added, with palpable respect: "The Chi-Coms are pretty wise with their money."

"Looks to me as if we'll get a bargain for our eight," Lowery said in clipped tones, as if to end discussion of the subject. He and Blake turned one way, Santos and Nicholson, according to their instructions, went in the other as if they were not in the same group. As Blake and Lowery climbed into Lowery's Morris, Freeman was still beset with doubts.

"Shouldn't we be sending off this dope about the Shape to the Typhoon party in Hainan? And also, right away, to Washington?"

"No problem to Washington. We'll have to see how much we can get through to the sub, now. She's practically on the beach at Hainan."

17

AS SUCH THINGS USUALLY GO IN WAR, THE *MAKO* DIDN'T
have its maximum difficulty with the Chinese Communist patrol boat
at the expected moment. The anticipated cataclysm petered into an-
ticlimax—only to explode later, when least expected. The real trouble hit the boat and the one hundred and seventeen souls aboard in
a moment of relaxation, when they thought they had thrown off the
inexperienced pursuer. After lying still on the ocean bottom for twenty-four minutes, the submarine had blown her negative tanks and ris-
en to one hundred and fifty feet depth. At Commander Wilson's order,
she had started engines, and was edging along at five knots under battery power, when it happened.

On the surface, the Communist patrol craft *Yu Min*, command-
ed by a twenty-four-year-old lieutenant in the Coastal Patrol Force,

Hainan District, had given up his depth-charge chase; then, through some innate streak of stubbornness, he had turned back and was almost directly over the *Mako*.

The skipper in question, Lieutenant Jo Li-ren, had decided he could not give up with such an ignominious result. In this, his first action against a hostile submarine, he had completely muffed the job. So he had retraced his watery steps, as well as he could remember them. This might be disastrous to his career, because any unauthorized trips were banned according to the current regulation on excessive use of gasoline in government vehicles and boats—but he was not about to give up, yet.

This time, at about the same spot of ocean surface where his Sonar man had made the first contact, there had been a fresh new, strong signal. The Sonar operator had called out to him: "A firm, loud ping in my machine, Captain—" 'Ping' the international onomatopoetic word among submariners. "A very loud ping, Captain. We must be almost directly above the enemy." They had known it was an enemy, because there were no Chinese subs in the vicinity. Lieutenant Jo, a sliver of a man with the tense energy of an exclamation point, had reacted even more violently than at the time of the last submarine contact. That time, his first encounter with the enemy, he had thrown three brackets of depth charges needlessly, at too great range. Now, with a strong Sonar signal, he knew he might really do some damage, and redeem himself for having wasted fuel and explosive in his first exposure to action. His heart yearned for the sight of oil slick and floating debris.

He bawled out the commands: "Rig Number Two and Number Four launchers! Prepare to fire!"

Scurrying sailors flipped the switches of the two Y-shaped launching cradles nearest the stern.

"Fire!" With two squirts of sound and white smoke, the heavy arms flung the barrel-shaped charges outboard, and they splashed in the PC's churning wake.

Twenty-five fathoms below, the *Mako* was slipping along all oblivious of the deadly ashcans being launched against her. The radar man in the conning tower at the controls of the SUBRAD machine had been troubled with a low ampere reading on his QR7J capacitator and the cloudy sweep behind the indicator of his SUBRAD dial wasn't clearing as it should. He wasn't worried, because the boat had secured from General Quarters five minutes before, and there had been nothing that looked like a blip recently. He was cussing out the capacitator which had caused him so much grief. He'd have to get the chief radar man to come and look into it, quickly—in any situation they couldn't afford to be without the SUBRAD signal. He was trying to make a sparking contact between the two poles of the 7R section with the blade of his screwdriver. His logical conclusions: The SUBRAD capacitator was Goddamn fucking shit —maybe even a shit-fuck.

One deck below, in the Control Room, the Sonar man listened with one earpiece, the other earphone lifted from a sore spot above his left ear. He had stopped, shaken by the tension of the previous hour's activity, to light a cigarette. He wanted to do two things: light a cigarette and rub his ear. And in that second, he heard a violent, loud sound in his one workable earphone: "PING-PING-PING-PING!" He shouted out: "A contact! Must be right overhead."

Farther aft on the same level, Captain Eric Hope had hauled up a case of C-rations and stacked a rectangular mass of the oil-paper-covered boxes on one of the multi-tiered bunks next to him. The men of his detachment spread out along the corridor of the torpedo room. He was saying; "We'll have five-in-one's which Sergeant O'Connor will be hauling ashore for us. But for the expected confusion of our landing operation, each of us will have to have a day's rations in his pack."

Hank Musgrave, his posterior jammed into the narrow angle between the second and third level in a tier of bunks, was watching Hope unfold a list preparatory to calling out the roll for distribution of rations, when the noise came: "CRRRUMMMPPP!," like the violent snap of a sail in a wind squall. In that second, the boat shuddered as if someone had smashed it with a fist from above, the boxes of C-rations bounced from the bunk and cascaded onto the floor, a light bulb exploded with a sharp bang in the overhead and showered flakes of glass onto the heads of the group, and something hot struck Hank on the back of the neck. In the instinctive reaction, he put his right hand on his mastoid and felt something wet. Probably only oil—there was no pain.

On the conning tower deck, Commander Wilson was startled as he heard the blast above and felt the sub shake under the impact. He knew very well what was happening.

He jumped to the telephone and dialed: "Sonar? What have you got?" Another huge CRRASSH! burst above them, and the sub jumped, the lights blinked, and the Captain jumped to the SUBRAD operator's table.

"Don't you have anything?" he barked at the radar man. "Goddamn it, Sonar shows a contact right on top of us." He leaped back to the phone and flicked a number. "Cob—take her down a hundred feet, give it maximum revolutions. Full left rudder! And fast." Again, as in the previous alarms, he leapt to the navigator's desk to check the indicated depth on the chart. In a second, he was back at the phone: "Cob, the chart shows we're got a hundred feet to go. Watch the soundings though, give me a yell if we're nearing one-hundred feet clearance." Another heavy blast came from above, shaking the boat. A black column of liquid squirted from a pipe in the bulkhead. An oil valve had popped. Commander Wilson flipped the switch above it. And in the same movement, he ordered Hammond, the navigator: "Double-check on the depth with your chart, Hammond."

From behind him, Commander Wilson heard the SUBRAD operator call out: "SUBRAD's working again, Captain! I've got the enemy, upstairs. Looks like the same size blip we had before— a PC."

Wilson told Hammond: "It's a good thing we've got some depth right here. Watch the DRT—we're going to try a sharp turn again. But this time, he's right on top of us. He'll probably run out of depth charges before the turn. We'll try to get down before he can load his Y-guns again." Wilson had studied the intelligence photos on the patrol craft of China in the area, and he knew every lump of the forty-meter PC by heart. He knew the armament fixtures could vary greatly, but that the standard forty-meter PC, known to American servicemen by the code name 'Jacky,' had three sets of Y-guns, and this one had apparently just finished firing three braces. It would take a few minutes to roll out the replacement tincans, and in that time, the *Mako* might make her escape again. He thought coolly: That Chinese schoolboy up there is learning fast. What rotten luck to have our SUBRAD go out that moment!

He wondered what damage might have been caused by the charges. Maybe something topside, maybe the top of the sail. He hoped: not the snorkel, please! Because pretty soon he was going to have to do some snorkel-running to recharge his batteries. Today's run submerged had been a severe drain on electrical power.

Wilson dialed the Cob in the Control Room level. "Cob, I want maximum speed while that joker upstairs is recharging his Y-guns. Run out for about five minutes at max revs and make a sharp turn."

"Aye, aye, sir."

He flipped the dial to the Electronics Counter Measures Operator. "Bentley, we've got that PC right on top of us. We're going to run out and try to shake him. Give him the maximum treatment, the RUSE business. This time, we've got to run our screws while we go down. I want his Sonar thrown off good and proper."

"Aye, sir."

*

In the after-torpedo room, the Special Force detachments simply sat and waited. Hank Musgrave carefully wiped the squirt of warm oil from the back of his neck with a handkerchief. The first depth-charge impact had loosened an oil valve, and a black stream was dripping now from the pipe on the bulkhead. Sergeant Bissell, sitting next to him, found it amusing: "New top secret weapon. They pee hot oil on us."

An odoriferous crewman came charging into the compartment, rummaged in the thin locker compartment beneath a bunk, and seized a wrench. Hank asked him: "What's going on?"

The crewman turned back momentarily as he fled, wrench in hand: "Feel the boat shake, sir? We're making max speed to get away from that fucking guy." He was stepping through the hatch, but still talking: "It's another fucking PC. Fucker is right on top of us."

Hank looked up grinning. The extraneous thought darted across his mind: Why is it that servicemen use their favorite word so much more often when they're farthest away from women?

The faces of the Special Force group reflected concern in varying degrees. Hank sensed that this time, the sub was close to being sunk.

The group sat silently. The compartment was empty except for a talker with earphones on his head, and a wired harness supporting a speaking tube. They could read in his face the same tautness which they all felt.

The talker was listening raptly to the chatter on the sub's intercom system. At last, he spoke into the mike: "After-torpedo room aye, aye, sir. Negative report."

Bissell, aggressive as usual, burst out with the question on everyone's mind: "What's goin' on up there in fuckin' heaven, Mac?"

A seaman answered briefly: "Cap'n's going for four hundred feet. Contact's still with us—but his bearing is different, thank God. Cap'n's talkin' about the Commie loading up his Y-guns." He gave his attention to the earphones again. And at that second, two more crashing sounds clanged from beyond the steel hull and above: TRAANG! CRANNK!

The sub shook, like a terrier after a plunge, but the impacts were less violent. Hope said: "That didn't sound so close! Maybe we're shakin' him." In a second, there came a third smash from above, this still fainter than the others.

The talker suddenly volunteered information: "Looks like he's turnin' away."

Silence. The group sat for long seconds, and then, on the PA system, they heard: "Captain speaking. Sounds as if the Commie is turning off. Looks like we shook him this time, too. But we're gonna play it good and safe, and shut down until he's well away from here." There was a measured hesitation, and the calm voice came back: "We took some damage from the first run. We're trying to find out just how much. We're expecting a report pretty soon from Damage Control. As far as we know now, none of the boat's major functions is affected."

On the higher deck, in the conning tower, Commander Wilson put down the intercom phone and turned to the SUBRAD operator: "What are you showing now, SUBRAD? What's he doing?"

SUBRAD still had his eyes fastened on the hood of his electronic device. "Looks like he's going around in a circle, sir. And about one thousand yards off!"

"He probably thinks that he's right over us, and he's looking for oil slick and pieces of submarine." Two more thuds came from outside the hull, and then a third, and this time they were only distant burps.

"Good! Good! He's shooting in a bone yard—and I'd be surprised if he's got any more tincans left. They're probably rationed, like everything else in China."

Substantiation came with the slowly moving seconds: no more crumps and crashes from the direction of the PC. The SUBRAD man reported: "Looks like he's shovin' off, Captain. He's bearing 44-true, and twenty-five hundred yards out. . . ."

"Good."

Commander Battersby came skinning up the access tube from below. He was short of breath. "Looks like we've got damage to the snorkel, Cap'n," he reported.

Wilson scratched his chin. "Not good. Cob says we're almost out of battery juice—too much running at speed. If the snorkel's out of commission, we won't be able to recharge the batteries except by surfacing."

"Let's hope the Commies don't have any good radar round here," Battersby said. "Tonight, we can surface and take care of everything."

"We're going to have to surface before that," Commander Wilson said. "Even if we don't run our engines, there's not enough juice for the air-conditioning and fans for more than an hour or so." He stepped to the navigator's desk and peered over Hammond's shoulder at the chart. "This our position?"

"Nineteen miles off Cape Tung Ku, sir. Right here, the chart shows about four hundred and forty feet depth."

Wilson turned to Battersby. "You better take the Conn, Joe. And bring her up to two hundred feet, easy, and don't use up too much juice. I'm going down to get twenty minutes sleep. It's been a long day's night."

"Okay, I'll watch 'er. And I'll call you in twenty-five minutes. Shall I secure from General Quarters?"

"Yes, you better. The crew had better get what rest they can. In forty-five minutes to an hour it's going to be real bad for a while. Better go back to regular watches, and some of them can get some sack-time, until the next GQ. Meanwhile, maybe we'll take a chance and send through another radio message for an airdrop. We can try, anyhow. And send a runner to pass the word to Captain Hope. He'll be tearing."

Ten minutes later, the Cob called the Conn and reported to Commander Battersby: "We got a rundown on the damage to the snorkel tube, sir. There *is* some. We can't be sure how much until we get near periscope depth and we can run up in the sail structure and have a look. But the snorkel seems to be shut off."

"What's our depth now?" Mentally, Battersby was cussing out the traditional submarine design which renders the sub commander in his conning tower blind as a bat while travelling submerged. His 'eyes' are scattered all over the boat. More than anything else, he has to be a telephone operator: to hang on the telephones constantly to get the dope.

"We make our depth to be ninety feet, sir." The Cob hesitated, and added: "And we've got enough juice for another twenty minutes running."

"Very well. If we shut off the screws and use the electrical power only to run the air-conditioning and fans, how long can we stay down?"

"Maybe an hour," Cob said. "Not enough to last until dark, by a long shot. It's only two-twenty, and it'll still be sunlight when we run out of all power. But if we could surface for a few minutes, maybe we could fix the snorkel fast, we could travel at periscope depth and recharge the batteries, and we can run submerged again."

"Okay, Cob. We'll do that in ten minutes. Meanwhile, see how much more you can find out about the damage to the boat—especially about the snorkel." These old Cobs, Battersby thought, were like mothers to these boats. They knew every damn convolution and wrinkle in them, and Colvin probably has a psychic wave for every bit of damage caused by the enemy's Y-guns. Colvin had been with this boat for eight years.

Battersby bent over the navigator's desk to watch the charting of the boat's position. Hammond looked up from his work. "According to the DRT, we should be damn near in sight of Hainan. If we surface, we should be able to get an upside-down mirage of the mountains, refracted over the horizon. And much too damn close for airdrop monkeyshines."

"We would be just about off Cape Tung Ku, right?" Hammond looked up and Battersby saw that his eyes were red and puffy with fatigue. "How many hours have you been at that damned desk?"

"Since twelve o'clock last night. But I'm not tired."

"Not much, you aren't. I've seen more wide-awake faces on night watchmen at seven A.M. Can Percy Smith relieve you for the next four hours?" Lieutenant Percy Smith was a stand-by navigator on the sub, and he also had the collateral duty of mess officer.

Hammond was not pleased. "If it's an order, sir, fine. But if I have an option, I'd like to stick around and see what's going to happen, right now. I couldn't sleep, anyhow, when we're about to surface in broad daylight off the coast of Hainan. If I have any choice, I'd like to stick with it during the surfacing—and *then* sack out."

"Okay, fine. . . But you'd better get Percy Smith so he'll be primed to take over when you go off."

Battersby hurried back to the ship's telephone and phoned Lieutenant Frisbee, the damage control officer, in the control room below. "Frisbee, this is Battersby at the Conn, and I want you to make sure that main ballast tanks and pumps are all okay. The Cob tells me that there's a negative damage control report except for some trouble in the snorkel."

"Aye, aye, sir. I just talked to the Cob and he told me. You're going to surface and check the damage to the snorkel, right?"

"That's right. But I want you to check all your circuits and pumps before we start blowing our main ballast. If we should have to dive right away, I don't want to be stuck up there with a Commie patrol boat."

"Aye, sir. We'll run over 'em and give you a quick report before we surface."

Battersby called out to the man at the radar hood: "SUBRAD, have you got anything on the scope?"

"Negative, sir." That meant that there was probably no water-craft within three miles range of the submarine.

Then there was the check by telephone with the Sonar operators at the Control Room level. Here, too, a negative result.

Lieutenant Frisbee called back: "Electrician's Mate tells me there are a couple of bum circuits in the main ballast tanks. But we can see how they function when we surface. If the tanks don't clear fast, they might not flood very fast either. Also, we've got a few fuses out. We can fix those fast enough."

"Okay, let me know when you're ready."

In the after-torpedo room, the telephone-talker had relaxed, since the signal to secure from General Quarters had been sounded, and he was waxing much more talkative with the Special Forces people assembled for their briefing. "Commander Wilson has gone off and the Exec has taken the Conn," he announced in the general direction of Hank Musgrave and Sergeant Bissell. "Sounds like he's planning to surface—some trouble with the snorkel he wants repaired. He's running through a check with the damage control officer."

Sergeant Bissell had an instant reaction: "Pretty tough titty comin' up on top when we're so close to China. Ain't we supposed to be practically on the beach?"

The torpedo room talker answered the question: "Nineteen miles off Cape Tung Ku, wherever that's at."

Captain Hope unrolled a chart of the Hainan east coast, spread it on a lower bunk, and the group crowded around him to look. He measured off the distance of nineteen miles due east of Cape Tung Ku. "Not too much water around here. Looks like the Atlantic coast. Plenty of sandbars."

Sergeant Veracruze was examining the coast west, on the approaches to Hoihow in the Hainan Straits. "It looks like just about enough water to float this boat, where we're going, there at Point Meng Wan," he said. "They must need fifty feet of water."

A crewman in worn dungarees popped into the compartment from the forward extremities of the ship. He held a piece of paper in his hand. He looked around the group, and announced: "I have a message here for Captain Hope." Hope took the message, and read:

XXXX FOR HOPE OPERATION TYPHOON. NEW INFORMA-TION FROM HONG KONG SOURCES RELIABLY ORIENTED INDICATES SHAPE IS TWENTY-FIVE MEGATONS SAME CON-FIGURATION AS ENIWETOK BOMB WITH A-BOMB TRIGGER SURROUNDING HYDROGEN BOMB AT BALL CENTER. MAYBE FURTHER INFORMATION NEXT FEW HOURS. ATTEMPTING LAY ON NEW AIRDROP. WILL ADVISE XXXX

Hope passed the message over to Gresham. Gresham studied it, and for the first time since Hope had known him, a broad-beamed smile crossed his face. "Now we've got some dope," he said. "At last, we can make some calculations." And excitement squeezed excess verbiage from him: "Man, that's a Big One, even among the Big Ones."

The public address system blatted out: "All hands, prepare to surface." And the fast-paced voice of Commander Battersby came on.

"This is the Exec speaking from the Conn. We're going to sound General Quarters, because we're going to surface in dangerous waters. But we have no radar or Sonar contact with any enemy. Repeat, as of the moment, we have no contact with the enemy. But want all hands to look sharp at battle stations—anything can happen." A second later, the tinpan dinging sound of the General Quarters alarm was sounded.

When the knife-bow of the boat broke water, the local weather was squally and overcast—and the submarine was alone in short, choppy seas.

The moment the deck was clear of water, the work party of two men and the Cob, and two lookouts popped onto the open bridge at the top of the sail structure.

The bridge space was jammed with people. While the lookouts swept the horizon, the Cob and his two assistants checked the damage to the snorkel tube. The Cob called through to the CO, who was now back on duty in the conning tower level.

"Cap'n, we've got a lot of bent metal up here but the insides seem okay," he said. "I think it'll take us at least an hour to patch it up. And we'll have to get some more metal-plate workers up here. It'll be a tight squeeze, but we should be able to do it in that time. Anything showing on the radar?"

The Cob stretched to help the two crewmen working over the bent housing for the snorkel. "How's it look, Jonesey? Do ya think the tube is bent?"

"Nope," Jonesey said. "If it was, we'd might as well give 'er up, and take 'er back to Pearl Harbor. We can't hardly fix none of that kind at sea, if we had two weeks."

The Cob smiled nervously, He knew that a bent snorkel tube was a shipyard job, a major overhaul which would necessitate derricks and drydocks. But he wanted to hear a judgment from the authority on snorkels, Chief Howard Jones. Jones might not know much about some things, but he knew as much as anybody the Cob had ever run across about the care and handling of snorkels. Jones was a slow, deliberate Alabaman with a very primitive sense of the importance of time. The Cob knew that he would have to be goosed even here in the incredibly dangerous position of surfacing amid Chinese patrol vessels on the coast of Hainan. Exactly how much and how to goose him was the particular knack of the Chief of the Boat.

"I'll send up Bennett and Hodges to work on the plating. Gotta get this done fast—you understand, Jonesey. We might get jumped any minute by another PC."

Jones growled: "Can't get a whole crew up here on the bridge. Ain't room enough to let a belch or fart."

The Cob was still being considerate: "Okay, I'll go below—that'll be one less. But remember, Jonesey, right now this whole operation depends on how fast you can fix this sheet metal."

Chief Jones was still growling: "Okay, okay. We ain't up here for our health."

The Cob's temper vibrated: "Then get it done, Goddamn it!" He knew that a calculated lash at just the right moment might do the trick. Jones smiled.

"Send 'em up fast, then. And tell Bennett to fetch his hacksaw and drill." He pushed at a tire iron he was forcing under the bent top of the snorkel plating. The normally smooth shield now looked like a bashed fender after a head-on collision, and some of the sheet-metal around the bridge railing had been ripped off and jammed into one of the folds.

Jones summed up the situation: "This is going to be a fuckin' bitch kitty." At that moment a spray of heavy drops of rain swept across his broad back. "Fuckin' rain, too, it's shit-ass," he growled. But he and the other snorkelmen bent to the job. "C'mon, Jack, give it the heave," he called out and MM1C Jack inserted his tire iron to uproot an especially twisted convolution of bent metal.

In the conning tower level, Commander Wilson and Battersby were both busy. "As long as both of us are on, Joe," he was saying as he looked up from a check of Hammond's dead reckoning tracer plot on the Hainan chart, "we can check everything fast. I can watch radar and navigation as long as you will keep an eye on Sonar. We'll head due north and get past Cape Tung Ku. At last, we can make some speed while we recharge the batteries."

"Aye, aye," said Battersby, "I'll keep all my fingers and toes crossed. And hope the ECM throws off the Commie radar."

✳

Half an hour later, Chief Jones and his three assistants were still muttering curses in the rain at the top of the sail structure, and there was still no sign of an airdrop; but the large trunk-shaped mass of the snorkel had re-assumed the smooth contours of an aluminum pullman case. Jones broke away to call the Cob on the sound-power phone: "It's comin' along all right, Cob. We might be through twelve, fifteen minutes. Be through in five minutes if the fuckin' rain would stop. Swimmin' with our clothes on. Swimmin' and a long way from the best swim I ever have, that's a joke. But the best shower I had for three days." As his job seemed to be coming to a successful conclusion, Jonesey was positively jovial.

Jonesey was going on with his talkative streak: "Ain't any blips on that radar yet?"

The Cob knew when to be firm for maximum effect. "No, ain't any. And you better buckle up your ass and get that job done fast, Jonesey—because we might be gettin' some of those radar contacts any minute now."

The Cob had been phoning from the control room and when he hung up the phone he acted on Chief Jones' question and hurried over to the SUBRAD operator's panel. Two radar-men sat at this console, the main SUBRAD panel—the console above in the conning tower was only a Repeater Set, so the Conn would have instant information on any contact. "You got anything that looks like anything, Pirelli?"

Pirelli didn't look up from the SUBRAD hood. Bob Greene, bis assistant, was fiendishly busy in the second desk chair, trying to get his surface radar to give him a good reading.

Pirelli recognized the Cob's voice and answered without looking away from the job: "Nothin' I can see, Cob. You want me to knock wood?"

"No, I'll do that," the Cob answered, and rapped a knuckle against his close-shaven head. He turned to Greene: "What are you getting, Bob?"

Green, still fiddling with his dials and rheostats, and plainly exasperated with the perversity of the machine, answered: "I've got a lot of little blips over to the west—bearing about 205, true. But it could be just this newfangled goddam fried-egg machine. Have you got anything over there, Pirelli?"

"No," Pirelli said. "But don't forget I haven't got any range with SUBRAD. Maybe ten miles at the most. You can go forty with your fuckin' machine, if you can ever get it un-fucked."

Greene said: "If these really are blips, you should be able to get 'em on your screen. My scale shows about 7,000 yards—about three of 'em out there, and one in here about 4,000. But maybe it's just static."

Colvin turned away and sped back to the receiver of the sound-power telephone near the helmsman's wheel. He spoke into it: "Lookout, this is the Cob. Have you got anything to the west bearing 205? Radar says there are some blips up there at 4,000 and 7,000 yards."

The muffled voice seemed to be in pain. "Can't see nothin' up here, Cob. It's still pissin' down rain and the binoculars don't help none. Visibility's about three feet."

After a moment's silence, the lookout went on: "Ain't nothin' I can see over there. Nothin' but fuckin' rain!" He added, hastily: "Cob? Jonesey wants to talk to you. Wait one."

The familiar, drawling voice came on: "Cob, looks like we'll be through in about five minutes."

"Fine." The Cob picked up the regular ship's telephone and flicked the switch for the Conn: "Commander Wilson?—the Cob speakin'. Had a report from Jones with the work party up on the snorkel that they expect to get through in five minutes. No radar or SUBRAD contacts. There's a possible indication over in the west, bearing about two hundred. But we're not sure—4,000 to 7,000 yards."

Wilson answered quickly: "Good, Cob. Tell 'em to keep a sharp eye out." He added, "I've got the ECM people sending out jam signals for the Chinese radar. We've just been damned lucky they haven't got through and picked us up yet. There must be all kinds of radar stations along this beach. So—keep an eye on the work party on the snorkel tube. We've got to get on our way. How's the battery recharge going?"

"Fine, sir. About three-quarters charged already."

"Good," Wilson said. "Tell the lookouts to keep a sharp eye out. Should be a C-124 coming out of Thailand to make the airdrop. Same bird that tried before when we had to dive. If he can find us— and if the Commies *don't* find us."

In the after-torpedo room, five of Hope's group sat on the multi-tiered bunks, the chart of Hainan still spread out on one of the bunk surfaces. Nooley, Gresham, Paisan Veracruze, and Hank Musgrave had remained after a runner from Commander Wilson came by to clear the torpedo room of all unnecessary people.

Some of the Operation Typhoon men had sacked out in their bunks in the torpedo room, others had gone forward to other crew quarters and a crew of three torpedomen were standing by the sleek fat shapes of the underwater projectiles. The torpedo crew were still busily checking through electrical connections, voltage readings, the settings of propellers and impellers.

Hope, back from the Conn, had a suggestion: "We're pretty much in the way here. We've got some things to talk about still. So why don't we go down to the mess compartment. Nobody's feeding there right now, and there's a table."

There was a grunted assent. The group started forward for the mess table. And the luxury of five hundred cubic feet of unoccupied living space. Now that the mid-afternoon soup-down was over, there were at least eight square feet where the maps could be spread out on top of the table marked with acey-deucey and chess boards. Hope unrolled the Hainan charts again and put his hand-drawn maps of the H-bomb base on top. He used his black-bladed K-bar knife to weight one edge of the charts and a pocketknife to anchor the other.

"Still no final word about the airdrop. The crew topside are really jumping—trying to fix the bent snorkel, Captain Wilson is trying to locate the plane with NRP. He'll pass the word if he gets 'em. Nothing we can do, right now. I want to know if Major Gresham will explain what the business of the Bikini bomb and all that means, and what it will mean to us when we get to that Shape. Maybe you could fill us in."

Gresham didn't answer directly. He looked extremely flustered, he glanced at Hope and then at Musgrave and he stammered: "Maybe I spoke too fast when we got the message. Eh-hem—the details about the H-bomb Shape are about as highly-classified as anything in the world." He glanced uneasily at Hank again. "I don't think we're all cleared for Top Secret."

Hope followed Gresham's meaning immediately, but incredulously. Then he laughed. "You think that anyone who is going to go in and help take out this bomb is not privileged to have complete information about it? Is that it? You mean you can't tell Musgrave?"

Gresham's lower lip was firming in lines of stubbornness. He deliberated, then said peremptorily: "I believe the information should be restricted to those who are going to have direct contact with the bomb—the actual raiding party."

Hank said: "Whoa! Just wait and back up a minute. As far as I know, I'm going to be going along with that party you speak of— because I happen to know something about the language."

Hope was still laughing. "My God, this *is* a surprise. Here we are on the coast of Hainan and the Commie patrol boats might blow the hell out of us any minute, and we might not even get to the damned island—and you're worried about who's got what clearance! Anyhow, Hank *is* cleared for Top Secret—he *is* an employee of the CIA —and he is going to be in the final raiding party when we hit that Shape." Gresham looked around at the faces of the others, and smiled his wry half-grin.

"Sorry. I guess anybody who's been exposed to the Shape for so long gets a little jumpy. Even here—in the middle of this kind of a mission."

"*Especially* here, in the middle of this mission," Hank said, laughing.

Three crewmen suddenly ran through the passageway toward the after-torpedo room. A seaman who was sitting in the corner of the mess compartment with a talker harness on his head, explained: "Cap'n is orderin' torpedo tubes ready. Fore and aft."

Nooley said: "Sounds as if we won't get to Gresham's briefing after all."

"If something does happen," said Hope. "We're not going to be able to do anything about it. So we might as well go ahead with the briefing. We're only passengers here." Gresham had turned over Hope's hand-made map and was drawing on the back of it with a pencil,

"Okay," he said. "I'll draw a picture of the Bikini Shape, and you can see what I mean. Also—it probably should help some in our planning of what we have to do."

"I should think so," said Hope.

Gresham had drawn a circle within a circle—the outer circle studded with projections like the detonators on a floating mine. The inner circle was much smaller than the outer. He filled this inner circle with pencil scribblings so that it was generally dark. Then, he divided the outer circle with lines which laid it out in wedges. "Hope," he began, "you probably understand the general layout of the nuclear bomb—maybe the others don't." He stopped as if thoughts were churning hard in his head and he was struggling to find the exact words for them. "This ball-shaped object is probably four feet across and these detonators on the outside are the things that set off the implosion. The ball is at the head end of the bomb shape—which is overall probably twenty-five feet long. This is a big baby, one of the biggest. It's probably got a bang at least a thousand times more powerful than the Hiroshima bomb—or the previous Chinese atomic firecrackers.

"The outer part of the big explosive ball is divided into segments. All these segments shaped like wedges in the outer circle are what they call Ring Lenses. These are all set up to go off simultaneously with an electrical charge, and when the implosion is over—" He still struggled for words. He felt as usual during an explanation or presentation that there was such an overwhelming barrier between the other people and him that words seemed the remotest way of bridging the gap. He struggled on: "You know the atomic principle: When two masses of fissionable material, of a certain size—I mean plutonium or uranium—are jammed together, you get an explosion."

He was so wrung out from the effort of public speech, and suffering so palpably, that Hope sprang to his rescue: "I don't think we all know the principles of the H-bomb."

Gresham looked relieved. "All right. Well, this inner circle here is the heart of the hydrogen bomb. This is the stuff that makes the *big* bang. But it takes the atomic explosion to set it off.

"The old-fashioned Eniwetok configuration had the atomic bomb on the outside, with the hydrogen elements—deuterium and tritium, at the center. There's a tritium booster on the outside too—but I won't go into that. The atomic elements are squeezed in—imploded, around the hydrogen elements, in this configuration. It takes the million degrees heat of the atomic explosion to set off the hydrogen bomb—and the longer the implosion pressure is kept up, the bigger the yield—the Bang."

Gresham could see the glazing of non-comprehension in Veracruze's eyes. He felt that most of the others seemed to be following him.

"So, to take out the bomb, what we have to do is to set off a Point One detonation—that's a low order detonation—in one of the outer Ring Lenses, that will smash in maybe one Ring Lense and the one next to it, and it will wreck the outer bomb, and if I do it just right, it will probably raise hell with the deuterium and tritium in the inner bomb—but it won't set off either an atomic or hydrogen explosion." He thought that over quietly for a minute. "I hope. That is my plan."

The seaman with the talker-harness sitting at the corner of the room burst out: "Cap'n has a hot contact and they're trackin' him. But we can't submerge! Sumpin' wrong with our main ballast valves. Looks like the old man's gonna fire torpedoes . . . He's turnin' the boat to bring the forward tubes to bear." The instruction in nuclear physics, the plan to destroy the hydrogen bomb, all of the convoluted scientific considerations vanished before the sudden shock of old-fashioned submarine torpedo attack.

※

In the conning tower, the Exec was training his sight through the rearmost or attack periscope, and the Captain hovered over the desk of the radar operator. On the operator's repeater instrument, he could see two definite blips at about 3,000 and 4,000 yards, the slivers of white light emergent behind the sweeping needle of the radar tracker as it rotated.

He jumped to the phone receiver and switched to the Cob in the control room below. "Cob can't you clear those damned ballast tanks? What's the holdup?"

The Cob's voice rasped in the receiver: "A couple of the valves are stuck, Skipper."

"Can't you do it with the negative tanks alone and the diving planes?"

"No, sir. Main ballast has to go, or we can't hack it. Somebody has to get out on the deck and see what's holding the valves. Something must have got bent by the depth charges. We need a volunteer to go out and—I'm the volunteer." He clicked off and Wilson knew he had bolted for the forward hatch to scramble up on the wet deck and make his own check.

Wilson called out to the Exec: "Have you got those two PCs on periscope?"

"I have 'em. One about 3,000, the other one about 4200 yards. But they seem to be moving in the same direction we are. Not toward us."

Wilson jumped back to the radar desk and called out: "That's what the radar track shows. Maybe they don't have any radar and they haven't seen us. It's pretty damn stormy out there."

The Exec called out to the Skipper: "Are the tanks cleared yet? Can we dive? They'll spot us any minute."

"We can't. Cob's gone on deck to check the main ballast valves."

"Have you secured the lookout?"

"No. Might as well keep him up there until we're clear to dive. The work party hasn't finished with the snorkel repair job."

On the slippery deck, the Cob and a sturdy sailor named Elgin, safety ropes around their waists and the buckles threaded into the deck grooves, ran down the line of main ballast intakes and fell upon one valve-frame which was deeply dented. With crowbars, they began to pry the damaged metal vent. The large curved piece of metal resisted the crowbar applied by the Cob. Elgin jumped beside him, and the ballast intake moved. They heaved together, and at last, the steel lid snapped to open position like the intake valves on both sides of it.

"I think that's got it!" the Cob shouted. "Come on, let's get below—but fast!" Elgin dashed for the forward access hatch, and the Cob, with one quick look-around the deck of his beloved boat, followed.

In the conning tower, Commander Wilson was shouting through the phone to the diving officer in the control room on the deck below: "As soon as the repair party gets in, I want you to take her down—quick! And let me know!"

"Aye, sir—" The diving officer, Lieutenant Holloway, broke off to switch to the PA channel. His voice crackled through the loudspeakers: "Lookouts and work party clear the bridge. Secure all hatches . . . Prepare to dive . . . Prepare to dive . . ." But the klaxon didn't sound, Holloway hadn't turned off the PA system mike and his voice sounded distantly as he shouted to the seaman handling the diving valves and vents: "What is it? Are the valves still bent? Which ones? Can't we dive without 'em?" Then Holloway must have noted that the PA system channel was still switched on, and it went off with a snap.

In the conning tower, the Exec kept his eye at the eyepiece of the attack periscope. "I've got the nearest Commie boat in the scope!" He called out to the Skipper. But at that moment, the Skipper was answering his ring on the ship's phone.

Lieutenant Holloway was saying: "You can't get them all clear? Then blow 'em all — negatives, too! And hit the diving planes as hard as you can. The first PC has spotted us. Get 'er down somehow!"

In the bright round lens of the attack periscope, Joe Battersby could see the rakish low shape of the patrol craft, a long lean gray sliver with a twenty-millimeter Oerlikon barrel jutting against the sky on the bow deck, three men around it. As he watched, they seemed to move aft. The gun barrel appeared to train slightly upward. The boat was making a sharp curve. "She's turning towards us, Cap'n." Battersby saw the men around the gun mount moving in a circular, rolling motion. They must be turning the magazine into position on the gun. He saw the gun barrel coming down, saw the shoulders of a man between the two half-arcs of the shoulder braces. Battersby noted the bone in the teeth of the boat as she charged, now a white moustache below the steep V of her strakes. She was head-on towards the submarine now. The magnifying power of the periscope brought the charging enemy frightfully near. Battersby sang out: "He's coming!"

Wilson was bellowing: "I can't get down! Blasted valves are stuck! Better fire some fish!" He called out to radar: "Give me a track! What's his closing rate?"

The radarman called out: "Bearing is 274-true. He must be closing at twenty-five knots!"

"He'll be *here* in four—five minutes." Wilson jumped to the ship's phone and dialed the forward torpedo room: "We've got a target 2000 yards, bearing 274-true. Ready One, Four, and Six! We're going to turn into him for a head-on shot."

He switched to the helmsman: "Turn her to 274-true. We're going to fire torpedoes!"

Commander Battersby held the eyepiece of the periscope firmly on the approaching patrol boat, as the bow of the submarine swung around toward it. The muzzle of the Oerlikon was down now, pointing directly at the periscope, and the knobs of men still clustered around it, the one triggerman leaning forward now, with the bracket of the two shoulder rests framing his head. The Exec saw a pale yellow winking of flame flicker in the dark mass of the gun, and short dashes of tracer bullets, white streaks coming towards the periscope. "He's firing!"

In that same moment, Battersby saw the second of the two patrol boats. It was a boat of the same shape, possibly a thousand yards beyond and a couple of miles to the right and she was also charging.

He called out: "I see the second blip. He's a PC like the first. And he's heading for us too. If you fire, Will, you'll get two for one."

Wilson was already acting on that suggestion: "Stand by to fire One, Four, and Six. Check your outer doors. Final bearing 271. Mark the bearing! Shoot!" The Exec reached down to carry out the order. His palm jammed down on the doorknob-sized fire button beside the periscope. He could feel the distant shudder as each of the tubes went: ONE!—THWUNNKK! TWO!—THWUNNK! THREE! —THWUNNKK!

The Skipper had jumped to the Number One periscope and its brighter field. They both watched the churning white wakes scooting towards the onrushing target—Number One, farthest advanced, on the left. Number Four closer in towards the sub. Number Six, just beginning to show her luminous white trail.

"Number One is going to miss!"

Battersby shouted: "Looks like the PC's gonna run right into Number Six, He's not combing the wakes. He's just charging."

The Cob was climbing up the ladder from the Control Room, next to the Exec's position on the attack 'scope. The Cob announced as he uncoiled on the deck: "Diving Officer's ready to go! The valves are fixed." That moment, the ship telephone jangled, and Wilson jumped away from the Number One periscope to pick up the receiver.

"Ready? Then, dive, dive!" He shouted to Battersby: "Stand by to fire again—set up the tubes—in case we can't submerge!"

Battersby saw the shape of the foremost Commie patrol boat as larger than ever, still charging, still with the wide white moustache of foam beneath her high wooden cheeks, the blinking of the yellow flame from the gun, the white dashes of tracer curving toward him. He heard a brief rattle, as of stones on a distant window. Would it be the shells hitting into the sail structure? The submarine was diving now, he could tell.

He heard the distant sound of the PA, somewhere in another world, "Dive! Dive!" and the two hurried ooga-oogas of the warning klaxon. They were going down, and the damage of those shells he had heard hitting could be great, or nothing. He looked away from the periscope for one second to see the Cob scrambling to his feet with a silly grin on his face, and heard him say: "We hacked it!" The image of the first PC was almost off the binocular field, but he glimpsed the explosion: a billowing flash of orange, the rolling flame fading into black smoke. He frantically turned his reticle upward and caught a vision of the second of the patrol boats still charging. But where the hell was the third torpedo? It must be out there.

In his frantic search to find the last torpedo and the second patrol boat, he had lost the first. He whipped the reticle downwards, saw the bright orange glow of the fire still burning, the smoke boiling out black—and black forms of men plummeting from the flames into the water. There were probably a lot more of the crew still on the boat—and those on the bow with the Oerlikon had probably had it. More people were jumping and the shape of the boat was lengthening, because it was turning. Now, he could see the jut of the second Oerlikon, the one on the stern, and the long squat shape of that stern, with blobs of humanity moving on it. The forward part of the boat was swallowed up in flame and the column of smoke thickening and towering above the stern.

Battersby had to keep on adjusting the reticle as the submarine dived, and the steel plates of the deck tilted underneath his feet. In the brightly colored binocular, he saw two more men dive from the immobilized stern—and one loyal soul still at the tilted prong of the Oerlikon barrel. He was trying to turn the barrel to bring it to bear on the spot where the submarine had been. But the submarine was going down fast, and all he might have seen at that point would be the top of the sail and the masts of the periscopes and snorkel sticking above it.

The rolling contortions of the orange flames underneath the column of smoke bubbled and boiled and rolled out with a sudden orange projection, and two more figures dived from the stern. The Exec saw them go, and in that millisecond, he watched the loyal gunner turning his Oerlikon barrel to bear on the disappearing trace of the sub. He saw the flash of the yellow muzzle blast, and the darting red tongue of the explosion rolling toward the gunner, projecting a sheaf of sooty smoke in his direction, swallowing him up.

In one second's blink—he knew he would have a fraction of a second only before he lost his vision through the periscope and the sub plunged below periscope depth—he flicked the recticle up towards the horizon, and desperately sought for the shape of the second patrol torpedo boat.

He couldn't find it! In the breathless excitement of the moment, he was training the periscope to the south, instead of the north, a mistake which might gain or lose the image in the disappearing seconds.

Now, in a flick of vision, he saw the curving wake of the torpedo. It was going wrong, it was turning. Something had gone kook with the gyro. It was turning sharply like a hooked shot on a golf course.

But where was the second PC? Then he saw it, still charging, the white arc of the curving torpedo reaching out like a twanging bowstring toward the foe. It might even hit! Thank God the guidance mechanism went wrong! And that was the moment when the lens-circle grew dark and streaky, periscope depth was lost as the sub plunged deeper. Battersby called out: "I've lost my periscope." He pulled his face away from the heavy tube and called out to the SUBRAD operator: "SUBRAD! Have you got a track on the second PC!" As he said it, he saw that Wilson was standing behind the SUBRAD and regular radar operator, and Wilson called out to him:

"She's stopped in the water—must have been a hit. A lucky hit!" He turned to the SUBRAD operator: "What do you show on the second blip?"

The voice of the SUBRAD operator seemed muffled, but everyone in the conning tower heard it: "The blip is only half-size, Captain! Looks like he's been cut in two!"

An outcry between a shout and a cheer roared through the conning tower. One voice, the voice of the Cob, seemed very distinct: "Got 'im! Got 'im!"

The Captain jumped to the PA system mike: "To all hands—well done. It looks like we nailed 'em both!" They could hear the roar running through the passageways of the sub. The Captain's voice went on, through the inter-phone: "We're diving to two hundred feet. There may be another PC out there, still."

The Captain went on, via the PA channel: "Now our battery charge is almost finished, and we can stay down for a little while. We'll probably just lie doggo until the sun goes down. Then we'll have ample time to get to our pick-up point by two o'clock tomorrow morning."

Below, in the after-torpedo room, the leading echelon of the Typhoon detachment and the talker were listening fascinated to Commander Wilson's cool summary. Paisan Veracruze voiced what they were thinking: "He ain't even upset. Like nothin' happened!"

The calm, hoarse voice rasped on the PA speaker: "Now I'm going to give you a more detailed run-down on what occurred. We don't seem to have any more radar blips at the moment." And he began a matter-of-fact summary of the action against the two patrol boats.

18

AT SEVEN O'CLOCK IN THE EVENING, THE *MAKO* WITH HER 217 men was sitting on the bottom, at a depth of 212 feet. They had been lying quietly for more than three hours, their Sonar and SUBRAD listening for the patrol boats which came in a never-ending progression.

Initially, there was the survivor of the three boats which had attacked her. This patrol craft had rushed over to the half-blips of the wrecked PCs. Apparently she was picking up survivors.

Then, about an hour later, two more boats came up to help. Battersby and Wilson studied the shapes in the SUBRAD screen, the three white slivers shimmering on the black. And Wilson had growled: "Looks like they're sticking together for mutual courage."

Then the boats had departed in three different directions, apparently on search segments,

A few minutes later, two more boats approached from different bearings. They, too, met up there, the blips bobbing together on the

SUBRAD screen. Then they went off, evidently scouring ocean segments in search of the Yankee submarine, and then three more blips appeared—possibly the first three returning.

Then, at five-thirty, the last three blips shoved off together, heading north, probably towards a common base near Hoihow or on the Chinese mainland side, fifteen miles across the Straits of Hainan.

But the rest of the afternoon, for the *Mako*, had been easy. Not one additional depth charge was dropped on them. And Commander Wilson summed up the feelings of all aboard when he said on the PA: "Thank God for SUBRAD, the most valuable of all Uncle Sam's submarine secrets. And thank God the Commies don't have it."

With the intelligence of the SUBRAD and the Sonar, the submarine commanders could formulate a good picture of the hunters topside: each had three screws, all were apparently fast patrol boats of the thirty-meter "Jacky" class, same as those they had met and sunk.

Down below in the bottom mud, waiting for the sea to clear above, the crew grabbed sack time.

Commander Wilson summoned Hope and told him: "Captain—I'm sorry. We blew the airdrop again—with too much assistance from the Commies. And it looks as if we're too Goddamn far in now to try it in the dark. We'd have to illuminate and that might finish the mission; even if we used infra-red they'd probably intercept. Can you hack the job with what you've got?"

Hope hesitated. "It's not too bad. Somehow, we'll manage it." He turned away: "And thanks for keeping us all in one piece."

Wilson smiled. "We're not there yet."

In the tiny ward room, Major Gresham continued his briefing for the five leaders of the Typhoon operation.

The receiving radio of the ship was kept open, but no dispatches were sent, because even the primitively equipped Chinese

Communists might have enough gear to unscramble their ECM signals. Besides, at 212 feet depth, as a practical matter, neither sending nor receiving would be apt to be very successful.

In the Conn, Commander Battersby and Cob Colvin, were checking over the valves and hydraulics of the ballast tanks, and discovering that apparently the twenty-millimeter shells fired at the boat had damaged nothing vital in the hull. But Battersby estimated: "It'll probably be two days before we can make a good check of the sail structure."

"Maybe late tomorrow afternoon, when we get in the clear," Colvin said, and smiled, "*if* we get in the clear."

At five o'clock, Hank Musgrave had climbed into his top-tier bunk, and he was dreaming troubled nightmares of Mary. Mary was in the back of a Communist patrol boat, they had taken the bandage from her face, and she had a great squashed nose of dreadful Jello-like red between her two blackened eyes. She was being held down while two Chinese, a thin one and a chunky one were going to hit her again in the pulpy nose. He fought against the dream and waked himself, and heard the now-recognizable dry voice of the Exec saying on the PA speaker: "All hands, we're going to surface to periscope depth to run on snorkel and finish our battery charge. Later in the night we'll need all the charge we can manage."

A pause, and the dry voice went on: "We have only thirty-six nautical miles to make before we reach the rendezvous point. We will probably encounter much heavier enemy radar surveillance as we come closer to the target area. The snorkel will present a minimal radar hazard, but we'll continue to run the danger of being spotted by their Sonar apparatus. When we finish charging our batteries at snorkel depth, we will probably stay submerged until we surface for the transfer of the raiding party to the Chinese junk off Point Meng Wan. Of course, we'll be running our Electronics Counter Measures machinery full blast."

Commander Battersby put down the telephone and switched off the conning tower phone-board. He grinned at the Cob who was standing near him: "At least, that's the plan—barring any sandbars which might have appeared on the bottom since the 1925 Coast and Geodetic Survey."

Below, in the messing compartment, the eighteen men of the raiding party had been assembled for yet another briefing session. Captain Hope was saying, as he turned away from the chart of the coastal area stuck on the wall: "The fact remains that all of our plans will have to be contingent on what we find out on the scene. The Intelligence we have so far is conjectural. We'll just have to play it by ear."

✳

It was ten-fourteen P.M. on a satisfactorily dark night at Farmer Dinh's house in the eastern reaches of the port of Hoihow, Hainan. In the smudgy light of a kerosene lamp unsteadily burning tung oil — kerosene oil had been preempted by government fiat, and only miserable tung oil was available—a group of four people in black Chinese peasant costume huddled over a table: Farmer Dinh, his wife Hahn, the Cordier, Wing On, and his son, Wing Run.

Wing beamed a wide grin of satisfaction: "And it seems that the Chek-koh near the house of Driver Pung were also making a more or less routine check on Comrade Pung."

He laughed. "I'm glad I didn't do anything—precipitous—about Comrade Pung. He has brought some late information about the changes in the base at Ching Tu. Very important information. Have you had a report about the junk? Is it going to be on station at the correct time tonight?"

"Yes, Comrade Wing. A home has been prepared for our new guests. It will be in one of the sheds where jute is stored, not far from the dock."

"And have there been messages during the day from our friends across the water?"

"No, I've been very cautious about operating the radio for anything but service messages to the junks out on the fishing banks."

"Very good. Then Run and I will remain here through the night, so that we will be on hand for the maneuvers later on, when the junk comes in."

"Excellent. Surely, if you tried to move out here after the curfew, you would have difficulty. My friends in town tell me that the police are enforcing the curfew very strictly during the last few days. Is that correct?"

"Absolutely correct, Comrade Dinh, and that is going to be one of the problems we will face in moving these visitors from here to the vicinity of the base. Because of their distinctive appearance, and their size, we will not be able to move them in daylight—and at night, the Chek-koh will be harsh in enforcing the curfew."

Dinh stood up. "So let us adjourn to the fishing house near the dock. My trusted servant and radio operator, Nhu, is on duty there."

✳

In his favorite small office on the second story of the White House, President Landers was considering the problem of informing the Seventh Fleet of Operation Typhoon with Admiral Joe Bloom-field, the Chief of Naval Operations, Special Presidential Assistant David Soloretha, and CIA Chief Charles Hudibras. The Chief Executive was restless and uneasy, and now, instead of sitting as the others were, he paced up and down, looking out the window toward the press gate and executive offices of the White House west wing.

He was saying: ". . . but Joe, we're going to have to hold the Seventh Fleet in position at least until the day before the Communist anniversary. We must further the illusion that we are unaware of what's going on in Hainan. If the Commies get wind of the fact that we have a landing party on Hainan, they'll make it impossible for us to get at the installation."

Admiral Bloomfield said: "But shouldn't we let Admiral Kerr in on the overall strategy, Mr. President? Certainly he's a trustworthy government employee, with access to Top Secret."

The President turned and faced Admiral Bloomfield: "Now listen, Joe, you know how hard it is to keep the number of people who know about this to less than twenty-five or thirty—and that's too many. I understand that Kerr wants to know what's going on, and how he fits into it—what field commander doesn't? But I think for the time being we'd better keep him in the dark—let him carry out his orders, and later on, we'll make sure he knows all about it— when it's over."

The President turned towards CIA director Charles Hudibras. "Charlie, how is the landing party progressing? Have they got ashore on Hainan yet?"

Hudibras puffed his pipe. "They're just about to, Mr. President. In the next couple of hours."

The President's face flushed. "You mean they're not even on the island yet! Goddamn, they've been two days on that pig-boat, haven't they? What's holding 'em?"

Hudibras smiled faintly and indicated Admiral Bloomfield with his pipe stem. "That's Joe Bloomfield's baby, Mr. President. Delivering the raiding party is a Navy job, not mine."

The President chuckled, and the agitation left his face abruptly. "Passing the buck, Charlie? Old Army game applied to naval affairs?"

Salty old Joe Bloomfield accepted the buck with good humor. "Charlie's right, Mr. President—it is our responsibility to get the people in—and it would have been much better if we'd had a nuclear submarine available—in which case we could have made better time, and delivered the people onto Hainan last night.

"But under the circumstances, the best we could do was to throw in a Sailfish class boat, really a modernized World War II design. Even though the *Mako* has been Guppy-ized—our jargon for changes in her hull and power plant to make her move faster underwater— she's lucky to be able to make eight or nine knots submerged." His kindly, bluff face suddenly grew stern, "I'd be derelict of my duty as a commander if I didn't point out that the submarine commander ran tremendous risks and overcame them successfully—thus far, at any rate—to get to his assigned station on time. The *Mako* was intercepted by a number of Chinese patrol boats and had to sink two of them. It was a complicated story, I don't know exactly what happened, but I don't believe that the Chinese suspected anything unusual. They thought this was a regular American submarine on patrol in their waters. They made the first attack. But ONI says they've announced nothing about it. Probably, they won't."

The President protested: "Was it a good idea for us actually to attack two of the Chinese patrol boats? I should think they'd want to be as inconspicuous as possible, and try to exercise all the arts of stealth they were capable of—why should they take time to engage the enemy?"

Admiral Bloomfield stirred uneasily in his chair. "We don't know the facts yet, Mr. President. As I say, it's a complicated story, the story of that engagement. There were probably some facts we don't know about—perhaps they were on the surface trying to recharge their batteries when they were surprised."

"Don't they have a snorkel so they can recharge their batteries while they're submerged?"

Bloomfield, the line sailor, answered: "Mr. President, back here at headquarters we are strong on theory. We have all the latest double-domes to equate all kinds of new patterns of thought and invent all kinds of new theory. But the people out on the battleline have to make-do with whatever they can lay their hands on, and the most practical, foolproof ways of utilizing whatever equipment and manpower is available.

"I would suggest that despite the holdups and the action—which must have been a very brave and expert one—Commander Wilson, the skipper of the sub, somehow has managed to get into position close to the rendezvous point off the coast of Hainan, and exactly on scheduled time—in spite of all the difficulties."

The President smiled: "You're absolutely right, Joe, and God knows I should be sensible enough of these field considerations. After all, I had to 'make-do' as you say, with very primitive material and other resources as an Army officer in the China-Burma-India theater in World War II. But I've been too long here in the city of the double-domes, and I've forgotten."

He sat down. "And maybe you're right—maybe Admiral Kerr, since his moves are going to be so important to us for the next few days, should be admitted to the fold of those who know about Operation Typhoon and the Chinese hydrogen bomb. I'm sure he's as trustworthy as they come."

"The *most* trustworthy, Mr. President. And by the way, sir, it would be more than simple consideration for him if Admiral Kerr were told about the H-bomb on Hainan. Because—and this is always more than a distant possibility with such a risky operation as this— the raiding party might not make it. I hate to think about that eventuality, but it is a possibility. If Operation Typhoon should not work, we should invoke that back-up plan we spoke about—and send the Seventh Fleet into a strike against the Hoihow base."

The President said: "There you go with your back-up plan again. I told you, Joe, this one has got to work."

"You're right, Mr. President—it's got to work." Admiral Bloomfield tugged at his eyebrows and smiled. "But in any case, if everything should go wrong—remember Murphy's law—and if the Seventh Fleet commander knew what the situation was, he would have formulated all sorts of plans to take out this installation. Remember, the attack bombers from the *Enterprise* can knock out this installation very effectively, if necessary."

The President laughed again. "This time let *me* be the authority, Joe. This kind of war doesn't follow the old patterns of massive assault and moving armies and fleets. The one thing we don't want to do is transpose this whole episode into a conventional war.

"The raiding group slips in, destroys the hydrogen bomb and makes its exit—I hope without too many casualties—and the whole thing will be so precisely done that the Chinese won't utter a peep about it publicly. And the whole story will be sat on, I hope, until the nebulous time in the future when I write my memoirs of presidential days."

"You also are a good field commander, Mr. President," said Admiral Bloomfield. "And I'll pass on the word under the Top-Top Secret heading to Admiral Kerr. Undoubtedly, he will work up a stand-by plan for an emergency air strike, in case it should be needed."

The President nodded his head and smiled: "Old ideas die hard, don't they, Joe?"

19

October 13

BOTH OF *MAKO'S* NAVIGATORS, LIEUT. COMMANDER STAN Hammond and Lieut. Percy Smith, were working over the chart and the DRT, when it came time to surface off Point Meng Wan. Hammond pointed to the designated rendezvous spot and inquired: "Do you check me out on this location, Percy? It's only the most important fix in all our lives."

"That's where my calculations come out, too," Smith said. "Do we surface?" He looked at his watch. "It's two-twenty-five. We're right on time like the Commuter's local."

"And I hope Murph the Surf's law is not operating tonight," said Hammond, "and that by some miracle, the Friendlies will actually be here with their junk."

He turned to Commander Wilson, who was standing by the radar operator's desk, with Commander Battersby. "It looks like we're here, Skipper," Hammond said.

Wilson lit a cigarette. "Pretty wild and wonderful that we haven't had more interference on this approach. No mines, no nets."

Hammond said: "Long coastline, short time. They haven't prepared. I hope,"

Wilson told Battersby: "Take her up, Joe. This time, I'm going to use the Number One periscope. We'd better go to periscope depth first, until we can identify the signal. What's the signal—SRO?"

"'Standing Room Only': the sign they put outside a theatre that's all sold out? I hope this one isn't."

"Isn't what, Skipper?"

Wilson laughed. "Sold out."

Commander Battersby stepped to the telephone console and he switched to the control room: "Diving Officer: up to periscope depth, Blow the main ballast tanks and the negative tanks. Skipper wants to see if we can pick up the visual signal from the surface."

"Aye, aye, sir," the Diving Officer replied. In a moment, the PA system crackled. There were three honks on the klaxon: "Prepare to surface to periscope depth." Next came the usual whooshing sounds as the main tanks were blown clear. Commander Wilson hit the 'Up Periscope' buttons. The heavy tube slid up in its collar of grease and clicked into position. Wilson grasped the heavy rubber grips and swung the eyepiece around.

"Better take the attack 'scope, Joe," he instructed the Exec. "Two lookouts are better than one. But keep an eye on the Conn while we level out, too. I want to concentrate my eyes on this one detail, looking for the signal."

Water was running down the sharp, shiny eye of the periscope. Wilson turned the field of view upward to orient himself by way of the night world above, spotted the tall diamond-profile of Orion, the belted warrior, and knew that the 'scope must be trained on the southern horizon. He lowered the binocular to what was evidently the shore-line—marked by a faint glow of light where the horizon sheltered a town. Above the glow he could see looming mountains. That would be the Wuchi mass on the southern part of Hainan. As his eyes grew used to the night light, he could make out a nearer hilly mass: probably Point Meng Wan, where the South China Sea slopes into Hainan Straits. He swept the black mass of the sea in a northward direction, and found no marine lights. His heart began to sink: Murphy's Law?

The junk should be sending her blinker signal from a bearing of 275-true, if the *Mako's* position was correct. But they could be anywhere in this general vicinity, and the fishing boat might be winking its signal a quarter of a mile to one side or the other and still be approximately at the coordinates.

Wilson swept the horizon again, called out to Battersby, who was squinting into the attack periscope: "You see anything, Joe?"

"No, sir. But did you spot that floodlight over there, bearing about 220?"

"Yes, what do you make it out to be—a town?"

"Hell, no, sir. That must be the airfield. They seem to have got the floodlights on—and I think I just saw a plane take off."

Commander Wilson swung his 'scope to the indicated bearing, and observed that the dim glow had grown into a far brighter light— possibly the bright floodlamp glow of a high-voltage power plant. "They must have just turned them on," he said, "when I went by there before, it only looked like a village. Probably they're practicing a little night flying, and taking a chance to illuminate briefly. I'll betcha they shut off in a minute, as soon as the planes are off—they'll probably turn the lights on again when they come back to land." As if to acknowledge his prognosis, the lights flicked off, and in their place there remained only the faint glow of the village.

Commander Wilson completed his sweep of the horizon, and this time found a white running light to the north.

"I've got a running light to the northwest, bearing about 310, Can you make it out?"

Battersby swung his 'scope in the indicated direction. "I've got 'im," he responded. "Looks like a junk to me, and he's moving."

"You've got great night vision, Joe. I'm gonna have to keep you on this lookout duty while I conn the ship. All I can see up there is a light. But—Holy Mackerel—he's signalling! The angle is difficult. Can you make him out?"

Battersby held the bright globe of his binocular on the flickering light. "That's 'S'! He's goin' on. R, That's R. But now, now it's M. SRM. That must be it! Just one letter wrong. Shall we surface?"

Wilson took a deep breath. He flipped the switch to the control room and reached the Diving Officer: "Okay—take 'er up." He switched on the PA system, and announced: "This is the Captain. To our visitors. We're about to surface. If everything goes according to plan, your gear will be unloaded through the after access hatch— above the after-torpedo room. In a moment we're going to sound the General Quarters alarm. It'll probably be some time before disembarkation. We've picked up a signal and we think we have the correct contact. Signalmen Rubinchik and Halsey report to the conn— on the double."

So at two thirty-two A.M, at the assigned coordinates to the east of Point Meng Wan, Hainan, the long, black shape of the U.S. submarine *Mako* split the surface chop with all the punctuality of the Westport Express arriving in Grand Central Station. Sea water still gleamed along the sides of her sail structure as the hatch on the bridge level creaked and popped open, and five men in flight jackets squirmed out: Signalmen Rubinchik and Halsey, Commander Joe Battersby, and two lookouts. Commander Wilson had elected to stay below in the conning tower level, the better to coordinate the complicated business of a sea-transfer.

Now the submarine moved slowly in a northward direction, the Pointer Stars directly above her bow. To the northwest a large fishing junk, with a sail rigged on her foremast, moved slowly with a quartering wind. A light blinked from her deck: "S—R—M."

"Okay," Wilson replied promptly. "Send away."

Signalman Rubinchik raised the long tube of a signal light, aimed it at the junk, and expertly flipped the shutters: "SRO—SRO— SRO."

He shut the light off and waited, and this time, the light from the junk blinked back: "SRO—SRO."

And Signalman Rubinchik uttered a faint cheer. "Hoo-ray. This time they got it right."

Battersby called into the sound-power phone: "Skipper, she's answering SRO. I guess we're on."

Down in the yellow light of the conning tower enclosure, Commander Wilson spoke to the Exec: "Okay, I'll hold her on this course. Shut down engines." He growled into the PA channel: "The Typhoon detachment stand by at the after access hatch. The junk is coming alongside. We'll use the rubber raft to move you over." And he turned to Commander Hammond, and Lieut. Percy Smith, as they sat at the navigator's tiny desk: "It's incredible, gentlemen— somehow we managed it."

In the after-torpedo room, the eighteen men of the Typhoon Force bunched at the foot of the steel ladder leading upward into a tiny passage. The Cob and Seaman Bennett were already on the ladder hauling the bulky black package of an uninflated life raft with them. Sergeant Veracruze and Muley Muhlbach were dragging canvas-covered bundles towards the ladder.

The PA system in the compartment grated: "Captain Hope, I'm sending a work party down to help load your gear up to the deck level. Just get yourselves up on deck and onto the junk. Leave the loading to us." There was a pause, and he added: "We'll be here same spot Saturday at two A.M. The honor of the U.S. Navy depends on it and besides that, we'll do it. Good luck with the job."

At five minutes after three, Hank Musgrave was still standing on the open afterdeck of the *Mako*, with Lieutenant Helmantholer, Sergeant Bissell, and Muley Muhlbach. The Cob and two crew members were still with them, superintending loads being sent from the sub to the junk. Six loads had been completed.

The rubber raft, paddled by Sergeants Espinoza, Hing, and O'Connor, moved midway between the sub and the junk, and both ships were dead in the water.

Hank looked up to the open bridge, and in the starlight could make out four figures there. One would be Commander Battersby. Battersby was sweating out every boatload between the two craft — and, Hank knew, watching every glimmer of light in the surrounding waters. The sub commander had made one of those incalculable decisions: Whether to risk damage to the hull by having the junk come directly alongside—in which case, any ineptitude on the part of the Chinese sailors might damage the hull—or to take a chance and load by the slower means of the rubber boat, with the possibility that a Chinese patrol vessel would show up at any moment and precipitate catastrophe.

On the last two trips, a Chinese sampan had at last been un-shipped from the junk to help haul passengers and gear across. The sub commander had taken advantage of the time as well to check over the damage to the deck of the sub and patch up three twenty-millime-ter holes in the top of the sail.

Sergeant Bissell squinted upward at the sail of the *Mako*. "This half hour must be the longest year in their lives," he said.

Hank smiled: "Except maybe the half hour when they come back to pick us up, on Saturday morning."

The life raft was edging close to the submarine's hull now, and the rubber doughnut bumped against the bulge of the main ballast tanks, and gingerly moved towards the stern deck. That moment, Hank heard an ominous familiar sound overhead—the droning of an old-fashioned reciprocating airplane engine. Then, two pale green points appeared against the sky, their glare spreading across and blot-ting out the starlight. To the north, the sky shone a bilious pale green, and the points themselves seemed to be moving in small oscillations.

"Parachute flares!" Bissell said. "Looks like they're really after us."

The Cob analyzed the spectacle. "If they are, they're a helluva long way off."

The flares were descending slowly, and as they slipped closer to the water, they cast a wide sheet of unearthly apple-green on the waves. In the embarrassing bare illumination, Hank could see two junks green-hued, with bat-sails far to the north, and on the seaward side of them, a pale Communist PC ploughing towards them at full speed. But the garish sheet of light fortunately hadn't spread as far as the submarine and the friendly junk.

Hank looked up at the bridge, and could make out the shape of a man bending over the rail; it was probably Battersby: Now the voice called out to them, a tense cry: "Cast off! Cast off! We're leaving. Cob, get below."

Hank, Muley, Helmantholer, and Bissell hurried into the boat, Muley and Bissell manhandling the ammo box into the life raft. Sergeant Hing was shoving off with his paddle from the steel hull. The Cob flopped into the sub's cramped access hatch, disappearing in a blink. The steel lid closed with a crash. It seemed only a moment they had been making only a few paddle strokes, when the men in the life raft heard a hissing of water along the bulbous upper flanks of the sub, a line of phosphorescence flared along it, and the black metal edges began to sink. Hank watched fascinated as the sail structure began to move forward and downward in the same quiet pattern, and soon only the top of the bridge could be seen above the bubbling water. Gracefully, amid the mildest of whirlpools, the submarine disappeared. The rubber boat was alone with the fishing junk in Hainan Straits.

There were only two paddles in the rubber boat, and Sergeants Hing and O'Connor were using them urgently. There was nothing for the passengers to do but watch the pendant green flares descending on the water.

As the flares drew closer to the water, the light brightened on the Communist patrol boat and the two junks near it. Incredulous, Hank watched orange pencil-streaks of fire darting from the patrol boat in the direction of the junks to the north.

The zips of fire arched above the junks, curved downwards towards them. Another burst of fire from the charging patrol boat, more arches of orange tracer, and then they heard the rattle of the guns. Hank's breath was coming short, but automatically he was estimating the distance of the firing. Sound travels about a mile in five seconds— it took about twenty seconds for the sound to bridge the distance. The Commie PC must be four or five miles away.

But his calculations could be off—he was rattled, like everybody else. Sergeants Hing and O'Connor were scrambling to move the boat faster.

The tracers arched the sky again. Hank clicked his stopwatch. This time the firing seemed to plunge directly into the foremost of the two junks. With a sudden movement like the flick of an eye, the junk sail collapsed. The junk-man was probably cutting off his power to let the patrol boat know he would stop. Then, with one bright final flash on the water, the green illumination vanished into black.

Bissell shook his great bald head: "Looks like the natives are restless tonight."

Hank said: "The Commies probably put out a call about the submarine contact, and they're shooting at most anything."

Bissell hawked and spat over the side. "Well, if they're lookin' for us, they're five miles off," he said. "And that's fine with me. Fucked up, that's the way it is with war. When the enemy is more fucked up than we are, that's great."

Helmantholer said: "We better duck this rubber boat as fast as we can."

They had almost reached the low bow of the friendly junk, and they could see a group of Chinese crewmen standing there, faint silhouettes against the sky.

They jumped aboard the prow, and were met by Hope and a wiry, lean-faced Chinese in black sharkskin. Hank bowed, and the thin man smiled, apparently happy that some of the American barbarians had learned proper politeness.

Hope was explaining: "I think this is the captain. Nooley tried some of his Hainanese on him, but no savvy."

"Let me try," Hank said while the others hauled the ammo aboard, dragged the rubber boat on deck and pulled the chains of the bungs so it would deflate, Hank essayed his sing-song Cantonese: "*Nay-ee woo-ee 'm woo-ee Gwang-doong wa-ah?* Do you speak Cantonese?"

The thin captain was thunderstruck. It was enough of a shock to see so many of the round-eyed long-nosed barbarian ghosts in one evening, without having one of them speak a familiar language. Hank repeated the question, and then the captain broke into smiles: "*Ngaw-aw woo-ee Gwang-doong wa-ah.*" The captain went on to say that his name was Ching Nam, that he had been to Canton many times in the course of his life at sea, and that he had lived there for a year. Therefore, he said, his Cantonese was passable.

Hank said, in Cantonese: "It is always pleasant to hear a familiar language in a strange place. It's like hearing a stranger call you by name." Hank remembered having heard this very phrase from Mary, and she attributed it to Mo-Tzu. "Wasn't that what Mo-Tzu said?"

Captain Ching Nam was astounded. "A stranger who knows our sages! That is a wonder."

Sergeants Hing, O'Connor, and Veracruze were still folding the wet, intractable shape of the deflated rubber boat when the faint grinding sound of an approaching propeller-airplane was heard again in the northern sky. Two more bright green points of light appeared and blossomed into a searchlight glow spreading wide over the water, turning the junk and everything around it a garish chartreuse. The captain and three of his crew wore expressions to match the deathly pallor. They chattered at a frantic pace.

Ching Nam composed his face with a palpable effort and turned to Hank: "My comrades of the junk feel that the same patrol boat will intercept us. It is our belief that all you *May-gwak-yun* must be hidden below our fish cargo. We are very sorry to ask it, but all your group must be in false bottom of the boat. It is where we carry what might be called incorrect cargo, a secret hold. Is not pleasant down there, but necessary—and time must not be lost."

With that word, he rushed off to the after-hold of the ship, where a group of crewmen were moving hatch-covers. As Hank was translating for Captain Hope, Ching called back over his shoulder, "Please, quickly."

Hope followed Captain Ching's meaning and fell in behind him, shouting: "Operation Typhoon, on the double." Ching led the group, with a flickering tung-oil lantern, through an open hatch and into a definite wall of the stench of fish, both fresh and pungent antique.

A crewman jumped in beside Ching, brandishing a pitchfork-like instrument, and a minute later another crewman joined the party. They immediately started shovelling the pile of flickering silver bodies, while the captain stood by with the lantern. A hatch panel, soaked with water and blood, was disclosed beneath a three-foot depth of the still-squirming catch. The crewmen threw aside their pitchforks and sprang down to lift off the cover, while Ching called out: *"Maw-len! Maw-len!"* which Hank correctly understood to be a Hainanese command to rush.

Hank peered down into the secret compartment: an evil-smelling bilge no more than three feet deep in the center, but probably long enough for eighteen men to take shelter in, if they didn't try to stand up. At the bottom, below the rickety floor-boards, there was a glint of water. Like all bilges, this one would be foul, and Hank had instant visions of the Typhoon crew staggering ashore blind seasick on Hainan Island.

Hope had a more immediately practical approach. He turned to Hank: "Hank, what about our gear? And will he thump on the hatch as soon as the danger is over, so that my people can get out?"

Hank relayed the question and answer, while Captain Ching made frantic motions as if to throw the raiding party directly into the bilge: "He says the crewmen will bring the gear down right away and stow as much of it as possible in the bottom, and hide the rest outside where they can. But he says the main thing is to get below quickly, and that it may be two hours before the danger will be over."

Hope said: "I hope it'll be sooner than that—that'll be after five o'clock, and we'll be coming up on daylight. It'll be time to land."

While Hank was translating, Captain Ching barely paused to listen. Instead, he kept motioning to the raiding party to go below, and repeating, *"Maw-len!"*

Before Hank could finish, there was an outcry of crewmen's voices from above. Hank heard a couple of distinguishing cries, particularly that now-familiar word: *"Maw-len! Maw-len!"*

Three more crewmen, wearing the usual peasant uniform of black sharkskin, came running down the open ladder from the outside deck, hauling the American cargo in heavy canvas covers, and Special Force rucksacks.

The detachment manhandled their gear into the secret compartment with a great profane grunting and groaning, but their complaints were not the slightest bit leisurely, because muffled shouts came from above, and the loud thudding of twenty-millimeter cannon: patrol boat shots across the bow. The crewmen shoved the Americans below, jammed the hatch on top, and shovelled the layers of fish back with their pitchforks.

Down below, in the dark and the stench, the men lay against the bilge, and swore to themselves in silence. They felt the heavy bumping of another boat alongside the junk, and heard heavy engines roaring. They held their breath as the Communist patrol came aboard. They listened to the sounds of the scuffing feet as the Commies descended the ladder into the fish-hold, and they picked out the authoritative, violent voices of the patrol-boat sailors as Captain Ching was questioned.

Then the voices grew fainter, there were more bangs and bumps as the patrol vessel was boarded, and the renewed sound of powerful torpedo boat engines. Came the rattle of the junk sails being hoisted, the boat began to heave uneasily with the seas, and Hank knew she was under way.

Bissell, as ever vocal, voiced his discontent: "Why don't that guy let us up? The fuckers have fucked off."

Veracruze tested the weight of the hatch overhead with a palm. It didn't budge. "Because we got three feet of shit over us, that's why. And they ain't about to shovel it away for a while."

Veracruze was not in favor of unnecessary expression, especially the profane kind. "You look pretty fuckin' shit sick, O'Connor," he said.

He crawled over some intervening stretched-out feet and legs to the forward reaches of the compartment, braced his back against the curve of the bilge, lifted his head as far as possible to get air, and retched.

A few minutes later, they heard footfalls on the hatch, and Captain Ching called out in Cantonese: "Captain Hank, you must remain below. There are other patrol boats ahead. We do not wish them to find any trace of you."

Hank translated, for all present to hear, and was struck by an idea. He called out, in his best Cantonese, his loudest voice: "Captain Ching, we must have the hatch open, for air. Our people will be too sick otherwise."

Hank heard a responsive footfall above, and further pleaded his case: "If you will leave the hatch open we will stay below. If a patrol boat appears, your crew can cover us over in a minute."

Hesitation, then a scraping and thudding on the hatch, as the fish were pitched off again, and at last, the rough, odoriferous lid lifted.

In a moment, the hatch was put aside, and the good air came rolling in palpable layers. "I never thought the air in this hold would smell so good," Sergeant Bissell said. "Ah, the fresh mountain air— flavored with shit fish—but delicious."

*

Twice more, before they reached the beach, the hatch was thrown over the hold, and oceans of fish speared over it. Each time, the air of their dungeon grew incredibly foul within seconds, and a wave of mal de mer swept through the compartment.

Then the hatch cover was mercifully lifted, and Captain Ching appeared in the aperture. He sought Hank's face, and explained: "We have weathered the storm. We are approaching dock."

Hank translated, and Sergeant Bissell said: "Musgrave, tell the gentleman thank you very much for the fuckin' pleasant sea voyage."

Hank looked at his watch. "Can we come up now?" he asked Captain Ching. "It is still dark, isn't it?"

"Yes, your men may come on deck."

Hank translated, and Hope said: "Okay, everybody up, let's get on deck and get the gear ready. Sounds like we're almost there."

Up on deck, Hank found the night as black as ever and ahead of the boat, he could see dim spots of yellow light across calm lagoon-like water. He asked Captain Ching if that was the destination.

Ching nodded. "Yes, that is the farm of Comrade Dinh, the jute grower. Also he owns this boat and two other junks, everything on them, including radios. He is very acceptable 'tiger' to the Tau Muk Village Chief—because very clever manager. Continues to bring in good catches of fish and manufacture good rope from jute."

The junk had dropped sails and was being poled in towards shore. The crew members walked up and down the gunwales, leaning against the long sticks. As the junk drew closer, Hank could see a lantern held high above the heads of a group on a pier. The man holding the lantern swung it slowly from side to side. Captain Ching indicated the man and explained to Hank: "That is Comrade Dinh."

Dinh lowered the light as he evidently saw that the Americans were on deck. He put the lamp down and walked forward to the edge of the dock. "Good morning, flen," he said, offering a large part of the English which he remembered from the old days before Chiang Kai-shek's debacle. "I bid you werrco. Suggest get from ship immediately. It safe here not."

"He kids us not either," said Sergeant Bissell.

"Who captain here?" Comrade Dinh wanted to know. Hank thought: He *does* know the mechanism of efficiency—the importance of the good commander.

Hope jumped to the dock and extended his hand: "I am. Captain Frank Hope. And your name is?"

Comrade Dinh was confused by the flow of strange language and by the extended hand. He had a distant recollection that the hand was to be touched in some way, a foreign-devil custom, so he seized Captain Hope's thumb vigorously, and bowed three times.

Three other figures had come up into the faint light of the lantern: a woman and two other men, and they were jabbering furiously. Hope called out: "Musgrave and Nooley, interpreters, front and center." And in the same breath: "Everybody off the boat. Make sure your gear's all disembarked."

The two men with Dinh were still talking rapidly and Hank knew it must be the Hainanese dialect. Dinh tried another bit of English. It sounded like: "Man Rook On," unidentifiable, but the gesture was clear—the nervous wave of the arm to the men, to follow him quickly. Dinh bounded away, seized his lantern, and started into a path through tall wet swamp grass. The other two Chinese jumped in behind him, while the woman hung back, waiting for the Americans to intervene before she followed her husband's trail.

Hope picked up an Armalite and his rucksack, and quickly ordered Veracruze: "He's going to take us someplace—probably the place we'll be hiding out. Better stay behind with the gear, and I'll come back and we can lug it. Keep the men under cover, better get security out, until we come back. But no shooting. Knife—if necessary." He motioned to Hank and Nooley, Muley Muhlbach, and Sgt. Bissell, to follow him; and he hurried after the shadows of Dinh, and the other two men disappearing into slick elephant grass as tall as a man.

The night seemed black, although as his eyes grew accustomed, Hank could see that the stars still twinkled. But they had faded, the sky would soon show faint green tints in the east.

He fixed east by the heavy coils of Leo, low on the horizon. That was the direction from which they had come, that would be the direction of their escape, if any, two and a half days from now, after the job was done. An infinity of time! Eons of hideous struggle, between now and then.

Sgt. Bissell was moving ahead of Hank toward the wall of grass—elephant grass he remembered like a ghost from the Vietnam war —as he hurried to catch up with Bissell's rocking gait. Bissell was the last of the group following Dinh.

Hank hurried, his feet hesitantly seeking the muddy mound which was the path. In the dark ahead, he could barely see Bissell's broad head and shoulders rolling against the dim sky. Beyond the field of grass, graceful silhouettes of palms stood like poinsettias against the Stardust.

On the far side of the field of elephant grass, Hank saw that the procession was reaching a coconut grove, long lines of palms, and dry land under foot. Dinh was leading the way towards the light, another flickering lantern shedding the half-hearted glow of tung oil. Now, from the dark came the fetid smell of rotting coconut husks. Evidently Dinh was also a producer of copra. In America, he would have been only a mixed-subsistence farmer. Here he was relatively a very wealthy man.

"How do you like China?" he asked Bissell softly as they hurried along in the scent of copra husks.

"It smells too fuckin' much like Vietnam," he said, "And no broads."

"What about the broad with Dinh—the farmer? She looks pretty good."

"Nah. Didja see her open her mouth. She's got black teeth, like those country broads in Vietnam. They put fuckin' dye on 'em or somethin' to keep out the devil."

Hank said: "They said it was vulgar to show all that white bone when they opened their mouths."

"Anyhow," Bissell sighed, "she's got black teeth, she ain't got nice choppers like the broads in Saigon. Boy, did you ever know a broad that worked in the Capitol Bar in the Ville, named Binh? What a little Tiger Lady, wow! We all called her Sweet Lips. What a broad, what a fuckin' construction!"

Hank's mind was flashing back to his own beautiful broad, but Bissell broke the spell: "That broad! She wore a fuckin' sex worker's uniform—a pair of knee pads."

Bissell guffawed, his hoarse voice carrying in the still of the grove. "Keep it down, Bissell," Hank warned him in a whisper, and added tactfully: "Fun-ee—fun-ee joke." They were coming up to the thatched barn now, and Hank could see Dinh trying to make himself understood to Nooley, Muhlbach, and Hope. Hope's face was turned back hopefully to seek Hank's assistance in the communication problem. When Hank came up, the wiry farmer, Dinh, beamed with pleasure. He said in Cantonese: "It is good to find someone who can bridge gap of language between us."

"It is good my poor Cantonese has some utility," Hank answered politely.

Dinh picked up the flickering lantern and led the way towards the barn, saying in Cantonese: "I would like to conduct you to the house which will be your home on Hainan." Hank translated for Hope and the others, and in the same moment he noticed the cloud of black bugs thick as coal dust around the lantern glow. They were apparently the same maddening tiny insect pests he remembered from the swampy rice delta of Vietnam. Those bugs used to come on certain nights in incredibly thick waves, stupid as moths struggling for hara-kiri in the light, or lemmings heading blindly for the sea. He remembered how the black bugs and their brothers the green ones would besiege your nostrils, ears, and eyes with determined, exasperating fury, and he stayed a couple of steps away from the light, as Dinh led the way into the barn structure.

Hank had felt an itching sensation around his wet ankles, the prickling of large-caliber mosquito bites. "They feel like big ones, too," be said.

"At least," said Nooley, "I haven't noticed any leeches."

"We can't be sure of that," Bissell offered sagely, "until we check our crotches. What the buggers call home."

Dinh led the way into the musty darkness of the barn, which combined the ripe smell of the black rice-mud with the stench of stale hay. Hank noted that the floor was mud, with a sprinkling of straw over it, and in the back of the enclosure, piled-up stacks of jute fibre, tied in plaits.

Bissell moved a flashlight beam around the room. In the illumination, a fleet of large spiders were revealed on the inside of the roof. They scampered for cover. He studied the mud floor. "No green snakes I can see, yet."

He turned to Hank. "Better ask the guy if we can get some more straw. Otherwise, this'll be like a mud bath—with eighteen guys walkin' in it."

Captain Hope, who was dumping his rucksack against one wall, agreed and he added: "Better ask him, too, if he's got any fresh water around here. Have to have some raw material to put the halizone in."

Hank turned to the job while Captain Hope, Muhlbach, and Sergeant Bissell shoved off to retrace their steps and bring in the rest of the detachment. Major Nooley looked almost at home as he propped his longbow in the corner and his quiver and armguard on a local pile of straw.

"This is the forest primeval," said Nooley. "We fell into it with a sudden muddy thud."

"A fishy thud first, then a muddy thud, and I hope we'll bust out of here without a thud two and a half days from now."

"And not too many thuds in-between," said Nooley. "Except the important thud at the Commie airbase."

An hour later as the first green lights of dawn were blotting out the night, a home for the Typhoon detachment had been fashioned in the jute storage barn of Comrade Dinh, farmer and fishing-boat proprietor in the eastern reaches of Hoihow. Dinh had built a fire, and heated a wooden bucket of water for them, while they stayed under cover in the barn.

Zave (for Xavier) Espinoza, mess sergeant of the group, made coffee in a bucket and passed out combat rations. Dinh suggested in Cantonese that "your men can regain sleep," and he added: "Your troops are too conspicuous by daylight. It is better that they remain within during daylight hours."

Hank translated, and Hope passed out the order to his crew as they munched their C-rations: "Farmer Dinh here comments on something pretty obvious about us—in the daylight we're conspicuous. Most of us better stay under cover all during daylight, and maybe we can mount a small patrol or two and find out what the situation is. We've got some Vietnam survival kits with black peasant clothes—and we'll use those on our people that have to move around in the daylight. Sergeant Veracruze has got some brown stain that we can use on our faces and hands—or just plain mud, and there's plenty of that.

"Even so, we couldn't exactly double for the local yokels.

"Farmer Dinh here suggests that we catch some sleep. We'd better do that, because tonight we're gonna be up, and we're gonna be operating. Dinh says there's a curfew at ten o'clock in the evening, and we might get caught moving around after that, because the cops get thicker. He says that there are cops all over the place most of the time, and he doesn't think we'll have much chance to make any big move except at night before the curfew."

He indicated Wing On and Wing Run, who were standing stiffly beside Farmer Dinh. Dinh's wife had gone. "Our Friendlies here, Mr. Wing and his son, and Mr. Dinh, will be going over the maps with us, and showing us the lay of the land. I'll send our Sergeant O'Connor, Sergeant Hildebrand, and PFC Trotter to post security around our camp here during the day. They'll wear the black peasant suits from the survival kits, and stay under cover. They can't afford to be seen. Mr. Dinh here promises to post his own security, and he'll tip us off if anyone is coming. Meanwhile, I want you all to start on chloroquin and Polymagma. Sergeant Roberts will hand it out. We're back on our old Vietnam diet again—dysentery bugs, no-go pills and chloroquin."

Sergeants Wohl and Hildebrand were getting out the black pajama suits for their guard duty, and some of the other men had already stretched their sleeping bags on straw pallets. Hope announced: "One more thing: Sergeant Hing—we want to see you." Hing moved to the officer group—Captain Hope, Gresham, Nooley and Helmantholer all standing together—and stood at attention. But he was shaking his head:

"I knew I'd be volunteering for the patrol, Captain. I'm the only one of the bunch that's got natural protective coloring."

Hope laughed. "That's right. But think about others of us who are going with you. We're completely the wrong shade. How do you think we feel?"

Captain Hope unrolled his chart of the Meng Wan area, and told Hank: "Hank, tell the Friendlies that we want to go over this geography and prepare for our patrol—whether they approve or not. We can't just sit here all day when we're practically out of time."

*

The patrol wore canvas and leather jungle boots, Vietnam style, but black pajamas top and bottom, and no other identifying equipment except C-rations stuck in pockets, and a minimum of weapons. Eric Hope and Hank wore webbing belts with canteens, and black-bladed K-bar knives. Hope, Veracruze, and Hing packed .45 automatics. "We'll share the weapons and water," Hope said. He had swung a pair of binoculars over his shoulder, under his shirt. Their faces were daubed with mud to simulate a non-Caucasian shade.

Dinh had made a series of nervous objections, as they were winding up for a takeoff at five after ten, and Hank was about to translate for Hope. But Hope still studied the route marks he had made on his chart. At last, he folded it up and stuffed it in a pocket.

"This map is one bit of equipment I'll have to be sure to dump if we get jumped."

The other members of the patrol, Sergeant Hing, Sergeant Veracruze, and Nooley stood by while Hank was translating Dinh's complaints.

"Dinh reminds us that he warned us against going anywhere at all before sundown. He says he can lead us along these trails and we might be able to reach the house, but that if anyone is suspicious, we will have no chance of escape."

"How about we compromise, and ask him how far he thinks we could go safely today with a small patrol, and be a little closer in for tonight," Hope said. And tell him or not, as you think best: "We've got to get a look at the layout for ourselves—we don't have time not to."

Hank translated, and Dinh and the Wings appeared satisfied. At 10:31 A.M. the patrol was moving across rice paddies at the extremity of Dinh's farm, and passing a neighboring farmer as he plowed with a wooden harrow behind a water buffalo. The Wings and Dinh waved, the farmer waved back briefly without exhibiting undue interest, and Dinh, leading the group, kept them well away. Dinh looked back sharply to see whether the neighbor was taking a second glance. He was not. In these days of greatly increased police activity in eastern Hoihow, it was apparently bad business to be too curious about anything.

From the neighbor's farm onward for the next two or two-and-a-half miles, the trip went well, phenomenally well. They skirted the rice fields and moved into a woods of scrub evergreen, the path well-worn among pale jade-colored undergrowth.

Then the forest suddenly grew tall, and thick. They waited for thirty minutes and Dinh and Wing On went ahead to scout before they moved into the tangle of thick ferns and thorns among the tall trees. Before he and Dinh started, Wing advised Hank: "Tell your friends to watch the ground. Green snake is common—carries much poison."

Hank told him they all knew about the krait, from Vietnam. Sergeant Hing, looking down at his thick-soled leather-footed jungle boots, laughed: "I'm not worried about steppin' on a snake myself— but how about those poor little bastards—if they did?" The Chinese Friendlies were barefoot except for thin slices of old rubber tire held in place over the soles of their feet, like Japanese *Zoris*,

Hank reminded him: "You were in Vietnam, Hing. You know how these little guys make out with bare feet. They've got tough skin, and besides, they're faster than we are when it comes to kraits, scorpions, leeches—any of the hazards of the road."

Hing sat beside Hank while the Americans and Wing Run stayed with them and waited for the other Friendlies to return. Hing said: "I *should* know about my people, I've spent enough time in Asia." He continued softly. "In the jungles at Mang Buk and the rice swamps at Camau. But I always worry about them. Probably because not very far back, my folks were little buggers just like them. It'd be good if we could remember everything they knew, and still add on what we picked up in civilization, But I guess we can't."

Hank commented: "You're a Special Force trooper. You do pretty well with backwoods tracking, survival in the jungle and whatnot."

"Yeah, that's right," Hing said. "But it's not the same. Did you ever hear of the East-West Center?"

". . . Is that the Federal study center in Hawaii?"

"Yes, sir. I was a student there for one scholarship term."

"I thought that was a graduate institute."

"It is," Hing said. "About two-thirds of the students are graduate students. I already had my M.A."

"And you're still a sergeant! What happened, did they bust you down after too much R & R? With a background like that, you should be a Third Secretary or a Vice Consul."

Hing was smiling. "I don't want to be up at the top of the barrel. I'm a good Zen Buddhist," he said. "I'm still hanging around the bottom, and waiting for my *satori*. To get *satori*, you have to be at the very bottom, looking up."

He went on seriously: "Anyhow, Asia's got a lot for us, we have a lot for them. Mainly, they're working their way out of the Middle Ages, and they need a lot of help."

"They seem to have developed a couple of scientific lines," Hank pointed out. "For instance, the H-bomb."

By this time, Dinh and Wing On had returned from their patrol and Dinh was telling them: "*Serng wah-ee* Hank, Captain Hank. After this jungle, we reach an open rice padi—many padis. It is rice commune of *Kiung Shau*, Communist attempt at collective farming. If we can cross, we will be in the farm of my friend—the friend who owns the rice farm overlooking the airbase." Hank looked at his watch: two-fifteen. He could see that Dinh had a proposal he was building to . . . He waited.

Dinh took a deep breath and went on: "I do not wish you to think that we are small heart, lacking in courage. But in previous discussion, you said it might be wise to stop a certain distance from the vantage point.

"Patch ahead is most dangerous part of our trip. We suggest course of wisdom is to wait until 1500 in afternoon in edge of thick jungle. At 1500, next group of workers come on and will work in the fields until sundown. Chief of the Commune is trying heroic measure to increase productivity.

"When new work force comes to area, many people will be moving through the field. More work for Chek-koh. We will be less noticeable."

Hank relayed the proposal to Captain Hope, and Hope was impressed. "Makes sense. We probably need something to eat again, anyhow. So we can take a break now—and then go on. What was it, six o'clock this morning that we had breakfast?"

Hope asked if Dinh and the Wings would lead them to a spot away from the path where they could have some food.

Dinh said: "If you will follow me, I will lead to hiding place which may be useful in next day or two."

Hank translated, and Hope picked up the idea immediately: "If the pressure is too great on Mr. Dinh's farm, we should probably move to the new place tonight, all of us."

After the translation, Dinh said: "First, you must see the hiding place. Perhaps too small, too demeaning."

He led the way on hands and knees through an animal track, a rough tunnel through the greenery. The arch of the track was frequently no more than two feet high, and the American group struggled to slip their larger bulk through behind the Chinese.

At last, they came to a pile of brush, which Dinh pushed aside to disclose a cave entrance in the red earth. He climbed down and disappeared in the blackness of a tunnel. Hope and Hank followed, and Hank lit a match. He saw a crudely hewn shaft, possibly ten feet long, and three feet high, with a pile of straw at one side in the rough shape of a bed, three sacks of rice on the other, and a mud floor. The other Chinese followed, and after them, Veracruze, Nooley, and Hing. Hing had a small penlight which he turned on, and he reported cheerfully: "Well, here we are back in the club."

Hope asked Veracruze: "What do you think about this for our hangout?"

"Not room enough," Veracruze answered. "But we could dig the tunnel out a little more."

"It isn't very comfortable," said Nooley. "I'd hate to live in it after a rain. But security is a kind of comfort. Is this place really secure?"

Captain Hope whipped out a C-ration box from his pocket. "We'll have to investigate this question of security with Mr. Dinh," he said. "Meanwhile, let's have lunch."

There were enough rations for the Chinese as well but this time they confined themselves to the biscuits. Hope was able to find out through Hank's translation that this jungle area was wasteland, that Chek-koh patrols checked through it occasionally because of its proximity to the airfield installation. "But," said Dinh, smiling happily, "even most zealous Chek-koh agent would not be likely to follow animal trail to cave here."

Hope passed around his canteen. "Johannesburger 1959," he said and Hing relished a draft of halizoned water.

It was time to go. Hope made his decision: "We'll move our camp here tonight." He smiled. "That is, of course, assuming that we *get* back to our camp, tonight."

They started on all fours through the animal trail and soon were back on the main path, following Dinh towards the edge of the Commune.

In a few minutes they could see the end of the jungle ahead through thinning vegetation, the lustrous emerald sheen of the rice fields spread out beyond. Dinh led the way from the path to the fallen trunk of a giant breadfruit tree. There they crouched, still under cover of the forest.

"Chek-koh! Chek-koh!" Dinh was hissing. They had already learned the word. Chek-koh, the Commie Secret Police, meaning approximately "Big Brother Surveyors." Here on the Commune, the Chek-koh had dug in.

The rice-terraces were a patch-quilt of varying shades of green and brown—lakes of *padi* in various stages of cultivation. Across the terraces, scattered thick as salt, the white conical sunhats of the workers—each marking a figure in dark sharkskin.

It was easy to see what had caused the expression of dismay on Dinh's part. About a hundred yards from the nearest edge of the fields, a detachment of laborers were digging a lengthy trench, with a squad of blue-uniformed Chek-koh police superintending. Fifty yards to the left, where the rice terraces petered out into a mangrove swamp, with the gleam of open water beyond, another detachment of laborers, with Chek-koh supervisors, were digging another redoubt. Evidently, from what Dinh had said, the airfield was beyond the next rise, in a low-lying area. Somewhere on that height would be the small farm of Dinh's friend, which Dinh counted on using as an observation point where they could watch the airbase.

Hope said quickly: "I get the picture. The boys in the blue uniforms are secret police—right? They're digging in, and we're stymied."

Hank checked it with Dinh in Cantonese. Dinh said shortly: "Absolutely correct."

Hope indicated the lower margin of the rice terraces where the mangrove swamp stretched thinly to the sea. "Ask him if we could backtrack and find our way through that mangrove swamp and get around the Commune that way."

Hank translated, and Dinh divined the meaning before the translation was through: "It would be dangerous—especially with people so easily identified as non-Chinese. Still, perhaps our best approach."

Hope had another idea: "Is there any other way to get to the airfield? How about the far side—the west side?"

Dinh shook his head after translation of the questions, and Hank translated his answer: "He says the other side is the main approach from the port of Hoihow. That's where the road is, and that is very heavily guarded. This is the only workable access, from the east side. There is an approach which could be made from the mountains to the south, but they are very high, rough, and full of bad insects and animals, and it would take many days to get into position there on foot."

Hope asked: "If we marched all night around this flank, could we get into position in the South before Friday morning?"

Dinh answered: "No less than four days steady march from here — even at a run."

A gloomy silence afflicted the group as all understood the bad news. Then Sgt. Hing screwed up his courage: "There's still the unfinished business of this patrol. Maybe we can't all make it across the mangrove swamp. But I'm the one with protective coloring. Maybe I could get through with my fellow Asians here, and get back with a hand-drawn map."

Before Hank could translate, Dinh said anxiously: "Whoever is to move, it would be best that the movement should be now, during the change of the workers' shift."

Hing was already getting ready to go, resigned to the fact that his offer would be accepted and mumbling to Hank: "I've thought of this a lot in the last two years. My only regret is that I have but one life to give for Fuckin' Asia."

Captain Hope was deciding. "Okay—if Mr. Dinh and the Wings want to try it, if they're equal to it—"

Hank looked around at the five sweat-drenched Americans and the three Asians who seemed relatively unexercised in their black sharkskin. "They're equal to it. You remember Vietnam. These people—even when they're fifty or sixty, walking ten miles and creeping through animal trails is no more than a step to the corner drugstore for us."

Hope smiled. "Maybe they're uneasy with so many May-gwok-runs. Especially since we're depending on Dinh to lead the way. Ask 'em. Would they like to go ahead with just Sergeant Hing?"

Hank relayed the question: "Would Dinh—and perhaps the others, too—prefer to go ahead with one American; Sgt. Hing, who could most easily pass as a Hainanese, to the farm of Dinh's friend, overlooking the Communist airbase?"

Hank waited while Dinh and Wing On discussed it rapidly, almost gruffly, in their native tongue.

"What's going on?" Hope wanted to know.

"I don't know," Hank said. "It's something I don't understand. And if we don't make up our minds pretty fast—we're gonna be having trouble with *any* movement, in any direction."

At last, the Chinese spokesman came back with an astounding answer: "Wing and I believe it would be wiser if Captain Hope, the commander of the detachment, and Mr. Musgrave, the only speaker of the language, should accompany our final expedition to the house of my friend overlooking the airfield."

Hank translated and remarked: "Well, I'll be damned! I thought they were going to find fault with the dangerous presence of such obvious foreigners on this last lap this afternoon. Instead, they don't give a damn about that—they just don't approve the idea of getting into the most dangerous position, without the American commander and interpreter. Matter of face, I'd say—or in the American idiom, status. They don't mind taking a chance of getting their nuts shot off, as long as they've got the head man along."

Hope said, with a sigh: "Well, that's a relief. Tell 'em the three of us will go—right now. That is, unless you have some practically unimpeachable reason to dissent, Hank."

"None that I can rightly reckemember," said Hank. "Except my usual, unreasoning and hysterical fear of death and dismemberment. Let's go."

20

HOPE GAVE RAPID ORDERS TO THE GROUP. "IT'S BETTER if you and Veracruze head back, Nooley. It's hard enough for our friends here to get stuck with Hank and me. At least, if the Chek-koh ripped off my hat, they wouldn't be looking at red-light locks like yours."

"Besides, you've got to go back to the camp and get the stuff ready to be moved tonight, while we try this end-run through the mangroves. And I want you to keep an eye on all the messages. I'll leave you in command till we get back. Tell Helmantholer to be careful with his radio transmissions. Remind him to use the counter-measure gear with the big radio—and not to use the little SCRs at all. We don't want to give the Commies any vector on where our camp is."

"I guess we'd better let Wing On go back with you. He knows the way."

Nooley smiled wanly. "I'll be practicing my archery," he said.

Hope grinned. "Okay. We'll go back through the jungle a little, past the dugout—and Musgrave, Hing, and I will make the end-run with Dinh and Wing Run."

Hurrying, they threaded their way along the path worn through the thick, thorny corridors of the jungle. They passed the shadowy tunnel which they had pursued to the secret dugout. Hank had blazed it in his memory: a pile of rocks marked it, rocks overgrown with propeller-shaped purple mallows. Then, a few feet further, came the bifurcation of the trail—one path leading back towards Dinh's jute plantation, the other winding in the direction of the thinning mangrove swamp and the gray lens of the sea. Where the mangroves began, Hank knew, their footing would grow spongier and spongier, and they might be swimming half the time as they tried to work their way past the Commune fortifications.

Nooley, Veracruze, and Wing On broke off and the small party plunged almost straight into the ghostly monochrome of the mangroves. The spread of short trees were one unending entanglement of roots, a gnarled spaghetti of knotty trunks in knee-deep brackish water. Dinh led the way, Wing Run following close behind. Like a young alleycat, Dinh bounded among the gray vermicelli, sometimes slipping into hip-deep holes, but always recovering his balance. They cut across the wide band of the swamp trees, the Americans thudding heavily in their jungle boots, slipping and splashing. But they were glad for the protection of American clothes, relatively proof against leeches and kraits.

The mangrove swamp was thick, an effective screen which masked their movement around the Commune. They could see some of the rice terraces above, through the black tree trunks—and the figures of workers moving. But it was one-way vision—the people in the terraces probably couldn't see into the darkness of the mangroves.

The party were progressing toward the sea, away from the Commune. Dinh's zeal to get away from the Chek-koh had led him clear through the belt of mangroves. Now they came to a wide salt marsh —a boggish swamp with tall, waving cattails. Beyond it, a space of mudbank, scrub trees and sandbar—a line of fishermen's shacks, with nets strung on wooden racks, and the thin insect shells of fishing sampans thick as fleas on the mud. In this distant fishing village, they could see trails of smoke uncoiling above the houses, and a few scattered fishermen moving in small groups—brown bodies in black loincloths.

Dinh decided to avoid the open reaches of the mud bar, and the fishing village, and try the middle-ground swamp. He led the way from the mangrove trees into the cattails, bounding with springy legs into marsh, wading the edge of a wide stream which seemed perilously uneven in depth. Twice, he slipped and fell into deep water as he walked up the bank of the stream among the cattails. Both times, Eric Hope and Hank pulled him out, spluttering. As long as they followed the river bank, Hank thought, they seemed glaringly apparent—much more so than they had been among the mangrove trunks, though of course they were farther from the Commune.

The little man halted, and squatted on a spongy riverbank in the lee of tall, bobbing cattails. He squinted across the marsh, focusing on the rising ground beyond the mangroves.

Hope squatted beside him. Dinh could see the perturbation in Hope's face. Hope turned earnestly to Dinh and asked the question in English. Hank knew what it would be: "Mr. Dinh, aren't you concerned that we are too obvious, out here on the swampy edge of the short? Wouldn't it be wiser to try to move farther inland among the mangrove trees?"

While Hank translated, Hope unfolded a water-soaked chart, and pointed to it with a finger indicating their supposed present location. Dinh smiled uneasily, as if uncertain that the identification was correct. Run grasped the situation. He oriented the map by the sun, and extended an identifying grubby finger to indicate a wide swampy river flowing to the sea from a wide thatching of mangrove swamp. "*This* side," he said in Cantonese. "And farm of Dinh friend is here. I know the way."

Run still struggled to make himself understood in fragmentary Cantonese. "It is many times—*sheung shi*—that I have made fishing in river here—with *ue foo*, fishermen."

Dinh's fingers were drumming nervously on his leg. Hank interceded with diplomatic tact, in his best Cantonese: "Young Comrade Run understands you are expert guide of entire area. However, he submits safer route would follow closer in mangrove trees, not so far exposed on edge of the sea."

Hank explained quickly to Captain Hope: "I can see why Dinh didn't want to take us out to the fishing village. But I think we're too far into this marsh. It's for the birds—swamp birds. We better let Run lead us back into the mangroves."

Through the cattails taller than a man, Hope and Hank scanned the green belt of rice terraces rising inland above the black line of mangroves. Up there they could make out hundreds of black-clothed, white-hatted worker figures, a pepper-and-salt of rice laborers. Among them, probably many Chek-koh. Could they see this far? Probably, if they turned binoculars this way. On the other side, from the edge of the sea, the fishermen might easily spot them.

Dinh was clearly sensible of the situation and all its dangerous overtones, and clearly he grasped the face-saving opportunity being offered him. He stood up in the shelter of a clump of tall cattails. He indicated the muddy riverbank winding in sluggish curves in the direction of the line of mangrove vegetation. "The young man, Run, can guide us from here to the *sap tey* trees. From the far edge of the trees, I will lead to farm of my cousin."

They were about to start, when Hing whistled sharply. "I see something moving—up there in the middle of those mangrove trees."

Hope unhitched his binoculars from the webbing belt underneath his black jacket. He quickly extended them to Hing.

Hing focussed and called out: "I see four—five blue uniforms. A Commie patrol."

Hing could see the unit leader, with a metal-stock Sudarev submachine gun, the Chinese copy called Type 54, familiar in Vietnam among the VC. One of the other dark shapes moving carefully through the closer end of the mangroves held a long-barrelled rifle. No other weapons were visible in the group.

"Can you tell which way they're moving?" Hope wanted to know.

"I'm not sure," said Hing. "They're facing this way, but the unit leader just turned around. They came from the far side, the west, and maybe that's as far as they're gonna go into the mangroves."

Hope licked his lips. "If they haven't seen us already, it'll probably be all right," he said. "That squad leader has turned away. He's moving back out towards the rice terraces." Hope saw the long arm of the soldier sweep in a gesture towards the luminous green of the rice terraces above the black wickets of the mangroves. "I think all we have to do is keep our cover here until they've gone."

Then there was another tense moment as the squad leader, evidently taunted by another member of the patrol, produced a pair of binoculars, and looked in the direction of the Americans through the two shiny black discs. He seemed to be sweeping a quadrant along the mud bar. Hope gave thanks that they had not chosen the mud bar, that they were instead in the tall cattails of the swamp, where the coverage was extensive as long as they hovered practically submerged in the water. Another item for thanks: Some favorable chance—or was it instinct?—had led Dinh to detour around the mangroves here, into the cattail swamp. Pure luck? An argument for the No-Atheists-in-Foxholes school of religionists? Good, anyhow.

At last, Hope saw the tall figure of the squad leader dropping deeper and deeper into the mangrove woods as he climbed back towards the Commune,

Hope motioned to Run—and he led the way along the swampy river bank, up toward the mangroves. As they reached the first twisted scrub trees, Hope suggested: "If I understand the geographic proposition, we're not too far from the farm of Dinh's cousin now. We're almost past the Commune. I think we'd better send out Dinh and Run, and maybe Hing, as scouts before we make this final lap. There could still be all kinds of patrols in this end of the mangroves."

Hank explained the plan to Dinh and Wing Run. Dinh nodded enthusiastically. Hank and Hope hunkered down in a hard knob of mangrove roots, a growth as dense as bamboo trunks in a jungle thicket. Both men were drenched in sweat, and they sank into the nub of horny vegetation with a sigh. The moment the other three men had gone ahead—with the agreement that Hing would run back to bring them the word—Hope unbuckled his canteen belt and field glasses and kid the soaked binoculars and his sheath knife and 45 pistol on top of a boulder.

"Man," Hope said, "I haven't felt this good since my first San Francisco week-end pass."

Hank laughed. "Before you get too relaxed, better check and see if we picked up any unwanted guests, hiking around in the swamps."

Carefully, the two Americans shed their black clothes, hung their sweat-soaked skivvy drawers over the nearest available rock surfaces —taking care that the surface of the underclothes did not openly reflect the sun—and they checked armpits and crotches. "Just damn lucky," Hope summed up after the thorough search. "Not even an itty bitty lonely little leech. This country isn't as bad as Vietnam— I think."

✳

It was still light when they saw the figures of Dinh, Wing Run, and Hing approaching carefully through the mangroves. Hope whistled softly to guide their friends back. In a minute, Dinh plunked down nest to Hank, taking the smooth rock seat which Hank offered.

Hank and Hope were slipping into their still-soaking black suits. It was clear from the faces of Hing, Run, and old Dinh that they had not run into any opposition.

Dinh said: "We must be fully prepared for any surprise. A Chekkoh patrol could be coming back at any moment, and we must make a workable plan for this event. I would suggest if the Chek-koh takes us by surprise, that you Americans must hide, and we will tell them that we are going to pay a visit to my cousin at the farm above the mangroves. Undoubtedly, they will release us with a warning to reach our homes before the curfew at ten o'clock."

"I hope we all do just that," said Hank.

✳

Dinh and Run led the way along the edge of the mangrove swamp closest to the rice Commune. The path had the advantage of being drier than their footing of the last two hours, although the screen of trees between them and the rice fields was skimpy, and they could see occasional figures of men moving. Fortunately, the light was fading, and the figures were only workers in black peasant garb. On this side of the Commune, they saw no blue-uniformed Chek-koh police.

But Wing Run warned: "There is Chek-koh outpost on this corner of the Commune, farther on. We will move deeper into the trees to get around it. Fortunately, it will be dark when we pass the post."

It was dark when they reached the edge of the rice fields belonging to Dinh's cousin. They hadn't run into any Chek-koh patrols or seen anything untoward and they hadn't come close enough to any of the Commune workers to establish any contact. The second shift Commune workers had left just before darkness fell.

Here at the edge of the rice fields which Dinh recognized as his cousin's, they halted, and Hing romped ahead to make contact. Dinh stayed behind with Hope, Hank, and Veracruze.

Hope looked at his watch. It was seven-thirty. He confided to Hank: "I hope the Commies decided to turn their landing lights on tonight, so we can get a look—that is, if you really *can* see the airfield from Dinh's cousin's farm."

Energetic Dinh asked what the *shwerng* was saying, and Hank replied judiciously: "He is wondering if we will be able to see anything of the base from your cousin's *padi*."

Dinh answered: "Please tell your friend that unless the men on the base have changed the appearance of it greatly, the view is quite good from Dinh Tzu's farm. And unless they have changed their practice, will be turning on their lights several times during the night, because aircraft fly."

*

They heard splashing sounds in the dark from the nearest *padi*, and Run and Hing came back to them—this time with another

Chinese who was plump and lethargic as Dinh was energetic and wiry. Dinh bowed to his relative, Dinh Tzu, and introduced him to the three Americans.

Dinh Tzu bowed deeply to Hope and Hank, a separate bow for each. There was enough light left in the sky so that Hank could make out Dinh Tzu's features. There was some similarity between his face and the older Dinh's.

Dinh Tzu led the way in the dark along a muddy divider between rice fields, across a line of banana and palm trees, and turned towards a tall-sided house where a faint glimmer of light could be seen through a small window. In a few minutes, he led the group through a low doorway.

After introducing his family Dinh Tzu led the way from the house, and out into the night now brightly lit with stars. In a few minutes, he took them across a series of muddy rice paddies, to the divider on the outer edge of the fields. From the embankment, they looked across a lower series of slopes, and perhaps half a mile beyond, they could see the pale-blue pinpoints of lights turned on, the Communist airbase—with something dark, like a cloud, hanging over it. Beyond the lights they could see little except the long white concrete road of the runway stretching southward towards the shapes of the mountains.

Dinh, speaking in muted tones although they seemed to be well out of earshot of any unfriendly persons, detailed the spectacle below them.

"On occasion they will turn on the searchlights, and will sweep the dark. But only one searchlight at a time: they do not have sufficient current to run more than one beam at any one moment."

Hank asked in Cantonese: "Which is the house where the big bomb is kept?"

Dinh waved vaguely at the line of blue pinpoints: "It is difficult to see bomb-house in darkness." Hank wondered if Dinh knew where the bomb storage house actually was, or whether he was disoriented, or perhaps the Commies had changed the geography down there, moved everything around, and Dinh didn't want to admit that it was unfamiliar.

But at that moment, a sudden blaze of floodlights spread a sheet of illumination across the field just beyond the shadowy white road of the runway. In the yellow sheet of light, they could see a phenomenon of camouflage; on tall bamboo poles, a wide, dark net illuminated from below. The bamboo poles, like vastly overgrown toothpicks poked up into the green folds of the camouflage fabric. From the vantage point of Tzu's rice padi, Hope's patrol could make out the dark, simulated rice fields painted on top of the camouflage landscape, and underneath it, lighted by floodlights, the teeming scene which it was supposed to conceal—buildings, trucks, guns, cement-mixers, the ant-horde of hundreds of people smudged across the center of the irregular rectangle of light. It was like looking into the wings of a theatre, seeing the stage as the audience saw it, and at the same time watching the scene-handlers working in full view.

"Behold!" the older Dinh said excitedly. "See what they do around the bomb building!"

Hank translated for the others, and indicated the crowd of people at the center of the lighted area. They were densely concentrated here, moving around the nucleus of a large torpedo-shaped object faintly masked with a long drape of cloth, The object was supported on a wheeled platform, ahead of it a tow-truck pulled, and around the platform a triple-layer of blue-uniformed Chek-koh police moved, to insulate the Shape from the mob of dark-clothed technicians and workers trekking with it. These police would be a-bristle with subma-chine guns.

"Perhaps this is the movement which we have expected, to a new storage house underground," Dinh explained. He pointed out a shad-owy concrete cave opening well ahead of the procession: a paved con-crete ramp sloping down into a sharp-edged dark hole. The ramp lay a long distance beyond the moving bomb platform, perhaps half a mile away.

"Do you think they still plan to drop the bomb Sunday?" Hank asked.

"That is as our informants have told us. It is still the schedule."

The bomb procession stopped momentarily, and a murmur of ag-itated questions in English overtook Hank. The Americans were won-dering what was happening, what they were missing in Cantonese. Hank began to translate carefully all that had occurred.

Hope's insistent questions concerned access to the bomb. He wanted to know what was beyond the patch of light; in the light they could already make out two formidable fences ranged between them and the new underground vault.

The picture was as they had gathered from the Hainan sourc-es Arthur Lowery had relayed to them: an outer rim-fence of dou-ble-strand barbed wire on this side—an A-frame with strings of wire on both arms of the A. And farther in toward the precise concrete mouth of the underground storage area, a high single belt of cyclone fence, with barbed wire at the top. There were gates in both those barriers, with guard stations—a larger one at the inner gate. But the Americans were on the backside of the field. The main gate, where the roads came in from Hoihow, was on the side away from them.

Hing, hunkered against the wall of the paddy-divider, estimated the fences like a demolitionist preparing for his job. "It's the back door all right. But it could be a bitch—with those floodlights on. No place to hide."

Captain Hope was busy making a map-sketch of the area.

"It looks as if the floodlights are mounted along that two-story building on this edge—where the light begins."

Hank translated, and Dinh replied: "That building is the house of the guards on this side. The lights are suspended from the walls."

"He agrees," Hank said. "He says it is a guardhouse."

Hope extrapolated: "If we could take out those lights—knock them all out at once—maybe then we could operate."

But Hank had a second thought: "What if they've got a separate circuit for the searchlights? Did you notice the searchlight towers?"

Hope nodded. "I saw it, all right. That tower on the left, there— with the two searchlights on top. But maybe we can cut the cable. Seems to be a generator there at the foot. You see the generators?"

"Yeah," Hank agreed. "But there's going to be a helluva lot to do, tomorrow night. Maybe we could just shoot them out."

"At this point," said Hope, "it looks like we could use about three times as many people as we've got, for this job."

The Chinese guides were restive under the tide of the agitated talk in the alien language.

Dinh asked Hank in Cantonese: "Can our knowledge of the airfield be useful to illuminate some matter for the American commander?"

Hank translated, and Hope, long experienced in frictions between cultures, responded properly: "Okay, Hank. Ask him what's beyond the floodlit area? And isn't there any way we could make an approach from that far side, by the main gate? It looks like a strip of jungle beyond those buildings, where the roads come in. Maybe we could use the woods for cover."

While Hank was translating, the Americans were fascinated to watch the slow-moving column, the sprawling escort of humanity accompanying the greatly-esteemed bomb, reach the concrete slope and the sharp-edged cave which would evidently be the new home of the machine. A squad of blue-uniformed police who had been guarding the entrance were moving rapidly toward the bomb, almost dancing. It was clear that the time was one of hearty celebration. Hank thought if they're blowing their tops tonight, when all they're doing is moving the damned thing, think what a Mardi Gras they'd have if they ever could drop it on the Seventh Fleet.

Dinh was answering Hope's question about the far side of the floodlit area: "Tell *Shwerng* Hope: far side is more difficult than this. Like this side, is protected by a double fence, reinforced with thorny wire. But on far side are also many more buildings, more roads, gun positions. Many more people. That is side where roads come up from town of Haiko. And beyond buildings, hills covered with jungle, Would be very difficult to make approach that way."

As he spoke, Hank heard heavy, rumbling, thumping sounds, like the bass beat of artillery, coming up from the direction of the procession. Hing was busy making notes and Hank borrowed his binoculars. At last, focusing the lenses, Hank saw the first marching men of a military band, in blue uniforms, coming up from the geometric, dark planes of the underground storage vault towards which the H-bomb procession was moving. It was a shock to see the line of musical instruments—worn Asian drums and brasses in weird shapes, instruments in curves which were comical and clumsy by our standards: shapes like nightmare specters, with sounds to suit; broken bugles, drums that made shattered rhythms, horns that skidded like tires on wet pavements—so that you almost ducked for fear of the anticipated crash afterward.

Now, with the Asian Conservatory Band coming up out of the earth to meet them, Hank thought, the column with the Shape really took to swinging—the periphery of technicians beyond the Chek-koh guards *were* dancing! This *was* a Mardi Gras, as the Chinese H-bomb nosed toward its new underground repository.

With the binoculars, Hank could see that there were large steel doors at the entrance to the downward-sloping ramp. They appeared to be sheet steel, now they had been swung back to allow the passage of the Shape. Hank shuddered; they could be formidable obstacles to the progress of the raiding party.

That moment, Hing nudged him to get the glasses back. Before returning them, Hank swept them quickly along the shielded Shape. He saw, along one open seam of cloth fluttering in wind, the flank of a metal ball structure, with prongs of detonators on it like the surface of a mine. Apparently, the huge, ball-shaped heart of the bomb rested at the front of the open girder shape.

He passed the glasses back to Hing and was too startled with what he had seen to be able to speak. They watched with awful concentration, saw the solid wedge of the advancing military band reach the head of the bomb column, flank it neatly on the far side, and then adroitly wheel and fall in behind the procession—the bomb procession in their work-uniforms pirouetting like mad Chinese Opera dancers.

The head of the column had become a tongue of life now in the concrete drawer-pull of the ramp, the band was almost to the spot in the concrete where he imagined the downward grade began, and where he had glimpsed the folded doors with the binoculars. Then, suddenly, the sheet of illumination died, the lights went off, there was nothing to break the blackness but the dim yellow headlamps of the tractor vehicle which towed the Shape. The lights glimmered faintly against the tunnel wall. And the noise, dancing, all the excitement seemed to have disappeared,

Hank's voice came back with a rush. "What happened? Did they have a power failure? Or would there be an alert?" he asked Dinh in Cantonese—and at the same moment he noted that Hope, near him, was sketching furiously in a notebook in the dim starlight.

While Dinh had not yet begun to answer, the response to Hank's questions was apparent. In the darkness, a sharp-edged beam of white light lanced across the field to grope the dark, then fix on the yellow glow of the headlamps marking the bomb procession.

"That's probably the answer to the question about the electric lights," Hope remarked. "The floodlight circuit is different from the searchlight circuit. The floodlights blew, the searchlight was turned on to cover for them—and there was enough juice in the searchlight circuit just for one beam at a time. That should help us with our plans for tomorrow night."

That moment, as if to substantiate what he had said, the floodlights went on again, and in a few seconds, the smoky beam of the searchlight flipped off.

"Nice of them to illuminate everything for us," Hope said. "Good luck is sure with us on this go-round—this far, anyhow."

In the floodlit rectangle below, they could see the end of the column disappearing into the concrete cavern, the gyrating technicians slipping in like an eraser-smudge of disorder after the moving rectangle of the band. And then, the steel doors closed, a sheen of gray intervening to shut off the tail of the column. At last, the floodlights went off again, the vast block of the airbase was dark, with only a scattering of blue points of light on the carpet of darkness.

"We better start the trip back home to Dinh's farm—before the curfew begins," Hope said. "And Hank—I want you to ask Dinh a lot of questions as we go—about distances, and the time it all will take."

"I'm for that," Hank said. "Does it look good to you so far, Eric?"

"I dunno," said Hope. "I'm not sure until we find out about the distances. It could be something—or plenty of nothing. And this new concrete bomb vault is going to be real tough, We won't be able to use any rocket launchers in there. We'd incinerate ourselves with the back-blast. But at least we've got some good, hard G-2 that we can believe."

"Do you think we've got enough strength in Operation Typhoon to do the job?"

"Like I said, I dunno. Maybe it'll be okay—or maybe nobody can do this job, not with a whole division. I know just about everything is in the timing—like everything else in life, only in this case, a helluva lot more so. We've got a tough session of agonizing reappraisal, like they say, tonight when we make our plan. Right now, I'd say we better get back to the camp, get on the horn and send through a May-Day call for a lot more help with this project. It won't hurt to ask. Or maybe I've just got the faint-heart heebie-jeebies. We've got to do some powerful thinking."

Before they splashed into the mangroves from the edge of the rice terraces belonging to Dinh's cousin, Hope instructed Hank: "Tell 'em we'll be back here tomorrow night. That'll be the time for our job—but don't let 'em know that yet."

21

ON THE WAY BACK, THEY KEPT TO THE MANGROVES AND stayed away from the cattail swamps and the fishing village. And as usual in war, chance turned a trick against them in the moment when the danger seemed to have passed, when they had least expected trouble.

They had almost passed the borders of the Commune rice farm. Then, a sudden splash of searchlights, thin needle-beams of light, split the blackness from that direction: fractious white arcs breaking the tangles of mangrove trees right at ground-level.

Like a frightened animal tribe, the Hope patrol slid into the water around the base of a knot of mangrove trunks. Dinh, Run and Hing fell on the side closest to the lights. Hank and Hope plastered themselves against the other side of the intertwined trunks. The outburst of searchlight activity was possibly one hundred yards ahead of them and in the direction of the Commune.

"Looks like the same Goddamn patrol we hit before—but they've got their flashlights now," Hope muttered. At the same moment, Dinh was uttering a related thought in Cantonese.

Hope whispered: "Looks to me as if they're moving in this direction. Better ask Dinh if he thinks we can get around them on the sea side, or if we should just stay here until we see what they're gonna do."

The translation took the usual long time, and Hank transmitted Dinh's opinion: "Suggests we stay here, because they'll probably make a quick look around and then go back where they came from."

But the patrol fortunately dawdled in their progress. They moved some fifty feet across the path of the Hope group. Almost dead ahead now, they halted as if they had reached a dense line of mangrove trunks. They flicked their lights in a compensating burst of activity through the low-lying trees, in all directions.

Hank often remembered later the protracted anxiety of that moment: that one of the almost accidental sweeps of the searchlights would graze across the knot of mangrove trunks where the Hope group had taken cover, three of them still unduly prominent on the same side as the Chek-koh patrol. Then, with the same slow-motion horror one feels in moments before a gruesome accident, the agonizing inertia of the most dreadful moment of a nightmare, the trouble struck.

Hank saw the one searchlight beam separate from the others. He saw the skinny white reed of the beam glance in a westward direction, and then, slowly and inexorably, begin a sweep across a row of mangrove trunks, and sit like a prowling mosquito, on the closer side of the mangrove cluster where Dinh, Run, and Hing were sprawled.

In that moment, it seemed that more than half their bodies were out of the water, and in that moment, they were moving! They had started to climb to a more sheltered position on the side of the trunks farther away from the Chek-koh patrol.

Now, in the steamy white glare of the searchlight, Hing seemed to be altogether out of the water except for his shoes. His black peasant costume stood out against the gray mangrove trunks with intaglio brilliance. When the light struck him, he froze in motion, like a dancer caught in a stroboscopic illumination. And the glare held absolutely stationary upon him, as if the anonymous Chek-koh soldier-on-patrol might be relishing his sudden discovery in the dark.

In that moment, Hank felt his heart chill as he saw that Dinh was still moving! Instinctively, Hank let out a hoarse whisper in Cantonese: "*Ting jee-ee!* Stop!"

Despite the whispered warning, Dinh continued to move. At last, much later, he froze, in the somewhat awkward position of a man in the middle of a leap over a hurdle—his legs spread-eagled as he had tried to twist his body over a high-flying mangrove root barrier. In the moment's illumination, both Dinh and Hing were painfully apparent although transfixed and motionless—but of the two, the smaller figure of the Hainanese seemed much more indelicately visible. Run was lowest, skillfully hugging the base of the mangrove knot.

Then, still at the same painful pace of incipient tragedy and present nightmare, another flashlight beam flipped into the sky close to the one targetting Dinh and Hing, and still with the same agonizing slowness, it moved, a snowy laser of light, across the rows of mangrove trunks, over the black sheen of swampy water, and it came uneasily to rest next to the first searchlight beam. The beam did not fall exactly into the same slot as the first. It covered the figure of Dinh with double intensity, and spread out farther to the west to embrace nothing but further twisted fragments of mangrove trunks and roots and fortunately it missed the figure of Sergeant Hing.

The positioning of the lights was from a direction directly opposite to Hank and Hope. And, with an incredible turn of fate, the first of the two successful enemy searchlights had unaccountably flipped off.

Now, over the spaghetti of the mangrove roots and between the spiky trunks, Hank could see that the remaining searchlight included only the blatantly obvious figure of Dinh. He heard a faint whisper from the dark next to him; Hope with the growl of instinctive command: "Hing! The light's off you. Come on, make it to this side of the tree. But fast. Double time!" Hank heard a scrabbling sound and knew Hing was unfrozen, hastening to carry out the order.

And, as if in almost the same breath, Hope went on, in a hoarse whisper: "Hank!—if we can get Hing over to our side of the tree, we'd better get ourselves forty or fifty feet away from here to the west. The patrol will pick up Dinh and Run. It's all right—they've got proper identity cards, the curfew hasn't started yet! Tell Dinh in Cantonese what we're up to!"

Hank translated fast, speaking as low and clearly as he could, lying low in the black water, against the rough mangrove roots. Before he could finish, the harsh order came from the direction of the Chek-koh patrol, while the light held on the figure of Dinh! "*Dau cham! Dau cham!* Halt! Halt!" In that second, Hank saw through the mangrove frame, the small, squirrel-like face of Dinh frozen in fright. For that moment, Dinh seemed incapable of movement, then slowly, he pulled himself into a central gathering of forces and began to stand up in the searchlight beam.

Meanwhile he said in a hoarse whisper to Run: "*Durng lai!* Get up! We'll tell them we've been visiting my cousin." Run stirred, his legs twitching, then slowly he, too, began to rise from the black water, to stand towering above the older Hainanese. And Dinh was shouting in

Mandarin in the direction of the Chek-koh lights: "*Ting choo!* We are farmers. Do not shoot! We have passes."

There were further harsh orders—"*Su tien !*" and "*Den ! !*"—from the direction of the Chek-koh patrol. Hank felt the compact form of Hing slide into the water beside him, and Hope's command from the other side: "I'm heading west."

"I told Dinh it would be twenty meters," Hank supplied.

"For that twenty meters," said Hope. "You and Hing better stay right behind me while I creep."

Hank watched the long shape of Captain Hope moving through the water, with barely a ripple. Hing was following with the same expert progress, the muscular body causing only slight irregularities in the black water. Behind them, on the other side of the mangrove which had been their refuge, Hank could see two Hainanese standing up in the glare of several searchlights, now, the trance-figures moving toward the white electric eyes of the patrol. It seemed that the patrol was fully occupied with the discovery of the two Hainanese, the lights were not roving through the surrounding area at the moment. Thus far, the three Americans were in the clear. And old man Dinh, with rare, instinctive military perception, was creating a divergence by speaking very loudly as he approached the Chek-koh. His language was unfamiliar; undoubtedly, Hank thought, it was Hainanese, but Hank caught a couple of familiar Mandarin phrases: "*Shem ma shih? What's going on?*" and "*Poo yow chow chee! Don't get excited!*" I hope, Hank thought, that if they ever give out medals to "indigenous personnel" in Washington, old man Dinh will get one, for whatever it's worth.

Then, in a space of time which seemed only a few seconds, Hope was sliding around a gnarled base of mangrove roots, as thickly-twined as hoses in a big-city fire. Hope was making the leap over the wall of roots into the comparative cover of the far side, away from the Chek-koh patrol.

Now, Hing followed in his commander's wake, his compact body edging over the fence of roots, inch by inch until the dark shape had disappeared on the far side. Then it was Hank's turn. He glanced behind him apprehensively and saw it was okay: the Chek-koh patrol fully occupied—five searchlights concentrated in one area, trained on the two Hainanese. Both of them talking now, both with hands extended in the air, and in the accumulated light, Hank could see the torsos of five or six Chek-koh clustered around them. Inexpertly, he began to climb the high barricade of mangrove roots.

In a squirt of effort, Hank skidded over the rough barrier of the trunks, and slid into the dark sanctuary where the two soaked, panting Americans waited, just arrived in the protection of the knob of mangrove roots. Hope had already pulled himself back up to the edge of the root-barrier, to peer over in the direction of the Chinese patrol.

The shouts continued loud from the direction of that mangrove thicket where Dinh and Wing Run were accounting for themselves. The mill-race of Communist questioning seemed, if anything, to have mollified in tone. Hank heard an identifiable Communist voice warning, in rapid, southern-accented Mandarin: "Don't you know you're supposed to be home by ten o'clock? Only an hour to get there. Hurry! Or you'll get shot."

Then, there was a flicking-off of several of the bright searchlight beams. Only two remained on the black water and twisted mangrove trunks. The two Chinese prisoners were dismissed, they went stumbling through the slick black swamp in a south-easterly direction, away from the patrol—and a couple of Communist soldiers were laughing, making rude jokes about the peasants hurrying home to their loving wives, who must be insensitive to their bad odor. The

American group around Hank waited quietly for their Chinese friends to circle back to them.

*

It was ten minutes later, when the wispy bright beams marking the progress of the patrol had moved back towards the west and south, in the direction of the Commune, that Hope heard a faint whistle in the black to the east indicating the approach of a possibly friendly presence.

The whistle was repeated, and at last, the thin voice of Farmer Dinh: *"Serng wa-ee? Serng wa-ee?"* Hope mimicked the whistle, and Hank whispered:

"Nay-ee ka-ee Dinh? Was that Dinh?"

The answer trembled on the moist air: "Dinh. Dinh. *Ngaw-ee haw-ee Dinh."*

Now, raising their silhouettes against the starlit sky, the little mosquito Dinh, and his tall young friend Run showed themselves boldly. They staggered through the black water, stumbling over roots and trunks, and the three Americans studied them intently from behind their mangrove barrier. "It looks like them all right," Hank whispered, and Hope muttered assent. Hope called out, softly:

"Over this way. This way."

At the same time, the high-timbred voice of Dinh had begun to ask Hank to relay questions to Captain Hope: *"Serng* Hank—please tell *Serng Wa-hee* Hope that we must hurry back to the farm. And must not your group move tonight, as we had discussed earlier this night?" Already, Dinh was answering Hope's question, before Hank could translate. And he was explaining: "The Chek-koh patrol asked repeatedly if other people with us. We believe they will come to jute farm to search for hostile presences."

*

They picked their way carefully through the dark hurrying, feeling some familiarity now as they threaded through the mangrove swamp, and reached the lagoon-like stretch of water between the mangroves and the jungle strip on the edge of the Commune. They could see flashing searchlights in the Commune rice fields, but the Chek-koh patrols seemed to be far off. A dim light, yellowish in shade, burned in the area of the emplacement on the side of the Commune close to the jungle. And in its faint glow, the shadowed figures of coolies could be seen, still chopping at the earth with shovels.

The Americans were not challenged again as they worked through the edge of the rice farm next to Dinh's and reached the dock where two fishing junks were tied up. It seemed a long time before they passed the fishing pier and were making their way through the tall elephant grass, into the palm grove toward the shack which was the American headquarters. As they came closer to it, Hank was pleased to see that no light showed—his compatriots were lying properly low.

As they came within a hundred yards of the shack, they heard a soft familiar American voice: "Who goes there?" In that second, the snick of a bolt as a weapon was cocked.

Hope called out: "It's Hope, Muley." And the familiar shaven-head-ed figure stepped out of the shadows, his Armalite at the ready. He measured the distinctive shape of Captain Hope.

"Sure glad you got back, Captain. We were sweating you out."

Back at the hemp-shack, the returning detachment found Lieutenant Helmantholer and his communications crew set up with their equipment. The radio key clattered a rapid-paced message. Hope recognized the shadowy figure sitting at the radio transmitter: "Helmantholer! The heat seems to be on. Better knock off that transmission as soon as you can. The Commies may have their intercepts out, and we're gonna have to be moving camp tonight."

The others of the force had gathered in the dim, acrid-smelling shadows of the jute shed. Hope could see a dozen faces around him, the dim visages were more felt than seen.

"Everybody better get out in the air where we can talk," he said.

Outside, in the starlight, they clustered around Hope, and Gresham, Nooley, Veracruze, and the others were bombarding him with questions.

Hope shut them off for a moment as he instructed Hank: "Better tell our Chinese friends that we want to move right away. We'd better not even stop to eat until we can move to the dugout over there in the jungle."

The ordinarily silent Major Gresham was pushing an agitated inquiry: "Did you get a look at the field? Can you see any of the approaches?"

Hope laughed. "Better than that, Gresham, we saw the shape—and we could see where they're putting it." He groaned. "A new concrete storage place, underground. And troops all over the place."

Gresham groaned, too. "Are we going to be able to get at it?"

"I don't know," Hope said. "As soon as we can get our stuff into the new dugout, I'd better send a message back to Hong Kong, asking for an airlift. Maybe an airdrop of Chinese who have the proper protective coloring, and forged papers for a diversionary attack if nothing else—if that can all be done in one day."

"A pretty big order, Captain," said Bissell. "Even for Uncle Sugar. Beg pardon, 'Unifollum Siella,' in the new code-alphabet that's so perfect for Asia."

Nooley said: "A miracle—that's what Uniform Sierra needs: A sense of urgency about counter-insurgency. But Unifollum Siella hasn't got it yet. We always prepare for another war: the last one."

The move to the new headquarters was carried out uneventfully, until they were less than a hundred feet away from the underground dugout, crawling on hands and knees through the animal track in the thick jungle.

That moment, a piercing shriek carried across the rice paddies from the direction of the airfield. Creeping through briars and under tangled foliage, sweating under their vast pack-burdens, the column of men froze against the ground. Hope told them softly: "I think it's only a jet, warming up."

At that moment, a white beam of light raked the sky from the direction of the Commune and the airbase.

"They're just practicing," Hope said to Gresham, behind him in the animal track.

Gresham pulled himself up next to Hope, brushing a stubborn wait-a-minute vine from his face. "What if the Commies change their minds," he said, "and decide to make the drop tonight?"

"Could be. It always could be. But we've got to work on the assumption that our dope is correct—that their H-hour will be 0400 on the sixteenth." He looked at his watch in the reflected glow of the searchlight beam. He shifted the mountainous load of his rucksack, brushed the tangle of vines away from the wet structure pyramiding above his back. "It's 2350 now, October 13. We've got fifty-two hours before they plan to take off with their H-Bomb. Fifty-two hours. But the *Mako* comes back the fifteenth, so for practical purposes, we've got only twenty-eight hours and ten minutes, to do all our business."

"At least, they're giving us light so we can set up camp," Hank muttered as he crawled up behind them in the animal track amid leaves and branches snowy-white in the reflection of the searchlight beam. Ahead of them, they could see the wiry torso of Dinh. Dinh had reached the dugout which was to be their new home, and was waving them on.

That moment, they heard the fluttering screech of a jet plane just over them, and another behind it. The two aircraft flicked across the searchlight beam, and were lost in the dark beyond. The first aircraft was rake-tailed, with a tiny delta wing, the second a slower blob of a plane, larger and clumsier. A moment later, two more dart shapes like the first roared overhead, plunging into the white searchlight beam momentarily, zipping through it, and into the darkness beyond.

"Quite an armada," said Hank. His face was a wide white patch as he bent his neck to follow the receding aircraft. "I read it one Tupolev-16 and three MIG-21 fighter escorts."

"Probably four MIGs with the Tupolev," Hope corrected. "Two in front and two behind. We just missed seeing the first of them. Anyhow it's the attack force all right."

The lights went off, and the Americans looked after the jet-thunder fading in the sky. Hank said: "They *think* it's their attack force."

"Yes," said his friend. "And we're going to change that idea of theirs—somehow."

22

October 14

IT WAS THREE O'CLOCK AT NIGHT AND THEY WERE FAIRLY
settled in their new lair when it began to rain. Dinh had gone back
to his farm. Run had stayed with them during the setting up of the
camp. Veracruze, Hildebrand, and Muhlbach had chopped one end
of the tunnel a good three feet farther, so that there was more room
in the muddy enclosure below the earth's surface, and Veracruze had
just reported to Captain Hope: "You might not see us here in the dark,
Captain, but we're all accounted for."

The rain came with a series of gusts from the China Sea. Hope
ordered Veracruze: "Paisan, I want you to rig extra canvas tarps over
both entrances to the dugout. We've got to keep out as much rain as

we can—or this'll be an underground swimming pool. And better rig the Lister bag with an open top—at least we'll have water to drink."

Hope and Veracruze were both outside the dugout, and the rain sluiced around them. Such heavy overcast darkened the night, they could barely sense each other in the gloom of the heavy jungle.

"Is Helmantholer under cover?" Hope asked. "Is the radio stuff all down there?"

"Yes, sir. I don't know what kind of signal he's getting, but he's under cover." Hope unfastened the canvas blind. He flipped his weight through the opening, projecting a squirt of rain into the stale-smelling dugout atmosphere. He bumped into sheltering forms in the darkness.

"Where's Helmantholer?"

"Here, sir." The answer came from the far end at the mole-blind enclosure.

"Are you ready to send?" Hope asked, and Helmantholer answered quickly: "Yes, sir. I don't know whether I can send without being triangulated, but I'll keep the GVB gear on, and I'll try."

"You think the Commies have got sophisticated radio-direction gear?"

"They've got it in Peking, but probably not down here in the boondocks. I hope."

"Okay, I want you to send a message back to Lowery in Hong Kong." Hope spoke to all and sundry in the close enclosure: "I'm going to show a light here, a flashlight, but I'll watch it. I'll make sure that the trap over the entrance is pulled tight. I want you all to be careful with lights. This is a pretty thick jungle, but we don't want any glimmers in these woods."

Then he spoke to Helmantholer: "I've encoded the message for Lowery. Here's what it says:

BOMB POSITION HEAVILY PROTECTED. NEED REINFORCE-
MENTS FOR OPERATION. SUGGEST POSSIBLE AIRDROP ON
SOUTH SIDE OF AIRFIELD BETWEEN COORDINATES 95471
AND 63546. POSSIBLY CHINESE NATIONALS WHO HAVE
FORGED IDENTITY PAPERS AND ARE PROPERLY TRAINED
AND INDOCTRINATED. NEED DIVERSION FOR ATTACK
WHICH TO BE MADE 2100 14 OCTOBER. ADVISE SOONEST.
COM TYPHOON."

*

He put down the message: "Might as well try. Even if we do end up
doing it all ourselves."

*

It was hours later, the sun had come and was distilling light
through the mists of the jungle, when the answer was heard. The
tired and wet raiders had sacked out in their muddy den, and Wing
Run had stayed with them, as exhausted as any. The rains had stopped
about 4 A.M., and Helmantholer had removed the canvas blind at one
end of the tunnel, and set up his aerial there, with air and sun above
him.

Helmantholer, standing the radio watch himself, with earphones
clamped to his head, was dozing as he sat on a steel ammo box in
front of the receiver. In the faint light filtering through his hatch
to the outer world, he faced the figures of the men of Operation
Typhoon, plus the one Chinese ally, strewn the length of the tunnel.
Some of the men had unfolded sleeping bags, others slept in exhaus-
tion where they had fallen. Most had strewn elephant grass over the
mud for attempted insulation. Like Nooley, Hope still wore the black

peasant sharkskin costume he had donned the day before. Next to Hope, almost part of his body in the same mud puddle, lay Musgrave. Beyond, arranged precisely in a squarely placed sleeping bag, Major Gresham slept in apparent comfort.

Helmantholer reached over to tap Sergeant Hanson on a sleeping bag at his feet. The sergeant stirred: "Huh? Huh??"

"I got something incoming from Hong Kong. Get me the code book. It's in my knapsack, over there."

It was 6:15 o'clock and the jungle birds were chattering, when Helmantholer finished decoding the message. He stopped a minute to re-appraise it before taking it to Hope:

FOR COM TYPHOON FROM TYPHON HEADQUARTERS NEGA-TIVE YOUR REQUEST INSUFFICIENT TIME CARRY OUT PLAN GOOD LUCK XXX LOWERY.

*

Helmantholer studied the message again and looked up at Sergeant Hanson who was peering over his shoulder.

Helmantholer saw that Hanson mirrored the sinking feelings he knew inside. "If good luck will win this war, we shouldn't have to worry," Hanson said. "Right, lieutenant?"

Helmantholer smiled wanly and picked up the message-sheet to take it over to Hope.

He moved down the length of the tunnel and gently shook Hope by the shoulder. Hope awoke immediately and stared up at Helmantholer with wide eyes, his face bristled and white. "Did you get an answer from Hong Kong?" Even in his sleep, the question was almost automatic.

"I did, Captain. Not a very good answer." He stuck the paper under Hope's eyes. Hope turned on his side and Musgrave woke up, too. Hank leaned over Hope to read the message.

"My God," said Hank. "So what now?"

Hope scrubbed his bristly cheek with a palm. "It just means we're gonna have to do it all ourselves—no manna from heaven."

"But didn't you once tell Freeman Blake yourself that you thought an airdrop would be a waste of effort? Wouldn't Lowery be a goof-ball to reverse the field and send in a drop now?"

Hope grinned self-consciously. "That's right. One of the times when I wish I hadn't been so smart, before. I just hoped he'd forget what I said. I thought maybe Freeman Blake would somehow jump at the chance and send in one of his DC-3s loaded with Chinese Nationals with all the proper papers—the thing we probably should have had in the beginning."

"But if your first reasoning was right, the DC-3 would have been shot down, and all those lives lost."

Hope laughed uneasily again. "Things look a little different now from what they did back then. If I were the overall commander, I'd send the DC-3 in, and take my chances."

Hank struggled up to his feet, stretching. The tunnel wasn't tall enough for him to reach more than a half-crouch. He sank again to a sitting position. "Too little, too late. The fate of the first wave in any operation. And later on, too much of the wrong things. So what now?"

Hope reached in his pocket for the crude map he had drawn of the Communist base, the hiding place of the bomb, and the barriers and guard stations around it. "In hindsight, what we should have done was train a bunch of Chinese, sell them on the idea that the Commies were a bunch of bums and ought to be thrown out, and send them in on a submarine with forged papers to do the job. But we didn't. So we've got to make it pay off this way."

"My God! A revolutionary doctrine!" Hank said gravely. "You're beginning to think like a Leninist! You'd go so far as to try to sell nationals of other countries on the idea of guerrilla activity to subvert a Communist government?"

Hope didn't smile. "I guess it's too late this time. And it doesn't matter. We'll do it our way and we'll make it work."

"A real Can-Do Marine," Hank said. He pointed to the labored diagrammatic sketch which Hope had unfolded. "What's the non-objective art?"

Hope turned the sketch-map so that Hank could see. "X is the bomb-hole, you remember that," he said. "These are the two fences, and here are the guard stations through the fences. These circles are the searchlight towers, and this big rectangle is the area they cover up with light when they've got their floodlights on. Our H-hour is 2100, and I chose that because Dinh says that's the time when they change the guard. But there are some items that have got me pulling out my hair. Like how we crack that H-bomb safe."

A couple of sleeping forms stirred in the tunnel. Veracruze, still clothed in his black peasant's costume, stirred and stood up, his black tunic and trousers streaked with chocolate-colored mud. "What time's the briefing, Captain?" he asked.

"At 0930," Hope answered. "Plenty of time to do everything."

✳

By nine-fifteen, Captain Hope had drawn a new map of the Communist base. With the help of Sergeant Hildebrand and PFC Muhlbach, he held up the backside of the map under the cone of sunlight falling through the open entrance of the cave. The other officers and men of the detachment, and their persistent Chinese ally, Wing Run, were bunched in the tunnel-like dugout.

"We're not gonna be able to do anything in daylight," Hope began. "That's one thing we learned in our reconnaissance mission yesterday. As soon as it gets dark, we can start moving our stuff up to this rice farm overlooking the airbase. It is situated right here and it belongs to Dinh-Tzu, a relative of Dinh, who owns the jute plantation where we landed. I'd say it's about a mile from this rice farm to the backside of the first fence the Commies have put up.

"As soon as it gets dark, we'll move our stuff up to Dinh-Tzu's place and get ready. We'll have until just before nine to get across the rice paddies and up to the edge of the first fence. The guard changes at that hour—2100—and I figure this is the best time for us to get through. The new men will be on and their eyes won't be used to the dark, yet—and if we're lucky, and Major Nooley can take out two or three of the guards right here at this gate, we'll get through the first barrier without having to fire any carbine, Armalite, or pistol shots.

"The first barbed wire we'll get through at the changing of the guard and with silent weapons. For the second one, we might have to have plenty of covering fire—all we can manage.

"I want the communicators to stay back here. We'll send runners back from the field if we need to send an urgent message."

He signalled to Hildebrand and Veracruze to fold up the map, and went on: "It's quite a far piece from here to the Dinh-Tzu farm. It's rotten walking, through a lot of mangrove roots and swamps, and we found out yesterday there are occasional Commie patrols through the area. That's why we'll have to travel in darkness and it'll be unpleasant. But you're all used to this kind of muck and we can do the job.

"After we've had some chow, we'd better sack out for most of the daylight hours—I want Sergeant Veracruze to post plenty of security

—and tonight, about 1800 hours, we'll have some more chow, have a final briefing, and get everything ready to shove off when darkness comes. Any questions?"

Muley Muhlbach raised his hand, and Hope said: "Muley?"

Muhlbach raised himself to a kneeling position, an intelligent adaptation to the lack of headroom in the dugout-tunnel. Despite the rugged ordeal of the last day, he had somehow managed to preserve a near-military appearance. He wore his green-spotted tiger suit and green beret, and he was freshly shaven. Where most of the others of the group were mud-stained, there seemed to be not a single smear on his uniform.

"Captain," he said, "we heard talk about maybe getting reinforcements. Do we get reinforced, sir?"

Hope answered quickly: "We had asked for a para-drop to help with the job. But the request was denied, because there wasn't time enough to lay on the drop, and too risky! But as the man says in the song, we can handle this job all by ourselves."

There was a snort of American laughter in the Chinese hole-in-the-ground. Hope went on; "When we get up to Dinh-Tzu's farm, we'll probably change some of our plans but we'll follow the general arrangement. Between now and tonight, we'll work out the details—we hope. We're going to take out that bomb—and to hell with the Commies!"

The lanky, youthful Wing Run had been listening in fascination to the flow of strange language. He caught the last sentence with the sharp ear of the Chinese for ringing slogans, and echoed it to the best of his ability: "To her with Comis!"

Hope went over his newly revised plan for skirmish-line tactics—now that he had benefited from first-hand observation of the target.

He diagrammed the way he would lead a single column through the wire, the order in which they would move—who followed whom. How they would fan out when they reached the bomb vault, and how each weapon—the M-79 elephant guns augmented by hand-thrown grenades, and the mass firepower of the M-16s would put out the curtain of fire they would need. Hope bad been thinking and planning very hard.

Hank went to sleep afterward with a kind of miasma of problems on his mind—how were they going to see to do their job in the dark? Why didn't Hong Kong send them sniperscopes, silencers, and other electronic gear in an airdrop? Even as he thought about it, he knew the rational answer: an airdrop would undoubtedly call the Commies' attention to them—and that would be fatal. And besides, as usual, there wasn't time enough.

23

October 14 (Continued)

HANK WOKE WITH FADED SUNLIGHT SPLATTERING ACROSS his eyes, the refracted sun from the open sky-hole visible beyond conked-out bodies on the wet floor of the dugout. He looked at his watch. It was 4:45, a good couple of hours, he knew, before Veracruze would be nudging the sleepers and saying, "Reveille, Reveille!"

Hank's hip was sore. He was lying on the side of his face. His eyes looked into close-layered, shiny green strands of elephant grass, a pile of which he had strewn on the muddy floor of the tunnel to make a bed. Through the strands of grass, the persistent, dark-chocolate color of the mud, and in the soft ridges of earth, the shine of water. His hip must be wet, bis backside must be lying in mud like that. That was why it was aching. Rust. He needed oiling.

He turned on his back, and the creaking hip felt better. One thing about lying in a hole in the ground, it was always warmer than being on top of it, where you got all kinds of vicious glacial breezes at night, even in these tropical latitudes. He had learned the virtues of digging into the ground for safety and comfort in Korea where cold had been such a tough problem.

He must sleep but he could already imagine Veracruze going down the line of sleeping bundles of men in the dim tunnel, growling: "Drop your cocks and grab your socks, Reveille!" Not with any personal intent, but simply chanting the age-old barracks rhyme like a nursery song.

No, Hank knew, he could sleep no more now. He would get up, get out of the dingy tunnel, away from the smell of mud, sweat, and cramped humanity, and breathe at least a few mouthfuls of air, good, fresh oxidized air, before the night and the beginning of what might be his last military action; in fact, it might be the last action of any kind on earth for all of them—and who would know what *karma* would come, if anything, after that?

Hank hauled himself to his feet, pushing away the heavy rubberized poncho he had thrown over his lower body. He folded it carefully, avoiding the sleeping men on both sides. He placed it on a pile of moist reed-grass and he was struck, as he moved toward the skyhole at the nearest end of the tunnel, with the peaceful expression of Hope, lying beside him, flat on his back, mouth closed, the calming impress of sleep stealing the tiredness from him, his face now free of weight. And, he found himself thinking, almost a dead Hope. It was almost as if he were previewing the deceased Hope, the body embalmed and daubed like an undertaker's confection.

Morbidity. He would survive and Hope would survive—and there he went, like the veriest of recruits who knew, who were positive that it would happen to someone else and not to them: the recruit, the merest, most optimistic recruit.

He looked over Nooley, conked out atop a sleeping bag, and Veracruze, on another bag next to him, and then one more of the pallets supporting Helmantholer. What, no radio operator? Jolted awake, he glanced at the opposite end of the tunnel. The Special Force was on the ball after all. Sergeant Hanson sat on the ammo box beside the big radio, earphones clamped over his green beret, and nodding sleepily as he tried to stay awake. But Hanson was not sending, or receiving, he was only automatically on duty.

Fourteen men and officers slept in the tunnel now, four would be on outpost duty: Espinoza, Roberts, Wohl, and Polk, watching over an imaginary square rigged in the jungle about the mole-hole. He would have to be careful, when he emerged through the skyhole into the outer world, not to venture too far—not more than a few feet —or he might invite a knife in the guts from one of the sentries. Stepping over the inert form of Hope, he stumbled, and Hope woke instantly. Hank saw the pale-blue eyes watching him quietly. "Going out for some air? Wait, I'll come with you."

When they poked their heads out of the skyhole, the headroom situation was worse than ever. In the animal track which led past the hole in the ground, the passage of beasts had worn the dense undergrowth to a maximum height of perhaps two-and-a-half feet above the turf. The best they could do was crouch under the canopy of vines and branches.

"I guess I was wrong," Hank said. "I thought this would be better—but it's a lot better in the mole-hole."

"As far as headroom is concerned, anyhow," said Hope. "But the air's better here."

Hank said: "Do you think they can hear us, in the hole?"

"I don't think so. Why?"

"Because I want to ask you something top secret—top secret for right now, anyhow."

"Go ahead."

"How do my chances really look, to you? I couldn't ask you back there, but—well, a lot of things have happened to me in the last week or so. I've met a number of people who've changed my thinking on a lot of things. I've picked up a bunch of new friends I can trust. Like the skipper of Operation Typhoon—a Can-Do Green Beret type."

"Thanks for the compliment."

Hank looked across the narrow span of the animal track to the thin, tense face of his friend. Hope had settled into the coolie squat so familiar in Asia: feet flat on the ground, body hung down from the knees and jack-knifed upward from the hips in a relaxed, yet flexed position. Asians could rest like that for hours. Hank was squatting in the uncomfortable fashion of Western man, with tense metatarsal arches and leg muscles. He hastened to rearrange himself into the more comfortable Asian stance.

"What I want to ask you about was *not* how it looks about our getting through this thing," Hank said, "but your opinion on what you would think about Mary Wu. I mean what you would think about Mary Wu and me on the assumption that the Typhoon Force gets through, and makes it back to Hong Kong?"

Hope looked at his friend quizzically. "You mean whether you and Mary should get married, and all that? And take on her kid and all the Chinese family?"

"Approximately that."

Hope answered: "I think I told you once in Hong Kong that I'd like to get me a nice clean China girl for a wife myself, and have plenty of golden-colored children. Probably that's the solution of the world's problems."

"Even if the China girl is out of the Asia Ballroom?"

"There are some clean girls among the dancehall types, too. I wouldn't ask too many questions about her vocation, in Hong Kong, where there are fifty people for every job." He grinned his wide white smile. "The particular individual we're talking about, I'd say, is plenty clean. Her mind is clean, hard, honest—and bright. Besides, she gave up the dancehall bit, and went straight. Certainly as straight as we are."

He reached into a pocket of his camouflage suit, pulled out a plastic envelope, found a small box of matches in it, and lit one. He moved the flame to his left arm where a dark-brown beetle-shape clung to the flesh. The flame singed the leech and it fell clear. He went on: "Right now, I'd say it's a pretty academic question. I'd say when we're on board the *Mako*, well away from Point Meng Wan and heading out into the China Sea with plenty of water between us and the Commie patrol boats—I'd say that'd be the time to think about it. That is *if* you're alive and if we really *are* heading out into the China Sea. It's premature now, to say the least."

"You really think our chances are that bad of getting out of this alive, right?"

"I wouldn't give any long odds on it," Hope said. He lowered his voice: "I didn't want to say anything about estimated casualties on this job when I gave the briefing before. But any commander has to go through some kind of rough estimating. I'd say fifty-fifty. I'd say we'll be lucky to get back to the submarine with half of our people —and in that other half, the one left behind, could be you or me."

Hope regarded Hank calmly, and he smiled. "So we finally got around to the question I thought you were asking me in the beginning, anyhow." He looked at his watch. "It's still damn near two hours before I wake the boys. Maybe you better have another try at some shut-eye."

Hank said: "Can't sleep. I keep thinking about too many—premature matters. I'll stay awake and I'll be on hand in case you need any unskilled labor. I know you're going to be a busy man from now on."

But Hank *did* sleep. He drifted off, weight squarely on his sore hip, under the light of the animal-track, the low dome worn in the underbrush by passages of furtive beasts.

On the flag bridge of the *USS Enterprise*, flagship of the United States Seventh Fleet, some 475 miles south of Hainan, Vice Admiral Andrew Kerr turned to receive a folded paper from Captain Morheim.

Morheim was saying: "Another directive from the Big Chief, Admiral. Communicator just got it."

Admiral Kerr mumbled thanks and walked to the edge of the deck to read the dispatch. He glanced down at the angled flight deck of the great supercarrier, now nearly empty of planes and strangely placid with none of the hellish roaring sounds of launching and recovery. Two of the squadrons were flying, the third below decks. Kerr glanced at the message, and called out to Captain Morheim, who was starting to climb down the ladder to the next deck: "Lew." Captain Morheim reversed his direction instantly and came across the deck.

"It's more direct orders from the Big Chief," Kerr told the Captain from beneath graying beetle-brows. "He wants to turn us around, and there's a lot more specific instruction. If you're going below, better send my flag secretary up—and Lew—better lay on a meeting of the flag staff, and your CAG and senior officers in the flag office, fifteen minutes from now." Morheim saluted sharply, and Kerr acknowledged with a half-wave, half-salute.

Admiral Kerr studied the message-sheet again. It said:

COM SEVENTH FLT FROM COMINCH TOP SECRET CHANGE COURSE TO DIRECTION AWAY FROM HAINAN DECOY WORK OF APPARENT APPROACH CHINA COAST WELL DONE STOP OPERATION TYPHOON CHIEF HAINAN REQUESTS SUP-PORT STOP HAVE DECLINED REQUEST FOR AIRDROP REIN-FORCEMENT BUT IN EMERGENCY MAY CALL ON YOU FOR LAST MINUTE BOMBING EFFORT IF PLANS FAIL STOP WILL ADVISE.

Admiral Kerr growled: "Now they tell us."

✳

It was nearly eight o'clock and a thoroughly dark night, when six-teen men of the Typhoon force, with Wing On and Wing Run, and lit-tle mosquito-like Dinh, arrived at the rice farm of Dinh's cousin, Tzu. Two of the force, Lieutenant Helmantholer and Sergeant Hanson, had been left behind with the radio in the tunnel, a safe communications center.

The sixteen men of the Typhoon group had run into no trouble with Chek-koh patrols as they labored through the black mangrove marshes. No one challenged them in the narrow waist of mangroves just below the Commune, where the earlier patrol had been stopped. This night, strangely enough, there were no flicking flashlight beams from the direction of the Commune, and they encountered no Communist patrols. And this time Hope, Hank, and Sergeant Hing found their way through the treacherous footing with more facility than Dinh and Run. The corner of a wild Chinese tropical island was becoming home for the Americans.

As they climbed up the slight grade to the outward dike of Tzu's rice farm, they heard a familiar whistle from the direction of the farm. It was a recognition signal, the same constant faint whistling Hank knew well from Vietnamese military phone conversations during military actions. Their Chinese friends here on Hainan apparently knew *the* same need for continual identification and reassurance.

Hank guessed that the whistler was young Tzu. Hank and Hope echoed the call, and Hank called out, adding in Vietnamese: *"Cat ma? Dinh-Tzu?* Who's that? Dinh-Tzu?"

Surprisingly enough, Dinh-Tzu answered with complete familiarity, as if the language were his: *"Ben phai."*

Hank knew *"Ben phai"* was the Vietnamese word for "right" and it struck him that it was only natural there should be intertwining linguistic roots between this island and the landward area to the west. He tried again with Vietnamese: *"Dai-uy Hope,"* and again he hit a responsive chord:

"Foon ying" came back from the dark, meaning approximately "welcome" in Cantonese.

Dinh-Tzu led the way toward the farmhouse. Hank walked just behind him, the other members of the force strung out in Indian file along the narrow padi dividers. Hank was finding that with a mixture of Vietnamese and Cantonese words and phrases, he could maintain a kind of contact with Tzu.

Now, half-turning to face Hank as he followed a path he could have found blindfold, Dinh used his newly discovered communications link to cultivate a deeply ingrained aspiration: *"Tsim shui tena,"* he said, using the Cantonese word meaning "secret diving boat." And he added:

"May-gock-yun" and *"Toi,"* meaning "Americans" and "I." He repeated the word for submarine and added: *"Va"* and *"con nit"* meaning "Wife" and "children." The total effect was easily recognizable: he wanted to insure a passage in the American submarine for his family and himself. There was a quick train of extra material in the local language which Hank missed. He decided the basic question deserved a courteous answer: Dinh-Tzu had made up his mind that after he had assisted the Americans in their raid, he would face a dismal and probably short future on Hainan. It was time to get out, and the round-faced youth was willing to chuck everything here for the gilded unknown of Hong Kong and America.

Hank answered in patched Vietnamese: "Your cousin Dinh and Wing On have already asked the *Dai-uy* to go on the secret diving boat. He has told them they can go."

Enough of this permeated Tzu's consciousness so that he was pleased. Hank saw the Sash of his white smile in the dark. And Hank explained to Hope, next in line behind him: "I've been taking your name in vain. I told Tzu you might consider taking him and his family along on the *Mako*."

Another white grin, this time from Hope: "Why not? Won't be much left for him here, after tonight. He heard about the gold in the Hong Kong hills, too?"

The party threaded past the thatch-roofed building which was Tzu's home. It was dark, the wife and children evidently taking cover inside.

The party went beyond the house without stopping, and Tzu led them across the far fields toward the airbase. As they walked along the muddy, narrow top of a padi divider, a glow of light rose over the edge of the fields nearest to the Communist base. First there was a faint, indirect white glow which silhouetted the line of pack-laden men trudging along the high muddy curb, and then the white, smoking pencil of a searchlight leaned against the sky. The sharp edge of light held low over the strip of runway. But this time, there was no shriek of jet engines, and no floodlights illuminated the darkness among the buildings nearby. Hope, at the head of the column behind Tzu, started at the sudden flash of light. Hank, next behind him, saw him jump and Hope passed it off with a nervous remark: "Like going to the john and finding you're on television."

Hank said: "No problem. They haven't even turned the floodlights on, this time." Looking ahead over Hope's shouldering, laden figure, Hank saw the unit commander's left arm raised against the white glow. Hope's first and second fingers were overlapped in the universal hand signal against evil luck.

"I've got my toes crossed, too," he said.

Despite the single searchlight beam lying over the runway, the Hope force seemed secure for the moment. The target area, spread out under the large camouflage nets on this side of the runway, was dark except for a faint glow around the underground bomb vault. Evidently, despite the protection of the spreading net above, the enemy wasn't taking any chances with excess light this close to the big morning. A searchlight might hang over the runway, and there was a faint cluster of lights at the far edge of the camouflage net, where the road came into the Main Gate, from Hoihow. But the critical area of the vault, although thoroughly covered by the large camouflage net, was only faintly illuminated.

✻

The searchlight was still on when they reached the outer limits of Tzu's fields, the shimmering beam still lying low above the runway. Then the light disappeared, the runway area went black.

They had ranged themselves along the mud retaining wall of Tzu's outermost padi field—which meant they were protected against sudden-silhouetting light; but they were standing in rice water over their knees. Tzu, Run, and Dinh instinctively knew the military art of concealment, and they crouched now on Hope's left hand, with Hank, Nooley, Gresham, and Veracruze on the other side. The heads of the others of the detachment were visible beyond, the line extending almost to the next padi divider.

Hope looked at his watch as he unshucked a heavy knapsack and hoisted it over the divider into the next muddy field. He spoke to Gresham: "I read seven-forty, that gives us an hour and twenty minutes. How does it look to you?"

Gresham in battle dress was a warlike figure, with Armalite in one hand, pack of demolition gear on his back, and a roll of fuse cord suspended over one shoulder like an aiguillette.

"Wait," he said. He laid the Armalite on top of the embankment, swung off his pack and set it beside the gun. Then, carefully, he extracted a package about the size of a binocular case. He unbuttoned the canvas box and carefully took out a hard black object— the same mysterious gadget Hank had seen in Gresham's hand when Gresham and Hope were talking, back at the tunnel. Then, Hank had been half asleep, half in a dream.

Now, as tense and awake as he could ever be, he saw instantly what it was—a Metascope, the infra-red scanning tube he remembered having seen once in Vietnam on a Special Forces night operation in the Delta, It was an optical device with an attached light which shone a beam invisible except through the scanning tube. Miraculously, with the gadget on, you could see a green spotlight illuminating the dark in the area toward which you aimed it. With it, you could read a map in the dark, or examine somebody standing in darkness without his knowing it. It had been developed in World War II, a great invention but hypersensitive to wetness. That was what had happened in that Special Force mission at Rack Gia—the gadget had been doused in a rice paddy and it had gone out. How like Gresham to have one and keep it a secret, and keep it dry, until now, the critical moment.

Now Hank could glimpse a clever plan which Gresham and Hope had evolved—a way in which the small force might accomplish a superhuman task in the target area—Gresham could do his work in the dark. Once they had blasted their way into the bomb vault, and kept up their volume of fire to neutralize the defenders, they could take out the bomb invisibly. With surprise on their side and in the dark, the small force might do this job under the noses of a vast protective force—*if* it was dark there, and there was enough confusion.

Now, Gresham unfolded the small handle on the scanning tube and carefully cranked twenty-five or thirty times. This, Hank remembered, would give night visibility for fifteen minutes or so.

Gresham levelled the device in the direction of the target area, and moved it slowly across the field below, as far as the lights at the main gate.

"What do you see?" Hope couldn't wait for the slow-speaking Gresham to report.

Gresham answered: "You know—the Metascope indicates whether they have any infra-red searchlights set up. They would be invisible without an infra-red scope like this."

Hope pressed: "Okay. Did you see any?"

"No indications."

"Good. They probably haven't had time to get infra-red down here."

Gresham handed the gadget to Hope. "Be careful," he warned. "It's our only Metascope." And he added: "You know, it's no good for seeing things in the dark at a distance—only up to about twenty-five feet."

Hope took a quick look through the gadget and handed it back. But he brought out his binoculars and aimed them at the distant light glow of the main gate, at the far end of the camouflage canopy.

"Looks like a last-minute load of something for the bomb coming through the main gate," Hope said. "I hope they don't get too many such last-minute ideas between now and nine o'clock."

Hope was instructing Hank: "I want you to ask our Chinese friends what the terrain is like between here and the first fence. I got some of that dope before from Dinh, but I want to know what it's like just the last one hundred feet before we get to the fence? Is it rice padi, elephant grass or jungle?" Hank nodded, and he was already beginning his questioning of Dinh-Tzu, because he would know better than any of the three about the terrain of this area, and now he had been able to improvise a bastard linguistic connection with Tzu.

24

THE LAST BRIEFING WAS TEN MINUTES LATER AGAINST THE final mud bank of Dinh-Tzu's farm. The sixteen men on the Dead Man's chest, all the men of the detachment were there except Helmantholer and Hanson, back at the tunnel with the radio equipment.

This was the first thing Hope referred to in his final briefing, apparently the uppermost item in his mind. "Trotter, I want you to stay here at Tzu's farm, with Tzu, Dinh, and Run, to be a runner back to the radio when we need you. I'm going to take a red flare in one of those fountain-pen cartridge mounts. If we get through the outer gate, no signal. If we can't get through, I'll shoot off the red flare.

"I want you to stay right here and keep a sharp eye out, and if you see a red flare, you're to get word back to Helmantholer at the tunnel—by walkie-talkie. We won't carry radio into the assault—too chancey. This has got to be an absolutely buttoned-up operation: maximum security. If anything goes very bad, you break out with the SCR to Helmantholer, and we'll get out a message to Typhoon headquarters in Hong Kong. Okay?

"It's very essential that this word should get back to Hong Kong, so that if everything goes completely wrong, they can implement some plan like calling in the Seventh Fleet to finish off the job. That is, if we fail; but we don't expect to.

"In a few minutes I'll go over our plan for the assault, but first I want to mention one other important point.

"That's our withdrawal plan. We've given a lot of thought to this. We may have a little trouble getting out. Dinh says there are machine guns mounted in the two searchlight towers, with squads that are supposed to be trained to aim along the searchlight beams. The Commies may illuminate with the searchlights. Fortunately, they only have juice enough to operate one searchlight at a time, Dinh says, and we will shoot them out as soon as they're turned on. Whenever you see a searchlight on, shoot it out.

"They might also turn on the floodlight system. So Sergeant Hing and PFC Muhlbach are detailed to rip out the cables supplying the current for the floodlights, when we get through the first barrier. We think that the electrical system is in the little guardhouse on this side of the outer fence. We're going to take this guardhouse quietly. We understand only three or four sentries are at this back gate.

"Major Nooley is going to try to knock off the sentries with his silent weapon. They might not die right away, they might start yelling, and they could give some kind of an alarm before we get all the way through that first barrier. But I don't want any shooting here. If the arrows don't kill them, we'll have to finish them off with the knife.

"Now, for the second barrier. Assuming that we get through the first barrier okay and there's no illumination, the second one shouldn't be too hard—even if a squad of troops is there. We'll get around them.

We'll have two men with bolt-cutters, Sergeant Bissell and Muhlbach will cut a hole for us."

He paused, took a breath, and charged on: "Now—the real bitch kitty. I was going to leave a covering force of five men on the higher ground just outside the outer fence, outside the barbed wire. But we won't. We need all the people we can get for the real tough job inside the inner fence, at the bomb vault, where we need maximum fire power.

"Once we get to the bomb vault, we'll probably have to shoot our way in. We'll go up to it in single file, I'll be out at the Point with Muhlbach. There'll be enough light at the vault so you can see my arm signal. I'll give you the skirmish-line signal, and the first seven men in the column move up on my right, the last seven on my left.

"I'll fire the first shots at the vault, and on my lead, I want you all to open up with everything you've got: Armalites, the three M-79 Elephant Guns—and all the grenades you can throw the old-fashioned way—with a strong right arm.

"We will shoot out every light we can see. The only way we can do this job, considering there may be fifty to one hundred people, troops and technicians, inside the bomb vault and around it, is to keep everything dark.

"Major Gresham has a Metascope, the infra-red gadget you remember from Vietnam. It didn't work very well there—it got wet too fast. But he's kept it dry. Inside the vault hell work in the dark with the Metascope with Bissell assisting him, while all the rest of us shoot out all the lights and all the people we can clearly identify as Chinese—except Hing.

"Major Gresham and Bissell will lay the C-3 over two adjoining ring lenses in the bomb and run out two separate three-foot lengths of time cord, which will give us a minute and a half to clear the joint.

Major Gresham will fire a green flare inside the vault as soon as he's lit the charge.

"From then on, we'll make a break as fast as we can for the place we've cut through the inner fence. We'll stop there for two minutes, then go on to the outer, barbed wire fence. Shoot out all lights everywhere—darkness is our best ally.

"We might have to use all of our firepower to crack through the outer fence on the way in. I hope not—if we do, we may ruin everything. If we're lucky, and if we do our job right getting through, they won't know where we got in in the first place.

"When we get back to the high ground outside the first fence, things should be all right until they find out where we've gone. By that time we've got to get out of here and we've gotta break all records getting across that stretch of mangroves east of the Commune. If they've got a vector on where we exited from the airbase, they may have scouting parties out in those mangroves. If we can get to the spot where the mangroves are narrowest—that part just below the far corner of the Commune from here—we'll probably be all right. From there on, the terrain is like a jungle—we'll follow the animal track and get past the tunnel, and we should be able to hack it back to Dinh's farm and get aboard the junk. Dinh says we have to be extra careful not to show light when we're getting aboard. Then, down into the false bottom of the fishing junk—stinky, but secure.

"Trotter, I want you to pass the word to the tunnel—I mean Helmantholer and Hanson—that we're on our way back, and they'd better get the radio gear secured and ready to go."

He added: "Each of you remember your single file order: I'll be at the Point, then Muhlbach, Bissel, Nooley, Veracruze, Hing, Gresham; then Musgrave—medical section, O'Connor, Wohl, and Roberts (who will be mostly shooting, not doctoring); then Espinoza, Jones, Polk, and Hildebrand."

He started to turn away, and remembered a vital item: "Our Chinese friends—Dinh and his wife and kids, Tzu and his wife and kids, and Wing On and his son will all be going with us when we go aboard the junk. There might be some problem bringing the children, but they're old enough so they won't make any unnecessary noises—and besides, they're Asians—pretty well-disciplined kids."

Again he paused, hesitated, as if feeling the speech was not rounded off enough emotionally. He fumbled ahead: "One thing that's good about our effort here is that it may be hasty and improvised—but probably not so much so as the Commie effort. You've seen that we've been able to send off some messages practically at will and we haven't yet been located by the Reds—you've seen that they haven't been very good with their patrols in this area around the periphery of the base. I'm not saying that when we run into them they're not gonna be tough and hard—but I think it is a fact that they're not as well prepared for this effort of theirs as we would be if we were in their shoes—not by a long shot. And we've got the best of all weapons on our side: surprise. We've got to take advantage of the odds, and keep alert for anything that might develop or anything they might pull out of the hat. So—we *will* bring this job off, and we'll do it right.

"I don't want to be corny, but it is a fact that the whole future of the world depends on what we do here, in the next hour or so. They picked the right people to do it when they gave us the job.

"So saddle up, we'll move out. We're going to stop first on the high ground overlooking the edge of the base and the first fence. We'll wait there until the guard changes at nine o'clock and the old guard detachment is gone off, and the new ones haven't got used to the night yet, then we'll move in and take over."

Dinh-Tzu, the man who knew the geography of the farm best, agreed to lead the party to the last high ground overlooking the outer fence of the base. He had willingly agreed to this, and Hope had said: "He might as well help us—we're going to make Americans out of him and his family."

Tzu led the way beyond his last paddy field across a series of muddy squares which must at one time have been agricultural land, but now they appeared to be only fallow acreage, harrowed and plowed, lying unplanted.

At last they came to a high mud wall which was a field-divider, and Tzu halted them. They ranged along the sheltered side of the embankment, standing hip-deep in viscous mud and a water overlay, and they looked down to a dark area where they knew there would be a barbed wire barricade and a guardhouse. Beyond the dark they could see the spiky shape of the camouflage net, supported by poles. It stretched far beyond, to cover the faint lights around the bomb vault, and a couple of hundred yards in the distance, the somewhat brighter lights of the main gate where trucks could enter. Under the spiked canopy, the poles were a bare black forest. The overhead net held the shadowy light and seemed to intensify it, a chiaroscuro pattern of abstract art, a primitive collage.

Hank, peering into the blackness, could only call on his memory bank to project the scene he remembered from the scouting expedition of the day before: this side of the camouflage net, the barbed wire barrier and the shack guarding a break in that obstacle. The guard station must be dead ahead in the dark. But it was a minor entryway, fed only by foot trails; a check-point where workers could enter, and it had been well chosen by the Dinhs and Wings as the point where the Americans could best mount a surprise assault.

Hank strained his eyes into the dark, and he picked out a dim yellow bulb which seemed too far to the left, and too close. But it must be the guardhouse, a light on it—no more than seventy-five feet away.

*

Near him, Hank could see Gresham's silhouette lighted faintly by the dim light from far off, under the camouflage net, the Metascope levelled at the guard station. Hope slid up next to Gresham, and Hank picked up fragments of Gresham's report: "It's faint . . . too far . . . can't see clearly. . . guard station . . . I think three people." Gresham was passing the Metascope to Hope: "Don't get it wet—or muddy."

Hank squinted along the line of the divider which separated the base from this, the last piece of high ground. He saw Nooley next to him, a bulky silhouette against the relative lightness of the sky, and the man's back was bent to string his bow. Now, Nooley would come into his own, the success or failure of the mission temporarily weighed on his shoulders.

Hank flipped the cover from the luminous figures of his watch. The time was eight-fifty-six, four minutes before the guard would be changed. Hank unshucked the Armalite slung on his shoulder, rested it against the mud wall. He wouldn't be able to use that for a while. He checked the wood-handled K-bar knife on his belt. Would he if necessary be able to stick someone with it? He never had. But he had killed people other ways. No problem, human motivation was automatic in the hurly-burly of a fight: kill or be killed. Survival is only the best reason for fighting.

From down below, a querulous, unsettled musical sound began, sour notes strung together with an abysmal disregard for harmony or the rationale of Western musical structure. Hank recognized it immediately: a bugle call, the musical tinkering which he had not heard since the days of the Chinese war in Korea, the calls which used to drift across the still air of no-man's land between the American and Chinese trenches. Probably, this would be the first step in the changing of the guard. They wouldn't turn on the lights. They were good at maneuvering in darkness, unless they had changed radically since the days of Korea.

Hank heard the thumping of military feet down below, and a sentence which he recognized.

"Ting jee-ee!": the challenge of the men on duty, as the new guard, possibly three or four men, appeared at the gate. The thumping feet stopped, and the challenge continued: *"Been gah ah?"*

In the still air, Hank heard a hoarse voice answering with what was evidently the night's password: *"Kawng-jeen sing lay!"*, meaning "Victory!"

Now there was the metallic clank of the bolt of a weapon being charged, and the same higher voice which had uttered the first "halt" continuing with the military routine of the challenge: *"Hahng mahee loy!"*, "come forward and be recognized."

Then there was the shuffling of feet again, the snap of arms being presented, and from the dark only twenty-five or thirty feet below them, a flashlight beam flicked on. The light was held low, and directed upwards, to show a broad, peasant face, the rough contours of Pithecanthropic eyebrows, nostrils, and mouth intensified by the light-from-below. Atop that face which was being scrutinized, a felt cap with a short visor, and a neatly traced red star. Below the star and the caricatured face, there was a hint of shoulders, the tense muscles presenting a weapon, apparently the popular copy of the Russian Sudarev sub-machine gun, the Chinese Type 54.

The light switched to the next face, another peasant aboriginal visage, the angle changed because the holder of the light had not moved, and the replacement guards were standing at attention. This time, below the face, Hank could see the glint of a black barrel, the folding metal stock and dull-gleaming ammunition clip held against the soldier's chest.

The light flicked to the next Chinese soldier, the illumination fainter with increasing distance, but showing more of the outline of the man: the cap with the star, the metal-stocked machine gun, the healthy peasant bulk of the soldier, the man with his weapon at "present arms" position.

Last, the light moved still farther, and now, with the distance, showed the shadow of a whole man, the cap not even visible at this distance, but the bulk of the body more apparent, the sub-machine gun snapped to attention with the same hard military precision.

Then the light flipped off, there was nothing but darkness down below. Hope whispered to Gresham: "Four coming on." Hope edged very close to Hank and now he asked in the faintest whisper: "Did you hear the password?"

"I think so. Listen: I'll say it slowly, *'Kawng-jeen sing lay'*, it means 'victory.'"

"Right. And we know about where they are."

The assault group had gathered as if by a magnetic force in the dark around Hope. Indistinct shapes clustered.

Hope whispered to Hank: "Tell each of them the password—*'Kawng-jeen sing lay'*—is that right?"

Hank nodded, and moving in the mud, whispered the password to every one of the raiding party.

Hope edged toward Nooley, and murmured: "I figure we're going to jump off in ten minutes," he said, "to give the early shift a chance to get away. Get Gresham's Metascope—and don't drop it or get it wet. Everything depends on that—and right now, on you."

Nooley nodded, too wrought-up to speak. He moved next to Gresham, Gresham took the Metascope from a plastic sack and carefully handed it to Nooley. Nooley took it gingerly, looked for a minute, and handed it back. Hank heard him: "Can't see enough at this distance."

Hope was whispering: "Okay—changed plan. I want Hing—he's still wearing his peasant suit—to go down ahead of the rest of us, and get challenged. He knows the password. I want you to be no more than five yards behind, with the bow ready to shoot. Probably, the sergeant of the guard will shine his flashlight in Hing's face. From the light, you can see enough to shoot, and get a couple of them down. Then, I'll have Muhlbach, Bissell, and Veracruze close by you, with their knives. Whatever you can't hack with the bow and arrow, they'll have to do with their knives.

"But I want you to kill that sergeant fast—before he can hurt Hing or shoot off a gun. Muhlbach, Bissell, and Veracruze will be around you to take care of whatever shows up. Okay?"

"Okay," said Nooley, his jaws clamped so his teeth wouldn't chatter.

Hing had gravitated close to Hope, and Hope began a long, whispered, careful instruction in Hing's ear.

By nine-fifteen, Hope had given whispered instructions to everyone on the assault mission. Then he nudged Muhlbach, who started over the mud parapet with Bissell going down the slope toward the guard station. Nooley, Hing and Veracruze, and Gresham followed a few yards behind, moving with slithering body contortions over the edge of the field-divider. Then, in rapid succession, Hank and O'Connor, Wohl, Roberts, Espinoza, Jones, Polk, Hildebrand.

The muddy bank which declined toward the guard station was surprisingly smooth. But there were spiky grain stalks in patches, rough and prodding. Hank was conscious that he was out of practice

with the piston-like movements of the knees and twisting of the torso to propel the upper body while the knees pushed alternately. The
others, he thought almost in panic, were so much more skilled. Fear
struck him that he might not be able to keep up with them on this desperate night. But Hope, he thought, like a nervous schoolboy in class,
seemed to have faith in him.

That moment, the mechanism of the attack whipped into action.
He heard the same growling voice, probably of the non-com in charge
of the detachment, the same man he had heard giving the answers to
the challenges before. Now, that hoarse, rough voice was mumbling
the challenge: *"Ting jee-ee!"*, the "Haiti" command.

There was a pause, an agonizing pause, and Hank knew that in
that particular spot of darkness where Hing was lying, a catastrophe
was striking. Hing, the only Asian of the group, couldn't remember
the password.

Hank screwed his courage and vocal chords and shouted: *"Kawng-
jeen sing lay!!"* There was another pause, probably because the Chinese
sergeant considered that the answer to his question was not precisely
in the spot where he expected it.

Then, with sudden presence of mind, Hing came through. Against
the faint starglow of the sky, the erect figure of Hing—the figure in
black sharkskin, with arms stretched upward in the universal gesture
of surrender—had emerged ahead.

And the hoarse enemy voice was going on with the mechanics of
the challenge, the command to come forward. And the voice, with an
edge of apprehension, added, *"Fah-ee dee!"* or "quickly."

Then came the mistake which they had all hoped the Chinese detachment would make. The sergeant turned on his flashlight to shine
it on the unknown intruder. The spot of light glowed in the dark like
a white heart, a perfect target; from it a beam fell faintly over the

tense figure of Hing and the man behind the light. There were strange sounds in the stillness: the slap of a bow-string, the wet thud of an arrow hitting into something solid, a man's faint grunt, surprised, impacted, curiously faint. Then, the flashlight flipped, a form tumbled to the ground, the light bounced and spread a cockeyed beam onto a hillock, and in the reflected light, beyond it, something large, a human form, was sunk on the ground. The human sound of suffering, the language of pain without national color, hung on the air: *"Ah—yee ray-arrrgh,"* the liquid, turkey-gobbler sounds of a human organism in shock and pain. Hank waited a dreadful moment for the outbreak of chattering machine-gun fire. It didn't come. Only thudding sounds, agonized sounds of men knocked breathless—the dagger crew of Hope's assault detachment striking.

Another sound of human agony—almost a scream—rang through the darkness. It was a voice choking and shouting at the same time, a nightmare cry repeated twice, with gurgling undertones. The Chinese outcry was hauntingly familiar. What was that word, shouted and strangling at once? *"Tsz mo! Tsz mo!"* Hank knew suddenly: "Sweet Mother! Sweet Mother!" A man stricken hard and smothering in his blood. From here, low on the ground—only the dim reflection of the distant lights showed on the sky. Hank saw two figures of men silhouetted against that glow, close together—an arm moving like a piston, both falling. The third cry was truncated, ended in a violent gasp. *"Tsz . . ."* the cry running out with a shudder like a broken steam whistle. An American had hit him again and shut him off hard, expertly killed him.

Someone, a form outlined against the light, was running back towards Hank. Hank's knife was in his hand, the sharp-edged hilt in his palm, the running figure was too big for a Chinese. He recognized Hope and called out, abandoning the password. "Eric! Eric! Here!"

Hope stopped short and squatted beside him. Hank saw the lean face twisted in an agony of excitement, the tight dark beret draped over the head—his gesture of loyalty to the Special Forces.

Hope said: "We killed all four. Veracruze got knifed. I think he's dead. Where's O'Connor?"

Hank squirmed to his feet. His left hand touched Hope's right, and he felt the thick, warm liquid running on it, blood. "Are you hurt, Eric? Blood!"

"Somebody else's. Where is O'Connor—the medical section?"

"Should be right behind me."

O'Connor appeared that moment, a shouldering form with a large haversack rising suddenly against the sky. Two men behind with large packs—Roberts and Wohl.

"I'm here," O'Connor's voice shook.

"Come on." Hope's voice was tense, but steady. "Veracruze got knifed. I'll take you to him. Roberts and Wohl—follow us."

Before they could move on, another bulky figure had risen against the night sky: Bissell. He waited, saying nothing, knowing that if Hope had word for him, he would pass it on.

Hope did. He said to Bissell and Hank: "We've got to get on through the post. Come on."

He led the way at a trot across the rough field dimly lit by the light from the storage vault perhaps a half-mile ahead of them beyond the pattern of the second fence. He stopped next to the shack made of un-painted wood, the guardhouse in the first barbed wire. In the same shadowy light reflected from the bomb vault half a mile away, Hank saw a large form stretched out on his back, his head propped on a rucksack: Veracruze, now hatless, his mouth open, gasping for breath.

O'Connor knelt beside him. He bent close to examine the dark, viscous stain across the broad chest. He flipped a pair of shears from his knapsack and expertly cut away the thickened cloth. Hank could see the gleam of gore.

O'Connor mopped at the wound with a wad of gauze, and bent one ear close to Veracruze's chest to listen for a heartbeat. Roberts and Wohl knelt beside the two men.

O'Connor grasped Veracruze's hand and wrist. He tried to smile: "Paisan—Paisan. You hear me?"

Paisan's eyes opened wide. Hank could see them moving absently. "I—took two of the bastards with me. I want—you to tell Joe—my brother—will you?"

Hank said firmly: "I will. He will know—all about it."

The eyes stopped moving and froze, the dark pupils fixed, staring at the sky.

O'Connor laid Paisan's hand gently by his side, and closed the eyelids. He spoke to Wohl and Roberts. "Too bad. Paisan's had it."

Bissell had come up, and Gresham, and Nooley, hatless and tousled-haired, still looking like an oversized peasant in black sharkskin, wild-eyed, clutching his bow and quiver. They were a row of disordered, wild, and vari-costumed giants in the streaked light. Hope told them: "Paisan is finished. No time to waste. Roberts—find the guard phone and rip it out. Muhlbach has cut the lights. We'll head for that next fence. Now!" He started at a run through the narrow gap in the wire next to the guardhouse. And, running, Hank saw two rag-bags of Chinese bodies near that gap, like two dark bundles of clothes thrown on the barbed wire. Those would be the two that Veracruze mentioned, they were near his body, two less of the enemy sworn to Communism, Paisan's last contribution to a lifelong effort.

The Americans were running now in the faint, reflected light from the bomb-storage vault. Hope had decided to bolt for that fence, taking his chances of being spotted in the shadows. Undoubtedly, when they came closer to the guardhouse in this last barrier, they would take cover and make a careful, creeping approach. The worst was to come.

The ground was rough, covered with low shrubs, but there were no people in this part of the enclosure. Dinh and Wing had chosen it with great skill. It was the back door to the bomb installation. But where had the first guard detachment—the one which had been relieved at the barbed wire—where had they gone? Was Hope worried about them? Hank wondered, his brain beating with his quick-thumping steps as he ran; they must be somewhere hereabouts. Probably they had gone to the guardhouse at the next fence. Hope probably knew. He seemed to think of everything.

Hank hoped devoutly: Let them not be able to turn on the flood-lights. If they did, the Hope detachment would be naked in no-man's land, caught in the light for all to see, and shoot at.

They were still running. Ahead, silhouetted against the dim lights of the bomb storage vault, the bulk of a house—and there were lights in it. And ahead, over the house, supported by tall bamboo poles, the beginning of the camouflage net.

The forest of poles supported it. And it stretched far beyond the lights of the bomb vault. This was the area, from the edge of the hut onward to beyond the bomb vault, which had been illuminated by the floodlights before. And Hank now, piecing together the bits of memory from the time when they had looked down at the floodlit rectangle from Tzu's farm knew this was the critical, inner area where he had seen the bomb-truck moving, with its attendant guards and technicians and celebrants, toward the bomb vault. And then, somewhere to the left, would be the searchlight towers, probably well to the left, well outside the scope of the camouflage net.

The strength of Hope's master plan was dawning on Hank: Hope had known that the guards of the outer fence, when they were relieved, would be coming to this inner barracks building at the edge of the inner fence. Hope, as always, was way ahead, a thinking soldier.

And now, looking toward the edge of the camouflage net and the poles supporting it, and the barrack-like shape of a building, Hank saw Hope's running figure stop, suddenly, next to a sturdy bamboo pole support for the camouflage net. Now Hope had stopped and was wigwagging a signal with his arms. The men thudded up to him. He was kneeling, they were panting, snorting for breath, struggling for air, as they knelt or slipped to the ground beside him.

Hank knelt next to Nooley, facing Hope. Nooley was a wild man still, a black-clad, frenetic red-haired giant. Hank thought Nooley must get another peasant hat, his supposed disguise was instantly penetrable without it—and the long bow on his shoulder also made his costume-cover ridiculous. It didn't matter—they would all get the works if they were spotted.

On the other side, as Hope began to speak, Hank saw Muhlbach, the sleeve of his green tigersuit ripped from shoulder to elbow, a wad of bandages showing through the aperture. Muley, too, must have been hurt in the passage of arms at the first fence. But he seemed cool and orderly as ever, the bandage neatly in place.

Hope was whispering: "The last fence—coming up. Bissell— you've got the bolt-cutters?" Bissell, who had been squatting, half-rose, and flipped a canvas scabbard at his waist upward. It was a sheath for cutters which must have been about the size of hedge-clippers.

"Yes, sir."

"Okay," Hope acknowledged. "Let Hing take the other pair of cutters, when we get to the fence. The Commies had better not illuminate." He squinted into the dark. "You all here?"

Voices answered softly: "Yes, sir. Yessir. Yessir."

O'Connor asked: "We leave the stretcher here?"

"Yes." Hope seemed to swallow. "From here on, we can't carry our wounded out. No time. If you get it bad in the legs, just make them pay for it. Thank God, all of you know what this is all about."

He gulped. "You know by now that Veracruze bought the farm." He paused, and went on, his voice thickening a little. "He did it well. A soldier to be proud of." He went on, now coolly again: "Muhlbach, are you all right?"

"Fine, sir."

"Good. Nooley: You okay?"

"Okay." His voice was foggy.

Hope sensed Nooley's discomposure fully, and told the other men: "Major Nooley's arrows cleared the way for us, back there at the wire. He did as he was supposed to: killed one Chinese and wounded two others. A Can-Do Marine." He hurried on: "Hing and Muhlbach and Veracruze helped finish it. Hing—you did a great job— that took real guts. You better give your coolie hat to Major Nooley. He needs it much more than you do.

"Okay. We'll have to go more carefully from here. Stay spread out. Take advantage of cover, stay on the ground between runs. You'll live longer. Follow my lead. We'll get through the wire over there. And one more thing: If I get knocked off, Major Gresham and Nooley take over—in that order. After that, Sergeant Bissell, Mr. Musgrave. Let's go."

He moved off at a trot, his body bent over, and the column followed in Indian file: Muhlbach, Bissell, a canvas bolt-cutter scabbard flopping from his belt; Nooley, the bow on his back making him two feet taller; Hing, carrying a knapsack now, over his black coolie jacket, an Armalite slung over his shoulder, his head bare now since he had given his coolie hat to Nooley; Gresham, composed, quiet as ever.

Hope ran until they were one hundred and fifty feet from the house, the gate station in the second fence. Then he hit the deck, and Muhlbach and the rest came in at intervals of a couple of yards behind.

He went back to Gresham, flopped beside him. He indicated the gate in the barbed wire fence to the right of the house structure, dimly lit by a string of yellow bulbs, and whispered: "It looks like a couple of squads of men here. Too many to take on. We'll cut through the wire on the left side of the house, where it's darker, and circle around." He was panting still.

He took off again, running at a crouch, hit the ground, waited, jumped up and ran again through a field of knee-high scrub, the others following.

At last, he reached the fence, and sprawled there, in the scrub brush at the foot of the fence. Muhlbach, Bissell, Nooley, Hing and Gresham joined him rapidly. Then Hank, O'Connor, Wohl, Roberts, Espinoza, Jones, Polk, Hildebrand.

All were lying low in the grass, all panting from the ran. But on the other side of the fence, no sentries appeared, and as yet, there seemed to be no reaction from the first guard station where they had broken through the barbed-wire defenses. No new lights were shown from the direction of the bomb vault.

The fence was about eight feet high, heavy-gauge steel, with three strands of barbed wire at the top, angled away from the bomb vault. Hope whispered to Bissell: "Let's go with the bolt-cutters. I don't think they've had time yet to electrify the fence."

Bissell flipped out the large cutters from the scabbard, gave a pair to Hing. He took a deep breath, and said: "Here's where we fuckin' well find out."

Bissell's heavy arms jammed his bolt-cutter against the fence. No streaks of sparks, no electrical arcs, no flashes of incandescence—nothing. He knelt behind the bolt-cutters and began to apply maximum muscular heft. Hing pitched in with a will, near him. The surface of the fence above flexed and bent as the two men worked, snipping the steel links. At last the fence shuddered and Bissell growled: "Bastard's comin' now."

Suddenly a flash of light danced from the far edge of the field, from the nest of lights where the road came in from the town, the main gate. Bissell stopped with the cutters, the men in the grass started. There were two moving lights, headlights of a truck or large vehicle, yellowish in color.

The truck was heading in their direction, the lights bounding, dust filtering through the beams. Then the vehicle turned and headed for the storage vault, evidently following the curving road which led to the bomb vault from the main gate.

Hope muttered nervously: "Hurry up, Bissell. We got to follow that truck."

Bissell and Hing worked frantically with the bolt-cutters. The fence shook with their movements. Hank asked Hope: "Will they turn on the floodlights?"

"I don't think so. They've probably got a lot of technicians working in the vault now trying to do everything at the last minute, and they've got to use all the current they can manage for that work. What worries me is whether patrols check the guardhouse where we came through, or whether they phone there. It's funny there haven't been any patrols along the fence here. Thank God, they haven't got things organized yet. The enemy can get more fucked up than we are. Thank God, they frequently are."

The fence was shaking as if in a heavy wind. Bissell grunted, there was a clatter of falling wire—and a hole in the mesh large enough for a crouching man to pass through. Equal to the situation even in a time of maximum tension like this, Bissell showed the way with a sweeping movement of the hand, like a maitre d'hotel indicating a table: "If you please, gentlemen!"

Hope said: "When we get there—I'll make it fast: If we can get in behind that truck, fine. Memorize where this hole in the fence is. See that guardhouse over there? That's the best way to mark it. Let's go."

He dodged through the break, the others following, and they were running across the open field beyond, in the dark, in the order he had indicated.

The field was rough, dusty, still broken into shadowy patterns by the forest of bamboo poles which supported the artificial sky of the camouflage net. Right now, the fabric sky rippled. It was torn up there and a wind must be flipping it. Hank, thudding along behind Hing, faintly seeing the charging figure ahead against the reflected light from the automobile headlights and the faint glow of the bomb storage vault, had lost sight of Hope and Muhlbach at the head of the column. Fear rushed through his head with the pounding of blood: What if he couldn't see Hing? Hank could head for the automobile lights, and the lights of the vault, but—to arrive alone, winded, panting, by himself at the center of the Chinese camp!

What was the Chinese password? Victory— *'kawng-jeen sing lay.'* And the American password for tonight! Hallelujah!" One of the old American Asia war shibboleths with plenty of "l's" that the Chinese would have trouble with—*most* Chinese, except a thoroughly Americanized Asian like Hing. It was all in language, language changed everything, people were the same otherwise.

Never mind. There was Hing. There, the dark figure running, against the bounding yellow lights of the truck. The truck had stopped, outside the ramp of the vault. The engine was being raced, Hank was close enough to hear the challenges and response, and now bright new lights went on, bright glaring floodlights high up at the far end of the ramp. The two white eyes glared across the slope of the concrete, throwing the truck into sharp silhouette, splattering across the forest of pole supports, reflected by the underside of the camouflage net. That moment, Hope waved his arm and hit the deck, and the others followed suit.

They lay there panting, and ahead, in the faint white light across the rough ground, Hank saw the shadowed shape of Hope, at the head of the column, raising his body gingerly, in the lee of a bamboo pole, looking ahead.

Now, they were on top of the prize, and they could hear Chinese voices, the voices of men bolstering their courage against the unknown in the dark by trying to be rough and military in their commands and responses.

Hank estimated it was only another seventy-five yards to the truck, now. He could see the six or eight soldiers of the guard detachment around the truck, in the light, and he wondered if there were any outposts. Didn't they have any security? What Hope said was true: Every army has fuck-ups, sometimes at the most important places. But you don't hear about the fuck-ups on the other side, where everything is kept covered. All you ever know about them is when finally, in this or that particular battle, you are startled to find out the enemy has lost. On our side, the slightest little fuck-up gets blown up into a federal case—as in the ill-starred Vietnam war.

Evidently the truck had been cleared by the sentries. Underneath the great glaring floodlamps, at the foot of the white concrete ramp that angled downward below them into shadows, the shadows began to move and as they moved, Hank could see that the shadows were doors; two tall dark solid doors which opened slowly to reveal at first a crack of light, then a widening picture of the underground vault, in a bath of white fluorescence. In the light, a modern Brueghel of peasant-technicians, a close-packed army of skilled workers in coveralls; lower-grade workers in blue peasant uniforms, and, near the opening of the gate, the stocky figures of Chek-koh troops in dark-blue. There must be sixty people visible in the crowded picture, and, Hank thought with a shudder, at least twenty Chek-koh troops at the gate, not counting those outside.

Among the crowded, moving, talking, busy figures inside, at the center of the room, Hank stared at a heavy four-wheeled stand where the bomb Shape sat, now mostly assembled and ready to go, a black, oversized torpedo with high fins on the tail; a pointed, smooth nose, and behind it, within the still-open girder construction there the central, mine-like H-bomb mechanism, a mine covered with flyspecks of detonators and a squirming forest of tubing—like the mangrove tangles the Hope Force had penetrated to get there— but these were *steel* forests. Around it, a cluster of workers in blue shirts had gathered— around the target, the great globe of H-bomb power with nose-cone and tail-fins now in place fore and aft of it.

The truck was starting to move forward toward the ramp. The two bright white eyes of the floodlamps stayed on, and the shadowed light reflected from them across the ground. Hope gave the signal: one arm straight up, the other at right angles. The men moved like darting sparrows to positions left and right of him. It was deployment they had practiced many times, the effective skirmish line, rapidly assumed.

Hope's Armalite spoke first with a crashing sound that brought a cascade of breaking glass, smashing the white illumination of the floodlamps, leaving untouched for a moment the picture of the room within: the technicians, the workers, the crowd of people around the Shape, still brightly lit, the bar of night sharpening around it into a black frame.

Came the crashing, descending curtain of fire, an implosion from all sides: the lights of the bomb room went out. There, now only darkness broken by the slashing of sub-machine-gun fire, the thudding flashes of grenades.

The moment the lights went out, Hank began moving, jerking a cartridge into the chamber of his Armalite mechanisms. Against the distant light reflections from the main gate, he saw the silhouettes of Hope, Gresham, and Bissell moving fast in the direction of the now-darkened ramp down into the bomb vault—Bissell's arm up in an overarm throw—a grenade being tossed.

He lost the silhouettes in a moment, but caught them against the glare of fire coming from the bomb vault. An earth-shaking flash as the grenade went off. Near it, people were firing out, into the dark.

He rushed toward it in a crouch, felt the downward concrete slope of the ramp under his feet, made out the bulk of the truck which was still stopped ahead on that slope. The car's lights were out. Shooting all around, a cascade of thunderous firecrackers. A streak of tracers flashed ahead, from the vault; some Chinese idiot had loaded these embarrassingly detectable self-locators in his submachine gun. Someone was shouting in there—shrieking, someone hurt, terrified by the awareness that he was hurt, like a child. Ricochets whined from the concrete walls. But nothing close, nothing that cracked, as really close ones do.

He ran on down the slope, past the flank of the truck, bumped someone hard, smelled a scent of garlic like something sharp-edged, knew it was a Chinese. He waited a part of a second for an identifying password, none came, he swung his Armalite around and blasted. The recoil was nothing, typical Armalite smoothness, but he sensed the impact of bullets on something there, something human falling hard on the concrete.

His brief burst had flashed in the dark. It brought an answering spurt of fire from beyond, in the dark cavern of the vault, to the right. This time, bullets cracked the air near him. Instinctively, he hit the deck.

A white light flicked on suddenly, shockingly, ahead, in the bomb vault. In that moment of brilliant black-and-white, Hank saw the action arrested as by a stroboscopic beam. The light was in the back of the bomb room. Arrested by it were a wide panel of Chinese technicians and workers—a startlingly large number of them with mouths opened in shock and surprise, and human wreckage, a half-dozen bodies twisted and bloody. Scattered among them, figures of dark uniformed Chek-koh troops, some simply standing, a few in squatting, aggressive postures with levelled weapons, two at the left end of the panoply at that moment firing, with yellow flashing from their sub-machine guns.

There was a powerful rhythm of movement away from the bomb, the motion frozen in mid-flight away from the wrecked and bloody humanity strewn on the floor—more of the same at the left end of the room where a tangle of bodies, still moving, had been smashed down by their flood of grenades and Armalite fire, partly his own.

In that second, he was startled, too, to see that the surprised inhabitants of the room were spread all over it—no particular concentration now around the bomb. One would have estimated that they would instinctively cluster around it. But the assault had driven them off base. Three men in blue jumpers stood beside the bomb, evidently technicians who had been working with specification sheets, and they still held the sheets absently. Near them, a worker in blue pants and brown shirt crouched with an open book.

He's studying a correspondence course in nuclear physics, Hank's thought flashed. In the same moment he thought: *I must shoot out that floodlight—where is it?—a single flood, that white eye at the back of the room.* He swung his Armalite around to bear on it.

Hank saw something moving, very close to him. A man's arm, flinging out. He saw the body move, a Chinese in dark Chek-koh uniform; the head lifted—an exceptionally dark skin, almost black. He saw the lips twisted, the teeth showing incongruously in a grin, blood running down the side of the face in a sheet, the close-cropped head hatless. And the blood poured from a wound somewhere high on the head. The man's arm reached for a Sudarev sub-machine gun lying between them, the ammunition clip towards Hank.

The movement of Hank's Armalite was detoured in that blink of a second, and the weapon's burst started up-angled and continued in a movement across the light. The barrel skinned towards the man's head, a few feet away. The bullets zipped toward the head, the red, ripped flesh and it fell over, the body twisting with it. The smell of cordite hit him like a wave: dead men, ripped apart. Bloody Communist, bastard, the good kind, dead. Better him than me, since they're the ones who want to fight. If anyone's going to puke, let them puke—they started it and kill the bastards! That's the job we have to do!

Beyond, Hank glimpsed four of the Hope Force moving on the slope down toward the bomb, Armalites in their hands. Hope, in the lead, looked back, startled; Gresham, his gaze fixed on the bomb,

Hing, and Bissell behind him, both firing into the crowd of people, in an offhand position, as on a target range. Two people falling there.

In the din of the firing, all around and behind, something shattered the floodlight in the bomb chamber. In the dark, Hank was on his feet and moving in, bumping past Chinese in the scrimmage, sensing the hard scent of the sour fish-sauce exuded from their bodies. He skated around them, boring in towards the bomb, incredulous that he had not been hurt, no sharp knife-point piercing his envelope of flesh, no bullet impacting him in the uproar of the firing and the pungent cordite smell, the dinning of the firing hammering his ears.

In the glimpse of light before it was put out, the Hope Force had seen targets indicating that fire was whipping like a sheet into the wall of people spread across the bomb room, into the humanity massed across the bomb-expanse. Men dying, men hurt. As he ran, Hank heard the turkey gobbler cry of blood in the throat: "A-rrrghhhgh!" Someone hit close by. If the firing continued like this, the way to the bomb would be cleared, the self-protective mechanisms in the enemy human flesh automatically pulling it away from the onslaught.

Hank bumped against a metal edge and a human body in the same moment, and heard the American voice: "Hallelujah, Hallelujah, Goddammit! Is that Hank?"

"Right." Hank saw that it was Hing.

"I'm tryin' ta fix fuckin' door so we can get in and out." Fire erupted from somewhere across the room, a far corner, Hank saw the orange muzzle-blasts in the dark, muzzles sharply indicated and pointing toward him. Chinese fire from the far side. The Chinese would have fallen back because of the tremendous volume of the American fire hammering into the vicinity of the bomb, smashing into it and everything alive around it, but Hank knew the small-arms fire wouldn't blow the bomb—that had to be done carefully, scientifically, with local wads of C-3.

He saw someone fall near him, somebody hitting against his legs. It would be Hing, the feeling of a person where Hing had been was gone, Hing was down, and there was enemy fire from across the room. Hank raised his Armalite and fired in that direction, a long, paper-cutting burst zapping through the dark.

It was Hing, there on the concrete floor. The floor was whitish in color, and he could see Hing's black shirt, body flat on its back, now, one arm bent at the elbow, the finger flopping above it. Hing's voice, gasping: "Ne' mind me. Get the door!" Hank, stunned, saw a pool of dark spreading on the white floor from Hing's chest. Like an automaton, Hank turned to find the thick metal edge of the door, where it had been shoved by Hing, and pushed it further, pushed it wide open. It was very heavy, it weighed a ton.

He felt Americans coming up behind him, two or three. "Hallelujah!" he said.

"Hallelujah—Hallelujah! Hallelujah!" they replied.

A figure emerged from the direction of the bomb, outlined against the orange flowers of fire blasting from the deep end of the vault. "Hallelujah!" the shape said.

It was Hope. Hank heard Hope's characteristic cool voice with an order: "We've driven 'em away from the bomb. Aim your fire over there, on the right side. That's where they are, what's left of 'em. I'll fire that way. Follow my lead. Keep your fire away from the left side of the room. That's where Gresham and Bissell are! With the bomb! They've got the Metascope!"

Hank felt the blast as Hope's figure was firing from a crouch position ahead of him. The Armalite flashed, a fast paper-cutting rip. Across the room, three or four orange spots of enemy fire winking. It was incredible to look so closely into the enemy guns and not be hurt. He felt a snapping across his face, a queasy sound like a crackling nail-on-blackboard. Too close. There must be scores of Commie dead and dying in the room, but many live ones over there, firing. He crouched to avoid the fire, swung his Armalite to bear, squeezed the trigger: "Brrapp! Brrapp!" An answering burst, two bursts from their direction. Somebody grunted, behind him. One of the Americans. "Madre Mia!" Espinoza? Espinoza had been hit. "Aaarrggh! Maria!"

Wohl's voice behind: "I'll help him."

Above the din of the firing, the pungent scent of cordite, he heard a man's voice, indeterminate in direction, but ahead somewhere and loud, a Chinese: *"Weft! Weh! Weh! Sheung piu. Sheung piu! Weh!"* A Communist on a field phone, trying to raise another headquarters. *"Sheung piu!"*—that meant "Trademark." The code name of a headquarters, probably. Where was that guy? He was trying to make a report, to get some help. Where was he? Driven by adrenalin, a strength as often men to make one survive, Hank's senses seemed to locate the voice with precision. It was on the right, still crying: *"Weh. Weh! Sheung piu!"* The voice, somewhere far to the right. Hank raised his Armalite and fired: "Brrappp! Brr-pp!" He had reached the end of his clip. He would have to stop, change clips, quickly. Had he knocked out the voice? Probably. There was no more *"Weh-ing"* from that direction. But the firing was a deafening cross of sound from all sides: The Americans firing practically over his head, and enemy muzzle-blasts flashing angrily from across the room. He crouched to change magazines in the dark. The clip! Where? He fumbled frantically—found it. He seized it with a grip of death, a ten-ton contraction, and rammed it home in the M-16.

He knew he would have to be moving, toward the left where the key men of the group, Hope, Gresham, and Bissell would be working at the bomb.

Hank was vectored to the center of action by firing on the spot. In the flash of muzzle-blast, he saw the largish figure of an American, perhaps Bissell, his gun pointed down as if shooting into the floor. In the orange flash, he saw the dark beret and hunched shoulders above the shaft of Armalite. A Chinese right at the foot of the bomb had tried to stake a claim to life that Bissell was brushing aside.

Hank moved closer and shouted the password above the unending din of firing: "Hallelujah! Hallelujah! It's Musgrave. Musgrave."

The firing ended where Bissell stood, "Over here! Over here!"

On the side of the room towards the ramp and the gate, a burst of fire continued. In the dark the flashing of the muzzles, our guns, five or six Armalites firing. They seemed to be pointing towards him. Hank knew they were firing into the far end of the room, where most of the enemy had been driven. From that end of the room, two or three muzzles flashed, but confusion had smashed any rehearsed organization, surprising catastrophe had chopped their will to fight. Momentarily, only momentarily. Hank knew the Chinese would rally. But let not that rally come too soon.

The Commie guns must have seen the burst of fire from Bissell. It was short, but prominent, and from a most sensitive direction, the direction of the bomb.

"Kraaddtt! Kraaddtt!" Ten—twelve bullets cracked close by. A slew of bullets smashed something behind Hank, there was a cascade of breaking glass and objects falling—no shouts of anyone being hit.

Hank crouched, an automatic defensive reaction. He heard Hope's voice sounding out clearly above the firing din:

"Hank—Bissell— Gresham! Don't shoot from here at the bastards. It'll draw too much fire. We've got to work."

Hank moved up toward the bomb, creeping, "Hallelujah, Hallelujah!" he said.

And Bissell answered: "Over here, look out! Slopies all over the place, all over the deck! They got knives!"

Hank stood up. No snapping of bullets. He was close enough now to sense two figures of men bending over in front of him—and there, in the dark, the telltale, pale-green glow of the Metascope reflected on an eyebrow. That would be Gresham, leaning over the 'scope, looking into the innards of the bomb—a mistake. His eye should be closer. The green light could be visible to someone with sharp eyes, even in the flashing shadows of the room.

Hank yelled: "Gresham—your eye's too far from the **'scope**—it shows!"

In a moment, the faint green smear was gone, Gresham had moved in. Somewhere, down there in the dark, he would be working over the curved surface, maybe molding a wad of C-3 over a detonator at that moment. Over the smells of the room, the powerful scent of cordite, Hank got a wet blast of C-3 stench—like cheese spoiled in a tin can.

Hank heard Gresham's voice, low but distinct: "Take the Metascope, Bissell. I've got this geography memorized, I need two hands to work the C-3. I want you to watch me with the Metascope while I work—especially over this tritium booster tube."

The pale-green light gleamed faintly as it passed from Gresham's eye to Bissell's. Then it was hidden, against Bissell's face. Bissell's growling voice said: "Go ahead."

A loud shriek rode over the din of firing—a scream like the cry of a loon. Hank remembered it from Korea: the signal whistle of a Commie squad leader. It seemed to come from the far side of the room. Was a Chek-koh non-com organizing something? An attempt to drive back to the bomb with a squad, to smash the Americans out of the room? By this time, despite the carnage and the continuing volume of fire, the initial advantage of the surprise attack must be wearing off.

Hope sensed it, too. Hank heard him shouting, over the din of the firing: "All of you guys—throw grenades! Throw at the right side of the room! That guy with the whistle." Hope's voice twisted off at the end as he threw a grenade in the dark. With a reverberation, a violent flashing of light, it exploded, and momentarily seemed to shut off the firing. Hope's voice followed, in crackling stillness: "Over there! Over there."

He tossed another grenade, it went off, and the others were throwing, too, the blasts like orange furnaces springing; "Crranggang! Crrannggg! Craanggg!"

Someone from the American side was launching another blast with an Armalite. But no answering fire, for the moment. Then, a single blast, one shot alone, from the Communist side.

Hope's voice called out: "Somebody from the ramp side shoot a flashlight beam over there. Maybe they're knocked out. Maybe they've gone out a back entrance."

Hank knew Hope's reasoning was right: If Hope aimed the flashlight himself, it might draw fire on the bomb, and onto the men doing the critically important work at the bomb stand. But the Force should know immediately if the enemy in the bomb room was knocked out, or gone.

A light flashed from the ramp side of the room—an American beam fixing the enemy side of the room with a layer of white light: bodies tangled there, a debris-pile of bodies, partly moving. Next to it, two Chinese technicians in blue jumper suits standing, staring vacantly into the light, blinking, next to the disorder. A blast of Armalite fire splattered in their direction. One figure disappeared abruptly, as if a trapdoor had been opened in the earth beneath him, swallowed up. The other still stood there, blinking, preserved by the ironic fates of battlefield physics. He still blinked, unarmed, into the light.

Hank was struck with the nightmare realization that the crowd of the enemy forced into the opposite side of the room had thinned greatly: *People had gone out the other side somewhere, to get help. Now, all hell would hit.*

Another American grenade smashed into the far side of the room with unendurable concussion: "Krracch!" Then, suddenly, no firing, no sound, the sounds has stopped, except for a refrain of whimpering, the crying of injured men, one very loudly shouting, from the far side: "A-A—rroww-rroww." International cry of terror and pain, the bully bastards asked for it.

Nearby, Hank could hear an American note of complaint, Bissell's growling voice: "Somethin' wrong with Goddamn Metascope. Somethin' fucked up. Can't see."

Gresham, cool and dry: "You've got to see. Got to make sure the C-3 is molded right. Is the image faint?"

"Yeah, it's faint. Nearly gone."

Another voice, from close by, Hope: "Maybe the charge is worn down—maybe needs winding. Give it to me, Bissell, I'll wind it up again, and look."

"Here it is," Bissell's growling voice.

The scraping of the crank seemed loud in the concrete cavern. There was no shooting now. Hope's cool, efficient voice was clear: "Image is faint. Still can't make it out."

Gresham's thin voice: "Can you see the blasting caps? In the C-3. Is it shaped right, around those two ring lenses?"

Hope's tone was heavy with disappointment: "I still can't see it. Something wrong with the Metascope generator?"

In the tautness of the moment, Bissell was growling: "Wait. Let me use a flashlight. Not so risky now."

Before Hope could stop him, Bissell's light snapped on. In the narrow angle of light, Hank saw the curved surface: a cushion of yellow C-3 molded an inch thick, a bomb-detonator plug sticking out of the middle of the plastic mass. Gresham's hands were nervously inserting a bronze-colored blasting cap, black-and-yellow time-fuse coiling from it like festive clothesline.

Bissell's light held steady on the heart of the bomb. Gresham's hands were still working over the plastic mass, inserting the second blasting cap at the far side of it, where it curved to what Hank knew as another lens charge on the outside of the bomb.

"We'll take out two ring lenses with this charge," Gresham's dry voice sounded as unemotional as a lecturer in a college classroom. Their initiator is already in place—a Point One detonation will wreck it. A Point One detonation—enough to ruin their mechanism. They'll never fix *this* bomb. They'll have to start—"

He didn't finish. The quiet across the room was smashed, in a long burst of sub-machine-gun fire from there. The narrow cone of light from Bissell's hand fell, up-ended, and hit the floor, bounding, flipping a flattened beam across the concrete.

Hank saw a figure falling, and he recoiled from a heavy blast of fire from somewhere near where Bissell had been standing. That would be Hope returning the fire across the room, and someone, one of the Force was down next to him, and the light still on; would it be Gresham who had it?

Hope bent over. In the light, Hank saw him reaching. The light angled downward onto Gresham's thin face; the body on its back, mouth open, a flap of tongue protruded, eyes bugged open, cheek bones skeletal.

Hope stood up, his voice crackled in the darkness: "Bissell! Give me the light here—on the bomb. Gresham's had it! I got the Commie that killed him! Shine the light!"

The light flipped back to the bomb. Hope's long hands moved in the beam, his fingers checking the projections of the detonators the moulded blanket of the C-3 over the curve of the bomb.

Hope's voice in the dark. "Hold it steady, Bissell. I'm going to light the fuse. First, is anyone wounded?"

Wohl said: "Only walking wounded, sir. Not too bad. Three dead, here in the cave. Gresham, Hing, Espinoza."

Hope glanced around the room for only a second, the impact of those deaths hurting him. Then, "Bissell, when I light this fuse, turn out the light—and fire the green flare!"

The light revealed Hope's long fingers moving, a lighted match closing on an end of time-fuse, the flame touching another match jammed into the end of the fuse, moving fast to another length with the same lighting mechanism, both fuses sputtering. The flashlight flicked off, a bright-green glow smashed over the room, and Hope shouted. "Let's go! All of us—go. Up the ramp. Fast. Go! Shoot out every light that comes on. We'll meet at the hole in the fence. Go!"

The remnant of the green flare was sputtering on the concrete floor, squirming and dying. Hank stepped over the supine, spare figure of Gresham. Another good American gone west, dead against the bully, the dictator of the world. Hurry—taking too long. In the same glance, Hank saw the two chugging, sputtering flame trails of the time-fuses. Hope looked at him: "Go!"

Hank thudded up the concrete slope, seeing, ahead, a bright glow of light, at the top of the slope—unbearably bright. Had the Commies turned on the floodlights? If so, it would be sure death, up there. And the reinforcements would be coming—all kinds of troops rushing in to take out the Americans and save the bomb. But that was too late, now.

He must run, run. Faster now, since the fuses were racing. A few seconds to go, now. Go!

He reached the top of the slope. Saw the running figures of Americans, darting towards the forest of bamboo poles supporting the camouflage net. It seemed almost as bright as day under the net. The illumination was a reflection from new, bright lights glaring in a white cluster around the main gate. Somewhere over there, a siren sounded, wailed. A slew of headlights, charging recklessly among the poles, like toy trucks going mad—three, four—reinforcements. But there was no system. The trucks bounced in several directions, he heard their engines screaming. Confusion! Good.

And there was no sweeping machine-gun fire, and, except for the trucks, no signs of reinforcements. The Commies were still recoiling from the attack, the weapon of surprise had knocked them, stunned them. Could the bright lights at the main gate be shot out—could we do it—or were they too far away?

The explosion, behind in the bomb vault, any minute, now.

Currowww! The crash came surging up behind Hank like a shockwave, a force like a wrestler picked him up, smashed him onto his face, sprawled him onto hard earth just beyond the start of the downward ramp. Thunder ran up his back. A wave of heat full of prickles. More thunderclaps, and an idea: It's done! Done! The dreadful, rolling clatter and crashing as of an accident kept on rolling behind him, and he smelled a stench of burning, like rubber. Hank looked back to see the white slope of the ramp blackened. Heavy objects falling around him, debris, pieces of metal and concrete, like stones, a hailstorm of concrete stones. But no nuclear detonation. If there had been, he wouldn't have known. At all.

From where he lay, Hank saw the foremost of the trucks, those probably carrying reinforcements, stopping, the others halting behind him. Four sets of headlights, stopped now, a half-mile, 800 meters to the west.

And in the same moment, the white glare over the field intensified many times. Floodlights were on! From ahead, Hank could see them burning white. From the direction of the large guardhouse in the second fence barrier, a line of lights, their illumination spreading over the uneven ground between there and where he lay. The Commies had restored the broken power line at the guardhouse. Now the floodlights would have to be shot out. He swung his Armalite around to bear on the row of fixtures. Others had already done so. He heard a storm of American sub-machine-gun firing, Armalites blasting, from close by. Five, six guns blatting.

But the lights were still on. In their glare, a scattering of figures of men running among the poles. Were they ours or enemy? Can't we shoot out the lights? That second, he lined the row of bulbs above the sights of his M-16.

He fired, a short burst. No effect on the lights. Nothing. His sights must be way off. The range must be 250 yards. In the glare of the floodlights he looked at his sight-scale hurriedly, flicked the indicator reticle and aimed again. The front bead levelled on the bright left end. He fired a long burst, twelve, fifteen shots. No visible effect, the line of light blazed as before.

He saw the Hope Force running ahead: Four, five figures moved fast among the bamboo poles. Still two men in kneeling position firing. No, three, one farther to the left, two to the west. Firing at the lights. He saw that the trucks with the yellow lights were moving again, charging over the rough ground, toward the bomb vault.

They must shoot out the lights. Why couldn't they get them out? He aimed again, and saw that there were many black spaces in the line of lights now; the Americans were getting the range, knocking them out. But still, too many. He squeezed off a burst, a couple of links in the line of lights blanked out. Now he had it—the range! And it was time to change his clip. He fell to the job. Blasted clip stuck.

The firing of the others was having its effect. The flood of light was dimmer, fainter, but still too bright. He saw one of the kneeling rifle-men get up and start to run at a zigzag angle toward a bamboo-pole support. The light was still bright enough to see that it was Hope, the tall, lean, racing figure.

The other two were running as well, now, diagonally among the poles, and farther on, he saw two other figures dart, the larger shapes of Americans, not Chinese—progressing toward the guardhouse and the hole in the fence.

The time was late. Getting much too short. He jumped up and ran in the same direction, his eye on the bamboo pole which seemed to be Hope's objective.

Where was the enemy machine-gun fire? Where were the enemy reinforcements? Late—and confused. Good. Out there, the four trucks with the yellow headlights seemed to be taking forever with their trip toward the bomb vault. That was fine. But his body was tense for the expected impact and sound of machine-gun firing from across the field. It hadn't come. His mind throbbed with anxiety as his feet thudded across the ground, heading for the bamboo pole where be thought he had seen Hope.

There was no shooting from the other side. He kept running, faster toward the pole ahead. Wasn't that the pole where Hope had gone?

A dreadful moment—Hope might not be there. Still, no recognizable enemy fire.

Another light broke over the field with the impact of a shell. A wide, smoking lane of light was laid over the field from a white searchlight circle beyond the camouflage net. Somehow, those clowns had cranked the searchlight around so the beam lay underneath the camouflage net, streaking a wide white road on the underside.

They had seen the floodlights being shaken down, knocked out by the fire of the Americans. Some Chinese engineer officer had managed to bend the searchlight beam underneath the net, to try to bring the light to bear on the Americans.

But the beam was in the wrong place. Instead of lying directly over the ruins of the bomb vault, it was over towards the main gate, halfway between the vault and the main gate. It lay over two bouncing shapes of trucks, trucks with yellow headlights. Hank could see lumps like sacks of potatoes crowded in the open backs of the trucks, in the moment in which they flashed across the searchlight beam. Troop reinforcements. Some of them had certainly piled out of the trucks—getting ready to fire, in the direction of our muzzle-blasts. But why no firing?

Then, two more trucks, led by the yellow headlights, moving on, passing through the white searchlight track, closer to the bomb vault. Hank saw eddying smoke in the headlight glare showing the wreckage of the bomb vault.

Suddenly, the wide white track of the searchlight beam died, disappeared, probably shot out. When the light went out it was clear that the floodlights were much paler now, many of them had been destroyed. But some were still on, there was still the glow of light and shadow across the unevenness of the field. And ahead, at the foot of one of the poles, Hank could see three crouching figures— big

Americans with dark berets, packs and the spikes of Armalites above them: Hope, Bissell, and Muhlbach. Hank slid happily in beside them. There was no need for passwords in the light. Hope was squinting off towards the barracks building: "Some Chinese over there. Coming this way. We're sunk if we can't get those lights out."

Bissell said: "The searchlight's cockeyed lookin' for us at the bomb vault."

As if to substantiate him, the smoky white track glared instantaneously across the field and rested on the blackened concrete ruins of the bomb vault.

"That's it," said Hope. "But thank God we're out of that beam now. In a minute, they'll start firing. Machine guns! Maybe they'll crank the flak batteries down and fire zero-elevation!"

Hank was still panting from his run as Muhlbach squinted up towards the floodlights on the guard's building. "On the left side, there're a lot of lights still on." He pointed up at the battery of lights atop the square of the guardhouse. Farther out to the right, there were only a few spots of light remaining. "Shall we get 'em?"

Hope swung up his Armalite. "Let's go." He squeezed off two long bursts: "Brrrappp! Brrappp!" The others started firing, the four muzzles darting orange.

"Looks like y' got some," Hope said, squinting in the direction of the floodlights. It seemed that now, abruptly, half of the lights at the brilliant end of the floodlight battery were blacked, the light was notably fainter. "That's good," he went on. "Let's hope the searchlight boys didn't see our muzzle-blasts."

Machine-gun fire was coming from the direction of the searchlight stand. But it was angling toward the bomb vault, not toward them. Red balls of tracer fire curving over the ground, following along the beam of the searchlight, bouncing off the concrete ruins of the vault, angling up, neon dashes snubbing into the sky.

Other machine guns joined the firing: One, two, three red curves, arcing into the ground near the bomb vault.

"Wasting their fire," Hope said. "Maybe they'll hit some of their own troops coming up." Now, in fact, the four trucks bringing reinforcements had halted, apparently just beyond the searchlight beam, and in the reflected light, the mass of troops at the back of the trucks was moving slowly, like night-crawlers in a pail. Spurts of fire—red flashes and tracer zips—came from them. The firing jutted against the sky in every direction. Still confusion!

"The ones that worry me are on the other side," Hope said. "Coming out from the guardhouse. But at least it's darker over there."

The machine guns at the base of the searchlight tower were still firing, the red lines ricocheting beyond the bomb vault, some close to the trucks. Large, thudding orange-red flashes, flower-bursts, smashed the night near the main gate. "Crrrampp! Crrampp! Crampp!" An anti-aircraft battery had fired—hysteria! They would kill their own people. The shells exploded on the field, near the trucks—red-black smears in smoke, the sounds like skidding tires, the shells landing: "Crroom-roomm!" More artillery fired. "They're shooting each other! Good shooting, Commies!"

"Okay," Hope shouted over the commotion. "We've got to make time. Before they come in on the back side of the field. If you see any strange people on the way, remember their password is *'kawng-jeen sing lay!'*"

He hesitated a moment, squinting at the huge, angry white eye of the searchlight. Beneath it, the blast of a machine-gun muzzle with arcing balls of red tracer still streaking from it. "We'd better knock out the light," he said. "But I'll fire alone. We don't want too much muzzle-blast or they'll be on our necks."

He flattened himself in a prone position and took very careful aim at the glaring white eye. "Brrrapp! Brrrapp!" The cyclops orb of the light disappeared, blinked out in smoke. Gone. Now there was only the faint reflected light from a few floodlight beams remaining on the side of the guardhouse. Hope stood up. "Follow me!" He began to run, diagonally toward the next bamboo pole, generally in the direction of the guardhouse and the few remaining floodlights there at the top of it.

25

HANK WAS RUNNING, ENDLESSLY, A BLIND FORCE DRIVING him as he tried to follow the figures of Hope, Bissell, and Muhlbach. The nightmare! They had disappeared into the bamboo forest of poles ahead. He clung doggedly to a shadow he thought was Hope, moving in the direction of the few light bulbs still burning on the guardhouse.

He was sure he saw Hope ahead, the tall shape darting, then his taut nerves snapped back toward more firing behind him: a storm of tracers and a cascade of small-arms fire crackling where the bomb vault would be. The ack-ack battery had ceased its wild firing across the field. Some of the reinforcements in the four trucks must have reached the vault. They were firing at anything that moved there, and some things that didn't. And to the west, the booming flash-fires of artillery: the ack-ack guns firing on the flat—leaping yellow flashes where the shells were striking. Firing at their own people.

A searchlight went on, again. The same kind of white beam, lying low over the bomb vault: the second of the two searchlights outside the camouflage net; following the same futile pattern as the first. Orange streaks of machine-gun tracers bounced in the dark below the light beam.

The machine-gun firing went on, the searchlight stayed on, and he looked back toward the guardhouse, and the moving shadow-shape of Hope was gone, vanished.

Hank searched frantically among the bamboo forest: nothing. His eyes flitted from one pole to the next: no wraiths there. He was looking too quickly, he might miss an important shadow. In his anxiety he had lost his top-priority target, the people he must follow. His life depended on it, and he had lost it. They had evaporated, where?

The way to find the Hope Force—the searchlight. The men of the Hope Force would be trying to knock it out. He could spot their muzzle-blasts. He scanned the dark stretch in the direction of the guardhouse, and heard the characteristic liquid squirt of an Armalite, and another—seeming to come from that direction. Instantly, the searchlight beam dropped into darkness, shot out. But he had missed the muzzle-blast that did it.

Why was he so desperate to find the Hope Force? He should give it up—head for the break in the fence on his own initiative, meet them there. They would be there. His blasted cowardice, his craving for the reassurance of company. He must go on his own.

That very moment, when he had decided to give up the hunt for muzzle-blast, he saw *two* muzzle-blasts—two orange blooms among the bamboo poles on the way to the guardhouse, and, less than a second later, the "brapp-brapp!" of the two Armalite bursts above the continuing rattle of enemy small arms from the bomb vault vicinity.

They would be out there, perhaps Hope, Bissell, and Muhlbach. He must get there. His resolution to be independent had suddenly gone.

He was running, fast, toward that spot indelibly marked on his mind, his brain pounding with determination to make it.

His boots thudding, his blood pounding, he should see them now, right now. But instead, he saw the wrong people! Five or six figures of men moving, away from the guardhouse, scurrying like rats. Their figures were the wrong shape, too small—Chinese! He was sure of it.

He hit the ground, and that second, heard the Communist challenge, a high-pitched, nervous cry: *"Ting jee-ee! Been gaw-ah!"* Halt! Who's there?

Hank called out, maybe too fast, the remembered password: *"Kawng-jeen sing lay!"* Victory!

He raised his head—and that moment, the world crashed onto him—a heavy curtain of black, with white lights glittering over his head.

He didn't go out. His view grayed, almost blackened; things around him were moving very slowly, beyond his control. Agonized, unable to move, he saw three Chinese in dark uniforms squatting in front of him in the lightening grayness, two holding Sudarev-type sub-machine guns. And one of the Chinese clutched an Armalite, Hank's own weapon!—gingerly pointing it in Hank's direction, dubiously palpating the stock.

Hank tried to move. He must get closer to the Chinese before the gun went off. But he couldn't move. Every muscle weighed a ton. Something was broken in his head. Blood ran down into his eyes. His heart was fading, thumping too hard. Let it go, he thought. It's finished. Relax. Sleep. Be killed. He was too tired, too tired to fight. End it. Go. Let it go.

But he saw the Armalite move in the Chinese hands—and his will suddenly drove him, he's got *my* gun, he's going to kill me with *my* gun. The hell with that, the bastard!

A blast of energy swept over him, exploded him into action. He grabbed the wet gunstock, his strength rammed against the enemy.

Locked wet clothing and flesh battering him, Hank clung like death to the plastic stock of the Armalite. The man was strong, his strength magnified like Hank's by the life struggle. They rolled over, something sharp pricking into Hank's back on the ground but he didn't feel it as pain, only an annoyance; death was too close and little pains faded.

In a second's glance Hank saw three Chinese standing motionless beside him, watching, their sub-machine guns dead in their hands. In that moment he realized they were unable to shoot at the moving target. Hank rolled over, saw close-up the enemy's two grimy hands locked on the barrel.

They flipped over again. Hank was bending the weapon away from the foe's hands I He could move the gun against the maximum strength of the Communist. For a moment he read the Chinese face: a face twisted, terrified, a man who knew he was losing his grip on the gun!

Hank thought in neon characters of life and death: *I mustn't get too far away from the Commie or the others will drill me. How can I turn the gun around and fire?*

With a snap, the gun broke loose. There was no time to think, and Hank saw a gleam of steel somewhere down below as they rolled over. The Chinese had a knife! Hank flipped the gun around and squeezed the trigger. The gun shuddered close to him, the muzzle-blast blew back in his face, the enemy's face exploded in a shower of blood. Warmth, wet. The hostile grip tensed like a vice for a moment, then fell back, and in the same second a sheet of firing ripped all around Hank. He hung on hard, rolling over with the enemy, knowing his life depended on clinging in that death embrace.

Fire seemed to be exploding all around him but not *toward* him—a strange sound, a sound nervously off-key from what he had expected and dreaded. It was American fire: the characteristic rapid "brappp" of an Armalite, of several Armalites overlapping! He glimpsed someone falling there, a Chinese body, rammed against the ground. He saw Hope's lean figure at a crouch, the Armalite flashing in his hands: Hope, Polk, Muhlbach, other Americans, a number of them.

Wohl sank to his knees, close by, then fell over backwards, turning and twisting.

Hank flung off the dead Chinese, the teeth bared below the rest of the smashed head. Steel dental work! Incongruous array of metal, grinning. Hank struggled to his feet, slamming away from the red hand which had somehow tangled his gunsling. His shirt soaked, thick—blood and sweat. He whipped the gun free, swung it around sharply because behind Hope's crouching, firing figure he could see in the shadowy half-light a Chinese swinging a Sudarev.

Hank aimed and fired in one movement. The burst chopped off short, but the enemy fell. Hank's clip must have run out. Hope swung and fired a long burst into the falling body.

The fight was still raging. Some thirty feet away, enemy fire flashed, two or three sub-machine guns blasted. It had been a patrol—probably from the guardhouse. Hank glimpsed the squatting forms of three Americans to his right, two of them firing in the direction of the enemy.

Hank had two grenades still. He yanked a pin and heaved the pineapple in the direction of the enemy firing: six-seven-eight-nine—BLAMM! The flash of the grenade seemed lost in the openness, but the blast was shaking.

The enemy fire had stopped, the concussion was still ringing. Hope ran over toward the enemy where the grenade had gone off, he wheeled and seemed to be firing into the ground. He stopped, searched the ground, and ran back. "We finished 'em," he barked. "Who's hurt here?"

Hank saw that there were six or seven Americans there. Muhlbach's voice: "I got another rip: the same arm. But not bad."

Hope said: "Roberts, fix Muley's arm. Anybody else?"

Polk said: "Wohl. Wohl's got it bad. Over here."

Hope jumped to Polk's side, they knelt beside a fallen form. Wohl's voice said: "Don't wait. I had it. Get!" The body twisted on one hip.

Polk brought his head near Wohl's chest: "Dead."

Hope said: "To the fence. Quick." He led the way, running skillfully at a half-crouch toward the nearest bamboo pole, the others stringing behind him, still in an approximation of their original order, discipline persisting.

*

They reached the hole in the fence, miraculously without an enemy contact, slipped through to the far side where Hope kneeled and the others sprawled, panting for air. Behind them, now, at the ruins of the bomb vault, all kinds of firing rattled like a hailstorm. There was firing at the spot where the machine guns would be at the base of the searchlights, and machine-gun fire from the direction of the main gate. In the confusion, plenty of Chinese Communists were being shot tonight by their own people. And Hank thought we're giving them back some of what the VC did to us in Vietnam in the ambushes. Or in Korea or in China or with the Huks or in Malaya. This time we gave some of their own medicine back. The language they understand and respect. His father used to say: "If you're going to be kind to a mule, first you have to get her attention. So give her a good belt on the head—then she'll listen to you because you're speaking her language. That's the way it is, negotiating with the Commies." His father was smart—he had only *read* about the Commies and still he knew.

Hope was saying: "We'll wait here for two minutes. I'll count off who's here: Musgrave—Bissell—Polk—Roberts—Muhlbach. That's it. Wohl and Jones and Hildebrand had it on the way here. Did anybody see Nooley? Or O'Connor?" There was no answer.

Hope warned harshly: "Somebody coming!" He slid down to a prone position, and Hank saw a largish American figure, a figure with a wide object like half of a door under one arm.

"Hallelujah! Hallelujah!" Hank recognized the big body of Nooley, hatless, in his black peasant garb.

Hope confirmed Hank's conclusion: "Nooley! Over here!"

Nooley found the gap in the fence. He was panting, hard. A large object fell to the ground as he collapsed. It was longer than a door. "I brought a board—to help get over the outside wire."

Hope squinted in the direction of the gate through the outer, barbed wire barricade which the Force still had to pass. The lights were on again there, a group of Chinese figures visible, moving around. Hope levelled his binoculars.

"They'll probably have a squad in there by now, patrols all over the place." He picked up the board Nooley had brought, "You're right, Nooley—we'd never get through that spot again. We'll have to get over the wire on this board. And fast!"

He looked at his watch. "Two-and-a-half minutes gone. Let's move! Polk, Roberts, bring the board. You and Polk can take turns carrying it. I'll pick the place, where the wire looks low."

✻

Again, no patrols. At the last minute, as Roberts and Polk were laying the board up the slope of the barbed-wire A-frame, the yellow headlamps of a truck charged towards them at a frenetic, chattering pace, from the direction of the main gate. The seven men flattened themselves against the ground, but the truck turned away, headed for the guard post through the wire, and Hope guessed: "Reinforcements. They'll be sending out more patrols along the wire, any minute. They still think we came in the front. Good!"

It was taking the enemy an incredibly long time to respond, and with amazing imprecision, Hank thought, as he waited for Hope and Muhlbach to precede him across the board, over the wire. But the enemy reaction was probably no more inexact, more imprecise, more misdirected or out-of-joint than the reaction of a thousand American and South Vietnamese garrisons hit by surprise attack during the Southeast Asia war.

It was Hank's turn to get over the lumber. He hurried, crouching and catching a trouser leg on an obtrusive bend of wire. As he moved, it tore the flesh, the rip was sharp, and in that same second a wave of dizziness descended on him. The bash on the head—hitting him now. He stopped a moment while the cone of pressure pushed down on his scalp. He was near the top of the board, the narrow wooden band of safety above the layers of barbed wire.

If he collapsed, if the red-mist of dizziness took him, he'd fall into the belts of jagged wire and he shivered. He bent his body over double and his consciousness cleared. Better.

He got across the board, slid into the ground, next to Hope and Muhlbach. The others were following fast: Nooley, Bissell, Polk, Roberts, that was all, the remnant of the Hope Force. The rest were gone, except for Helmantholer and Hanson, waiting back at the tunnel, and Trotter, somewhere in-between the tunnel and Dinh-Tzu's rice farm.

Dinh-Tzu, Wing On, and Wing Run, and old Dinh, and Dinh-Tzu's family would be waiting for them, a pitiful selection of their belongings wrapped up in bundles. But with Dinh-Tzu guiding them, they would probably get back to the tunnel, to Helmantholer, Trotter, and Hanson, in record time—if they were lucky.

26

October 15

AND THEY *WERE* LUCKY. LIKE THE VICTORS IN TEN THOU sand surprise attacks in military history, from Cannae to Pearl Harbor and Bien Hoa, Chu Lai and Hiroshima and Hamburg, they got away with scarcely a flick of trouble; they made their way to Dinh's sea-coast farm without being detected and were not even stopped this time by the coastal patrol. Scores of Communist parachute flares were dropped in the dark of that early morning, and the ten remaining men of the Hope Force, with the ten escaping Chinese spent an odoriferous three hours in the fishy hold of the junk. But they had no major troubles in the junk. Only the patching-up of injuries with Roberts' aid kit, the inevitable shuddering, second thoughts about the raid on the bomb vault, the haunting realization of the closeness with which death had missed them, and agonizing twinges of remembrance of their friends left behind, sacrificed to the new and desperate kind of war.

When the junk had delivered them to the familiar long black shape of the *Mako* off Point Meng Wan, the rugged faces of Wilson and Battersby looked awfully good. That crowded slip of a pig-boat seemed like home.

But it was a long time before they could enjoy it. From the first moment they spotted the *Mako* there were again endless tense hours and many scares with the patrol boats. However, most of the time the men of the Hope Force were dead asleep. Compared with the mission on the island, this was a pipe—danger, like everything else, being relative.

After twelve hours of running, they were one hundred miles south and east of Hainan—but still they travelled at snorkel depth, recharging batteries.

Wilson and Battersby had given up their cabins to the Chinese families, and a kind of Hong Kong ghetto had been set up in this end of officers' quarters. And the Asian guests were allowed to use chopsticks in the sub's mess compartment—and were given clothes-washing privileges among the sanitary facilities.

At a distance of one hundred and fifty miles that night, well clear of Hainan and almost straight south in the China Sea, the Chinese passengers were transferred to a junk. Hank told them for Commander Wilson that their entry into Hong Kong had been arranged. That it was better this way, since the mission was very secret. It would not be good if they came in to Hong Kong on a U.S. ship of war. He told them they would be met on arrival, and welcomed. And he made a mental resolve—and a note—to make sure that all this would actually happen.

Roberts, the head "Doc" in the Typhoon group, was busy fashioning fresh dressing for Muley's left arm, Bissell's right foot, and Hank's head and back. Most of the Force were busy with reports, and all were quiet. But Muley was suddenly talkative as Roberts worked on his arm, and spoke to Hank: "Hank—do things seem different to you? I think the whole world is different—even a different color."

"You can color it grown-up now, I guess," Hank said.

"What does that mean?"

"It means you have a new, and pretty basic standard to check everything against. Like bedrock. You're lucky to have that standard — most Americans never do."

"Just pretty Goddamn lucky," he said, with undisguised irony.

"You are," Hank insisted. "To be alive after that if for nothing else. And also for what you've learned. What you've seen—it probably won't help you to earn a living, but it will give you something a lot of people never have, a perspective."

"Thanks a lot," Muley said.

October 17

Out of sight of land, and fifty miles west of Hong Kong, the Hope Force transferred from the *Mako* to another familiar United States ship, the destroyer *Edson*, and the *Edson* headed east for the last, most peaceable segment of the Operation Typhoon involvement.

That afternoon, as Lantau island was in sight and the tall towers of Hong Kong would soon be showing on the eastern horizon, Hope gathered the remnants of the Typhoon Force on the fantail of the destroyer, with their massed belongings. This was the task force now: Hope, Bissell, Polk, Nooley, Roberts, Muhlbach, and Musgrave, and the three of the communications section, Helmantholer, Hanson and Trotter. They wore civilian suits borrowed from the *Edson* crew, and the clothes fitted them with notable imprecision. There were fresh bandages among the group, swatches of white—most notably, Hank's partial turban, Muhlbach's arm immobile in a cast, Bissell's right foot a vast white sculpture.

Hope was saying to the group, his face seamy, haggard and worn despite many hours of rest: "Pretty soon, we'll be disbanding, going our own ways—until the nest time."

He smiled and it seemed very hard for him to smile: "This has been a rough one. Very few people know about it, very few people probably *will* know about it, until a long time has passed."

He fumbled in a pocket and pulled out a piece of message-paper. "But Helmantholer has decoded an important message, which you will all want to remember—and I'll make sure that you all have copies. It isn't much in terms of money or decorations—maybe the decorations will come later—I'm sure they will if I have my way. But here's the message, and it's from the President:

'TO TYPHOON FORCE FROM COMMANDER-IN-CHIEF: BE-CAUSE OF YOUR OUTSTANDING BRAVERY, DEVOTION, AND SELF-SACRIFICE, THE GREATEST COMMUNIST CHI-NESE THREAT TO WORLD PEACE HAS BEEN ELIMINATED. THERE WILL BE OTHER THREATS, PERHAPS EVEN GREATER THREATS, BUT THE NATION AND THE WORLD OWE YOU A DEBT OF EVERLASTING GRATITUDE. MY LIFELONG ESTEEM AND THE RESPECT OF THE NATION ARE YOURS ALTHOUGH VERY FEW IN THE WORLD WILL KNOW HOW MUCH THEY OWE TO YOU.'"

Hope put the paper in his pocket. He looked off toward the towers of Hong Kong. "We left some good men on Hainan. The best men I knew—Veracruze, Gresham, Espinoza, King, Wohl, Jones, O'Connor, Hildebrand.

"What's left are still the best men I know, besides being the best soldiers. I'll always know that—and you know it, too. A good fighting man knows he's the best. He's Goddamn proud of it. As proud as I am of all of you.

"Thousands of good men—the best men—contributed to what we did, like the crews of the *Mako* and the *Edson*, the Seventh Fleet, the SAC people who stood by, ready to go. But mostly it was us.

"Some day, maybe, the world can use the good men, like you, to solve its peaceful problems. The world needs brains, guts, and strength, to build as well as fight.

"But first they've got a lot of high-priority military jobs to be done. Military jobs like we're used to, that are top-priority political jobs, too—because political and military jobs are getting to be more and more alike these days. Like ours."

He stopped, swallowed, and went on: "I just want to say 'Thank You' to each of you for your guts, strength, and skill. Soldiers don't get many thanks in times that are supposed to be peaceful. But somebody has to do the hard, dangerous jobs like this in a war called peace. You are the kind of men that people depend on to do these lousy jobs." He sat down.

Major Nooley popped to his feet. Now he was scrubbed clean, immaculate in his ill-fitting civilian clothes. "Captain Hope, we had a meeting without you last night. That was Musgrave, Helmantholer, Bissell, Hanson, Trotter, Polk, Roberts, Muhlbach, and I. We know that the best our CO, the Commander of the Typhoon Force, can hope for in the way of official recognition is the Order of the Purple Shaft, with palm, and a secret letter of commendation.

"So we've got the chiefs from this ship, the *U.S.S. Edson*, to do some expert handiwork for us."

He unwrapped a package done up in brown paper. He exhibited it proudly: a varnished wooden plaque in the shape of a shield, and at the top, a metal profile of a thick-necked man in a tight Marine collar.

"This," said Nooley, "is the standard bronze plaque given to the championship detachments, torpedo crews, bowling and yeoman teams on the *U.S.S. Edson*.

"But it's a lot more significant than that to us. Here, at the top, is the profile of General Merritt A. Edson, one of the U.S. Marine Corps' greatest combat leaders, and we give this to our idea of the greatest combat leader anywhere. It says: 'TO CAPTAIN ERIC HOPE. ONLY THE BEST OF COMBAT COMMANDERS IN THE GREAT COMMUNIST WAR, 1946 TO PRACTICALLY FOREVER,' and it's got all of our names on it."

Nooley extended the plaque to Captain Hope and smiled faintly. "We're sorry," he said, "that this token of our affection isn't a Porsche 911 or a Ford GT."

Hope took it and said soberly: "This means a lot more to me than a 911 or Ford T—and it will, to my kids, when I have them."

October 18

Hank walked in to see Mary by himself, in her apartment off Nathan Road.

He knocked at the door and she opened it. Still, the graceful, wide-set eyes with level candor, miraculously unmarked; an appealing, child's plate-face, the shape of a Chinese wedding cake, flawlessly modelled despite new, fine red lines along the jawbone, and a thin pink line along the nose. But it was the same delicate little nose, the shape preserved.

She wore a *Cheongsam*, the high-collared silk moulded over her small shoulders. She looked tall, her legs long in the slit skirt.

He kissed her carefully, and held her in his arms and looked at her.

"Your nose looks fine," he said. "It's just the same."

"But *you've* lost weight, my little *Fu*," she told him. "Robbing banks has worn you out." She indicated the bandage still wadded on his head. "And given you another bloody head."

"Not too much to interfere with what men are supposed to do to women."

"I hope not," she said. Her smile seemed cramped now by the scars along her jaw, but her face was still bright. "Your other jobs shouldn't interfere with the best part."

She was still smiling, and she said: "A smile is a woman's best asset, next to sex—and Mo-Tzu didn't say that."

Hank said: "Speaking of your assets, how is the best-behaved son I ever met, the one I like the most?"

"He's at a new school now and I know that you and I are going to make sure he has only the best of educations." Mary still smiled. She looked at her watch. "I'm going to take you over to see him," she moved closer, ". . . in about three or four hours. I may be getting very virtuous, but I still know what's important to a woman *or* a man."

"You're right, my little *Fu*," he said, touching her hand. "First things first."

Afterword

RT Would Go
A Crusade for Ideals and Survival
Ray E. Boomhower

In the months following the Japanese attack on the U.S. Pacific fleet at Pearl Harbor in the Hawaiian Islands on December 7, 1941, millions of American men pondered what would become of them as their country took its first tentative steps in the worldwide conflict. One of those who wondered what his future might be was a young reporter working on the rewrite desk at the New York office of the International News Service, Richard Tregaskis of Elizabeth, New Jersey.

Tregaskis had suffered several shocking developments since the surprise Japanese raid. He had been rejected for service due to his height (he stood more than six feet, five inches tall) and weak eyesight and had learned he had developed a debilitating chronic illness, diabetes. To get to the fighting, Tregaskis became determined to become a foreign correspondent for the INS, a news agency founded by newspaper magnate William Randolph Hearst. He kept after his boss, Barry Faris, to send him off as to cover the war, believing that the "closer I cam to getting killed in this career, the better my story would be, if I survived."

One rainy March evening Tregaskis learned that Faris wanted to see him the next morning. Tregaskis respected Faris, who, although physically undistinguished, could do any job in the newsroom. He particularly admired the veteran journalist for "his fondness for direct action—the shortest way to a point. This was characteristic of all great newsmen I knew—and it was the quality they had in common with the great military leaders I came to know, the leaders among the brave men."

Faris was polite and to the point, asking Tregaskis if he would rather go to London or Australia. Knowing that Faris did not "brook a 'think it over' kind of answer," Tregaskis seized his chance and made up his mind, picking Australia. Tregaskis was on his way to combat, pleased that "out there in the void of the future was a shape I had dreamed of: men at war in a crusade for ideals, and for survival."

From the Doolittle Raid, the Battle of Midway, and the invasion of Guadalcanal in the Pacific, to the invasions of Sicily and Italy, as well as the drives into France, Belgium, Germany, and back to the Pacific, Tregaskis followed the troops, paying the penalty many others paid in the war, including being gravely wounded by a German shell in Italy. "I gave that effort a lot of my own blood and I didn't hold back when it came to risking my neck to do what I was supposed to do," he recalled.

In doing so, Tregaskis discovered that he possessed an innate affinity for covering combat, writing his sister Madeline shortly after he had finished his Guadalcanal book that it was funny the way "this war business hits you, after you've been meddling around with it for a while. Action, and particularly some new variety of action, gets to be like a drug. You feel let down without it and with it you feel a sort of unhealthy excitement. And frightening—shooting at people and that sort of thing—comes to have a compelling interest, although you're fully aware of the unpleasantness of it." He even began to look forward to the next assignment, hating to miss any upcoming big battle, even if he had an opportunity to return to his family in the United States.

Tregaskis's willingness to go where the action was heaviest impressed me greatly as I researched his career for my book *Richard Tregaskis: Reporting under Fire from Guadalcanal to Vietnam*. The reporter's courage in combat also amazed the soldiers, sailors, airmen, and Marines he covered. One awed soldier told the correspondent, "How you guys go ahead and stick out your necks when you don't have to—well, it just beats hell out of me!" Tregaskis had a simple answer: "But we certainly do have to—that's our job."

Asked by the editors of a national magazine to return to the Pacific late in the war to follow the crew of a B-29 Superfortress as it prepared for bombing missions against Japanese cities, Tregaskis was asked by an editor, "Do you really want to go?" Without hesitating, Tregaskis gave an answer that any reporter who covered World War II would understand: "I don't want to go, but I think I ought to go." He went.

Richard Tregaskis Books

SOUTHEAST ASIA: BUILDING THE BASES

THE HISTORY OF CONSTRUCTION IN SOUTHEAST ASIA

CHINA BOMB: A NOVEL

GUADALCANAL DIARY

INVASION DIARY

JOHN F. KENNEDY AND PT-109

LAST PLANE TO SHANGHAI

SEVEN LEAGUES TO PARADISE

STRONGER THAN FEAR

VIETNAM DIARY

THE WARRIOR KING: HAWAI'I'S KAMEHAMEHA I

WOMAN AND THE SEA: A BOOK OF POEMS

X-15 DIARY

Other JMFdeA Press Books

CHASING THE SURGE

THE ENERGY INSIDE VALSIN'S CHOICES

PERSIGUIENDO LA OLEADA

SASSY FOOD